ADVAN

"The dynamics between Hunter and Tate - true friends and colleagues without being lovers - forms the heart of this intricate, riveting tale of a missing child, family jealousy, business skullduggery, and the deepest sort of betrayal. Hunter and Tate are a duo to root for. I'm looking forward to their next outing."

—Vicki Delany, national bestselling author

"Once again, Brenda Chapman serves up a compelling array of complex characters, disturbing situations and twisty plotlines. What's not to love?"

—Mary Jane Maffini, Author of the Charlotte Adams and Camilla MacPhee mysteries

"A wonderful book, beautifully written and engrossing. I was drawn in and carried along from the first chapter right through to the last page."

—Alex Brett, Author of the Morgan O'Brien mysteries

PRAISE FOR BLIND DATE

"...a well-crafted page-turner that explores the evil lurking in the shadows of the nation's capital."

-- *Ottawa Citizen*

"Never at a loss to weave a spellbinding story, Chapman has seamlessly made the transition from portraying police detectives to depicting an amateur sleuth in over her head ... The result is a credible, well-crafted story that will keep readers turning the page, and when finished, thirsting for more. Highly recommended."

-- *Ottawa Review of Books*

"Blind Date will hook you from its early pages and reel you in, holding on until its final page."

-- *Glebe Report*

"When I settled back with Blind Date by acclaimed author Brenda Chapman, I only meant to read the opening chapters, but I ended up reading late into the night. It was that good."

-- Dietrich Kalteis, *Under an Outlaw Moon*

"Exceptional start to a new series. Chapman's prose is clean and clutter-free, the action well-paced, and the twists and turns keep coming from beginning to end."

-- Judy Penz Sheluk, The Marketville Mysteries

"An amazing story that grabs you on the first page and doesn't let go until the end. Ella Tate and Liam Hunter make a great crime fighting duo. And Tony was quite a surprise. A very satisfying read." Five Stars.

— Patricia Bradley, *USA Today* best-selling author

WHEN LAST SEEN

A HUNTER AND TATE MYSTERY
BOOK 2

BRENDA CHAPMAN

Title: When Last Seen / Brenda Chapman

Names: Chapman, Brenda, 1955 – author

Description: Series statement: A Hunter and Tate mystery - #2
Edited by Allister Thompson. Cover Design by Laura Boyle
Published by Ivy Bay Press, First Edition March 2023

ISBN Trade Paperback: 978-0-9784284-4-0; ISBN ePub: 978-0-9784284-3-3; ISBN audiobook: 978-0-9784284-5-7

For Ted and your unwavering belief

Light thickens, and the crow
Makes wing to th' rooky wood.

— Shakespeare, *Macbeth*

CHAPTER 1

Ginger pulled back the curtain to spy on Charlie in the garden. He squatted on his haunches, petting the tabby from next door where it lay stretched out on the sun-drenched flagstones. The sight of her son's tiny back and bony shoulder blades always made her smile while turning her wistful at the same time. He wouldn't be her baby boy much longer. Soon he'd go to nursery school, where he'd make friends and she'd recede into the background of his world. David had already paid for the first term starting in September against her pleas to keep him home one more year. But for now, Charlie was all hers. The brilliant sunshine made his hair more golden than brown, more her colour than David's, in the halo of light. She let the curtain fall back into place and turned to the stove as the kettle whistled. He'd be fine by himself a minute longer.

She poured water over the teabag in her mug and got the apple juice out of the fridge while she waited for the tea to steep. She cut the juice with water and glanced at her cell phone lying on the counter while turning off the tap. The screen lit up as the phone pinged a message. She took a moment to check and regretted doing so right away. Another ad from the online pottery store where she'd bought her dishes. She hit *Delete* and read a second message from the moms' group. Tomorrow's session had been pushed back an hour, and they asked for confirmation that she and Charlie would be attending. She typed a quick yes and tucked the phone into her pocket.

The need to pee came on suddenly, as it did these days. She sighed and hurried into the washroom next to the kitchen. She'd learned to go in record time ever since Charlie started walking, an important skill she'd used over and over the past two years. He was a busy child, inquisitive and into everything, and couldn't be left alone for long, but at the moment he was enamoured with the neighbour's lazy cat, which would keep his interest until she returned. Less than two minutes later, she stepped through the patio door, set the cups on the table, and climbed down the stairs to fetch him.

The air was steamy in the mid-morning heat. July in Ottawa could be brutally humid, but Ginger didn't mind, since the stretch of days like this one never lasted long — well not long in summers past. Climate change had made the heat waves unpredictable and more frequent the last few years. She brushed damp wisps of hair off her forehead as she walked around the corner of the house. "Charlie," she called. "Come have a drink of juice." She'd fill the wading pool afterward and let him cool down while she pulled over a lawn chair and soaked her feet. The idea made her weak with anticipation, the physical longing for relief close to unbearable.

The scent of roses, blowsy with faded petals, wafted toward her from the bed lining the fence. She had checked out the names of the flowers when they first began blooming: astilbe with the feathery pink plumes, purple Russian sage, coneflower, black-eyed Susans, and blood-red bee balm. She wasn't sure how to keep this garden alive and thriving and reminded herself to check out websites when she had more energy. She glanced toward the spot where she'd watched Charlie and the cat from the dining room window, but they were nowhere to be seen. She cupped a hand over her eyes to cut the sun's glare, remembering too late that she'd left her sunglasses on the kitchen counter. Her voice rose several notches as she searched both sides of the walkway, looking through flowers and greenery for a glimpse of his blond hair and red shorts. "Charlie, where are you? Come here right now, darling. I'm too hot to play hide-and-seek."

Uneasy, she spun back the way she'd come and walked toward the open space of grass in front of the deck. The lot was wide and deep, with trees and bushes toward the back of the fenced-in property. She closed her eyes and pictured the shoreline beyond the fence. Three steps cut into the breaker wall led to a strip of rocky, sand beach that grew and shrank depending on the time of year and the water levels. At the moment, the shoreline was several feet wide lining this part of the Ottawa River called Crystal Bay. Britannia Beach jutted on a piece of land far to her right, while Shirleys Bay was visible farther upriver, the bookends to Rocky Point, the name of this affluent neighbourhood where David had moved them two months earlier after his business reaped a banner year.

A gate in the middle of the back fence swung closed automatically with a latch too high for Charlie to reach. Even so, she ran across the lawn to peer around the trees and shrubs and make certain the gate was properly shut. She unhooked the latch and pushed it open, stepping outside the fence to scan up and down the beach, but Charlie was nowhere to be seen. She mopped her forehead with the bottom of her shirt and took a deep breath to calm herself. Charlie hadn't gotten to the water. He wasn't in imminent danger of drowning. Three sailboats drew her eye to the distant Gatineau Hills on the Quebec side directly across the wide expanse of water. Even the hills seemed to shimmer in the baking July heat. She stepped inside the yard, spun back toward the house, and called his name, her voice now cross from anxiety. "Charlie, this isn't a game. Come to me now!"

A crow launched itself from the top bough of a pine next to her and cawed on its flight path above her head into the cottonwood trees on the other side of the fence. Crows had left her apprehensive ever since she read *Macbeth* in high school. She couldn't remember the words but knew that a crow or a raven sitting atop one's house was a very bad omen, a foretelling of death. She gazed at the blueness of the sky for a moment, wishing for clouds to filter the unrelenting sunlight that left her drained and lethargic. Her eyes dropped, and she scanned both sides of the yard again, more methodically now as she checked behind every bush and tree, calling Charlie's name at increasingly louder volumes and shorter intervals.

She reached the deck and hurried up the steps. Charlie liked to play hide-and-seek, but he had never lasted this long before jumping out giggling into her arms. She had no idea how he'd have slipped past her into the house, but she entered by the sliding glass door and went through each room regardless, returning breathless to the backyard five minutes later.

The worry had burgeoned into a nauseous panic. She jogged down the steps and arrived back at the place where she'd last seen him petting the cat. Her mind struggled to grasp that he was missing. A woman shouted her name from the other side of the gate. "Ginger, is everything okay? I heard you calling for Charlie when I was working in the garden a few minutes ago."

Ginger hurried up the path. The wire gate looked shut, but it wasn't latched and swung open at her touch. Her stomach flip-flopped, and a stronger wave of anxiety rippled through her. Ainslie Harvey stood a few feet away, still wearing her gardening gloves caked in dirt. The cat that had been with Charlie moments before meowed as it rubbed itself against her legs.

"Charlie's gone missing. It's not like him to stay out of sight so long." Ginger touched the gate's latch, the lump in her throat making her voice hoarse. "I think this was left open. He must have gotten out while I was pouring him a glass of juice. He was right there petting your cat when I looked out the window." She didn't mention waiting for the kettle to boil or dashing to the washroom. She didn't want to appear a careless mother. "I looked at the beach already. I'll need to search up and down the street now."

She'd never made any effort to befriend Ainslie or to respond to her overtures. She'd been tired and depressed by the move to Loch Isle Road, and making friends had been beyond her. Thankfully, Ainslie didn't appear to hold a grudge.

"I'll put the word out, and we'll all help with the search. Don't worry, we'll find him. You don't look in any condition to be running the streets." She looked meaningfully at Ginger's belly. "How far along…?"

"Eight months. Thanks so, so much for your help. I really am frantic."

"I know, but it's best not to panic. He can't have gotten far. You should stay home in case Charlie pops out of wherever he's hiding. When my boys were young, they got into all kinds of mischief. He might be playing and not realize how worried he's made you."

"I hope you're right."

"I'm sure that I am."

Ginger watched from the end of her driveway as

Ainslie rounded up three neighbours from the closest houses. They began the search on both sides of the street, calling Charlie's name every few steps. Most of the wide front yards weren't fenced with tall cedar trees and bushes providing privacy. Scanning the length of Loch Isle, pine, balsam and elm trees formed a canopy with long, droopy branches swooping high above the road. Ginger lowered her gaze and squinted toward the untended patch of woods across the road at the far end that pressed in on the cleared spaces and gardens as if waiting to reclaim its stolen territory. She shivered, not wanting to give credence to the ominous presence she'd sensed on evening walks as the sun began its descent behind the tree line.

Fifteen minutes in, watching her neighbours scour the bushes and yards, the worried feeling inside her chest had blossomed again to panic. They gathered mid-street ten minutes after that, and Ginger started toward them. Ainslie met her partway while the other women stared at her with concerned faces. Ginger waved her phone and tried to keep from falling apart. "I'm calling 911. We need more help."

Ainslie was out of breath, a sheen of perspiration glistening on her forehead. She nodded. "I agree. Wherever Charlie's gotten to, we can't seem to find him. Let's bring in the professionals." Her fake cheery voice scared Ginger even more. Ainslie had put up no resistance to bringing in the cavalry. The other three women exchanged sombre looks, their eyes signalling grim messages that they dared not say in front of her.

After the dispatcher assured Ginger that a search team was on its way, she made a second call to David. His assistant had to get him out of a meeting. Her husband's shout of disbelief reverberated in her head long after the conversation ended. Once the initial shock wore off, he'd calmed down and then grumbled that Charlie would be found before he got there, but he wouldn't be able to concentrate anyway until he knew for sure.

"I'm on my way, Gin. Don't worry, I'll sort this out," he said before hanging up, his presumption that he would solve the problem that she couldn't angering her even as guilt pulsed through her like hot lava. She retreated to their yard to begin a search of the grounds one more time.

"Charlie, please come to me," she begged over and over while searching the bushes and shadowy corners near the fence. The crow had returned and startled in the pine overhead, cawing its displeasure as she stopped and tilted her head back to stare into the branches. She spotted its dark shape on a bough near the top of the pine before its wings spread wide and it flapped away, a grating cackle receding into the horizon. She stood clasping her arms around herself and closed her eyes, face upturned into the relentless sun, while she tried to ignore the dark omen and the dread that coursed through her in sickening waves.

CHAPTER 2

Detective Liam Hunter took the call as he was packing up for the day. Officer Leduc had limited information but rattled off the basic facts. A three-year-old boy had gone missing in the Rocky Point neighbourhood several hours earlier. The police were swarming the area but so far had come up empty. She added that there was a distinct possibility that the boy, named Charlie McGowan, had somehow made it to the river behind the family's property, but it was also possible that he'd been abducted. Apparently, the mother had left the toddler alone in the backyard for a few minutes. Leduc concluded by saying that her sarge had asked that Homicide and Major Crimes be alerted as a heads-up in case he wasn't found before nightfall.

"I'll make a run out there. Thanks for your call." Liam looked down at the address he'd scribbled onto his notepad, glad they'd been notified before the trail got cold, hoping the boy hadn't drowned.

"Got time to make a drive to Rocky Point in the west end with me?" he asked Quade. "Missing three-year-old boy."

Quade looked up from her computer screen at the desk across from his. Her brow furrowed with concern. "Of course. Let me call my ex to pick up the kids, and I'll be ready to go."

He sent a quick note to their staff sergeant, Greta Warner, and five minutes later they were in his car, accessing the ramp to the Queensway.

"How long's this boy been missing, and do you have a name?" Quade looked up from her cell phone.

"Charlie McGowan. He's been gone a couple of hours now."

She clicked on her phone and studied the screen. "Nothing in the media. Do you have a photo?"

"Not yet. Let's hope he turns up before this goes viral."

Not that long ago, before amalgamation, Crystal Beach and Rocky Point had been considered the far west end of Ottawa. Now the city sprawled past these neighbourhoods to Kanata and had almost joined up with the communities of Carleton Place, Stittsville, and Carp, formerly working farmland. The Crystal Beach neighbourhood spanned the south side of the busy six-lane Carling Avenue. The McGowans lived on the pricier north side in the Rocky Point neighbourhood, which ran parallel to the Ottawa River.

Liam took the Moodie off-ramp and merged onto Carling. He drove a few minutes before turning left onto Rocky Point Road. The street wound its way through old tree growth and greenery to a stop sign where Liam made a left turn onto Loch Isle. Large houses set back from the road had substantial treed properties that backed onto Crystal Bay. The McGowan house was the last lot on the north side, next to a dead end. Liam scanned the mature conifer and cedar trees and trimmed bushes on both sides of the road as he coasted past police cars and emergency vehicles. There were countless places for a child to hide. A cop directing traffic waved him over. Liam rolled down the window and flashed his ID.

"How's the search going?"

The cop shook his head. "Nothing yet. We've called in the dive team." He pointed to a spot farther ahead. "There's a place to park in front of the fire truck."

"The dive team's a serious development." Quade turned her head to stare out the side window as Liam eased his car into the tight space. Neither of them would utter the worst-case scenario, not wanting to give life to the boy's fate. They got out of the car and walked the length of the road, nodding at a couple of uniformed officers going door to door. "They might not need our services after all," she added as she looked toward the police boat on the river. "Not if Charlie made it that far."

Liam didn't respond, trying to keep the heaviness from overpowering the slim thread of hope. "It's hot as Hades," he said instead.

"Going on two weeks of living in this furnace. Climate-change deniers have some 'splaining to do."

Her voice lightened, but her face remained worried. He knew she struggled, as he did, with cases involving children.

The McGowan house was a seventies two-storey. Flat roof and pale grey siding. A limestone wall, eye-height, extended along the property line between their house and the neighbour on the east side. Trees and bushes provided privacy in the front yard, and a small woodlot wrapped around the western perimeter, beyond the McGowans' fence and the street's dead end. He could see houses far off in the distance through the trees, but to get to them someone would have to access a road farther along Carling. The neighbour's house across the street was set back behind a half-acre of pine and balsam trees, spirea, sumac, and choke cherry bushes. Looking toward the McGowans, he spotted a metal wire gate to the right of the house. More trees in the backyard towered above the roofline with a view of the river merging into the cloudless sky. "Nice spot."

"It's like living out in the country. This is what money can get you. Makes my neighbourhood feel even more sterile. Hard to get a warm, back-to-nature feeling about concrete and more concrete." Quade shot him a rueful smile.

"It's secluded enough." Liam could see how easy it would be to abduct a child with sightlines so frag-mented by greenery and homes set far back from the road. On the other hand, if the child had gotten out of the yard on his own, he wouldn't have far to go before he was at the water's edge.

Another officer greeted them at the front door of the McGowan house. Liam recognized him from past cases, and they weren't asked to show their badges. The cop led them down the hallway into the kitchen and introduced them to Ginger and David McGowan, who sat close together in the breakfast nook, their hands intertwined and resting on the table.

"I'm sorry you're going through this," Liam said, taking the seat across from them. Quade tucked herself into a corner near the doorway. "I'm Detective Liam Hunter, and this is my partner, Detective Julie Quade. We're here to help find Charlie. Could you tell me what happened?"

David looked at his wife, and she withdrew her hands from his. She was a lot younger than her husband, and when she shifted position, Liam could see that she was heavily pregnant. David had to be fifty, and he guessed that she was early thirties, with long, reddish-blonde hair tied back and dark brown eyes rimmed red. Her voice was raspy from crying.

"Charlie and I were outside, and I came in to fetch some juice. I checked on him through the window, and he was playing with the neighbour's cat in our side yard. I believed the gate was shut, but…" She trailed off.

"It's not your fault." David grabbed her hand and squeezed. He looked at Liam. "It's really not her fault. We've only lived here since May, and the latch on that gate doesn't always catch. I'd meant to fix it but never found the time. I blame myself."

Ginger nodded without looking at him. David's hair was thick and grey and styled to look naturally windblown. His dress shirt had to be tailor-made. Liam wondered what he did for a living and whether his money made him a target. "This isn't a question of blame," he said. "No parent can anticipate everything that can go wrong when it comes to their children. Could Charlie have opened the gate himself?"

"Not possible. He was too short to reach the latch." David shook his head. "No, it had to have been left open and Ginger didn't notice. In her defence, the gate looks closed, even when it isn't. I could easily have made the same mistake."

An annoyed look crossed Ginger's face that disappeared as quickly as it came. She glanced at David before lifting her eyes to Liam's. She appeared to be selecting her words carefully. Her voice gained strength as she spoke. "I don't see how Charlie could have gotten to the river without me seeing him. I checked the gate at the back of the property a minute after I noticed him missing, and it was shut for certain. I scanned the beach and water, and there was no sign of him. I wasn't in the house long enough for him to go out the front gate and make it to the river before I started searching."

"Then hopefully he's somewhere close by and will be found soon. Tell me what you did exactly after you left Charlie alone in the yard." Liam wanted to pin down a timeline.

"Charlie said he was thirsty, and rather than haul him inside with me because it would have been a battle, I left him petting the cat. He's enthralled with the tabby from next door, which was happily letting Charlie fuss over him." She glanced at her husband as if to gauge his reaction. David stared straight ahead, but Liam noticed his hand squeeze Ginger's again in a show of support. She took a deep breath. "Anyhow, I left Charlie in what I believed to be our securely gated yard and went inside. I filled the kettle and checked on him from the dining room window. He was still crouched next to the cat, which lay stretched out in the sun. I watched him until the kettle boiled and returned to the kitchen, poured water over my teabag, got him some juice, and went back outside."

"Do you happen to know what time this was?"

"It was ten fifteen. I know because a message pinged on my phone, and that's when it arrived."

"So from the last moment you saw Charlie until you went back outside, it was how long, would you say?"

"Three minutes? Certainly no more than five, but I'd watched him through the window for most of that time." Her face paled. "Oh, wait. I dashed to the washroom, but that took half a minute. I also checked my email and returned one message." She started to stand. "I don't see how this is helping find Charlie." She turned to David. "We should be out there. He might not come when he's called by a stranger."

"I'll go. You stay here in case he comes home on his own. Have a lie down and try to rest."

"I can't stand this. I just want to hold him and never let him go."

"I know, babe, but they'll find him. We have to hang on. The doctor told you that stress isn't good for your pregnancy, so try to relax." David rested his other hand on her arm, but she shook him off and heaved herself up from the table.

"I'll be upstairs unless you want me to stay here?" She looked from Liam to Quade.

"We'll call if we need you." Liam spoke gently, trying not to add to her distress.

They listened until her footsteps reached the upstairs landing. David ran a hand through his hair. "I want to go outside and help with the search, if that's all right."

"We can go together." Liam signalled Quade with his eyes. "My partner will stay with your wife in case of any developments."

"I'll text immediately if there's any word," Quade said.

Liam followed David out the front door. The search team would already have combed the yards nearby, but they retraced their steps, calling Charlie's name as they went. David didn't stop until they had gone up one side of the street and down the other, dipping into yards and checking through foliage and behind bushes. The late-afternoon heat was bearable under the shade of the trees but brutal on the road where there was no protection. Liam's shirt stuck to his back, and he wiped the sweat from his forehead before it dripped into his eyes. He'd put on dark sunglasses and wished he'd thought to bring a hat. David, however, seemed immune to the heat. He moved with the prowess of an athlete: long, confident strides and square shoulders. Liam felt the nervous energy radiating off him.

They circled back to the McGowan driveway and stood together, Liam silent while David decided whether to continue searching or wait for the police to give an update.

"Only the beach side remains." David looked toward the river but made no move in its direction.

"Do you have any other children?" Liam asked, partly to distract him.

"Two by my previous marriage. Sara is seventeen, and Roddy's just turned fifteen. They live with their mother, Claudette, in the east end but visit on the weekends when their schedules open up." He shot Liam a look. "You know how busy teenagers can be."

"What is it you do for a living?" Liam hadn't ruled out the possibility that this was an abduction for ransom.

"I own a financial investment company. Our offices are in the east end as well, on St. Laurent Boulevard. I was there when Ginger called that Charlie was missing."

"How many employees?"

"Forty-some, but not all working out of Ottawa. We're considered mid-sized."

"And you've only lived in this house two months? You don't mind the drive at rush hour?"

"I stay late most nights and am often in the office early, so I miss the worst of it. A couple of days a week I work from home and avoid the traffic altogether." David scanned the tree line on the far side of the road as he talked. He dropped his voice. "If only I'd stayed home today."

"Don't do that to yourself, sir. None of this is anybody's fault."

"I know." He hesitated. "Ginger has that foggy brain women get when they're pregnant. Any moment of inattentiveness could be put down to that." They started walking toward the gate at the side of his house. He added, "We may as well cut through the yard and have another look for Charlie, fruitless as it might be. Standing still is driving me crazy."

So you do blame her, Liam thought, casting him a sideways glance. He wondered if Ginger sensed this, even though David had insisted he was responsible for the gate latch not being fixed. "Why don't you go inside and be with Ginger, and I'll come see you if there's any news?" Liam didn't want him to witness his son's body being pulled from the water, if that was the outcome.

Realization crossed David's face, and his skin turned ashen. "You're right," he said after a pause. "But you'll come get me if…"

"Yes."

"That'll be for the best then." David nodded once before turning and striding toward the back deck.

CHAPTER 3

After Hunter and David left to search for Charlie, and Ginger had climbed the stairs to her bedroom, Julie Quade took the opportunity to look through the downstairs. There was a time she might have felt bad about snooping into another person's private affairs, but that was before she'd borne witness to all the atrocities people inflicted on each other. She was usually amazed by the evidence guilty people left in plain view, either from ineptness or hubris. Sometimes she thought the perpetrators subconsciously wanted to get caught.

Houses had an aura. They gave off a feeling — happiness, grief, sadness, love — she couldn't explain it but knew to trust her first impression. As soon as she stepped through the McGowan front door, she'd sensed a home out of kilter, and not just because their son was missing. This kind of tension went deeper. She'd never told Hunter about her sixth sense. He'd have given her that lopsided smile of his and changed

the subject. Her partner never commented on other
people's opinions if he wasn't in agreement, unless
they affected a case. Sometimes he stayed silent even
when he was completely opposed to a working theory.
She'd come to learn it wasn't shyness, as she'd first
believed. He preferred to remain aloof, to distance
himself from conflict. She thought about all the open-
ings she'd given him to criticize their boss, Greta
Warner, that he'd neatly sidestepped. His reticence to
badmouth Greta made her redouble her efforts to
make him crack. What did that say about her?

She went through drawers, methodically, silently,
starting in the kitchen, even checking out the food in
the pantry and fridge. Ginger and David were into
healthy eating. Fruit, vegetables, whole wheat everything, kale, almond milk … they put her food choices
to shame. She opened the bottom cupboards,
searching for store-bought cookies, checked the
freezer for ice cream, and found nothing. *Poor Charlie*,
she thought. *Not an Oreo in sight.* Her kids would go on
a hunger strike if this was all she had on hand.

The house was an older vintage, but previous
owners had undertaken renovations. The wall
between the kitchen and dining room had been
removed, with an island separating the two spaces.
What might once have been a bedroom down a short
hallway off the kitchen was being used as an office.
His or hers? She entered and surveyed the space. A
glass and steel desk under a window looked out over
the backyard. Bookcases lined the walls, and a locked
filing cabinet sat to the left of the desk. Why locked?

She opened desk drawers but didn't disturb anything. That would be a step too far without a warrant.

The renovations hadn't reached the living room. A large picture window faced the street, but the room was nondescript and functional at best. A sectional couch and two chairs took up only a small part of the space, the rest of the room empty and waiting for attention. A glass coffee table sat in front of the couch. The off-white wall colour appeared dingy in the light filtering through the elms in front of the window. A toy box against the far wall and a high chair in the kitchen were the only signs a child lived here. Julie thought about her own place, every room crammed with toys and games and all things kid-friendly when her two were younger. In contrast, the McGowans' main floor was sterile and geared to adults. Charlie's books and larger toys must be upstairs in his bedroom.

She made it back to the kitchen and was walking toward the basement when she heard footsteps slowly descending the staircase from above. She changed direction, and when Ginger entered the kitchen, she was leaning against the island, waiting. "Are you feeling any better?" Julie asked.

"Have they found Charlie?"

"There's no word yet. Your husband is still searching with Detective Hunter."

"Then no, I'm not feeling any better." Ginger's hairline was dark with sweat from her nap and her face even paler than before she'd gone upstairs. She walked over to the patio window and looked outside.

Wrapping her arms around herself, she stood motionless, gazing into the backyard.

"Tell me about Charlie," Julie said to draw her back. "What kind of boy is he?"

Ginger didn't answer, not until she turned, walked over to the island, and sat on a stool facing Julie. "He's busy, always on the go. He's inquisitive, and his favourite word is *why*." She closed her eyes. "He smells like sunshine and baby shampoo and … he gives the best snuggles. He loves books, especially ones with teddy bears. He has a collection of stuffed ones."

"He sounds like a wonderful little boy."

"He's my world."

The back door opened, and David entered the kitchen alone. Ginger spun around to face him, half rising from her chair. "They haven't found him anywhere," David said. He walked over to his wife and put an arm around her. "But no sign that he went into the river. The canine unit didn't pick up his scent on the beach."

"Oh, thank God." She buried her face in his shirt.

"They're still searching the shoreline, but he's not in any of the places they'd have expected. Thankfully, there aren't any currents or rapids close to our stretch of beach." David looked at Julie. "Now what?"

"We start looking at other possibilities."

"Like abduction?"

"It's something we need to consider. Has anyone been threatening you or acting oddly this past while?"

Ginger and David looked at each other and then at her. They shook their heads, and David spoke for

them both. "We lead simple lives, all things considered. My business is doing well, but we're not rolling
in money by any means, not with the child support I
pay to my first wife."

"I rarely go out," Ginger added. "There's a mom
and me class Charlie and I attend twice a week, but
that's it since we moved here. I don't really know any
of the other families on the street."

"We'll listen in on your phones in case there's a
ransom call, and we'll have a victim support worker
here for a few days at least. I can recommend issuing
an AMBER Alert if you agree. This will be the
quickest way to have people across the country
become engaged, and we should get fast approval. Of
course, we'll continue searching in the meantime. Do
you have a recent photo of Charlie that we can
circulate?'

"I can send you one." Ginger said, standing. "I've
got lots on my phone upstairs."

"We'll do whatever it takes, anything you want,"
David added, "if it brings Charlie home."

"Of course," Julie repeated. She could see that he
was as distraught as Ginger over their son's disappearance. In her experience, most men wanted to fix
things instead of tuning in to what their wives were
feeling. Given the age difference between Ginger and
David, it was understandable that he saw himself as
her protector and perhaps didn't consider her as his
equal. Ginger showed signs of irritation whenever he
was too solicitous, obviously not appreciating his
efforts. If their son stayed missing much longer, the

fissures in their relationship would deepen — Julie had seen this happen many times before in stressful situations. If he blamed Ginger at all for Charlie's disappearance, time would exacerbate his feelings, and he'd have a harder and harder time keeping her from knowing … that is if she didn't already.

CHAPTER 4

Ella Tate stood with the other reporters across the street from the McGowan house next to the dead end on Loch Isle Road. Yellow police tape and two officers kept them from moving closer onto the property or walking to the front door and ringing the bell. She'd arrived after the local television stations set up their cameras, and she watched a CBC reporter filming a segment with the house as the backdrop. She turned when somebody called her name.

"How'd you get here so fast?" Sherry Carpenter demanded, trotting up behind her and panting in the heat. She didn't wait for Ella to respond. "Canard sent me as your backup. He smells a big story, and as our long-time editor, I'd lay bets on his nose being right." She looked up the road toward the line of emergency vehicles and cop cars while wiping sweat off her face with the end of her shirt. "It's like Fort Knox getting in here."

"We aren't being told anything yet, but the place is swarming with cops. They've got the canine units and dive team taking part in the search."

"So they think the kid escaped his yard and started roaming?"

"That's one theory. Kid's name is Charlie McGowan, by the way."

"Yeah, I knew that already." Sherry touched Ella's arm. "I want to thank you for putting in a good word for me with Canard. He told me the other day over a couple of beers what you did."

Ella waved a hand. "It just made sense to put you on the crime beat." She turned her face toward Sherry and smiled. "It's time we women started working together on these stories. Give our male colleagues the opportunity to report on health and fitness and family life for a change."

"A few men in the office weren't too pleased at my assignment, I can tell you." Sherry laughed. She tugged on the collar of her blouse. "This heat is killing me. I've been in air conditioning all day."

"I like the heat."

"You do look untouched by sweat. Kind of abnormal, really."

Ella shrugged. "A genetic trait." She paused. "Any background on the family?"

"David McGowan owns an investment company with forty-two employees. He turns fifty-one this year, but he made the top forty under forty back in the day. Previously married to one Claudette McGowan for twenty years. They have two kids: Sara, aged seventeen, and Roddy, aged fifteen. Shared custody, but the children live with the mom in Orleans."

"And his new wife?"

"Not much on her except her name is Ginger, she's thirty-three, and used to work for David's company as an admin assistant. She also took his last name, making for two Mrs. McGowans. A most confusing ritual in my opinion."

"Boss aging out of his youth leaves wife for younger model in the secretarial pool. A sordid story as old as time."

"You're too young to be this cynical, Tate. He could have taken up with the fair Ginger after the amorous Claudette left him for a younger man."

"Yeah, right. Not bloody likely. Has the first Mrs. McGowan remarried?"

"No."

"I rest my case."

Ella's phone buzzed at the same time as Sherry's started playing "Smoke on the Water." Sherry's fingers clicked open the message before Ella could get the phone out of her pocket. "An AMBER Alert's gone out. Must mean the police are leaning toward abduction. Canard's gut feeling was right."

Ella was having trouble getting her head around the randomness of an abduction. A stranger happened to be on this road for the five minutes when Charlie's mom wasn't watching him? What were the odds? Perhaps someone had been staking out the yard and saw an opportunity. More likely but still an uncommon crime. The boy making it out of the yard on his own and wandering down to the river seemed a more likely option. "If that's the case, why pick this particular child on a dead-end road in the middle of nowhere? Something's off."

"Who knows, but it could have happened. Random crimes occur all the time. By the way, I emailed the background info to you. Are you drafting the article for the morning paper, or do you want me to handle it?"

"No, I'll write it. I took a photo of the father and the cops searching the woods that we can use along with the AMBER Alert pic of Charlie."

"Good. Canard said to send your article to him today. He wants to get it online before the paper comes out. Well, I've got another story on the go about a shooting downtown, so I'm out of here but am available if you need me for more research or whatever."

"Good to know."

Ella stood in place, watching the house, after Sherry jogged back the way she'd come. She hadn't told Sherry that Detective Hunter was inside. She'd texted him earlier to send information to her cell when he had a chance. The television crews had made their way to the beach, where the dive teams were searching, and she was left alone, waiting for something to happen, periodically scanning the trees and bushes on both sides of the road, hoping Charlie would somehow magically appear.

The day was getting on. Shadows stretched long fingers across the pavement, and the breath-taking heat lessened to a notch below bearable. Ella's stomach rumbled, and she wished she'd thought to bring more food than the package of nuts and the smushed granola bar she'd found at the bottom of her bag. She'd finished the tepid water in her bottle an hour before. Police officers were still patrolling the road, but the earlier frenzy had slowed to more of a waiting game. She'd have to leave soon to get her story written and submitted by deadline. Canard had sent two pointed messages after Sherry left, asking for an update.

At last, the front door of the house opened and Liam Hunter and Julie Quade stepped outside. She hadn't seen Hunter since her return to Ottawa in late November, although they'd periodically corresponded by email about some of her true crime podcasts. His black hair was longer than she remembered, giving him the appearance of an undercover cop on a drug case. More likely he simply hadn't gotten around to seeing a barber. He was overdressed for such a hot day, and sweat stains darkened his cream-coloured shirt. He carried a grey suit jacket loosely in one hand. His sharp blue eyes spotted her almost immediately, and he said something to Quade before walking over to stand facing her. "Fancy seeing you here."

"What, you don't want to know how I've been?" She raised a hand to stop him answering. "Have you got anything more to tell the public than what's in the AMBER Alert?"

Hunter glanced at Quade, who'd started walking away from them toward their car, before he turned his intense gaze on her. "Just we haven't found any trace of him in the area surrounding the house or the river, so we're considering other options. That's all I've got for you. You're looking good, by the way. Cooler than the rest of us."

She shrugged. "I like it hot. Will there be a press conference?"

"Not sure how Greta … Staff Sergeant Warner plans to communicate this case. Are you working on your podcast or writing for *The Capital*?"

"An article for the paper, but I want to do an in-depth podcast. I'm up to seventy thousand followers and might be able to get the word out more widely to help find him." She looked at the house tucked in behind a metal fence next door to the McGowans. "I'm guessing no home security video cameras captured anything?"

"Not so far. The officers were checking on that possibility in the door-to-door search but came up empty. Most people aim the cameras around their entrances and driveways. A lot have doorbell cameras, so investigators are asking homeowners to check these too. Hopefully we'll get a lead. I'll run the idea of using your podcast past Greta." His eyes darkened. "I hate this type of case."

"It's a tough one. A three-year-old child."

"Yeah." He ran a hand across his forehead. "The longer he's missing…" He stopped and didn't finish the thought. "Look, I gotta get moving. Quade and I will be debriefing the team back at the station. It's going to be a long night for everyone if he stays missing. I'll be in touch when I can."

"I'll be on standby."

She watched him go, already writing the article for Canard in her head as she rounded the dead-end barricade to get to her car parked on the other side. Hunter hadn't mentioned the word "abduction," but she'd raise the likelihood as part of the story lede. He was right, though. This case already had grief written all over it.

———

SARA MCGOWAN HEARD the AMBER Alert signal on the flat screen as she stood in the kitchen drinking a glass of water. She raced into the living room in time to read the details of a possible abduction scroll across the screen. Roddy and her mom weren't home yet, so nobody heard her shout of disbelief. *Charlie's missing?* The alert said he'd been wearing red shorts, a bright yellow t-shirt with Yogi Bear on the front, tan sandals, and a denim ball cap. She closed her eyes and pictured him in the little outfit. He was all about bears and had told her on her last visit that he was going to be one when he grew up. Last seen in his backyard on Loch Isle Road mid morning. Her heart jumped. The timing was not good.

Dad's midlife crisis. That's what she always thought of whenever she saw Ginger and Charlie at her dad's house. Charlie was the reason her dad had left her mom … proof of the affair he'd been having behind her back. It had taken Sara a long time to go visit him in his new life, but she'd never gotten comfortable with "the other arrangement," as her mother called it — and now Charlie was missing. She could barely get her head around the idea. She'd refused to babysit the kid at the start but had softened as time went on and he became more interesting. She still didn't care much for Ginger, though, and only looked after Charlie when her dad insisted. Letting on that she'd grown fond of Charlie felt like a betrayal of her mother.

She bit her bottom lip and debated whether to call her dad or to act like she hadn't seen the alert. What would she say to him anyway? *Sorry the kid who broke up our family is gone? I was walking on your beach spying on Ginger around the time he went missing?* She could imagine how bad that would look. What if they found out she'd been stalking her dad and Ginger for the past year since she got her driver's licence? Watching their house. Following her dad to work. Tailing him on his social outings. Driving behind Ginger's car to the grocery store. The list had creepy written all over it. No, better to play dumb and keep out of whatever was going on.

A key rattled in the front door. She grabbed the remote and clicked off the television before scooting into the hallway. Her mom swung the door open and stooped to pick up a shopping bag before stepping inside. She jumped at the sight of Sara staring at her in the hallway and slapped a hand over her heart. "Goodness, you gave me a fright. What are you doing just standing there?"

"Checking my heart rate and stretching. I'm in from a run. Why are you so late, and where's Roddy?"

"I went for a drive and stopped to get some food. Chicken and rice okay for tonight?" She kicked off her sandals and walked past Sara without looking at her or waiting for an answer.

"I guess."

Her mom was acting funny, but then she'd been all over the map since her dad left some three years ago. Emotional and unpredictable. Sara trailed after her into the kitchen. Her mom was busy laying out what she'd bought on the counter and getting pots out of the cupboard. Sara grabbed a bottle of Gatorade from the fridge and leaned against the stove as she took a sip. She lowered the bottle. "So where's Roddy?" she asked again.

"He said something about visiting one of his friends. I expect him home for dinner." Her mother was definitely avoiding eye contact.

"Is everything okay, Mom?" She thought about bringing up Charlie's disappearance, but how would that look since she hadn't mentioned it when her mother first came in? Plus, there'd be a tirade at the sound of his name — there always was. Her mom probably wouldn't even care that he was missing. Sara decided not to risk her wrath and hoped she'd be somewhere else when the news broke.

Her mother rummaged in the cupboard and pulled out a bottle of red wine. "Yes, dear. I'm tired, that's all."

"I'm going for my shower then."

"And I'm going to pour myself a glass of vino and put my feet up after I get the chicken in the oven. Uncle Ivan is coming for supper."

Again? Sara thought the word but didn't say it out loud. She shot her mom one more glance under lowered brows before exiting the kitchen. She couldn't tell if her mother already knew about Charlie's disappearance and wasn't letting on. If she really didn't know, Sara wondered how the news would land. Her mom had never forgiven her dad for his betrayal and still made disparaging comments about Ginger and "the bastard child." Sara was becoming more and more uncomfortable as time passed and her mother's seething anger boiled and bubbled. Uncle Ivan didn't help. He liked to badmouth her dad whenever the two of them got into the alcohol. It might improve things if her mother got a new boyfriend, but she'd told Sara often enough that hell would freeze over before she'd trust another man.

And now Charlie's missing and Mom is acting stranger than usual — difficult as that is to believe. Please, God, don't let her and Uncle Ivan have done anything stupid. Please let Charlie be found and keep him safe until he comes home to Dad and Ginger and his teddy bears.

CHAPTER 5

"Yoo-hoo! Ready for some company and a chat?"

Ella got up from her seat at the computer, crossed the small space, and opened the door of her third-floor brownstone unit. Tony, her neighbour from the floor below, slipped past her with his dog Luvy trotting behind him. The dog scooted into her usual spot on the floor under Ella's desk. Ella dropped into her chair and bent to scratch behind the miniature dachshund's ears.

"You've been working long hours," she said, glancing up at Tony, who stood a few feet away in the direct line of the floor fan.

"It's a bumper year at the altar. I'll be keeping up this pace through September until every last bride is coiffed and hitched to the misery — or I should say the dream — of her own making."

"A fool born every minute. Do you get a sense of how many of these marriages are doomed to fail?"

"You speak from a place of disillusionment and a deep well of pathetic … ness. However, one in three marriages ends after ten years, making for repeat business the second time around. A win-win, truly." He tugged at one of her tufts of hair and pouted. "When are you going to let me cut this chaos, girl?"

"Yeah, just what you want to do in your time off. My hair can wait." She avoided Tony's grimace by spinning around to face her computer screen. "I'm on deadline and need to finish this." She absentmindedly pushed a stray strand out of her eyes before she began typing.

Tony leaned over her shoulder. "You writing about the missing university student?"

"No. A three-year-old boy's now disappeared in Rocky Point, which is in the west end. The paper's hired me to follow the case and write updates."

"Three years old. Gad." Tony shook his head. "A parent?"

"No. They thought at first that he got out of the yard and searched for him all afternoon and into the evening. They even had the dive team out since the kid's house abuts the Ottawa River. Another possibility is that somebody abducted him, but the parents are together and this isn't over custody." She stopped typing. "Meilin Hanon's story has gone cold. The police haven't any new leads."

"Perhaps this three-year-old's abduction is linked to hers?"

Ella considered the likelihood before shaking her head. "Opposite ends of the city. One's a child and the other's a Chinese exchange student at Carleton U. Meilin Hanon disappeared about eight months ago after a party. I don't see that the cases have much in common besides the fact they're both missing."

"It's terrible to think two kidnappers are on the loose."

"There's more than one evil person walking the planet, my friend, but Meilin's disappearance could be a suicide. That hasn't been ruled out. Little Charlie McGowan might have drowned."

"Hard to choose amongst all these happy scenarios. So, are you putting her story on ice while you work on this latest abduction?"

"Uh-huh." She added a sentence to the last paragraph and held up a finger for him to stop talking while she did a final scan of the text. "That ought to do it." She hit *Send* and angled her chair around to face him. "So what can I do for you, Tony?"

"It's more what I can do for you. I have Friday off and thought I'd celebrate by hosting a small dinner party."

"You want me to watch Luvy?"

"No, I want you to attend. Don't bring anything but your sunny self. For sure, don't cart along any of that wine your body somehow manages to tolerate. Your insides need a night off." He tugged at his t-shirt. "Gawd, it's hot up here. I should have dressed in my towel because sitting in this teensy, tiny apartment is like being in a sauna."

"I'm used to it. Who else is coming?"

"Well, Finn and Adele from down below. I've told

them to bring baby Lena, whom Adele assures me
sleeps from seven to seven. Also a few members of my
baseball team."

Ella didn't need to worry about Tony trying to set
her up. His ball team was composed of men who
proudly waved the rainbow flag. "You do know I'm
Adele's least favourite person, right? She can't seem to
understand that Finn and I have only *ever* been friends
since we met in grade school. I can only surmise that
she believes I'm a threat to their marriage, which I
categorically am not."

"All the more reason to get together over alcohol.
One's quibbles look insignificant while scarfing down
cocktails and chicken Kiev. It's time you two buried
the hatchet."

"There is no hatchet. She's just never taken
to me."

"She's your polar opposite — and granted,
appears to have a jealous streak to rival Othello's —
but that doesn't mean you can't be friends."

"Tell *her* that. I'm not the one doing the avoiding."
Ella motioned toward the door. "I don't mean to be
rude, but I have to finish some research before bed.
Time for you and Luvy to hit the road."

Tony stretched. "It *has* been a long day." He bent
and picked up the dog but turned when he reached
the entrance to the living room. "It's only now struck
me what Adele was talking about earlier. We met on
the front steps, and she said that she and Lena go to a
mom and me group where she met that woman in the
news and didn't know if she should contact her. I had

no idea what she was talking about and was in a hurry to get to work, so I didn't ask. Anyhoo, something for you to follow up on."

Ella turned from her computer. "Thanks for the tip. I'll try to catch Adele in the morning."

Insomnia had plagued Ella all spring, and the idea of getting into bed filled her with anxiety. She spent the next couple of hours reading up on child kidnappings, trying to tire herself out while waiting for the apartment's temperature to drop a few degrees. She could take the heat, but lying between sweaty sheets made falling asleep even tougher. The information was what she'd expected. The majority of missing kids in Canada were runaways, followed by parental abductions. Stranger abductions were rare — the last year of data, sixteen stranger abductions out of over forty thousand missing kids were reported. Ninety-two per cent of cases were solved within a week. Ella raised her head and thought about that. She mentally prepared herself to read the reasons why a stranger abducted a child and lowered her eyes: sex, ransom, mental issues, wishing to cause harm to the child or their family. Where did Charlie McGowan's disappearance fit in? All of the motives hurt to contemplate.

Weak moonlight filtered through the window, and she glanced at the time: 2:30 a.m., and dawn only a few hours away. She was weary enough that if she took off her clothes and climbed under the sheet, she might be able to sleep. All she had to do was put her head on the pillow, close her eyes, and relax. She decided to lie down on the couch first and see if she could clear her mind. Maybe ease into the bedroom when she was already drowsy.

At four thirty, she finally gave up trying to sleep on the couch and dropped her clothes on the floor as she made her way to bed, clicking on the fan inside the door as she passed. She kicked back the covers and pulled the cotton sheet over herself, then stared at the ceiling and cursed herself for being so wide awake. After a few minutes, she rolled onto her side and closed her eyes. At the very least she could rest until the sun came up, when she'd have to drag herself through another day. It wasn't as if she didn't have a lot of practice.

CHAPTER 6

Ginger walked over to the bedroom window and looked out across the backyard. The Ottawa River sparkled a brilliant aqua band above the tree line at the back of their property. David was at the beach, watching the police divers. He said that he needed to be outdoors, even if he wasn't able to do anything useful. He'd reassured her over and over the night before and again this morning that she was not at fault in any way for Charlie's disappearance. He'd said it so bloody often that she knew he actually did blame her for leaving Charlie alone in the backyard. His constant hovering and sad cow eyes were getting on her nerves, and she was happy when he left her for a bit.

The detective assigned to stay with her in case of a ransom call was keeping discreetly out of sight, setting herself up in the living room but ready to help if required. Ginger could hear Julie Quade speaking on the phone every so often, her voice a low background murmur that she found oddly soothing. She'd brought the detective a pot of tea earlier, and she'd been appreciative while insisting that Ginger needn't have bothered.

Ginger tilted her head back and looked at the sky. Her son was somewhere under the same blue canopy. Had somebody fed Charlie last night? Read him a story and rocked him before putting him to bed? She stifled a sob with her fist pressed against her mouth. She'd never been separated from him this long. He'd be scared and asking for her. He wouldn't understand why she wasn't coming to take him home.

She turned and crossed to his bed tucked up against the wall. He'd only progressed to the "big boy" bed two months earlier as a treat for being in the new house. He'd helped to choose the blue bedspread with the huge cartoon polar bear stitched into the fabric. She picked up his favourite teddy from where she'd laid it on his pillow the night before and squeezed the stuffed bear to her chest with both arms. The minutes were crawling by even as she dreaded each passing second without word that he'd been found.

The doorbell chimed throughout the house, and she froze, listening to the detective's footsteps hurrying from the living room into the hallway. She spun around and ran to the landing, leaning over the banister to look downstairs. Detective Quade and the two people in the foyer stared up at her.

"Mom and Dad. You've come." Ginger's voice caught, and tears filled her eyes.

"We took the early flight. Detective Quade tells us there's been no word," her father said.

Her mother met her at the bottom of the stairs and opened her arms. "Darling girl. Your sister sends her love. She wishes she could be here."

"Where's David?" Her dad was staring down the hallway and into the kitchen. His voice had taken on a harsh edge. The detective hesitated for a moment on her way into the living room. She glanced back.

Ginger held her gaze without flinching until Julie Quade resumed walking and disappeared around the corner. She hated the feeling that her every word and action were being scrutinized. Did they honestly suspect her or someone in her family of harming Charlie? "David's down at the river with the dive team." Ginger saw her parents' shocked faces and quickly added, "They would have found Charlie by now if he was in the water. They're going over the same territory as yesterday. He's not in the river, I just know it in my bones."

"Of course he's not," her mother said. "We have to stay positive. How are you feeling? This is a lot of stress on you and the baby."

Ginger rubbed her belly. "We're doing fine, although David and I are frantic about Charlie. We feel so utterly helpless." She'd purposefully linked herself with David so that her parents would believe them a united front. And they were, weren't they?

When it came to their normal lives and what really mattered, of course they were.

She herded her parents upstairs with their suitcases to settle them into the larger guest bedroom and to get them away from the nosy cop. Her dad had never hidden his dislike for her husband, based solely on the fact he'd been her married boss when they'd hooked up. Strictly old-school with no understanding of another person's unwillingness to stay in an unhappy marriage. David had been struggling back then and called her his saviour more than once. For the first time, she thought that she might have made a mistake phoning her parents the day before in a panic. She didn't know if she had the energy to defuse her father's criticism, spoken and unspoken.

Her mom waited for her father to leave them alone in the hallway. "I'll freshen up and will see about making some lunch, shall I? Have you eaten today, Ginger?"

"I can't keep anything down. Not with Charlie missing. I'm out of my mind with worry."

Her mother slipped an arm through hers. "You have to think about your other child too. The baby inside you needs nourishment and calm. I'll make some omelettes and toast if you have eggs and bread, and we'll figure out how to get through this. Charlie will be found, and you need to stay healthy so that you can welcome him when he comes through that front door."

Ginger rested her head on her mother's shoulder. If only her mom could have come without her father. She was a comforting presence and would stay quietly in the background. Ginger felt the familiar apprehension growing inside her at the thought of her father's abrasive observations that he could never keep to himself. Tensions between her and David were already running high with the stress of Charlie's disappearance. Throwing her dad into the mix would be like throwing gasoline on a simmering fire. Who knew when the explosion would come … or how much uglier their world could get?

———

LIAM WALKED with David into the house after the morning's fruitless second search of the Ottawa River and the shoreline. The likelihood of Charlie having wandered into the water and drowned was getting more remote with every dive by the police unit and every sonar image that came up empty, but drowning still could not be completely ruled out. The river was deep and wide, and his body might have been moved downstream where currents and eddies could take him in any direction. Yet a three-year-old boy wouldn't have been able to wade very far from shore. His body should have been relatively easy to discover, given how quickly the police divers had been on the scene and the size of the bay.

David's mood had swung from one of despair to hope and back to despair on the walk home from the beach. "If he's still alive and somebody took him," he said as they entered the house through the back door, "shouldn't there be a ransom call, Detective?"

"We're ready for one."

"That doesn't answer my bloody question now, does it?"

"I wish I could be more definitive, but every case is different." Liam didn't take issue. He saw himself an objective outsider, watching and assessing every action and emotion.

David gave him a sheepish grin. "Sorry, man. My anger isn't directed at you or the enormous effort being put into finding Charlie. I just feel so damn helpless."

"Don't give it another thought."

Liam looked past him into the kitchen. Ginger was sitting at the island with an older man who had the ramrod bearing of ex-military. A grey-haired woman, presumably his wife, was cooking at the stove. David half-turned and took in the scene. The face he swung back to Liam was a curious mix of resignation and long-suffering. "Lucky you. You're about to meet my in-laws," he said so quietly that Liam wasn't certain he'd heard correctly.

"Madeleine and Richard. We're so glad you've come to support Ginger." David crossed the floor and put his hands on the woman's shoulders before air-kissing each cheek. The man got up from his seat and stood at attention until David closed the distance and shook his hand. David motioned toward Liam. "Meet Detective Hunter. These are Ginger's parents,

Madeleine and Richard Halliday. They've come all the way from Halifax."

"Of course we're here," Richard snapped. "Wouldn't have it any other way. Is there news, Detective?"

"We're pursuing all the avenues, but no, nothing concrete yet."

Madeleine stood staring at her husband and opened her mouth to speak. He glared at her, and she stopped whatever she'd been about to say and turned back to the stove. Liam wasn't sure what to make of this silent exchange. He made a mental note to follow up later when he could get Madeleine alone.

David took the stool next to Ginger and put a hand on her forearm. "How're you feeling?"

"I'll be better after I eat something." Ginger turned her anguished gaze on Liam. "Shouldn't we have heard from the kidnapper by now? Is this wait normal?"

"There's no set schedule when it comes to kidnappings. If someone took Charlie, they could be waiting until the search quiets down." Liam didn't say that the more time that passed without contact from Charlie's abductor, the worse his chances were. He didn't raise the idea of kidnappers whose sole intent was to harm the child.

"Then you lot have to clear out so whoever took Charlie makes contact," Richard said. "I can't believe you're still roaming around, covering ground that's already been gone over while scaring this person off." A dull red flushed upward from Richard's collar line as his voice rose to a near shout. He was a bullish man with white hair combed back off his forehead and piercing dark eyes set close together. "Who's running this circus anyway?"

"Dad," Ginger said without energy. "Please stop."

"You're upsetting Ginger." David moved closer to her and took a protective stance. "This isn't the time or place."

"Well, somebody has to hold the police accountable." Richard glared at David before picking up his coffee cup and drinking.

Liam spotted Quade hovering in the doorway and sent her a questioning look. She shook her head and mouthed, *Nothing to report.* He turned back and addressed the family. "I've got to return to headquarters, but you can direct your questions to Detective Quade. She'll be replaced later this morning by a liaison officer from Victims' Services. We'll have someone on site until the abductor makes contact." He turned his gaze on Richard. "And yes, we'll be unobtrusive."

He met Quade in the hallway, but they didn't speak until they were at the front door, out of earshot of the others. "Greta says to go home and get some sleep when your replacement arrives," he said.

"I could use a nap. Have you managed any shuteye?"

"I grabbed a few winks at my desk." He looked over his shoulder. "Tensions are starting to run high. If a ransom call comes in, might be difficult to control the two men."

"I've already talked to Ginger and David. They've been coached on what to say if the kidnapper calls."

"Don't let Richard anywhere near the phone. He's a loose cannon."

"I noticed that right off. I'll warn my replacement."

"I'll be in touch after I get the latest debrief at headquarters. A new door-to-door search is going on now, and the dive team will wrap up later today. We have no leads unless the tip line comes up with something."

"Or the neighbours. They're still checking their home security cameras."

"We can hope. This is a wealthy street, so owners will have cameras installed to protect their property. There should be lots of video footage." He looked down the hallway toward the kitchen. "I have a bad feeling about how this is going to play out. This family … I can't put my finger on it, but there's an under-current."

"I feel the bad energy too." Quade opened the front door. "See you later, Hunter. Maybe, we'll catch a break soon."

Liam strode down the driveway and scanned the crowd of reporters and cameras set up on the street. Since the house nestled up against the dead end, they were able to spread out on the roadway without fear of being run over. The sun burned brightly, and he squinted into the glare, searching for Ella Tate. She was nowhere to be seen, likely carrying out some background research for another article or her podcast. He'd been looking forward to seeing her again, even if they didn't have a chance to talk. He tucked away his disappointment and continued walking down the road toward his car. He'd grab a coffee on his way to headquarters to keep alert for the next part of his day.

CHAPTER 7

Ella stepped out of the shower and wiped the steam from the mirror. This was the only time that her hair looked half-decent — soaking wet and plastered to her head. Once it dried, she'd resemble a cross between a startled porcupine and a shaggy dog. If she hadn't been in a hurry, she'd take the scissors to the mess. She shrugged at her reflection. One more day looking like this wouldn't kill her.

She dressed quickly in tan cotton slacks and a white t-shirt, stepping into leather sandals on her way downstairs to the main floor. She'd finally fallen asleep as the birds started their morning song and had overslept. Hopefully, Adele hadn't taken Lena for a walk and would answer her knock.

Ella rapped her knuckles on the wood and listened for movement inside, relieved when Adele yanked the door open. Her expression chilled when she saw Ella. She raised a finger over her lips to signal quiet and then drew the door partway shut behind her as she stepped into the hall. "Lena's just down for her nap. She had a cranky night."

"Her and me both." Ella kept her voice low. "I understand from Tony that you know the mom of the little boy who was abducted two days ago."

"Oh my God, isn't it horrible? Charlie's such a sweet little guy, and Ginger adores him. I can't imagine what she's going through. Did you know she's pregnant?"

"Yes. It's truly awful."

Adele ran both hands through her long hair and pulled it away from her face, winding an elastic around three times until the strands were captured in a messy topknot. She was wearing a loose-fitting blue cotton dress covered in white polka dots, and her feet were bare. She reminded Ella of a picture she'd once seen of a sixties flower child.

"Are you certain he was abducted? The news showed the police searching the river behind their house." Adele's forehead creased with worry lines. "Either scenario is horrific."

"The working theory now is that he was taken."

"Damn. I'll have to send a message of support to Ginger on Facebook. We belong to a mom and baby group. She moved out of our neighbourhood a few months ago but stayed in the group."

Ella's heart quickened. "I could prompt people to be on the lookout for Charlie by putting out something on my podcast. Do you think Ginger would agree to a short interview?"

"Now, why in the world would she want to do that?"

"Because I have over seventy thousand followers, many in media, but lots of regular Ottawa citizens too. Not everyone gets their news on television or through established channels these days, so the more ways to get the word out, the better. It only takes one person who sees or remembers something that could lead to Charlie's whereabouts."

Adele's mouth rose in a sideways grimace. "One would almost believe there's nothing in this for you."

"I'm a reporter. A good story or interview is always my goal."

"A strange rationale, but all right." Adele pursed her lips and took a step back inside her apartment, pulling the door halfway shut. "I'll ask Ginger, but only because she has to be desperate to try every avenue to get Charlie home. I'll let you know when I hear back from her."

The door swung closed, and Ella stood for a moment, staring at it. Adele's animosity had sharpened since Lena's birth. She couldn't think of a single reason for Adele to be so antagonistic except for the long-standing friendship between her and Finn, dating back to their teen years in Edmonton — pre-Adele. He'd always been like a brother, but Adele might not believe they'd never hooked up. Ella shrugged and started back up the stairs. Not her problem.

She hesitated on the second floor and looked at Tony's closed door. He'd been working long hours and had been uncharacteristically subdued since his ex-boyfriend Sander came by to collect the last of his things. Except for the constant blasting of Celine's "My Heart Will Go On" pumping through the floorboards, she'd never know when he was home. Was yesterday's visit a sign that he was done grieving for his failed relationship? She regretted rushing him and Luvy out the door, even if she'd needed to keep working. The flash of remorse over her lack of empathy caught her unawares. She could have been more sociable. It wouldn't have killed her.

She continued climbing to her third-floor garret. She was already late for a meeting and would make time for Tony later to assuage her guilt. In the meantime, she'd think of an excuse to back out of his dinner party. The last thing she wanted to do was spend a meal pussyfooting around Adele and pretending they had anything in common.

————

ELLA GRABBED a latte and found a seat near the back of the Bank Street coffee shop where she could watch the front door. She pulled a copy of *Roget's Thesaurus* from her bag and set the book in front of her. At 11:20, a petite Asian woman with straight black hair to her waist entered and looked around. She glanced from the book to Ella's face and nodded once before lining up to order a coffee.

"You must be Ella," the woman said as she slid into the empty seat across from her. "Sorry I'm late."

"I'm just glad you made it, Yina."

"I thought about not coming."

Ella noticed Yina's hands trembling when she lifted the coffee cup to her lips. Yina flashed a weak smile as she lowered the cup to the table. "If speaking with you helps find Meilin, I need to give it a shot."

"I don't want you to do anything dangerous, but if you can find out who she was with the night she disappeared…"

"I talked to Meilin's roommate, Joanne Freemont."

Ella felt the first twinge of hope. She'd tried numerous times to speak with Joanne, without success. Joanne had avoided the media after the initial onslaught and disappeared into the woodwork. She was one of the last people to see Meilin on the night she went missing. "How did that go?" she asked, somewhat optimistic.

"Joanne wants to forget that night ever happened."

"I can't say I blame her. Losing a friend isn't something you want to relive." Ella could write a book. She forced herself to stay in the present. "Did she tell you anything?"

"No, sorry." Yina paused. "She said she'd talk to you, though."

"She what?"

"Yeah, she said that she listens to your podcast. She likes your interview style and the fact you don't sensationalize."

"How do we set it up?"

"Joanne will be in front of the Art Gallery on Sussex tomorrow afternoon at four. She'll find you."

Ella's photo was on her podcast site and easy enough to find elsewhere on the web. Joanne would have no problem identifying her. "Let her know that I'll be there, rain or shine."

Yina nodded. She looked around the café, and her eyes landed on a man paying for coffee at the cash. She swivelled back around to face Ella. "I've gotta go. Good luck."

"Same to you." She watched Yina duck into the washroom, her face averted from the counter the entire time. Ella stared at the man who appeared to have spooked her. He was white, early- to mid-twenties. Long black hair tied tightly in a man bun. Thick, coarse beard. Short and squat like a wrestler. There was little that made him attractive to women … well, to her anyway. He took his coffee and bagel over to a table near the door and surveyed the room as he sat down.

Ella stood and glanced over at the washrooms, which were down a short corridor. She was in time to see Yina slip out of the ladies and disappear through the back exit at the end of the hallway. The man at the table didn't make a move even when Ella walked past him on her way to the entrance. Could Yina be imagining danger where there was none? Ella still had no idea why all the cloak and dagger, but something was going on that had these young women looking over their shoulders, scared to be seen in public. It had taken her five months to track Yina down and another month for her to agree to this meeting. As far as Ella knew, she'd made more progress getting inside Meilin's circle than the police. Even at that, she had no idea where this case would lead, but she was becoming more and more curious to find out.

CHAPTER 8

The day was not going well. Uncle Ivan had slept over and was still hanging around in the kitchen like a scavenger raccoon, even though her mom had left for the grocery store an hour ago. The two of them had sat in the backyard with a case of beer after dinner and were still at it when Sara shut off her light to go to sleep at midnight. She'd heard Roddy come home a half hour later and go straight to bed. He'd left for the mall as soon as he got up in the morning, telling her on his way to the bathroom that he was meeting friends and he wouldn't be home all day.

Sara stayed in her bedroom and played video games on her laptop between reading updates on the police search for Charlie. She was trying to outwait Uncle Ivan before she went down for breakfast, now lunch, but he wasn't going anywhere fast. Hunger was going to win out if he didn't take off soon.

Her eyes dropped to the computer screen, and her

heart fell as she read the latest report. The police were asking for anyone who had information about Charlie's disappearance to come forward. They had no leads. She focused on Charlie's wide blue eyes staring at her from the Internet. He had the sweetest face, with chubby cheeks and dimples. She wondered if he was scared. If he was alive. The AMBER Alert was still in effect, but the clock was ticking. She knew that the likelihood of finding him safe and sound lessened the longer he was missing. The thought that she'd never see him alive again made her want to throw up.

She shoved the laptop aside and stared at Drake's face hanging over her bed. She'd outgrown the posters of idols on her wall but hadn't thought about redecorating until now. She stood and jumped onto the bed. In a few quick motions, Drake lay in tatters on the floor. Once started, she couldn't stop until the rest of her childhood crushes lay in strips next to him. "I loved you once," she said to BTS before tearing their poster in two. "And you never once called." Destroying posters released some of her pent-up worry, but the anxiety returned as soon as she stepped off the bed and slumped into her chair.

Uncle Ivan was talking on the phone, his muffled voice carrying up the stairwell and through the closed bedroom door. Sara tiptoed across the carpet, opened the door, and crept closer to the top of the stairs to listen, but his voice dropped, and he ended the call before she heard anything interesting. He and her mom were up to something, of that she was certain. If it had anything to do with Charlie's disappearance, what would she do? She told herself to knock it off. There was no way they could be involved. Her mother would never stoop to something so evil ... *would she?* Uncle Ivan, now he was another story. Sara knew he'd been involved in petty crime since his teenage years. The miracle was that he'd never been caught except for a few minor infractions that hadn't included jail time.

She heard him stomping around in the kitchen before he clomped down the hallway and out the front door. *Thank God*, she thought and waited a minute to make sure he was really gone before she trod slowly downstairs, listening for the door the entire time. She was pouring a bowl of Raisin Bran, confident he wasn't returning, when the doorbell rang. *Please don't let it be him back again.*

The good-looking man standing at the door smiled and showed her his ID badge. She looked closely and compared the photo to his face. Detective Liam Hunter. Dark, wavy hair on the long side, five o'clock shadow, brilliant blue eyes that were studying her as intently as she was staring at him. "I'm here about Charlie," he said. "Is your mom home?"

And a sexy Irish accent. Icing on the cake. "She's gone out for groceries but should be back soon. Would you like to have a cup of coffee while you wait?" She wasn't sure why she invited him in but thought it might be because he felt unthreatening. His eyes were too direct to be a conman's, and she liked his smile.

He glanced from her to his car parked on the

street and back again. "Sara McGowan, is it? That would be nice. Thank you."

He sat at the kitchen table while she got the coffee ready. He didn't appear fazed by the mess left over from their dinner the night before or the stale smell of beer that she hoped the coffee would mask. She stifled a sigh of frustration. At least Uncle Ivan could have cleaned up while he was hanging around. He'd bummed enough meals that scraping a few plates was the least he could do.

She got busy stacking the dishwasher while she waited for the coffee to brew. The detective studied his phone screen as she worked and seemed comfortable with her tidying around him. At last, the coffee was ready and she poured two cups, sliding one in front of him before she got the cream out of the fridge. She prayed it hadn't soured as she plunked the carton next to the sugar bowl. He looked up from his phone.

"Thanks, Sara. Just what I needed. Why don't you join me?"

His request felt more like a demand, even though his tone was friendly. She took the seat at the far end of the table. "Have you got any news about Charlie?" she asked, glad to get the elephant in the room out in the open. She also thought he might find it odd if she didn't ask.

"Nothing yet. When's the last time you saw your half-brother?"

He was watching her, and she didn't dare pick up the coffee cup in case he saw her hand tremble. "Last week?" She said it like a question so he wouldn't be able to pin her down later. She added, "I don't spend that much time over there."

"No? I imagine not." He watched and waited.

Was she supposed to elaborate? The silence lengthened until she couldn't stand the discomfort. "He's a sweet boy, but my mom still has trouble accepting what happened, you know, with Dad leaving and all." She mentally kicked herself as soon as the words were out of her mouth. Why had she pointed him in her mother's direction? Detective Hunter waited a moment as if giving her statement due consideration.

"What happened, exactly?" he asked.

"With my dad? He and Ginger were having an affair, and she got pregnant with Charlie almost four years ago now. Mom took a long time to accept that he wanted to divorce her to marry Ginger." Sara shrugged. "I wouldn't want to stay married to somebody who screwed around on me like that." She paused. "He's still my dad, though."

"Of course he is. How do you get along with Ginger?"

"She kind of tolerates me. She'd like me to babysit, but I've only done it a few times. Mom doesn't like them to take advantage." Sara smiled before lowering her gaze to the sugar bowl. Where the hell was her mom anyway? She should have been back long before now if she went to the store. The detective seemed to read her mind.

"Your mother's been gone a while," he said before drinking from his cup. His hands were tanned and strong-looking. Confident. That was the word she'd use to describe him. "Does she shop in the neighbourhood?"

"Usually." Sara pulled her eyes away from his fingers and chanced lifting her coffee cup. She was relieved when her hand didn't shake. "We were getting low on stuff."

"Ahh. Does Charlie ever visit here?"

She nearly choked on her coffee. "No. We're not that kind of happy family." She thought about how much her mother hated the very idea of Charlie. How she'd refused even to meet him or have Ginger in her house. Sara shut her mouth to keep her thoughts from escaping.

The front door opened, and they stopped talking. Sara watched the detective while they listened to her mother walk down the hallway and into the kitchen. She must have seen the detective's car outside because she wasn't surprised to find him sitting at the table. "Is everything okay, Sara?" She looked at the detective with suspicious eyes before setting two bags of groceries on the counter. "Who's this then?"

"Detective Hunter. He wants to talk with you about Charlie in case we have any ideas as to who took him." She was adlibbing, but he didn't correct her. Sara tried to see her mother through his eyes. Curly black hair cropped short with a wedge of grey at the part and no real style to speak of. Pudgy belly that stretched her t-shirt to the max. Stained knee-length red shorts that she'd worn yesterday as well. There were lines under her eyes, and her face had a greyish tinge from last night's bender. Sara suddenly realized her contrast with the elegant Ginger was almost painful. Her mom had aged poorly since her dad left.

"Hello, Claudette." He had his ID out and held it up for her to inspect. "I understand you don't have any interaction with Ginger and Charlie." A half-smile softened his words.

"Why would I want to? They're the reason my marriage broke up." The lines around her mouth tightened with the aggrieved look she got every time someone mentioned Charlie or Ginger.

Sara willed her mom not to break into one of her rants as she shifted her gaze to the detective. He was watching her mother as if she was a curiosity he was trying to figure out. Claudette lowered herself into the chair kitty corner to Sara. "Mom doesn't mind if Roddy and I go visit them, though." Sara felt the need to defend her mother and was rewarded when the detective turned his stare on her. The relieved feeling didn't last long.

"How often do you visit them?"

"Wednesdays and every other weekend. We alternate holidays."

"Not as regular as that," her mom said. "Often the kids prefer to stay here, particularly Roddy."

"Is he home?" the detective asked.

"No, he's out with his friends at the mall. It's summer vacation, after all." Her mom looked over at the coffeepot. "Pour me a cup, would you, Sara? I've just sat down. And while you're up, put away the groceries. There's stuff that needs to go into the fridge."

"I can see you're busy, so I'll be on my way." The detective stood and carried his cup over to the counter. "Thanks for the coffee, Sara."

"No problem."

He took a step before turning to look back at her. "When do you visit your dad next?"

"It's supposed to be tomorrow. I don't know now with Charlie missing. Do you think ... will he be okay?"

"We're trying our best to find him."

"I hope that he comes home soon."

"We're all wishing for the same thing."

After he'd gone, Sara sat in the kitchen while her mom brewed a second pot of coffee. "You shouldn't have had him in the house without me here," she said for the third time.

"I heard you, Mom. I checked his ID before I invited him in, and he didn't try anything pervy. He's a detective, after all."

"The point is he could have tried something, and you'd have been all alone with nobody to stop it."

As if a man who looked like the detective would have any interest in me, Sara thought. She swallowed a retort and asked instead, "When did you find out Charlie's missing?" She studied her mother's face.

There was the briefest of pauses before she answered. "The AMBER Alert yesterday afternoon was hard to miss. I feel bad for them, but it's really nothing to do with me, or you for that matter. Maybe your father's sins are finally coming back around to bite him in the arse."

"That's an awful thing to say, Mom."

"Be that as it may, this does feel like payback, even if I wouldn't wish losing a child on anybody, your father included. However, I saw no need to ruin our evening by bringing it up yesterday."

So odd but not out of character, Sara thought. They'd stopped talking about anything sensitive after Dad left, pretending everything was normal, dodging land-mines. Nobody dared mention Charlie's name within her mother's presence. They'd learned after her first meltdown.

Sara took the milk out of the fridge and poured some over the bowl of Raisin Bran she'd never gotten around to eating. She was unsettled by the detective's quick departure and wondered if she'd said something she shouldn't have. He'd barely asked her mother anything. She picked up her bowl. "I'm going up to my room," she said. "See you later."

"Mind you bring your dirty dishes down when you're done," her mother called after Sara had started up the stairs. "I'm not in the mood to pick up after you."

CHAPTER 9

Liam was tired and ready for his bed, but the day wasn't over yet. He pulled into the parking garage at the Elgin Street station and made his way to the newly named Homicide and Major Crimes Unit on the second floor. The office was a hum of activity, all hands on deck, with Charlie missing and the unsolved disappearance of the university exchange student Meilin Hanon some eight months earlier. Staff Sergeant Greta Warner had assigned the Hanon case to a recent transfer into their unit, Kurt Auger, who led the team of Boots and Jingles and another new recruit, Rosie Thorburn. Boots and Jingles grumbled about reporting to Auger yet had no choice but to obey orders. Greta had pointedly kept Liam and his partner, Julie Quade, on the sidelines. Quade was angrier than he was about the snub, but then he'd never seen the point of fighting windmills. However, he thought that if Greta's aim was to sow discontent and escalate animosity amongst the team members, she was doing a terrific job.

Quade was at her desk when he arrived, her face drawn and her eyes bleary from lack of sleep. "I know," she said, catching his gaze levelled on her, "I look like hell, but you look ten times worse. I managed four hours of unconsciousness before my ex called to chew me out about leaving the kids with him all week. He seems to believe that I'm working overtime solely to mess up his social life. I'm guessing you haven't been home yet."

"I'll be taking a couple of hours after this meeting. I catnapped at my desk sometime in the wee hours."

"You're due for some serious slumber then."

"It can wait a while longer."

They spent the next hour comparing notes and catching up on the search, phoning contacts and checking with the call-in line to prepare for the team meeting. Quade signalled to Liam when the time came to gather up their information and follow the others into the meeting room. Greta was seated at the head of the long table and nodded at them as they took seats on either side of her, facing each other but avoiding direct eye contact. The team consisted of representatives from other units, including the call line, uniformed officers, Forensics, Victims' Services, Communications. It was a full house, and the mood around the table was sombre. Liam had somehow rallied a second, if not fourth wind, but his energy was beginning to flag. Thirty hours with virtually no sleep — he didn't have much left in the tank and hoped the meeting wouldn't drag on.

He looked sideways at Greta. She'd made him and Quade lead on this missing child case, but then the rest of the team was busy with the Hanon file, so she hadn't had a great deal of choice. He and Quade liked to share a case equally but took turns presenting as the lead. It helped to keep them sharp — this case happened to be his turn.

He found it surprising that Greta hadn't been her usual demanding self when it came to keeping her in the loop about every last detail. Her expression was stony as she stared over everyone's heads for a good five minutes before calling the room to order. He wondered if she was coming down with the flu or if she was being pressured from up high and feeling the stress. Two missing young people had everyone on edge. She appeared oblivious to the uneasy faces around the table as they took turns glancing at her. Nobody dared break into her reverie.

"Let's get started, shall we?" Her voice cut through the chatter, and the room fell silent. She cleared her throat. "The long and short of the Charlie McGowan case is that we have no idea what happened to him and no viable leads. Hunter and Quade, I turn it over to you."

Quade sent Liam a questioning look that he recip-rocated. Normally, Greta took charge and pontificated at length before asking anyone else to report. He had no idea what her brevity meant. Quade took the lead on the update, as they'd agreed. She gave the timeline

for Charlie's disappearance and outlined the neighbourhood search, the dive team's efforts and the two
door-to-door canvasses. She ended by saying that the
AMBER Alert and phone-in line had yielded nothing
tangible, but every lead was being followed up regardless. Liam sensed the frustration at the lack of
progress that he shared with everyone around the
table. Basically, they were no further ahead than when
the call came in that Charlie McGowan was missing.

Greta nodded at Lisa Flint, who was heading up
media and outreach. "Where are we with the media
plan, Lisa?"

Lisa opened her laptop. She was early thirties,
highly efficient, and had mastered technology by the
time she was old enough to work a mouse. She flicked
back her ponytail and scrolled through the screen.
"We need to keep Charlie's picture front and centre
on social media, and the AMBER Alert is of course
our main tool, but Twitter's a good second. We'll be
doing daily press briefings that will be covered both
locally and nationally by mainstream outlets." She
lifted her head. "Staff Sergeant Warner, I'm assuming
you'll be the daily spokesperson?"

Greta shook her head. "Quade or Hunter will give
the updates to reporters." She seemed to read the
puzzled stares. "I've been lead on the media updates
for Meilin Hanon and don't want these two cases to
get confused by the public."

Not likely the reason, but okay, Liam thought. The
media updates were few and far between nearly nine
months after Meilin's disappearance, and Greta had

never found a microphone she didn't hog on every case — until now. He felt Quade's stare burning into him but didn't engage. Whatever had prompted Greta's change in leadership, he wasn't complaining, but he could only imagine the speculation her uncharacteristic behaviour was going to generate around the water cooler.

After the manager of the call line and Forensics gave brief updates, Greta abruptly ended the meeting. Liam found himself next to Boots on the way out of the room. Boots glanced back at Greta. "What, no words of encouragement from our fearless leader?" He grinned at Liam. "Now, *that* was unprecedented. I hear she's been called on the carpet again."

"Oh yeah, what for this time?" Quade asked, sliding up behind them.

"Should I give you the list?" Boots put a hand on Liam's shoulder. "Go home and get some shut-eye, buddy. You look like death. We'll catch up when the time's right."

"Sure, leave me hanging." Quade scowled at Boots before saluting Liam and crossing over to her desk. She rolled her chair closer to Liam's once Boots was gone. "Something's going on with Greta. Any idea what?"

"Nope. I like this version of her, though."

"You'll get no argument from me. Anything I should follow up on while you go home?"

"Check in with the officer at the McGowans' and see how things are going with the family. I'd like to make a run over to David's work, but that can wait a bit."

"Any reason to focus on him?"

"Covering the bases, that's all." He hadn't told her yet about his trip to see David's ex-wife, but he would before they visited his workplace. This abduction felt personal, but he had no evidence that someone in Charlie's orbit had taken him, only a gut feeling that he wasn't ready to share. God knows he'd been wrong before. He thought of Ella Tate and how close they'd come to disaster.

Quade rolled back to her desk and picked up the phone. Liam made one more email check before shutting down and putting on his jacket. Quade hung up the phone and leaned back in her chair.

"Someone from Victims' Services is staying with the McGowans. Do you know Vanda Winters?"

"Can't place her."

"She says lots of tension simmering amongst the family members, but not unusual given the situation. No ransom request yet."

"Call me if one comes in. Don't worry about waking me."

"You sure?"

"I can a catch up on my sleep when this is over."

Ten minutes later, he drove onto the Queensway and cut across the city toward his house in the west end. He was relieved to see that someone, likely Hannah, had put his garbage can and recycling bins close to the garage. He hadn't been home since dragging the trash to the street Monday morning and had forgotten all about the bins. He had been organized enough, however, to text her after being called in to the McGowan case, asking her to drop by and feed the cat on Tuesday if she had a chance. He went around the house to the back door and stepped into the kitchen. Not only was the cat bowl full of food, but the kitchen was also tidied and dishes washed and put away. He found her note on the fridge.

Come for dinner when the dust settles. Love H.

He was so exhausted that he fell onto the bed with his clothes on. He remembered to take his phone and wallet out of his pocket and set them on the bedside table before pulling the comforter over himself. A moment later he was sound asleep.

CHAPTER 10

After a Tuesday spent working on the podcast about Charlie McGowan's disappearance, Ella knew the finished product wasn't her best work. The edited podcast was short on interviews or new information not already reported in Monday's *Capital* article. Ever since she'd broken ties with her anonymous source, she'd lost the inside edge. Still, she didn't regret her decision. After learning the name of a woman in Victims' Services who'd originally been working with her murdered cop friend Paul O'Brien under the moniker Felix, Ella had carefully researched the woman's life history. Vanda Winters was putting two kids through university and couldn't afford to lose her job if their secret alliance came to light. Vanda had insisted in a recent "Felix" email that she would continue feeding Ella information, but she didn't put up much resistance when Ella told her thanks but no thanks. "I sure could use you now, though," Ella said aloud. She decided to wait a bit before posting her podcast, hoping Hunter came through with an update within the hour.

She looked at the clock on her computer. Seven thirty — no wonder her stomach was grumbling. She stood and stretched in front of the window, looking down at the street. Adele, in a loose yellow cotton dress, was starting up the walkway, pushing Lena in a stroller while talking on her cell phone. Lena was nine months old, if Ella counted back correctly. Memorably, Finn and Adele's house had burned down the night of Lena's birth and was in the process of being rebuilt. Finn spent his days running his downtown gym while Adele stayed home in the rented ground-floor apartment with Lena. She'd return to her teaching job in September, and Lena would enter daycare. Ella had overheard Adele telling a friend that she was going crazy cooped up with a baby in a cramped apartment and couldn't wait to get her life back. Ella wondered if Finn knew that was how Adele truly felt.

Ella had just put a pot of water on the stove to boil spaghetti when she heard a tap at her door. Tony and Finn were both at work, so it had to be either Alex, her landlord, or Adele, since nobody else could enter the building without being let in. She yanked the door open to find Adele standing on the landing, holding a bouquet of daisies that she thrust into Ella's hands.

"These are my apology for being out of sorts earlier."

"You don't need to…"

"Yeah, I do. I also contacted Ginger, and she's agreed to speak with you if it will help get Charlie back. The police have given the okay as well."

"Why … that's wonderful. Thanks, Adele."

"Ginger said for you to go to her house at ten tomorrow morning. She'll be watching for you."

"Perfect."

"I have to get back to Lena. Let me know how it goes with Ginger."

"Of course. Thanks again — for the flowers and linking me up."

Ella watched Adele disappear down the stairwell before going back inside her apartment. She could hear the pot boiling in the kitchen and hurried to turn down the burner. She didn't own a flower vase and looked around for a container to hold the daisies, settling for an empty juice bottle that she pulled out of the recycling bin. The interaction with Adele had thrown her, and she couldn't decide what had prompted this change of heart. Whatever it was, she was grateful to have the chance to speak with Ginger McGowan. She was glad now that she hadn't posted her podcast online. Tomorrow she'd have a scoop that hopefully would help to bring Charlie McGowan home with the side benefit of sending her viewership numbers sky-high.

———

At nine the next morning she drove the car Paul O'Brien had left her in his will across the city to

Rocky Point and into the McGowan neighbourhood. The frantic activity of two days ago was over, the police presence all but undetectable. She parked after turning the corner and walked the rest of the way, enjoying the treed lots and bright midsummer gardens. She caught glimpses of the river between the well-spaced houses, the sun sparkling on the cold, turquoise water. Loch Isle Road was a peaceful place to live, as close to nature as one could get in a city of a million people. The most unlikely of places for the abduction of a three-year-old child.

A couple of reporters were set up across the street from the McGowan house. Ella kept her head down and strode past them on the other side of the road, quickening her pace as she started up the driveway. Canard had texted her the day before with instructions to write an update when there was movement on the case. Sherry was busy covering the gang shootings in the ByWard Market, so Ella was on her own. She had to get a story to Canard soon after lunch or he'd be breathing down her neck.

Vanda Winters answered the door. Her eyes met and held Ella's without a flicker of recognition, and Ella kept her own face devoid of emotion. She'd never told Vanda that she knew about her relationship with O'Brien and their Felix collaboration. Acknowledging each other now could lead to repercussions for Vanda that Ella would go out of her way to prevent. Vanda pointed down the hallway. "Ginger's waiting for you in the sunroom. She's fragile, so tread carefully."

"Of course. Has anyone made contact about a ransom?"

"No. We're hoping now that the police searches are winding down, the abductor will feel safer asking for money. My presence is being kept low-key."

"I won't mention anything about the police being on the premises."

"Good."

They passed the living room where an older man sat in a chair by the window, reading the newspaper. He had to be Ginger's or David's father. He looked at her over the rim of his glasses with a steely glare but didn't say anything before returning his attention to the paper.

"Richard Halliday," Vanda said quietly. "Ginger's father from Halifax. Her mom Madeleine is waiting with her in the back room."

"Where's David?"

"Working in his office off the kitchen. He said he'll sit in if requested, but I get the feeling Ginger would prefer he didn't."

"Perhaps I can get a soundbite from him after I'm done with Ginger." Ella wanted to meet Charlie's dad but was pleased to have Ginger on her own for now. Couples were tougher to interview together because they usually censored each other, sometimes simply by exchanging a look. One partner, more often than not, did all the talking.

The sunroom was on the west side of the house, a space with tall windows on three sides and four skylights in the ceiling. Ella imagined the room would

be unbearably hot by noon, but for now, the temperature was comfortable. Ginger was sitting on the
couch with her mother. Neither woman made any
move to greet her, so Vanda tactfully stepped in front
of Ella to make the introductions before giving her
the floor.

"I'm so sorry about your son." Ella picked up a
rattan chair and set it across from Ginger after Vanda
moved closer to the door.

Ginger's eyes followed Ella's movements. "Adele
said you have a large following on social media."

"Yes, I have about seventy thousand followers on
the podcast site and thousands more on social media.
I also freelance for the *Capital*. Your interview will
reach a lot of people. My hope is that one of them
knows or saw something and will come forward."

"That's our hope too." Ginger nodded at her
mother.

"I'll be editing the interview and won't reveal
anything the police are keeping back." Ella pulled a
tape recorder out of her satchel as the doorbell pealed
throughout the house.

"And the rest of the team arrives," Vanda said.
"Don't start yet."

Ella watched as a woman she didn't recognize
entered the sunroom, followed by Liam Hunter.
Hunter met her eyes and nodded. "Ella, this is Lisa
Flint from our communications team. We'll be sitting
in."

Great. More people to make Ginger clam up. "Are you all
set, Ginger?" Ella asked, trying to draw her attention

away from the others. She willed Ginger to focus on her face and was rewarded when their eyes met.

"Yes, let's get started." Ginger shifted on the couch, and Lisa Flint sat next to her, leaning against the arm of the sofa to give Ginger space. Ginger had to be seven or eight months pregnant, Ella estimated. Further along than anyone in the media throng outside had known. How would the stress she was under affect her unborn child? Hopefully, Charlie would be home soon to end this trauma. She checked that the tape recorder was working before asking her first question.

Ella: I know how difficult these past few days have been, and thank you for talking with me today, Ginger. Our goal is to bring Charlie home. Can you tell us about the morning Charlie went missing?

Ginger: *We were in the side garden Monday, two days ago. Charlie was playing with the cat from next door … you know, petting his head and talking to him. Charlie turned three only a week ago and has a passion for bears, but the cat next door comes a close second. It was such a hot morning, and Charlie was thirsty, so I left him for two minutes while I went inside to pour some juice and make a cup of tea. I watched him through the dining room window while the kettle boiled, and he was happily engrossed in the cat…* (she swallowed and her voice dropped away).

Ella: Did you make your tea and go directly outside?

Ginger: *I made a dash to the washroom and then went right outside. Charlie was gone. I thought at first he was playing hide-and-seek, a game he loves, but he always jumps out after a* *few seconds, laughing and giggling. I searched the yard and the house after checking that he wasn't somehow on the beach, and my neighbour heard me calling for Charlie. She came over and organized some neighbours to search the area outside the gate. When we didn't find him, I called the police.*

Ella: Was the gate closed? Could your son have opened it?

Ginger: (hesitated and looked at Lisa before answering) *The gate has a faulty latch that we'd meant to fix. We only moved into this house two months ago. It looked shut but might not have been. Charlie couldn't have opened it on his own.*

Ella: The police made a thorough search of the area, including a dive team on the river, but they've found no trace of him. What do you believe happened to Charlie?

Ginger: *Somebody took him. Whether the gate was open and he left the backyard on his own, or someone went into the backyard and got him doesn't matter. There's no other explanation. He was taken.*

Ella turned her head while Ginger was speaking and met Hunter's gaze where he stood off to the side. She knew he wanted her to go carefully without him having to say a word. She looked back at Ginger.

Ella: Do you have any idea who would take Charlie?

Ginger: *No, I can't imagine anybody doing something like this, but whoever it is, all I want … all my husband David and I want is for Charlie to come home. I wish with all my heart to look into the backyard and find him there. I can barely stand waking up in the morning without him.*

Her voice cracked, and Lisa signalled with her hand for Ella to wrap up the interview.

Ella nodded. "Ginger, my last question, if you're up to it, is for you to describe what Charlie was wearing that morning and any distinguishing features that would help the public to identify him. I'd also like a few photos to post on my podcast page with contact info for people to call or email if they remember anything."

Ginger wiped her eyes while her mother rubbed her leg in sympathy. Ella looked at Hunter, and he nodded his okay. "Last question then," Lisa said. "I'll send the photos and contact information to you straight away."

Ella taped Ginger's answer and stopped recording as she looked at Lisa. "How about David? Can I get a few words with him?"

"Actually, he has something he wants to say. I'll go fetch him."

Hunter told Ginger what a great job she'd done and reinforced the reach Ella's podcast had. A wall of silence and reserve was his default, but Ella had come to anticipate his moments of compassion that came when people were at their lowest point. They turned to watch David stride into the room with Lisa following behind. Ginger's mother stood and motioned for David to take her place next to his wife. He sat and reached for Ginger's hand. "Everything okay?"

"Yes. Your turn."

Ella sensed a change in the room's energy. A

realignment of the power dynamic. She took a closer look at David. He was fit, early fifties, with a shock of thick grey hair and eyes that openly scrutinized her. *Not a man to cross without consequences,* she thought.

"Are you ready to make your statement, David?" Lisa asked.

"Turn on your recorder." David sat forward on the couch and waited for Ella to cue him. "My wife Ginger and I beg whoever took our innocent little boy Charlie to bring him home. Leave him somewhere we can find him and there will be no questions asked."

Hunter moved to cut off David's statement, but David held up a hand to stop him. "I'm offering twenty thousand dollars to anyone who has information that leads to the recovery of our son. You can call the special number set up with the police. You'll also receive Ginger's and my undying gratitude."

Ella was aware of a stillness in the room after David finished speaking, and she glanced over at Lisa and Hunter. The look that passed between them told her that neither had known about the reward.

"When will you be posting your interview?" Lisa asked Ella, turning to face her.

"Tonight around five if all goes well. I'm heading home now to edit and get the podcast ready for upload."

"Good. I'll coordinate a statement for the evening news about the reward. I'd also like you, Ginger and David, to consider a press conference to appeal to the public. We could have that ready for the suppertime news if you're willing."

"Of course." David squeezed Ginger's hand. "We'll do whatever helps to bring Charlie home."

Ella picked up her tape recorder and bag. "I'll be on my way. Thank you again for agreeing to the interview. I sincerely hope this story helps to bring Charlie home safely. If there's anything more I can do, don't hesitate to contact me."

David stood and reached out his hand. "Thank you for doing this."

His skin was smooth and his grasp strong. Ella found herself momentarily distracted by the force of his stare before releasing his hand. "I'll see myself out," she said.

"I'll come with you." Hunter was on his feet and followed her through the house to the front door. They didn't speak until they were outside and walking down the sidewalk toward the street.

"That was interesting," Ella said. "I notice that David McGowan's reward announcement came as a surprise."

"They're having a hard time, as would anyone in this situation. He's a man used to being in charge. It's best if you cut out his sentence about there being no consequences if Charlie is anonymously returned."

"Of course. Have you got any leads at all?"

"None I can talk about."

"So that's a big no. Has there been a ransom demand yet?"

"No."

Ella stopped walking. "Surely whoever took Charlie should have reached out by now?"

Hunter pivoted to face her. "We think they're waiting for the police to back off. That's our hope anyway."

"Can I report anything else in my podcast that would help to find Charlie?"

"Getting people to watch for him is a start. We'll handle the rest."

She took a closer look at him. "You seem tired. Are you managing any rest?"

He ran a hand across his stubble and grinned for the first time. "I caught a few hours. Hopefully we'll make a breakthrough this weekend, and I can catch a few more."

"I'll let you know if I hear anything after posting the podcast, although I'll be telling listeners to use the police call line. Sometimes people ignore instructions though and send me a direct message."

"I'll check in with you. Take care, Ella."

"You too."

She watched him head back up the walkway to the McGowan house before starting down the road to her car. In addition to O'Brien bequeathing his vehicle to her, he'd willed her a cottage southwest of Ottawa near Perth. She'd sold the cottage and paid off her debts, put away enough to cushion her through the lean times, and sent the rest to her mother. Her mom had left her father in the fall and had little income. She'd taken some convincing to accept the money.

Ella couldn't part with O'Brien's car, though. She thought of him every time she sat in the driver's seat.

She'd lost both him and her brother Danny the autumn before, and bouts of grief still came out of nowhere and knocked her sideways. She'd always liked being alone, but these last few months she'd been spending more time by herself, trying to find her way out of the lingering depression. If but for Tony and Finn, she'd go days without seeing anybody. They were the lifeline keeping her from the bottomless abyss. Them and the thrill of tracking down a new story. The possible abductions gave her a reason to keep on going, perverse as that sounded. She needed to see these stories through, no matter the outcome. Their families deserved answers, and she needed a purpose.

CHAPTER 11

The family had gathered in the living room when Liam reentered the house. He could hear Richard's strident voice from the front hallway. "Why the hell didn't you take part in that interview? You couldn't even bother to be in the room with your wife."

"Ginger asked me to let her handle it alone. Madeleine was with her for support." David's voice rose in volume to match his father-in-law's.

"Of course Ginger would say not to disturb your work, but you should have been with her anyway. She needed you, and you were what, typing a memo on your computer? What kind of husband and father puts himself first like that?"

"I made a statement and offered a reward at the end of the interview. I was setting up the fund, if you must know."

"Well, you could have picked a better time to do that."

"Dad, stop." Ginger sounded more weary than angry.

Liam looked down the hall and saw Madeleine standing motionless in the kitchen doorway. He moved silently toward her and signalled for her to lead the way into the kitchen. She stopped at the island and stared out at the backyard. "I'm sure you've seen families fall apart before us," she said without looking at him.

"This is a level of stress most people will never experience, but you're right, we see people at some of the worst times in their lives." He wasn't sure how direct to be with her but decided she wouldn't entertain weakness. "The other day, when we first met in the kitchen, you wanted to say something that you held back. Can you tell me what that was?"

She turned her head. "You're observant. It … it was nothing important."

"Perhaps tell me what it was, and I can see if it fits in with any other information."

"It was more an omission than information pertinent to the case."

"Can you tell me what that was?"

He waited while she considered his request. Before she could respond, Richard filled the doorway and Madeleine's expression went from open to closed. Liam cursed the man for his timing. Had it been deliberate to stop his wife from talking?

"Are you getting lunch started?" Richard's question felt like an order, and Madeleine moved over to the fridge.

Her voice was conciliatory, verging on obsequious.
"I boiled eggs earlier and will get started making
sandwiches. I'll have the meal ready in two shakes,
although it's early yet."

"Well, people might be hungry after all this
nonsense."

"I'll leave you to it," Liam said. Madeleine
wouldn't share anything while her husband was in the
kitchen, and Richard was even now pulling out a
chair to sit down. It was time for Liam to return to
headquarters and coordinate the next steps in the
search for Charlie. He'd have a word with Vanda on
his way out and would ask her to speak with
Madeleine when she could get her alone.

———

THE OFFICE WAS HUMMING with activity, but the
frenetic pace of the last two days had eased. The first
forty-eight hours were over and with them the hope
for a quick resolution to Charlie's disappearance. The
sprint had become a marathon. Boots met Liam in
the hallway outside their block of offices.

"I hope your case doesn't drag on like our missing
person nightmare. Meilin Hanon's family in China is
pressuring the federal government to find her. Greta is
beyond peeved that we have no leads." Boots took a
sip from his coffee cup. "Did you hear she's under a
management review? There've been complaints."

"That's why she's not her usual self."

"If by that you mean her usual controlling, arrogant, argumentative self, then yeah, she's somewhat subdued. I like the change, personally."

"This could be an opportunity for her to reassess and grow."

Boots laughed as if Liam had told the joke of the year. "Greta is a bully in over her head. She has no clue how to run an investigation without letting her personal biases override logic. Kurt Auger is a personal friend of hers. She brought him in from Toronto and promoted him to deputy staff sergeant without a competition for the job. Very few people knew she'd made him permanent in the position, and the time to challenge the appointment is over."

"Quade passed her sergeant's exams. I wonder if she knows about Auger."

"If Quade found out he's been made permanent in that position without a competition, she'd be a complainant for sure."

"Are you one of the complainants?" Liam asked.

"Not me. My guess is Jingles, but he's being close-lipped about it. I also hear rumours she's been putting the moves on a detective in Guns and Gangs. He very well could have submitted a harassment complaint. Word is he's married."

Liam thought about the evening he'd gone for a drink with Greta and her suggestion that they go somewhere private to get to know each other better. He'd sidestepped her offer and fallen out of favour as a result. She'd even demoted him on the cases that he was lead detective.

Liam entered the office with a new reluctance. He

liked working on cases, but he detested the organizational politics. He planned to never rise higher than detective, knowing his strengths did not include managing staff or negotiating political channels. Quade wasn't at her desk, and he wondered if a fresh lead had taken her out of the building. He took his seat and began working his way through phone messages and emails.

Jingles stopped by ten minutes later on his way from Greta's office. "Staff meeting in ten," he said. "Message just went out."

"Thanks for the heads up." Liam put off making a phone call and got to the meeting room ahead of the throng. He took a seat next to Boots. Normally, latecomers had to settle for chairs around the perimeter of the room, but this time the participants were limited to the Major Crimes squad, leaving lots of room at the table. Quade entered behind Greta and took a seat to her right at the head of the table. Quade smiled at Liam with a sheepish expression that he had trouble reading. Her gaze shifted to the water glass in front of Boots as she avoided looking at him.

Greta got down to business. "This won't be a long meeting. I wanted to tell everyone at the same time in person that I'll be going on medical leave. I'm not sure for how long, but I'm starting chemotherapy on Monday and need some time to rest and see how the treatment affects me. In the meantime, Julie Quade has agreed to be acting staff sergeant with Kurt Auger continuing to lead the Hanon investigation and giving support in his deputy staff sergeant role as required. I know you'll give them both the same dedication and respect as I've always had from each of you." She turned sideways. "Anything to add, Acting Staff Sergeant Quade?"

Quade shook her head. "Nothing except that I'm here to support everyone on the team and to help oversee the investigations."

"Good," Greta said. "If you need to reach me, I won't be checking my email. Quade and Auger will be in touch weekly, so contact me through them. Right, if there are no questions, back to work and keep doing the unit proud."

Liam glanced around the table at the stunned faces. Nobody had considered that Greta might be ill. The idea would take a while to digest. Boots walked with him out of the room and over to Liam's desk.

"Do you believe her?" Boots asked.

"You don't?"

"Call me a cynic, but her illness seems opportune. I also question why Quade is acting while Auger's next in line." Boots left before Liam could reply. The rest of the team spoke to each other in hushed voices as they made their way back to their desks. Liam started answering an email and looked up as Quade positioned herself next to him.

"I wanted to tell you ahead of the meeting, but Greta vetoed that. Are you okay with this?"

"Okay?" Liam grinned. "It's about time you got some recognition. I'm thrilled for you."

Her grim expression softened into a smile. "You're one cool guy, you know that, partner?"

"So you keep telling me. Don't hesitate to ask if you need my help with anything."

"Rosie Thorburn will shift over from Auger's squad to work with you."

Liam looked across at Rosie. She had her head thrown back, laughing at something Jingles and Boots were saying to her. Her brown hair was tied up in a bun with loose strands trailing to her shoulders. She looked young, new to the job. "Sounds good." Even as he voiced the words, he was thinking that Quade's acting promotion would leave him shouldering the bulk of the investigation with only a rookie on his team for support. These were lean times on the force. Make-do times. He'd need to put in extra hours and hope for a break from the public. Ella Tate was on the case as well, working her reporter sources. She'd come through in the past and might again.

Quade leaned in and dropped her voice. "Auger isn't happy about my acting, but Greta was told to put me in. Something's going on upstairs, and her days could be numbered. But that's between you and me and the water cooler."

CHAPTER 12

The sun continued to bake the back patio, so Ginger dragged a lawn chair into the dappled shadows under the sweeping branches of the sugar maple. This was where she would have set up the wading pool for Charlie if he hadn't gone missing. She tried to get comfortable on the recliner, and the baby kicked as she manoeuvred into position. Through her sunglasses, she watched a squirrel race across the top of the fence and tried to think about nothing. For three days, she'd been in a state of terror and knew she had to gear down for the sake of her unborn child. She'd refused to take a sedative, promising David that she'd relax on her own.

Mercifully, her mom and dad had gone grocery shopping, and David was working in his home office. The victims' liaison officer was set up inconspicuously in a corner of the living room, monitoring phone calls, even though whoever took Charlie was staying quiet. This worried Ginger more than anything else.

What if this person had taken Charlie to hurt him or worse? How would she endure never knowing where he was or if he was being cared for?

She put a hand over her heart and forced deep breaths, in and out, in and out. Then she closed her eyes and pretended Charlie was playing with his teddy bears next to her on the grass. The hot breeze caressed her face and dried the tears on her cheeks. The trees swayed overhead, but the birds were silent, sleeping through the worst of the afternoon heat. Ginger welcomed the discomfort, needing to physically feel some of the anguish going on inside of her, to hurt like her son was surely hurting without her.

She must have dozed, because the next thing she knew, David's hand was on her shoulder, and his voice was speaking quietly into her ear. "We need to get ready for the media interview, darling. Are you feeling up to it?"

"Of course." She sat forward and rubbed her eyes. "Do I have time to put on makeup?"

"If you hurry. We have to leave for the police station in twenty minutes at the latest."

"Then help me out of this chair."

She bit back her annoyance at being left to sleep for so long. Even an extra ten minutes would have given her time to adequately prepare. She wondered as she hurried across the lawn to the back steps if her low threshold for stress was a result of Charlie's disappearance or hormones and her pregnancy. The heat wasn't helping to ease her discomfort with her own body or to lessen her irritability. David was being patient, but she felt sometimes as if he was humouring her while hiding his own frustration. She told herself to be kinder and less focused on herself. David needed her too, and she had to be there for him as he was being for her. She had to be the even-keeled wife he'd married and not this shrewish version of herself that she hardly recognized.

———

LIAM HAD INSISTED that only Ginger and David appear on camera and was pleased to see Vanda Winters settle Madeleine and Richard off to the side in the seating area, leaving the prime spots for the press directly in front of the table. He and Quade sat on either side of the McGowans. Quade presented an opening statement with a blown-up photo of Charlie on an easel behind her.

The reporters asked questions about the search that Quade signalled for Liam to answer. He began speaking while his eyes were drawn to Ella Tate making her way to an empty space in the middle of the row. Even in the heat wave, she was dressed in jeans and a black t-shirt under a jean jacket. Her blonde hair was a ragged mess, sticking up in tufts. She finally reached her seat and stretched out in the chair as if she was getting ready for a nap, arms folded across her chest, legs crossed at the ankles. Her unusual green eyes skimmed over him and focused on Ginger.

"So, you have no concrete information about what

happened to Charlie?" the CTV reporter asked when Liam finished his update.

"We're investigating every lead, but we need the public's help. Let me turn the mic over to Charlie's parents, Ginger and David McGowan."

David spoke first in a strong, even voice. He and Ginger had rehearsed what they'd say with Vanda, who'd assured Liam they were ready. "We're asking anyone who might have seen something that morning, no matter how inconsequential it might have appeared at the time, to step forward and call the hotline. We desperately want our little boy to come home. I'm offering a twenty-thousand-dollar reward to anyone who gives information that leads to Charlie's return." He ran a hand through his hair. "Please help us find Charlie." He turned the mic toward Ginger and sat back in his seat. They were holding hands under the table.

Ginger made a sympathetic sight, her bright eyes glistening with tears, the swell of her stomach making everyone aware that she was close to delivering another child. "My boy…" Her voice wavered. "*Our* boy only just turned three years old. He's never been away from us for more than a few hours. He's innocent and loving and doesn't deserve any of this. Please, if you know of anything that can help bring him home, call the helpline. And if you have Charlie, let him go and we'll come get him anywhere, anytime, no questions asked. You can carry on your life knowing you did the right thing in the end. He's just a little boy who needs his mom and dad."

Liam saw Quade lean forward and put her hand over the mic to cut off Ginger, who'd deviated from the script. She was promising immunity that they would never give the kidnapper. They'd prosecute even if Charlie was set free. She was giving the same promise David had when Ella interviewed them in their sunroom, the promise Liam had gotten Ella to quash. Had David put Ginger up to saying it this time, or was she acting on her own?

"Thank you, Ginger and David. We aren't taking any further questions at this time," Quade said, directing her gaze at the press. "The media kits have the phone number set up for people to call in with information. The contact number is also behind me on the poster. Thanks, everyone, for coming, and our wish is that Charlie is found quickly and returned home safely with his parents and family where he belongs."

The scraping of chairs on the concrete floor punctuated Quade's quick end to the news conference. She ignored the jumble of questions being yelled from reporters and herded the McGowans out the side door with Liam leading the way. Vanda Winters, along with Ginger's parents, followed them into the small meeting room across the hall.

"What happens now?" David asked.

"We wait to see if anyone in the public comes forward." Quade spoke in a flat voice and met Liam's eyes. He could see anger in the black depths of hers and knew she wasn't pleased that Ginger had gone rogue. He could already picture Ginger's empty promises as the lede in media stories and hoped the news release they'd handed out ahead of time would stifle the speculation. Lisa Flint would be fielding questions for the rest of the day, as if the team didn't already have enough to keep them busy. Quade looked at David. "Vanda will escort you home. Refrain from speaking with any media. We'll handle the inquiries from our end."

Richard had been unusually quiet, and Liam could sense the strain amongst all four family members, particularly between David and Richard, who glared at each other whenever their eyes met. The longer Charlie was missing, the more evident the fractures and dislike had become. Vanda stepped from behind Ginger so that she stood next to Liam.

"Can I have a word with you in the hall before we go?"

"I'll follow you out." He signalled to Quade to keep the others busy for a few minutes and slipped into the hall behind Vanda. "What's up?"

"Ginger. I should have realized she'd go off script, even though she agreed not to adlib. She's not handling any of this well."

"We'll deal with it. Nobody's to blame."

"Thanks for saying that. I wanted to tell you that I overheard Madeleine and Richard arguing. He was in Ottawa when Charlie went missing."

"He was?"

"Yeah, on business, apparently. Madeleine doesn't understand why he didn't say so from the start."

"It does make one wonder." Liam thought about

how much Richard disliked his son-in-law. If he'd arranged to have Charlie kidnapped, what would he hope to accomplish? Breaking up his daughter's marriage? Even so, would he do something so heinous to his family? Liam reached for the door handle. "I'll look into it. Thanks, Vanda."

"This is an odd case. No ransom call." Her voice dropped to a whisper. "Do you think Charlie is alive?"

"No reason to believe he isn't … yet."

Vanda held his gaze. "I don't know what will become of this family if Charlie doesn't ever come home. They're blaming each other, and that's as destructive to any relationship as a ticking time bomb. I doubt any of them will survive unscathed, regardless of the outcome."

CHAPTER 13

Ella watched the McGowan family and police reps file out of the media briefing. She remained seated while the other reporters chattered around her and gathered their paraphernalia in preparation to leave. Hunter had caught her eye once from his seat on the raised dais, but she hadn't responded to his stare. He seemed tired, eager for the circus to be over. Ginger had looked almost catatonic sitting next to him until it was her turn to speak. Her vow of absolution for the kidnapper if Charlie was returned had to have been her idea, judging by the speed with which Julie Quade had ended the scrum. She'd omit Ginger's promise from her next article, just like David's earlier attempt.

She checked her phone. Three o'clock, with an hour to kill before she met Joanne Freemont outside the art gallery on Sussex, a half-hour walk away. She'd planned to ride her bike, but the humidity had settled into the Ottawa Valley overnight, making the morning heat climb to the unbearable level by noon, so walking seemed the better option. She could nip into buildings to keep cool or ride the bus home. Before stepping outside the station, she changed into shorts in the washroom and took off her jean jacket, putting the clothes into her backpack. She ducked her head under the water tap and combed back her hair. All set to face the stifling heat, she stepped outside onto Elgin Street and began walking north, a sheen of sweat on her face and her t-shirt damp before she made it to the corner.

A street vendor was selling hotdogs near Parliament Hill, so she bought one and a cold bottle of water and found a park bench shaded by an elm. A girl in her twenties with pink hair and enough piercings to qualify as a pin cushion plunked down at the other end and talked loudly on her cell phone while Ella ate. It seemed the girl and her boyfriend had broken up, and he was trying to get back together while she wanted him to get his stuff out of her apartment and never to darken her door again.

Ella crumpled up the hotdog wrapper and stood. "Make sure to change the locks," she said on her way past and gave a thumbs-up.

The girl rolled her eyes and lowered the phone. "He thinks I'm bullshitting, but not this time. I'm done with that lying dick. His other girlfriend can have him."

Young love, Ella thought as she kept going down the hill, past the Château Laurier Hotel to the intersection. She was glad to be over that stage of life. She turned left on Sussex and strolled toward the National Art Gallery, an impressive modern structure rising to a glass tower that backed onto the Ottawa River. A giant metal spider dominated the square in front of the gallery. Ella skirted it and found a place to sit out of the line of visitors streaming through the main entrance. She pulled out her phone and pretended to read the screen while she kept an eye out for Joanne. The heat made her lethargic, and a headache had started behind her eyes. The people going in and out of the gallery moved slowly, drained by the humidity that made breathing an effort. Fifteen minutes after Ella sat down, Joanne ambled over and lowered herself onto a nearby concrete block, leaving two spaces between them.

"I'm glad you came," Ella said without looking at her.

"I almost didn't. You must have read all the nasty messages on social media."

"I'm sorry. People can be brutal when they remain anonymous."

"The media wasn't too kind either." Joanne wore a wide-brimmed sunhat and dark glasses. She was tall and slender, about nineteen, with long auburn hair tied into a bun at the nape of her neck.

"I'm not adding to the vitriol. I'm only interested in hearing your side, figuring out what really happened to Meilin."

"Will you tape what I say?"

"With your permission."

Joanne thought for a moment before nodding. "I

know you'll tell it straight. Your podcast is one of the few I trust."

"I appreciate you saying that." Ella paused and looked around. "Is there somewhere we can go where you'd feel comfortable speaking? It's a bit noisy here with the traffic and people walking past."

"Do you live nearby?"

"I have a small third-floor apartment in a house in the Glebe. We could catch an Uber and be there in ten minutes." The risk of having Joanne know where she lived seemed worth the trade-off for the privacy that would allow her to relax enough to share her story.

"Okay, let's do it."

The Uber arrived five minutes later, and they didn't speak until the driver dropped them in front of Ella's apartment. As they started up the walkway, Ella said, "Sorry, only a couple of fans in my place, but they'll give the illusion of coolness."

Lena's stroller was in the hallway, so Adele had either just come home or was on her way out. Ella led the way upstairs, pleased by the silence as they passed Tony's apartment on the second floor. If he were within, Celine, Cher, or Shania would be pumping through the floorboards.

Once inside, Joanne looked around Ella's small living room, furnished with a second-hand sofa, desk, and floor lamp before taking a seat on the saggy couch. "You live like a student," she said. "And a poor one at that."

Ella scanned the crowded space and shrugged. "I

keep meaning to buy new furniture but never get around to it." She couldn't see the point but kept this to herself. She had a bed, a corner in which to work, and somewhere for Tony to sit when he came by. What else did anybody really need? "Would you like tea or coffee while I get organized?"

"No, I've got my water bottle. I'll check messages while I wait. You weren't kidding about the heat up here. It's a sweatbox." She kicked off her sandals and tucked her feet under her on the couch, soon engrossed by her screen.

Ella set up the mic on the desk and got a chair from her bedroom so that they'd be kitty corner to each other while she asked questions. She double-checked that everything was working properly and recorded an introduction before calling Joanne over and handing her a set of headphones.

Ella: Thanks for speaking with me today, Joanne. Tell us about how you know Meilin Hanon.

Joanne: *I'm a second-year university student at Carleton and living in residence. Meilin was assigned as my roommate last fall.*

Ella: Do second-year students usually share rooms?

Joanne: *Not always, but a double is cheaper than a single. Meilin was a first-year exchange student from China studying English literature. Her English is really good, and she wanted to go into journalism second year.*

Ella: And what are you studying, Joanne?

Joanne: *Biology. I plan to go into nursing.*

Ella: How did you and Meilin get along?

Joanne: *She's an introvert, and I'm not, so it took a while for us to gel, but we were always friendly. We had a respectful relationship.*

Ella: What happened that last evening when Meilin went missing?

Joanne: (deep sigh) *I invited her to a party because she seemed homesick and had zero social life. I felt bad for her. She agreed, which surprised me because she was so shy, but I took that as a good sign. The party was at a downtown hotel…*

Ella: Who was hosting the event?

Joanne: *See, this is where people start judging. My work organized it for the staff. I was … an escort, but not the kind that slept with customers. I needed the job to stay in school. I never had the luxury of a well-off family, and my scholarship was only for first year. It's the reason I had to share a dorm room."*

Ella: I'm not judging you, Joanne. However, I know that social media was quick to blame you for bringing Meilin to what they've called a sex party. How do you respond?

Joanne: *Yeah, that's what they called it to get some readers. There might have been some hook-ups, but that wasn't the intent of the party. It was just a party. A social gathering.*

Ella: How did Meilin fit in with the other guests?

Joanne: (glanced at Ella and looked past her) *She was having a good time. She had a drink or two and was chatting with different people. A couple of times, she was up dancing. I kept an eye on her at the start to make sure she was okay, but I got busy myself. Someone told me she left around midnight. That surprised me because I thought we'd catch a cab and go back to residence together.*

Ella: You never saw her again?

Joanne: *The last time I saw Meilin, she was smiling, dancing, and looking happy. I have no idea what happened between the hotel and home. The people I know who were at the party say they have no idea either.*

Ella asked a few more questions to wrap up, knowing that Joanne and everyone at the event had been interviewed and investigated by the police. If one of them knew something about who Meilin left the hotel with that night, or if she left alone and got into trouble walking home, they were staying quiet. Joanne hadn't deviated from the police report, as far as Ella could tell. If she'd lied then, she was sticking to her story. Ella signalled to her that the interview was over and shut down the recording. Joanne took off her headphones but remained seated, watching Ella check her computer.

"It's true what I told you," Joanne said. "I go on dates with men, usually from out of town, but I don't have to sleep with them if I don't want to. We can negotiate, but it's ultimately up to me. I'm putting myself through university, and it's not cheap." She paused. "My dad's a plumber, and we're six kids. His pay doesn't stretch far even before he drinks half of it away."

Ella looked over at her. "And what I said is also true. I'm not judging you."

"Well, you're about the only one."

"I have a question, though."

"So ask."

"Why is everyone so scared to be seen with me?

You and Yina both went for the cloak-and-dagger rendezvous. Yina seemed on edge the entire time I was with her."

Joanne sat still for a moment before getting to her feet. She took a step away from the desk and stopped. "The people I work for are connected. They're nervous about protecting their investments. Since Yina and I have no idea if they're involved in Meilin's disappearance or not, we have to be careful who we're seen with. Added to that are the death threats from those anonymous online trolls. People seem convinced I brought the innocent, virgin Meilin to the party as a gift to somebody. I left residence and went into hiding, so yeah, I'm being careful. I'm not surprised Yina's scared too. She and Meilin were best friends in China. Meilin's parents are influential."

Ella had read a good deal of the online vitriol as part of her research. The bitterness in Joanne's voice spoke to the impact the social media onslaught had wreaked on her. Ella knew first-hand how public opinion could destroy a person. "Can you tell me the name of your agency?"

She shrugged. "Sure, why not? Juliette Dating Service. Good luck tracking down the owner, though. He keeps a low profile, and no, I'm not sharing his name. You'll have to figure that out on your own." She looked at her phone. "Look, I called an Uber, and it'll be here in one minute. Thanks for listening to my side of the story and for being open-minded. It means a lot."

"Are you safe, Joanne? Can I help in any way?"

The tough mask slipped for a split second before she gave Ella a wry smile. "I wish it was that simple," she said. "The problem with anonymous threats is that you can't protect yourself unless you find a way to disappear or to reinvent yourself. I'm planning on doing both. I've given up the escort business and dropped out of school, but I've got another source of income that I'm pursuing."

Ella listened to Joanne's footsteps race down the stairs, wondering about all the secrets she held, worrying about the danger she was in. The only way she could think to help was to uncover what happened to Meilin. Then maybe Joanne and Yina could stop looking over their shoulders and rebuild their lives without constant fear crowding in on their futures. Ella tried to imagine what new source of income Joanne had lined up and wished she'd asked, but something told her Joanne wouldn't have shared anyway.

CHAPTER 14

Roddy entered Sara's room without knocking and threw himself onto her bed. She was propped up against the headboard, reading a trashy romance novel that she slid under the covers as he was crossing the floor. Her mother would kill her if she knew her daughter was reading what amounted to soft porn. Why did they always put half-naked men on the covers anyway? May as well shout "perv."

"Where've you been hiding these past few days?" Sara asked. Her brother looked scruffy. His hair hung dull and lank almost to his shoulders, and a new breakout of blotchy red acne spread across his cheeks and forehead. She felt sorry for him, knowing he was bullied at school. He appeared to shrug off the meanness, but the taunts had to hurt. She should know.

Roddy rolled onto his back and made the shadow of a bird with his hands fly across the ceiling. "Trying not to be here."

"What do you think happened to Charlie?"

"No idea."

"Don't you feel bad about him being missing for so long?"

Roddy tired of making the shadow bird and crossed his hands behind his head. "I figure he'll be home soon as Dad pays the ransom."

"Nobody's asked for ransom."

"Not yet, but they will."

"How could you possibly know that?" She stared at his face, trying to get a read on him. Was he part of some plot to steal away their half-brother, or was he whistling through his ass? Her tone sharpened. "Are you involved in anything I should know about, Roddy?"

"Like what?" He turned his head and grinned. For a split-second she saw their father in him. Charming, secretive, full of bravado.

"Do you know anything about what happened to Charlie?" A stronger rephrasing of her original question.

"No. Stop asking me that." He rolled onto his stomach and picked at her bedspread. She swatted at his fingers. "I just mean that kidnappers always ask for money. At least in the movies."

She relaxed slightly but not enough to let it go. "Mom and Uncle Ivan seem to be out a lot lately. Have you noticed?"

"No, because I've been out a lot too."

She was getting nowhere with him, and frustration made her snap, "Did you want something?"

"Dad's been trying to reach you. He said he texted three times and left messages on your cell twice. You should call him."

She'd been avoiding talking to their dad since Charlie went missing. She had no idea what to say to him and Ginger, not even certain they'd want to hear from her with Charlie's disappearance on their minds. It seemed the time for indecision was up. "I'll call him then."

"Why haven't you? You had to know he was trying to get a hold of you. This is the day you usually go stay over."

"Because I thought he was busy."

Roddy laughed. "I guess that's the understatement of the year."

She heard the front door open, and Roddy scrambled off her bed. "They're ba...a...a...ck. I'm going to game in my room. Catch you later."

"Yeah, later."

After he was gone, Sara pulled the paperback from beneath the blanket and wedged it under her mattress before padding across her bedroom floor and into the hall. She stood at the top of the stairs and listened. Her mom and Uncle Ivan were in the kitchen, and their voices carried up the stairwell.

"This calls for a celebration," Uncle Ivan said, followed by the sound of bottle caps popping. Her mom screeched out a laugh, and then one of them turned on the radio. Some country song cranked up high. Uncle Ivan was wailing along off-key. He sounded half-cut already.

I've got to get out of here, Sara thought. *I can't take any more of them.*

She stopped by Roddy's room to let him know she was leaving for a bit. "If Mom asks, I've gone to a movie with a girlfriend."

Roddy glanced sideways at her and nodded before going back to his game. Thankfully, he didn't ask the girlfriend's name.

Hard to believe people earned a living playing video games, but Roddy told her he'd make a mint one day if he kept practising. She hoped he was right. Otherwise, his life was going to be one huge waste of space.

She trod as quietly as she could down the stairs and eased her way out the front door, pulling it gently shut behind her. The sight of her small, bug of a car made her smile, as it always did. Her father had bought her the older, second-hand vehicle in the States for her seventeenth birthday, saying she and Roddy could visit him more easily. She suspected it was really so he didn't have to pick them up and deal with their mom, but that didn't matter to her. A car meant freedom.

It was another steamy afternoon, the slight breeze doing little to ease the humidity. She could remember when the heat of the day was early afternoon. Now it seemed to peak closer to suppertime, and nights without air conditioning had become unbearable. Her mother told her and Roddy to complain to their dad so that he'd have a system installed in their house, but so far she hadn't, and Roddy was happy enough with his fan. Driving around in her air-conditioned car cooled her down enough to sleep most nights.

She took the slow route across the city to Rocky Point, cranking up the stereo and the air conditioning, singing along with the top forty. By the time she reached the Loch Isle intersection, the tightness in her chest had gone, to be replaced by a new sense of trepidation. What if her father wasn't happy to see her? How should she react to Charlie's disappearance?

Her dad's Beamer was parked behind Ginger's Volkswagen in their drive. A couple of reporters and a camera were set up across the road. She hadn't expected that but should have. Charlie's disappearance had been headline news since it happened. There was room to park next to her dad's car, and she slid hers into the space with enough of a gap to open her door. The heat hit full force when she stepped onto the pavement. She looked over at the reporters to find them staring back and ducked her head to run toward the front door before they recognized her. What happened to Charlie felt real for the first time. She knocked, and a moment later a woman she didn't know let her inside the foyer.

"Sara? I recognize you from photos. Is your dad expecting you?"

"And who are you?" She hadn't meant to be rude, but the words came out before she thought about how they sounded.

"Sorry, I'm Vanda Winters, the police liaison worker. I'm here for support. This is my last day, however."

"Has there been news … about Charlie?"

"Nothing yet."

"It's really … awful. Ginger must be going crazy."

"Everyone's having a difficult time."

"Of course." Had she misspoken by singling out Ginger? The liaison worker was staring intently, sizing her up. Sara tried a smile, but even that felt wrong. "Can I see my dad?"

"He's upstairs working in the den."

Sara looked past the woman's shoulder, and her heart sank. "Hi, Mr. Halliday." Ginger's parents — of course they were here. She should have figured that out too before driving over.

"Good of you to finally show some interest in your half-brother." Richard had moved into the centre of the hallway, and Vanda Winters disappeared into the living room.

"I didn't know if I should come."

"Why not? You're part of the family. Where's your brother?"

"Roddy's home. He … he feels bad but couldn't come over today. I'm to report back." She'd filled the silence with lies because Mr. Halliday always made her nervous as hell. She liked Mrs. Halliday, though, even if she seemed happy to let her husband do all the talking. The opposite of her own mother. "I'll just go see my dad then."

She felt his stare follow her up the stairs, but she forced herself not to turn around. "Fucking asshole," she muttered when she reached the landing. The door to the den was shut, and she hesitated until she remembered that her dad was the one trying to contact her, not the other way around. She strode across the thick carpet and rapped on the door.

"Come in."

Her dad turned his head when she entered, and she thought he looked tired. He smiled, though and stood, bending at the waist and opening his arms wide like he had when she was a kid. She crossed the room and slipped into his embrace. He hugged her hard before letting go. "I'm glad you came."

She wasn't used to this much affection from him and felt off-balance. Had she entered another universe where people did the opposite of what you expected? "What's going on, Dad?" she asked.

He ran a hand through his hair. "I'm beginning to think the worst. There's been no ransom note, and we're nearing the end of the third day. Ginger's in shock, and I don't know what to do to make this better."

"Maybe it's not up to you." She squirmed under his stare. "I mean, maybe this isn't anything you can control. You have to wait and hope whoever took Charlie does the right thing and brings him home." Even as she said the words, she wondered if something her father had done was responsible for Charlie's disappearance. He'd betrayed her mom with Ginger and left them for his new family. She'd learned not to trust him, even if she loved him and wanted things back the way they were before Ginger and Charlie came along to steal him away.

"You're a tonic."

"Why were you trying to reach me, Dad?"

"To make sure you and Roddy and your mom are okay." He paused. "I also need a favour, if you have time."

"Of course. I'll do anything to help."

"Spend a few hours with Ginger. She's stressed, and that's not good for the new baby. You've always had a nice way with her. Maybe help her with some chores. We're both coping in our own way. I know that my hovering is driving her around the bend, so I'm trying to back off. I'm handling a work crisis, which helps keep me out of her hair and my mind off Charlie because otherwise I'll go crazy. Can you stay over tonight?"

"I guess, if I call Mom, but just for tonight. I have to work at the Dairy Queen tomorrow. What about Ginger's parents? How long are they staying?"

"Who knows?" His expression turned grim. "It'd be better for Ginger if they left, but not my call."

"Her mom seems nice."

"Yeah, but Madeleine's got this nervous energy that isn't helping. As for Richard, I have to keep away from him or I'm going to lose it completely."

Sara wondered if she should reconsider staying. Then she remembered her mother and Uncle Ivan drinking in the kitchen. "I'll call Mom now to let her know I'll be spending the night. My usual room?"

"No, Madeleine and Richard are in it. I'll pull out the couch in here and will get it set up for you.

Thanks, Sara. Why don't you go check in with Ginger now while I finish dealing with this work mess?" His eyes darted to the laptop.

She watched him sit down at the desk and start working before turning to leave. He hadn't looked at her again once he began typing, but she wasn't surprised. When it came to work, he tuned out everything and everybody around him. It was something that used to drive her mother insane.

Ginger took a while to answer her knock. She was sitting by the window with a look of such sorrow on her face when Sara opened the door that she took a step backward. "Can I get you anything, Ginger? Some tea maybe?"

"I don't want … okay, some tea would be nice."

"I'll go make some. I'm really, really sorry about Charlie. I hope he comes home soon."

"Me too." Ginger gave a heartbreaking smile before turning again to look out the window.

Sara closed the door on her way out, leaned against it for a moment, and closed her eyes. *I hate this*, she thought. *Being in the middle. I wish that I could walk out of my life and start over somewhere else, somewhere with a normal family that doesn't lie and keep secrets.*

She sometimes dreamed about living alone in a big house near the sea. There were pear and lemon trees, and she owned a Black Lab named Sunny. She spent her mornings at the beach and played online chess in the afternoons with worthy opponents from all over the world. In the evenings, a boy she liked at school took her to dinner, and all the girls in her class wanted to be her.

Some mornings, the dream was all that got her out of bed.

CHAPTER 15

The day was waning into evening, and Liam was frustrated. The tip line hadn't yielded any credible leads, and the clock kept ticking. Charlie McGowan's chances of coming home alive were growing slimmer with every passing hour. The dive team had made another sweep of the river and shoreline, mercifully with no sign of the boy's body. More and more it looked as if somebody had taken him, and if not for ransom money, Liam didn't want to think about what was happening to the boy.

"Do you have something for me to do?" Rosie Thorburn was standing in front of his desk. "I've read up on the McGowan file," she added.

"Thanks for helping out. It's been a long couple of days, and I'm heading home for some sleep. Can you keep an eye on the tip line and incoming reports from officers in the field and call my cell if anything develops?"

"You got it. This case is as maddening as the

missing Hanon girl's file." She walked back to her desk and was on the phone when he finally left for the day.

Exhaustion hit him as he turned the corner onto his street. The pace of the investigation would be steady but not frantic from here on in unless they got a lead. Other work would eventually usurp Charlie's investigation, moving the case to the side of his desk, where it would sit like a throbbing toothache. He'd give it his attention when he could, the boy's fate never straying far from his mind.

Hannah's car was in the driveway, and he felt his mood lighten. They'd once talked about living together. It would have made his life easier, working such long hours in Homicide, but she hadn't wanted to uproot her boys. Losing their dad to cancer two years ago had been traumatic enough. She met him at the door and pulled him into a hug.

"Long haul?" she asked.

"You've no idea."

They moved into the kitchen, and she got busy making scrambled eggs and toast, knowing he needed a light meal before crashing.

"Where're the boys?"

"Overnight camp. The bus brings them back Friday morning." She set a plate in front of him and took a seat across the island after pouring them each a glass of red wine.

"You're not eating?" He pointed at her with his fork.

"I already did." She took a sip. "Tell me, is that missing boy any closer to being found?"

"No." He took a bite of eggs. "It's not looking promising."

"That's such a shame. His family must be going crazy with worry." She watched him eat. "I'm taking the boys to Toronto for the weekend after I pick them up from the bus and bring them home for a shower and change of clothes. Will you be okay without me?" Her smile was teasing.

He grinned. "Thanks so much for all you've done to keep my life halfway sane."

"What are sisters for?"

"I lucked out when I became your little bro."

He could hear her cleaning up in the kitchen as he got ready for bed, but he was sound asleep when she let herself out. He stayed dead to the world until his alarm went off at five the next morning. No dreams, just eight hours of sound, unbroken sleep.

———

HE SENT a text to Ella Tate before setting out for breakfast. The sun was starting its climb above the tree line to the east, and the heat was like a damp blanket covering the city. It was going to be another hot, humid one. Daisy greeted him as he entered the diner and waved the coffeepot in his direction. He nodded and took a booth where he could watch the door. The place was hopping with construction workers fuelling up before their workday.

Daisy was pouring him a second cup when he spotted Ella in the doorway, wearing a loose, black t-shirt, blue jean shorts, and flip-flops. "Make that two cups," he said, setting aside the sports section of *The Capital*. He raised an arm and Ella made her way to his booth and slid in opposite him.

"Hey, Daisy," she said. "I'll take the usual."

"Coming right up. And for you, sir?"

"Two over easy, bacon, hash browns, and white toast." Daisy moved away, and he looked at Ella. Her hair was still wet from the shower, her green eyes bleary. "Wasn't sure you'd get my message," he said.

"Lucky for you I woke up early. So why'd you want to see me?" She slumped back in the seat and reached for the coffee cup.

"Thought we could have a think about the Charlie McGowan case."

"Still got nothing?"

"Not a single lead. He could be in the river, although that's looking less and less likely, or someone could have taken him."

"What's your gut telling you?"

"I'd like to know more about David McGowan and his associations."

Ella sat quietly for a moment. "He was married once before Ginger and has two teenagers, if our research is correct."

"It is. He also owns a company of financial advisors in the east end."

"You think he's made an enemy?" Ella asked.

"It's something to consider."

"But difficult to uncover."

"We're looking into his finances on the quiet." Liam leaned back as Daisy set their breakfasts on the table.

"There you go. You two both look like you could do with a good meal." Daisy patted Ella's arm before sashaying over to a table of construction workers.

Ella smiled at Daisy's retreating back and picked up her fork. "So what can I do to help?"

"Perhaps start by interviewing David's first wife and teenage kids and his work associates for your podcast. They might be more inclined to speak with you than us. You have a way of listening that gets people to talk."

"I can do that. You have no idea how much I edit from those podcasts. People tend to tell me *waaaay* too much."

"Keep me in the loop so I know who you're approaching and where you are at any given time. I'll be available as backup."

"No need of that. I can handle myself." She scowled before taking a forkful of eggs. "Are you working on the missing university student case?"

"No, but I can pass info along to the team if you have something." He wouldn't be surprised if she did. If he'd learned anything about Ella, it was that she was resourceful.

"I met with Meilin's roommate, Joanne Freemont. She's defensive and paints herself as an innocent victim, even if she brought Meilin to the party where she disappeared."

"From what Auger said, Joanne went to ground and he couldn't locate her. You're putting his team to shame." He smiled. "Do you believe her?"

"I had the feeling she was trying to convince herself, as well as me. Something's got her and Meilin's friends scared. I plan to keep digging."

"I'm not convinced that's a good idea."

"I'll be careful."

He studied her bent over her plate and tried to swallow his worry. "I can definitely be your backup on those enquiries." *Who needs sleep anyway?*

Ella tilted her head to one side and met his stare. "Let's say I'll contact you if I ever feel in danger. Will that work?"

"I guess it'll have to." It wasn't as if she'd given him a choice. Meilin's case wasn't his to pursue, and he couldn't stop Ella from doing her job.

"I want to bring the missing ones home," she said quietly. "Their families deserve to know what happened to them."

"I feel the same. Everyone's in limbo, frightened of what's to come but needing closure at the same time, even if the outcome isn't good. Nobody can move on until they know."

"And not knowing can be the worst kind of torture."

CHAPTER 16

David's executive assistant agreed to give Ella a tour of the premises at 1:00 p.m. after running her request past David. Vanessa was certain the staff would speak with her about the desperate situation if it helped to bring Charlie home. Ella tucked away her phone, feeling slightly guilty about the slant she'd given her request, but not enough to cancel the visit. Hunter was counting on her to check out David's associations, and she had to admit that she was curious herself.

She walked to the transitway and caught the O-train across the city into the east end. From there, it was a short walk to McGowan Financial Services, located in a low-rise grey building on St. Laurent Boulevard. Vanessa met her at the door and gave her a tour of the office, introducing her to several of the financial advisors. Over half were men, most in their late-twenties and thirties.

"How long have you worked here, Vanessa?" Ella

asked. She looked to be in her late twenties, Asian with straight black hair cut in a pageboy. Tall and slim, dressed in a crisp navy suit.

"Goodness, three weeks?" Vanessa's voice rose at the end of statements as if she were asking Ella for answers, an affectation Ella never understood.

"Where were you before?"

"Seaway Digital. I like it here better."

"Why the change?"

"Pay raise? I applied last year and got a call at the beginning of July from human resources. Britt had already told me she was leaving, so I jumped at the chance."

Ella looked around the empty waiting room, thinking. "Who was David's executive assistant before you?"

"Britt Flambert. She had some family issues with her mother being sick and gave her two-week notice. Lucky for me."

"So no complaints?"

"Not so far." Vanessa grinned. "Say, would you like a cup of coffee? David bought one of those single pod machines, so I can make you any kind you want, including espresso."

"An espresso would be great." She wanted to stick around and assess the operation, get some of the financial advisors to chat with her. Coffee would give her a reason to linger.

Vanessa took a call on her cell after handing her a mug of coffee. She invited Ella to remain in the lunchroom while she went to talk with a supplier. "This could take a while, but please enjoy your coffee and come see me before you leave."

"Thanks, don't worry about me."

It wasn't long before one of the financial advisors entered the kitchen. His name was Jeremy Adams, and he'd been working for David two years. He was friendly but sidestepped all her attempts to draw him into a conversation about his colleagues or the state of the business and left with his coffee as soon as it finished brewing.

Ella was nearly done drinking her coffee and about to give up when one of the women advisors came in to make a pot of tea. Olivia Jones-Briggs dropped into the chair across from her while she waited for the kettle to boil. Olivia was attractive, slightly older than the other employees Ella had met, silver-blonde highlights, black-rimmed glasses on trend, tailored red pantsuit. They'd been introduced when Vanessa took her on the rounds, and Olivia greeted her warmly before asking, "Getting everything you need?"

"I am, thanks. So how long have you worked here?"

"I'm one of the longer-serving advisors — also one of the oldest at forty years of age in a few months. Gawd, I'm getting so damn old." She grinned. "It'll be six years next month since David hired me."

"You certainly aren't old. Is there a large turnover?"

"It's a competitive business. All the companies head-hunt."

"I imagine, but you decided to stay."

Olivia shrugged. "The location suits me. David also gives me nice bonuses."

"I get it. Has anyone left on unhappy terms?"

Olivia snorted a laugh. "No more than anywhere else. Office work isn't everyone's first choice." She paused. "An advisor, Winston Simmons, left in a huff around Christmas, but he hadn't been performing. Britt Flambert was David's EA, and she left at the beginning of the month and seemed reluctant to turn in her resignation. The admin assistants don't tend to last long, I might add. The pay isn't the best for all the hours they put in."

"Do you keep in touch with either of them?"

"Not usually, but I have their phone numbers if you want. Everyone shares where they are in case another better opportunity arises."

"Sure, I'll take Winston's and Britt's numbers."

Olivia pulled out her phone and started clicking. She read off the information and jumped up as the kettle boiled. "I liked Britt. She was good at her job."

"Did she give a reason for leaving?"

"Her mother had a health issue, so she decided to move back to help out. Peterborough, I believe, although I think she's still in town until the first of August. Her last day in our office was two weeks ago after she trained her replacement, Vanessa."

"Great, I'll see if I can catch her before she moves. And Winston Simmons?"

"He's still unemployed. David didn't give him a recommendation, so Winston might have to move cities to get work. We're a small community in Ottawa."

"I'm beginning to see that. How angry was Winston when he left?"

Olivia dipped a teabag by the string into her mug and leaned against the counter. "You know, slamming the wall with his fist mad. Typical for someone who was just fired. I'm sure he cooled down by the time he got home."

"Off the record, would you rate David as a good employer?"

She tilted her head to one side. "I'd say David works harder than anybody here and pays on par with other similar-sized financial companies. He's always friendly and engaged if you can get his attention. I handle a great deal of the staff issues and mundane details of the business so he's freed up to woo clients and keep them happy. He's called me his right hand on occasion."

"Do you like your role?"

"Again, large bonuses, so I can't complain."

"You must have been here when David was dating Ginger. How did that go down with your colleagues?"

"Nobody was aware they were dating until she quit and they moved in together." Olivia shrugged. "He wasn't happy in his first marriage, from what I've heard."

"No judgments then?"

"One's personal life has nothing to do with the business."

Ella left the office after this exchange. She phoned Britt and Winston in the train heading home, leaving messages with both. Winston Simmons was worth a closer look and might agree to an interview if only to get her off his tail. Next up, a visit to David's ex-wife Claudette, but for that trip, she'd take her car after a late lunch.

———

DAVID WAS PACING in the hallway at the top of the stairs as Sara came out of her bedroom. He stopped when she blocked his path. "What's going on, Dad?"

"Ginger's having a bad morning, and I need to go into the office." His eyes sharpened on her. "Are you leaving?"

"Dairy Queen, remember? My shift starts at two."

"I was hoping you could stay with Ginger today."

"Her parents are here."

"They aren't really helping. Any chance you could cancel your shift?

Typical that he didn't hesitate to ask her to change her plans without considering the inconvenience. "No, it's too late to get a sub," she said.

She was curious about his reluctance to leave Ginger alone with her parents. It seemed odd, but she was late and didn't have time to try to figure out what was going on with him. She thought that her dad stood to lose a lot of money if he and Ginger split, and maybe he was just trying to keep a lid on things. She had no doubt the two of them wouldn't last over the long haul.

He gave a half-hearted grin, one meant to work on her sympathies and perhaps to change her mind. "Well, I'd better tell her I need to go in to the office. Not looking forward to this."

Not my problem, she thought, but the guilty feeling that always came when she disappointed him flared anyway.

Mr. Halliday was in the hallway at the bottom of the stairs and watched her as she made her way down. He stopped her before she could get past him. "What's going on up there?"

"Dad's talking to Ginger. He has to go into the office for a bit."

"Bloody hell. Can't he stop thinking about work and focus on his family for one hour?" Mr. Halliday was like a landmine detonating. His face flushed beet-red, and she thought he might be having a stroke.

His anger made her defensive. Her dad wasn't perfect, but who'd want this man as a father-in-law? "People at work are still counting on my dad. I think worrying about them is helping him to cope. I guess you and Mrs. Halliday can step in for a few hours to help with Ginger. It's why you're here, isn't it? To help them out?"

His eyebrows went up and joined in the middle. His stare hardened. "You seem a chip off his selfish block. I should expect nothing less, I suppose." He moved aside to let her pass. "Have a nice day."

"Thanks, I plan to."

She stomped out of the house, but the rush of self-righteous indignation wore off by the time she reached her car. She got behind the wheel and stared up the driveway. Aside from Charlie, she didn't feel bad for any of them, Ginger and her dad included. She loved her father but couldn't deny that he was a self-serving liar and cheat. Ginger had cheated Sara's family too by stealing her dad away. Maybe the universe had taken Charlie as a way to show Ginger what loss and grief felt like. Sara thought about her mom and her downward spiral since she found out about Ginger. None of what happened was fair. Would she blame her mom for wanting to get even?

Sara was still pondering her jumbled mess of feelings after taking the Queensway east across the city. She pulled into her driveway twenty-five minutes later and jumped out of the car, hurrying inside to change into her DQ uniform. The front hallway was a sauna, and she paused to slip out of her sandals. It took a moment for her to tune in to her mother's face staring at her from the kitchen.

"What's going on with your father?"

Sara couldn't read her mother's mood but knew enough not to answer directly. "There's still no word about Charlie. I've got a shift in half an hour, so…" She took a tentative step toward the stairs. Her mom was halfway down the hallway. Her face was as pale as a bowl of cream except for the dark circles under her eyes. Sara hesitated. "Are you okay, Mom?"

"Why wouldn't I be? I don't want you staying over

at your dad's until this Charlie business is sorted. We shouldn't get involved."

"Where's Uncle Ivan?"

"At his place sleeping, I imagine. You heard what I said?"

"Yeah, Mom. I heard. I don't want to be over there anyway." She turned her back and climbed the stairs. Her mother's voice followed behind her.

"Your father needs to handle this with his new family. You're kidding yourself if you think he'll do anything but take advantage of your kind heart and spit it out when he doesn't need you anymore."

Are you talking about me or yourself? Sara thought. She reached the landing and forced herself not to look down the stairwell at her mother. She'd be glad to go to work for the rest of the day and be away from this house. She'd stop worrying about Charlie and the possibility someone close to her was involved. Pretend her life was normal as she filled ice cream cones and flipped burgers. Surely that wasn't too much to ask?

CHAPTER 17

The woman who snapped the front door open was not the put-together person Ella had been expecting. An uneven strip of white at the top of Claudette McGowan's head had grown out and contrasted with the dyed black locks. Her red shorts stretched uncomfortably tight at the waist and thighs. Ella smelled beer on her breath, even though it was mid afternoon. She thought that Claudette could be quite attractive if she put any effort into her grooming and felt a pang of sympathy for the unhappiness evident in her appearance.

"Yes, can I help you?" Claudette glared at Ella with undisguised suspicion.

"Who is it, Claudie?" a man's voice bellowed from the back of the house. Ella watched him barrelling toward them down the short hallway. He was tall and gaunt in high-waisted shorts and an untucked, white undershirt. His thinning hair was gelled back, and a scraggly goatee underscored his bony cheeks and pale grey eyes. Ella forced herself to focus on Claudette.

"I'm Ella Tate, a contract reporter for *The Capital* and a true crime podcaster. I was hoping to chat with you for a moment about Charlie."

The man put his hand on Claudette's shoulder and somehow wedged himself between her and the door. "Why don't you go back and finish what you were doing, sis, and I'll handle this?"

Claudette had been about to say something, but the man pushed her gently backward and shooed her with a hand. She glared at Ella but pivoted and left without putting up an argument. He moved so that he blocked Ella's view into the house.

"My sister's not speaking to any reporters. This is a family tragedy, and we ask to be left alone at this difficult time."

"I understand. I'm only trying to help bring Charlie home, so anything I can use to appeal to the public for information would be much appreciated. I'm not after a sensational story."

"Well, that would be a first." He looked her up and down. "You don't dress like a reporter."

"I'm not in front of the camera ... so..." She shrugged and smiled. "Claudette seems upset, which is understandable."

"Her ex treated her like dirt, and she's had a hard time getting over how low he brought her." He paused, looked over his shoulder, then back at her. "She feels awful about Charlie, but the kid's the reason David left her."

"And you are…?"

"Ivan Deerfield, her brother. Uncle to Sara and Roddy. Now, they're closer to Charlie, although not really that close. We got nothing to tell you except that we're hoping Charlie gets home safe and sound. You can quote me in your paper on that. So you have yourself a good day." He stepped back and shut the door. Ella heard the click of a lock.

She jumped down off the steps and walked toward the street. She hadn't gotten anything useful aside from an uneasy feeling and their names. A few moments later, she drove into a shopping mall parking lot and found a spot in the shade. She rolled the windows down and put her seat back before pulling out her phone and starting some Google searches, beginning with Ivan Deerfield.

———

SARA WIPED down the counter and made a final check of the room. The last group of teenagers left at ten to eleven, and she was hopeful of getting out of there on time for once. She crossed over to their table with a tray and collected burger wrappers and fry containers before cleaning the table with disinfectant in a spray bottle and a rag. The bell on the front door tinkled, announcing another customer as she straightened and glanced over. *Please let whoever it is order ice cream and leave.* She was relieved to see a lone woman standing at the entrance. She had a pretty face but wild blonde hair and was dressed in jean shorts, a t-shirt, and flip-flops. Her eyes were an odd shade of green, almost like the sage in her mom's garden.

"You still serving?" the lady called across the space.

"Of course. What can I get you?"

"A medium strawberry sundac."

"Coming right up."

Sara hurried behind the counter and set to work. After pressing the lever and adding a gush of berries, she slid the sundae in front of the customer and punched the price into the cash register.

"Thanks for this." The lady had already dug into the ice cream and was licking the back of the spoon. She pulled out her debit card and tapped the machine. "When do you finish?"

"I'll lock the door after you, so now, I guess."

"Do you have a minute to talk, Sara?"

She froze, fear pumping through her. "Do I know you?"

"No, but I'm working to help bring Charlie home. My name's Ella Tate, and I interviewed Ginger and your dad for my podcast. I just came from your mom's."

Sara relaxed slightly. She followed Ella's true crime podcast, *Crime in the Rear View,* trying to resolve the cases before the last instalments. Another thought struck her. "How did you know I work here?"

"You should make your Facebook account private."

"Oh." She'd been posting public updates from her boring afternoon, telling people to come visit her at the DQ. She had very few followers, so it seemed safe enough. Changing her privacy settings might be a good idea. "Okay, I can talk for a minute after I close up."

"I'll wait outside at a picnic table. It's cooled off a bit since the sun went down and is quite pleasant."

"Yeah, I'd like to get out of here, so I'll join you in a few secs."

Sara emptied the cash register and put the money in an envelope and into the safe. Most people paid with debit or credit, and the cash take was small. While she worked, she considered what Ella Tate might ask her about Charlie. She'd have to be careful and not let herself be blindsided into saying something that would cast suspicion on her family. Could that be why she was here? First that detective and now a reporter … no, this was only the media looking for a story, believing she and her mom and Roddy cared about what happened to Charlie. Luckily, she didn't have to fake her own feelings.

Ella was sitting at a table when Sara stepped outside. She locked the front door and slid onto the bench facing her. The night air was stinking hot after six hours spent in air conditioning. Ella had to be nuts to think this was a pleasant evening. The table was half in shadow, and she could hear cars passing behind her on Bank Street. Ella had finished the ice cream and was fiddling with her phone. She set it aside and leaned forward, both elbows on the table, focusing her full attention on Sara. "Tell me about Charlie," she said.

Sara's eyes watered, the worry she'd been avoiding hitting her. This reaction wasn't what she'd been expecting, and she ducked her head so the reporter wouldn't see. She cleared her throat. "He's a sweet little guy. Loves teddy bears and mashed potatoes. He's always busy and getting into mischief. I hope that whoever has Charlie is taking good care of him." She swiped at a tear before it rolled down her cheek.

"I'm so sorry." Ella paused, giving her time. Her voice softened. "Do you have any idea who might have taken him? For instance, did you see anybody hanging around when you were at your dad's house?"

Could Ella possibly have found out that she was the one hanging out and spying on her dad and Ginger? Sara dismissed the idea as soon as it popped into her head. She'd been careful, and nobody had been around that morning on the beach. She'd double-checked and knew she'd left before Charlie went missing. No, this reporter was just fishing.

"I can't think of anyone who'd take him. I wasn't at my dad's that often. This job keeps me closer to my mom's place on the weekends lately."

"That makes sense. Your mom isn't a fan of Charlie, is she? I suppose that's understandable given the divorce." The woman went still, watching her like a hawk studying its next meal.

"Mom's had a hard time."

"I met your Uncle Ivan."

Sara couldn't stop her grimace. "Lucky you."

"What does he do for a living?"

Mooch, she thought but said instead, "He works for

a roofing company but hasn't had any jobs for a few weeks. He says a break is okay because the summer heat wave was killing him."

"Does Roddy go over to your dad's much?"

"Roddy avoids going there as often as he can. He's been twice since school got out but only because Dad insisted. Listen, I don't want to be on your podcast. My mom doesn't want me involved."

"I understand." Ella was studying her with those peculiar green eyes. "I'd like to give you my phone number, Sara, in case you think of something that would help find Charlie."

Sara pulled out her phone. "Tell it to me, and I'll put it in my contacts."

"And just so you know, I never reveal a source."

Later, when Sara was driving home with the air conditioning up full, she decided not to tell her mom about Ella Tate's visit. She didn't want her mother and Uncle Ivan to know she'd talked to someone from the press; they'd go ballistic. To be fair, she hadn't told the reporter much. Nothing about her dad's lies and catting around on Ginger. She'd stayed silent because sharing any part of what she knew wouldn't help find Charlie. Better to protect all the family secrets, keep her head down, and pray they made it through without another implosion.

And hope that whoever had Charlie let him come home soon.

CHAPTER 18

Friday morning, Ella woke early, hot and sweaty under a sheet tangled around her legs. She reached out and angled the floor fan so that the air blew squarely on her face and then lay thinking, not eager to get the day underway. She'd dropped off sometime close to 4:00 a.m., three hours of unconsciousness if she calculated right. This heat wave, combined with too little sleep, had sapped her strength. She closed her eyes and imagined lying in a cool bath, eating one of Sara's strawberry sundaes. The image only made reality feel worse. She'd sent Hunter a quick update the evening before, letting him know about Winston and Britt and her plans to interview them. Hopefully one or both would be in touch today.

Sometime after midnight, she'd dug out the name of the owner of Juliette Dating Service where Joanne worked but couldn't find any physical location for his business or home. Wes Gilbert, self-proclaimed entrepreneur and business agent, had created a few layers of separation between himself and the escort service. She'd reached a dead end and had texted Sherry Carpenter to get her tech genius to sort through the final roadblocks to get his address. She planned to waylay Gilbert but would need to go carefully. First, she'd stake out his office, if she could locate it, and monitor his movements.

She couldn't hear Tony moving around in his apartment, so leapt out of bed to beat him to the shower before he drained the hot water tank. She'd keep the water cool to conserve some for him. The shower improved her mood, and she stood debating what to wear when Tony knocked and called through her apartment door.

"Hellooo. I've got coffee and muffins hot out of the oven. Pop down when you're dressed."

"Sure." *Why not?* If she'd learned anything about Tony, he was persistent when he had a bee in his bonnet … and his baking was to die for. She dressed in a white sleeveless blouse, flowered skirt that fell mid-calf, and leather sandals in an attempt to blend in with the work crowd. She ran her hands through her wet hair and left the sweatbox, grateful to step into the slightly cooler hallway. Tony met her at the door to his apartment with a cup of coffee. He handed it to her and pointed to a straight-backed chair in the living room next to a window with the sun streaming in. "Have a seat."

"What, you planning to interrogate me?"

"No, something much better."

"I'll play along if you feed me some muffins. What kind this morning?"

"Blueberry. They'll be done baking in ten."

She sat in the chair, and he whipped a smock around her. "Time to lose the shaggy dog, living-in-the-gutter look," he said, "much as it kind of suits you."

She spotted the scissors laid out on a nearby table. "Tony, you don't have to do this. I'm growing out the length and plan to trim it myself on the weekend."

"Over my dead body, girl. Now sit still."

She scowled but did as he'd ordered. His scissors clipped, and he gelled and sprayed to finish up. He took off the smock and shook it out. "Once your hair dries, you'll look like a million bucks."

"Thanks … I think." She waved away the hand-held mirror. "I'll look at it when it's dry."

"You are an unusual woman, you know that, Tate?"

A plate of warm muffins helped to ease her annoyance with Tony's subterfuge. He sat across from her, leaning on the table, both hands wrapped around a mug of coffee. "I have the day off to prepare for my dinner party. You are coming?"

"About that."

"I won't take no."

They locked stares until her shoulders sagged. "Okay, I give. What time?"

"Drinks at six. Casual dress, but please, no flip-flops."

"I think I can manage that." She picked up a third muffin and stood. "I'm heading downtown. Enjoy your day off."

"Anything I can do to help with your story?"

"Not now, but I'll keep you in mind."

She checked her phone in the hall and sent Sherry Carpenter and her tech genius Mark silent thanks. He'd found Wes Gilbert's home and work addresses easily, cutting through the firewalls and whatever other impediments meant to keep reporters like her out. "Gotcha," she said under her breath.

She caught a bus on Bank Street and got off at Somerset. She walked east to O'Connor and turned left. Gilbert's office was in a converted brick house tucked in between a Japanese restaurant and a florist shop — not the easiest location to hang about without looking conspicuous. She pulled out her cell phone and crossed the street. Luckily, O'Connor was a busy one-way with a constant flow of traffic, limiting the odds of anyone noticing her. She slid into the shadow between two buildings with a good view of Gilbert's place.

The night before, she'd unearthed a photo of Wes Gilbert taken at a gala. His hair was shaved at the sides and curly black on top of his head, oily and glistening like a beaver pelt. Black eyes, olive skin, short stature. A tall blonde woman in a sequined silver gown hung like a sparkly bauble on his arm. Ella hadn't been able to find any other pictures, certain he was camera-shy for a reason. She brought up the photo and checked it now and then as she watched people coming and going. Gilbert arrived at five minutes to ten, speaking into his phone as he strode along. He held himself like a larger man, self-assured and cocky: a businessman on trend in a cream-coloured, lightweight suit and pointy tan shoes.

She took snapshots with the camera on her phone until he disappeared inside the building. He left his office two hours later, and she trailed behind him to Beckta's restaurant on Elgin. He joined two male friends already sitting at the window table, a convenient placement for her to take more pictures. Two and a half hours later, the three men exited, shook hands, and Gilbert sauntered back to his office alone. Ella followed at a distance but decided she'd seen enough after he disappeared through the front door. He'd put in a two-hour workday, and it was getting close to four o'clock. She'd recognized his dinner companions from somewhere but couldn't place them … yet. She'd have to give it some thought and do more checking online.

Her phone rang as she started walking toward the closest bus stop. She checked the caller and swiped up. "Hi, Britt. Thanks for getting back to me." She listened. "Yes, I happen to be downtown and can meet at the Starbucks. I'll be there in ten minutes, tops."

She switched directions and headed north toward

Parliament Hill. Meeting David McGowan's previous assistant should give some fresh insight into his family and his business. Hopefully, she'd have something worthwhile to tell Hunter when this day ended.

———

THE STARBUCKS WAS NEARLY EMPTY, and Ella had no difficulty picking out Britt Flambert sitting alone at a table in the middle of the room. She had thick blonde hair to her shoulders and a slender physique. Ella guessed mid-twenties. Pretty. She waved at Britt before buying coffee and a doughnut, having missed lunch, and took the seat across from her. Britt pulled out earbuds and smiled. "You made it."

"I did. Thanks for returning my call."

"Happy to. My apartment on Nepean isn't air-conditioned, so I've been spending a lot of time in coffee shops. You said this concerned David McGowan and his family?"

"You do know his three-year-old son Charlie is missing?"

"He is?" Her eyes widened, and her smile disappeared. "What happened?"

"It's hard to believe you haven't heard. Media's all over the story. There was an AMBER Alert on Monday evening and all week." Ella stared at her more closely. Was she that clued out?

"I don't follow the news. I listen to music when I want to relax. I've mainly been in Peterborough since

I stopped work. My mother's sick with MS, and I can't take anymore sadness at the moment, which is all there is on the news these days. I get AMBER Alerts on my phone but never look at them. It's not like I could find a missing kid." She rubbed her forehead. "God, David must be frantic. He adores his little boy."

"The entire family is devastated."

Ella thought Britt's explanation sounded plausible, if not overly thought out. Charlie had been missing five days, and Britt had been busy with her mom. She was also of the generation that didn't tune in to mainstream media. Up close, Britt's face was skillfully made up, with rose eye shadow and fake lashes. Her lips were painted a warm coral. She'd taken care with her appearance, wearing a cream-coloured silk chemise, short black skirt, and red sandals. Bangles lined one arm, and a necklace with a single diamond nestled in the hollow of her throat. Ella couldn't imagine putting this much effort into her own appearance, especially not to sit alone in a Starbucks.

"I'm sorry to hear about your mom. You're moving back home, I understand."

"Thanks, yeah, she needs me, so I gave up my job and am nearly finished cleaning out my apartment. I'm leaving tomorrow, so you're lucky to have caught me in town. Say, do they have any idea what happened to Charlie?"

"No. He was playing in the backyard Monday morning, and his mom, Ginger, went inside for a minute. He was gone when she got back."

"Why, that's horrible. Did he wander into the river? I know their house backs onto it."

"The police searched for two days, but no sign of him in the water. They now believe that he was taken."

"Oh my God, how awful. Poor David and Ginger." She bowed her head and stared down at her hands holding the coffee cup as if in a moment of prayer.

"Did you like working for David?"

She lifted her eyes, and her face brightened. "I did. He was even-keeled with the staff. I've worked for bosses who go on rants, but he never did. He also didn't micromanage my work, something I appreciated after my previous employer."

"Do you know if anyone was upset with him?"

Britt tilted her head and thought for a moment. "There was one analyst named Winston Simmons that David fired a few months ago. He was definitely upset. Other employees came and went, but I don't know how many were fired."

"So you never heard anyone threaten David or complain about him behind his back?"

"No, nothing like that. I'm quite honestly having difficulty grasping that something like this happened to his son."

"How long did you work for him?"

"Almost two years. I was sorry to say goodbye, but I had no choice. My mom needs me."

"She's lucky to have you. Did you have much to do with the company finances?"

"No. Olivia took care of most of that, along with David and his accountant. Have you met Olivia?"

"Yes, she told me that she handled most of the HR and day-to-day. Would you say that's accurate?"

"I would. David's more big picture, looking after the clients." She fiddled with the handle of her cup. "Did Olivia say anything else about … David or the company?"

"No, we only had a brief conversation. I thought she seemed efficient. Competent, certainly."

"She's all that. David would have a hard time if she quit." Britt looked toward the door. "If you don't have any more questions, I still have some work to do at my apartment."

"I wanted to know if you ever met Ginger McGowan?"

"No, she was long gone when David hired me. I sure don't envy her now."

Had you envied her before? Ella searched her face, but Britt gave nothing away. "I guess that's all for now." She couldn't escape the feeling that she'd missed something by the relief in Britt's eyes as she began to stand. Ella reached into her pocket. "Here's my card if you think of anything else down the road."

Britt hesitated but took the card from her and thrust it into her bag without looking. "I can't imagine that I'd have anything to say that would help find Charlie, but if something comes up, you'll be the first one I'll call." She smiled before pushing in her chair. She turned and waved at the door as she opened it and stepped outside, a shaft of sunlight shining on her face for a moment, like a golden spotlight.

Ella sat sipping her coffee, replaying the conversation and sifting through Britt's words and body language for anything that felt off. She couldn't pinpoint something specific except that her answers had been short on information, almost too Pollyanna. Had Britt been playing her? David left his first wife Claudette for a younger, beautiful assistant. Britt was fresh-faced and attractive, and it didn't take much imagination to see a man like David tiring of twice-pregnant Ginger and wanting a younger, unencumbered replacement. Ella tried to picture Britt and David together and squirmed inside as the image came into focus and held. With a force of will, she blinked the idea away, reminding herself to follow the facts. She could be reading too much into his first divorce and affair. He'd been attentive to Ginger, from what she'd witnessed, and frantic about Charlie.

She pulled out her phone and checked the recording. Britt's voice came across loud and clear. She'd replay their entire conversation later at home, listening for inflections in Britt's voice that she might have missed. There was usually something new to learn.

A message had arrived while they were chatting. Winston had returned her call and invited her to meet in an hour in the west end at an address on Majestic Drive. She typed a reply and booked an Uber to take her home. She'd get her car and should have plenty of time to make the next interview with the person who, according to his colleagues, appeared to have the biggest axe to grind. Ella thought it might be time to check in with her backup, but only because she'd promised Hunter that she'd play it safe and didn't relish facing him later if things went south. She sent him a quick text before stepping outside into the relentless heat.

CHAPTER 19

Quade called a staff meeting early afternoon, and Liam joined the others filing into the room. He liked seeing his partner sitting at the head of the table, already sensing a positive change in the air. His colleagues appeared more relaxed and chatted amongst themselves while waiting for her to get the update underway. Laughter rippled around the room every now and then, unheard of when Greta was in charge.

"Hell of a difference," commented Jingles, sliding into the seat next to him. "I almost don't mind being here."

Liam didn't comment. There was no point stating the obvious or kicking Greta when she was down. Life was taking care of that without his help. Quade's eyes met his, and he gave a smile of encouragement. She returned a curt nod and called everyone to order.

"The long and short of it is that we have no

breaks in either the Hanon or McGowan cases, but I wanted to gather everyone to thank you for all your hard work. I know each of you has given up precious time with your family to put in long hours. This brings me to the latest edict from the pay grades above mine. Overtime is to be cut back forthwith on the Hanon file, and unless there's a lead in the Charlie McGowan disappearance, each request is to be rigorously vetted by me before I give approval."

"So we have to check with you before we can follow up on a lead after hours?" Auger asked.

"That's the size of it, yes. I'm going to make myself available though if you need my okay."

"I would certainly hope so." Auger looked around the table with an expression that invited everyone to join in his disgust.

Quade remained calm. "I know this is one more layer of red tape, but we'll have to abide by senior management's directive. Please do not go working on your own time without pay or without my approval. The union will get involved, and nobody wants that."

Liam could feel the goodwill in the room dissipating. Auger was talking to those close to him, and people's expressions became agitated. A disgruntled buzz started around the table. Liam motioned to speak, and Quade raised a hand to silence the room. "Detective Hunter, you have the floor."

He waited for the noise to die away. "We have no leads on Charlie McGowan's disappearance, and the search of the neighbourhood and river over the past five days has been thorough. No ransom call. No credible phone tips. It's as if a hole in the ground opened and swallowed him up. Unless we get a lead soon, we can carry out the investigation during regular hours. The force is on the lookout for Charlie around the clock, of course, and the tip line is working twenty-four/seven." The Hanon case was nine months old, and he doubted Auger could make a strong argument for unrestricted overtime if he couldn't for a case only five days old.

"To be clear, I'm not saying no to overtime." Quade looked around the table, meeting stares head-on until her gaze rested on Auger. "But you need to tell me why it's necessary. As we all know, the recent city council froze the police budget, including a hiring freeze. We're being asked to tighten our belts, and this is the result. Now, if there are no further updates, I suggest we all get back to work."

———

BOOTS AND JINGLES followed Liam to his desk. "Methinks a power play is underway," Boots said. "Auger sees himself next in line for Greta's job."

Jingles nodded. "Quade better watch her back."

"Great." Liam dropped into his chair and looked up at them. "All we need with two difficult cases is for him to stir it up."

"Who's stirring what up?" Rosie skirted around Jingles to drop a file on Liam's desk.

"My son's making minestrone soup for supper."

Boots winked and saluted Liam before he and Jingles headed toward their desks.

"Strange, but okay," Rosie said, watching them go. She turned and looked at Liam. "A few messages to follow up on from the tip line. I can handle them if you like."

He opened the file and glanced through the call log while Rosie stood waiting. "Nothing too promising, but thanks for looking after these. Let me know if anything develops."

"Sure thing." She took the file and crossed to her desk opposite Auger. Liam watched her for a moment before checking his phone. "Damn," he said after reading Ella's message that she was going to interview the man fired from McGowan's office. Luckily, she'd included Winston's address. He grabbed his jacket and texted a reply as he jogged for the exit, hoping he wasn't too late to prevent any trouble.

He chanced going over the speed limit as he drove onto the Queensway into the west end, bypassing the Carling off-ramp and exiting at Woodroffe South. Winston lived in a bungalow in a neighbourhood near Algonquin College. The houses were small and tired-looking for the most part, set on large, treed lots. He imagined this would be one of the next sections of the city to see developers buying up properties and replacing single-family homes with doubles and triples. The future was intensification as the city prepared to double within a few decades. No more large backyards or privacy in the new builds, victims of so-called progress.

He parked a few doors down and hurried up the walkway to Winston's front door. Ella's car was in the driveway, heat radiating off the front windshield. He was supposed to stay in the background, but Ella had indicated that Simmons could be aggressive in last evening's update, and he couldn't let her be alone in harm's way.

A Filipino woman holding a dust rag answered his ring. "Yes? Can I help you?"

"I'm looking for Winston Simmons. Is he home?"

"He's with somebody right now."

Liam held up his ID. "Can you take me to them?"

She looked from the laminated card to his face. "Has he done something wrong?"

"How often do you clean?"

"Once every two weeks."

So she'd have no idea what Winston was doing Monday … whether he'd showed up home with a small child. He paused, listening to voices in one of the rooms. A moment later, Ella and a man dressed in khakis and a button-down shirt entered the hallway. Winston's short, rotund body rocked from side to side as they walked toward Liam, his Friar Tuck haircut making him look even odder. Ella spotted Liam first, and a stony glare settled over her face. He waited until they reached him.

"This is a policeman," the housecleaner said before Liam had a chance to say anything. "He wants to speak to you, Mr. Winston."

Winston looked suspiciously from Ella to Liam. "You two know each other?"

"I should say not." Ella turned her back on Liam and held out her hand to Winston. "Thanks for the chat, and best of luck with that job interview."

"My pleasure."

She stepped around Liam without looking at him and was out the door, leaving him to come up with a reason for being there.

"So what is it you want with me?" Winston asked. He stood with his legs spread wide and his arms crossed. His face was set in a belligerent stare.

"I'm lead detective on the missing Charlie McGowan case and checking to see if anybody who worked for David knows anything. You were fired from his company last month, I understand."

"I was, but as I explained to Ms. Tate, I was out of town on Monday and can prove it. A friend and I drove to New York City for a three-day getaway. I showed her my receipts and a couple of date-stamped pics. She took photos of the lot. I suppose you want to have a look too?"

"No, that's fine." Liam figured Simmons would be less antagonistic if he didn't ask for proof, knowing Ella would share the documents later. "Can you think of anyone else who might be considered a disgruntled employee?"

"How long do you have?" Winston shook his head. "Okay, call me biased, but I'd rather eat nails than work for that bastard David McGowan. I wasn't in his company long enough to figure out where everyone else was coming from, if you know what I mean. The staff turnover is high, so read into that what you will."

Not what Ella had reported, but Liam didn't challenge him. "So noted. What grounds did David have for firing you?"

"It was his pit bull, Olivia Jones-Briggs, who did the honours. She said David had received a vigorous complaint from my main client about small returns on their investment. I was unceremoniously escorted out without the chance to defend myself."

"Could you have?"

"If they'd let me look at the books again. The company in question had made money, although perhaps not the amount they believed they deserved." Winston shook his head. "I'm not a miracle worker."

"The allegations are that you became violent." Liam watched his reaction.

Winston laughed. "I tossed a few files around. Punched a wall. The moment passed."

Liam wondered if the anger truly was over or remained lurking under Winston's smile. In either case, the conversation had run its course. "Well, that was all I wanted to ask for now. Thanks for your time, and sorry to have interrupted your day."

"Yeah, glad you heard my side. I'm not surprised if David tried to pin his kid's disappearance on me. He's just that kind of guy."

Ella's car was gone from the driveway when Liam turned toward the street. His cell pinged a message as he reached his car.

You need a lesson in being a backup, Detective … and no I

didn't need rescuing. W. wasn't in town Mon. Britt (David's previous EA) had nothing worthwhile to offer. All-around useless day. Forwarding pics of his receipts and photos from New York City.

Liam hit reply. *Thanks for trying. Sorry I botched backup*

He checked up and down the street before getting into his car. Ella didn't want his support, but he didn't regret knocking on Winston's door. They'd been lucky this time. The interview could have turned nasty, and she'd have been thankful for him barging in. He always operated on the side of caution when it came to his partners, which she was in a sense. She'd simply have to get used to it.

CHAPTER 20

Sara eased her car off the shoulder of Loch Isle Road into a spot partially hidden by bushes. She opened the windows and turned off the engine. The owner of the house couldn't see her car through the thick stand of cedar trees, and she had a partial view of her dad's driveway three doors down in the gathering dusk. It was cooler here in the shade, a good thing on this steamy summer night. She'd found the sweet hiding place soon after her dad bought the car for her and she began spying on him and Ginger. It was fortuitous that her little car was slate grey and blended into the foliage.

The reporters from across the street were gone for the day. No cameras were set up for on-the-spot reporting. Even the police cars were nowhere to be seen, although she knew an officer was likely inside the house. The thought that they'd all but given up on finding Charlie made her sad. She hoped he wasn't scared, wherever he was.

She wasn't sure why this compulsion to follow her dad hadn't abated yet. It had started by accident after he bought her the car last year. She'd driven over to see him one evening only to pass him on the road going in the opposite direction. He hadn't seen her, so she'd done a U-turn and trailed behind him to an apartment building downtown on Nepean Street. She liked the rush of following him incognito with the possibility of getting caught. The idea of becoming a private eye interested her, and she thought of this as practice. She had no idea whom he was visiting, but he stayed inside for an hour before she followed him home to Loch Isle Road.

Over the course of the next two weeks, he visited the same building six times that she knew about, always early evening. It got so Sara drove downtown and parked across from the building, waiting for him to arrive. The first thing she thought of — naturally, and as it turned out correctly — was that he was having an affair. He and Ginger had tied the knot a year after Charlie was born and had been married for a year when the trips to the apartment started, or at least when she became aware of his evening visits. It took a bit of sleuthing for her to find out the name of the woman. She should have felt bad for Ginger, but instead she experienced a certain satisfaction knowing that the cheater who stole away her dad was now the one being cheated on.

Sara scanned the street and took her notebook log out of her bag. She'd been recording every trip and making notes about who her dad and Ginger visited and how long they stayed. At first it was for something to do while she sat holed up in her car, and then it became part of the game. She liked asking her dad innocent questions about his week in front of Ginger when she went to stay over. She had to admire what a practiced liar he was. He was so good that she'd have believed his stories if she hadn't followed him and kept track of his comings and goings.

He'd stopped visiting the apartment building five months ago, about the time he and Ginger announced that she was pregnant again. *Coincidence?* He did, however, continue going out in the evenings on the same days of the week as before, usually to a bar in the ByWard Market, but not always. On those nights in the Market, she could never find a parking spot nearby and would go home rather than hang around. She didn't feel safe wandering alone in this section of the downtown after dark.

She didn't expect Ginger or her dad to go out tonight, but home was not where she wanted to be. Uncle Ivan was over for supper again, and he and her mom were into their fourth beer each when she said that she was going to a movie with a girlfriend. It never occurred to her mother that she didn't have any girlfriends. Her mom had stopped taking much interest in Sara's life except to criticize and to tell her to stay away from boys. Her warnings always included the words *grief* and *heartache*. Sara wouldn't have minded a bit of either emotion if a boy would look at her twice.

She was about to give up and go home when

brake lights went on in her dad's driveway. A few moments later, his car cruised by, her father looking straight ahead, talking into his cell phone. She waited a few moments before giving chase, keeping her headlights off until he was far enough ahead not to notice. She was lucky this old car still had a manual control. She checked the time on the dash. Ten after nine.

He merged onto the Queensway heading east, and she found it easy to hang back a few cars while keeping an eye on him. It was a relief when he didn't drive into the Market, turning onto a side street off Elgin after he took the Metcalfe off-ramp. She drove past as he pulled into a parking spot and turned right onto the next side street. By the time she'd hoofed it on foot back to Elgin, her dad was two blocks down and opening the door to a restaurant. She didn't dare follow him inside but walked past and looked in the window. The big surprise was that he wasn't meeting a woman, instead joining a table with two men already seated.

She pulled out her phone and opened the camera app, putting the setting on video. This time she sauntered past the window, filming as she went. One of the men at her father's table was staring at her when she glanced inside, and she lowered the phone. She dropped her head and picked up speed until she was well past the window. She turned off Elgin at the next cross street and jogged around the block until she reached her car, out of breath, with sweat dripping down her back. Once inside the front seat, she locked the door and fumbled with the ignition key, crying out in relief as the engine turned over.

The street was empty, but her heart only stopped pounding after she careened out of the parking spot, turned left on O'Connor, zipped under the Queensway overpass, and hung a left onto Isabella, finally merging onto the highway eastbound on her way home. The man's eyes had given her the creeps, and she checked the rear view several times, almost expecting him to be on her tail. She didn't relax until she slowed for the exit ramp and saw that nobody else was getting off the busy highway with her. The sick feeling in her stomach didn't disappear, though, even as she turned onto her street and spotted the lights on in their house. She had no doubt that the man in the restaurant had seen her filming his table as she walked past, and she had watched his eyes tracking her hand as she lowered the phone to waist level. He'd half-risen from his chair, anger radiating out of his eyes — nasty, snake eyes that she'd have a hard time keeping out of her dreams. For the first time, playing P.I. seemed less a game and more a dangerous reality. She could only hope that the man with her father had a short memory, and he'd already moved on to more important concerns.

CHAPTER 21

Ella stepped inside the front door and stopped for a moment to listen to Lena crying in Finn and Adele's apartment. The baby had worked herself into quite a state. Ella would have liked to spend time with Finn, but as if by silent agreement, they'd never met up alone once he moved his family into the same building. They had nothing to hide, but Adele didn't like their friendship. No point in throwing gasoline on the smouldering embers.

Ella climbed the stairs as quietly as she could, trying to slip past the second floor without Tony opening his door. It was a Shania afternoon. "Man, I Feel Like a Woman" blasted through the wall, masking her footsteps on the squeaky floorboards. The dinner party was tonight, and she planned to give it a pass. She smiled at her stealthy success as she opened her apartment door, only to be met by Luvy scampering down the hallway toward her. The dachshund jumped on her legs until she bent down to give her ears a scratch. She straightened.

"There you are, girl!" Tony appeared in the doorway to her living room. "I was writing a note and hoping to be gone by the time you showed up."

"We're supposed to use each other's key for emergencies only. Writing me a note is *not* an emergency."

"It's not just the note. I left some clothes in your bedroom. I'm thinking the blue sundress for this evening, but the mauve would do equally. Your hair dried fabulously, by the way. Mmmm-mmmm-mmm."

"I wasn't planning … oh, what the hell. I thought dinner was a few guys from your ball team and Finn and Adele. Doesn't sound like a dress-up evening to me."

"You don't want to be the only one in sweats. Trust me, girl. Come along." He crooked a finger and started leading her down the hallway.

"I'm not a charity case … or Eliza Doolittle. I'm happy as I am and don't need a makeover." She reached the doorway to her bedroom and looked at the clothes laid out on the duvet cover. She frowned. "Where did these dresses come from?"

"A client. She's about your size and was getting rid of some summer stuff. I suggested that I'd take whatever she didn't want off her hands."

"So, somebody's seconds. My own clothes are probably in better shape."

"I highly doubt it. She's not even certain she wore any of these outfits. Has a house in Rockcliffe but spends most of the autumn and winter in her Italian villa in Tuscany. Well, I have a charcuterie board to finish off. And you have time for a quick shower before drinks. Anon." He scooped Luvy up into his arms and squeezed past her on his way down the hallway and out of her apartment.

Ella stared at the closed door. "Italian villa? Tuscany? Really?" she asked it before she stomped into her bedroom. He'd laid out two dresses and matching sandals on the floor. She had to admit the dresses were lovely. The contrary part of her wanted to put on sweatpants, a tee, and flip-flops, but she knew wearing one of these dresses would make Tony light up like a Christmas tree. He never asked for anything from her and gave so much, seeming to know what she needed before she did. She didn't have a handle yet on what made him tick but was growing to believe he was a statistical oddity — a genuinely nice man with no agenda. He annoyed her … often … but she was beginning not to be able to imagine her life without him around.

———

AN HOUR LATER, Tony greeted her at his apartment door with a glass of champagne before guiding her into the living room. Adele was seated on the couch, dressed in a loose cotton caftan with her hair pulled into a messy topknot. Finn sat next to her. He smiled and started to rise to greet her before thinking better of it. "Hey Ella," he said, raising a hand by way of greeting. The baby lay in his lap, dressed in a sleeper and sucking on a bottle.

Ella looked across the room to three men standing by the window. Two she didn't recognize, but the third gave her pause. "Hunter?" she asked. "Are you on Tony's fastball team?" Tony played on a gay men's team, and she was quite certain Hunter didn't fit the profile.

"Hey Ella. Tony joined our police team this season. He's the reason we're not in last place." Hunter grinned.

The other two men nodded. They shook her hand and introduced themselves. Stefan and Erik. Both cops working in patrol.

Tony leaned in from behind her and whispered into her ear. "I thought you deserved a selection."

She turned her head. "What am I? Your school project?"

"I'm more like your guardian angel."

They settled into seats, and Tony brought out the appetizers. Jazz played in the background and candles glowed from every surface. Ella glanced at Hunter several times and thought he seemed preoccupied and withdrawn, although he spoke when asked a question. She also let the conversation float around her as she sipped on a glass of wine that Tony handed her in exchange for her empty champagne flute.

After Adele downed a quick second glass of champagne, she began talking animatedly to Stefan, who was sitting to her right, while Finn burped Lena and chatted to Erik. Finn excused himself after Lena nodded off and left to settle her in her crib in their apartment, returning with a monitor that he plugged in and kept close by. Tony finished refilling glasses, and Ella followed him into the kitchen to help serve the food.

"Ella, why aren't you chatting up one of the good men in blue? You look fabulous, and they're all single and yummy, so odds are in your favour. I double-checked their marital status and credentials before inviting them."

"Sometimes you're just too much, Tony. What if I'm happy being alone? Not everyone needs to pair up. Take a look at yourself, my friend." She stopped, horrified at what she'd said. Sander had left him bereft not so long ago, and she knew he was still grieving. "I'm sorry. That was insensitive."

Tony raised a hand, palm facing her. "No, I've overstepped. It appears to be my character flaw. I'll back off."

She put an arm around his shoulders. "I'm the grumpy one. You're just being kind. I'll make an effort to chat up the bachelors in blue when we sit down to dinner."

Tony grinned and fist-pumped the air. "That's my girl. You don't need to live your life as a recluse up in that garret, talking to the walls like mad Lady Macbeth. Now let's get this chow on the table before it congeals in the pots."

They gathered around the table ten minutes later, digging into a meal of Caesar salad, roast beef, York-shire puddings, roast potatoes, and gravy. The wine flowed, and the noise level rose pleasantly. They settled back as Tony served up chocolate almond cake with Amaretto cream and brandy with coffee to finish off the meal. He'd seated Ella between Erik and Stefan with Adele directly across between Hunter and Finn. Ella relaxed and smiled at Tony, who'd positioned himself at the head of the table. He'd gone to such lengths to get her a date that after another glass of wine she found his actions endearing rather than irritating. He caught her eye and returned the smile. She joined in the conversation and found herself actually having fun.

"And how did your interview with Ginger McGowan turn out, Ella?" Adele asked when there was a lull in the conversation.

"Good, and thank you again for setting it up." Ella looked over at Hunter. He wore a poker face that she guessed would get guilty people talking. No hint of what he was thinking or feeling or what he thought about her. It was disconcerting. "Any breaks on the case you can share with us, Detective Hunter?"

"Nothing to report."

"It's been an awfully frustrating week."

"Did your podcast get more followers?" Adele's voice cut above the chatter. "Because it doesn't sound like your show did anything to help find Charlie."

Finn put a hand on Adele's forearm. "I hear Lena on the monitor. Do you think it's time we go back downstairs?"

"You can go." Adele picked up her wine glass and

slid it closer to Tony for a refill. "I'm still enjoying my night out."

"Why don't I check on her?" Ella asked, jumping up before Finn could say no. "Is your apartment door unlocked?"

Finn nodded. "Thanks, Ella."

"I'll come with you." Hunter was on his feet. He patted Tony's shoulder on the way by. "Terrific meal, mate. Best food I've eaten in I don't know how long."

Ella led the way downstairs. She checked first on Lena in her crib in the small bedroom. She lay on her stomach, chubby arms spread wide, deep into dreamland. Her hair curled damply on the nape of her neck. Ella adjusted the blanket, and when she turned, Hunter was leaning against the doorway, the light from the hall illuminating him from behind. "Sound asleep?"

"She's sleeping like a baby." Ella grinned.

They stopped near the entrance to the living room. "Did anything come of your interview with Britt?" Hunter asked.

"Not really. She's in the process of cleaning out her apartment and moving to Peterborough tomorrow. There was one odd thing, though, that could be nothing. She said she hadn't heard that Charlie was missing. Claimed she doesn't listen to the news."

"It's possible."

"I would have thought someone from McGowan's office would have contacted her. She hasn't been gone that long."

"I'll keep that in mind. By the way, Winston's

receipts and story checked out, even if he comes across as slippery. Thanks for forwarding them to me. What about Claudette and that branch of the family? Any insights?"

"A lot of unhappiness living under one roof. Claudette's in a bad way. Drinking, letting herself go. I met her brother, Ivan Deerfield, who seems to be taking on a protective if not enabling role. Claudette harbours a grudge against David that appears to run coal-mine deep. I tracked down Claudette and David's seventeen-year-old daughter Sara working at a DQ on Bank Street."

"Did Sara have anything to say about Charlie?"

"Unlike her mother and Uncle Ivan, she genuinely seems to care about him. She and her brother Roddy don't appear to spend much time with their dad." Ella didn't say that she'd found Sara to be an introvert and socially awkward. These were initial impressions that might be too quickly made. She added, "It seems a stretch that the family had anything to do with Charlie's disappearance."

"Except that a simmering desire to bring someone down can make people do terrible things."

"I give you that."

They were standing close to each other, speaking quietly so as not to waken Lena. She could smell his aftershave and see the amber flecks in his dark eyes. He was staring intently into hers, and the moment stretched. He opened his mouth to say something when the phone rang in his pocket and broke the spell. He backed up two steps and turned, leaning into his phone. He asked questions but mainly listened. Ella started toward the apartment door to give him privacy, but he called to her before she stepped outside.

"They've found a body on the Ottawa River Parkway. I don't have any details."

"Oh my God. Charlie?"

"Possible. Can you let Tony know I've got to leave and thank him for me?"

"I'm coming with you if I can hitch a ride. The paper will want me to get the story."

He hesitated. "Might not look good to arrive in the same vehicle."

"You're right. I'll follow you in my car."

He seemed to weigh the fallout before saying, "Okay, but be discreet when we arrive on scene."

"I can do discreet."

His smile was half-grimace. "I'll have to trust you on that, since I'd prefer our unusual alliance not come to light if we can help it."

She smiled. "Reporting is all about building contacts and keeping them secret. You have no need to worry on my account, Detective."

CHAPTER 22

Ella could see the flashing red lights and line of police and emergency vehicles on the Ottawa River Parkway through the gap in the fence at the bottom of Churchill Avenue. She found a spot to leave her car on nearby Ferndale Avenue and jogged back to Churchill. The path through the gap led her across the Parkway, blocked off by emergency and police vehicles, and onto a bike path that paralleled the Ottawa River. Bands of trees and bushes lined the trail, making for a difficult trek through the woods toward the river in the darkness. Hunter was somewhere up ahead, having driven to join the rest of the team now scouring the brush and shoreline.

Derick Zukowski, a reporter with CBC News, had made it there ahead of her. He was watching the scene of activity from a distance, and she walked over to stand next to him. He was one of the twenty-some-things, always hungry for a story, never seeming to need sleep. They'd crossed paths often but never exchanged more than a few words. The first responders had already set up lighting that illuminated the scene, and from this vantage point, she could see the body covered by a sheet lying at the edge of the tree line, a few metres up from the water. The shape under the sheet was larger than a child's, and she felt momentary relief that it wasn't Charlie. "Any idea who the vic is?" she asked.

Derick glanced at her. "I got a glimpse of a woman. Long hair, youngish. It was hard to see much in the dark, though. She couldn't have been there any extended length of time or the animals would have torn her apart."

"Who found her?"

"A homeless man with a dog was searching for a good place to sleep along there. He flagged a cop passing by on Churchill after his mutt found the body. If not for him, this heat would have hastened the ripening, and the coyotes and raccoons would have had a go. Fortuitous for Homicide she was found so quickly."

"But not for whoever put her there. How'd you get here so fast anyway?"

He shot her a small grin. "Sources. You?"

"Same."

He turned his head sideways and looked her up and down. "Nice dress. Out for dinner?"

"I was. Luckily, we ate dessert before the call came in."

They stood in companionable silence, listening to snippets of conversation and trying to glean what they could. She watched Hunter squat next to the body and lift the sheet to have a look. He stood and talked to another detective. It took her a second to recognize his partner, Julie Quade. Ella pulled out her phone and sent Hunter a text, asking if there'd be a media update soon. She waited, but he didn't check his phone until five minutes later. After he read her message, he spoke with a woman who glanced their way before she went to speak with someone else. Ella sent a text to François Canard at *The Capital*, telling him where she was and the details she had so far. He called her back almost immediately.

"Sit tight and find out what you can. Your byline. Phone it in to me." He clicked off.

Ella lowered her cell and looked at Derick. "Where's your film crew?"

"On their way." He looked over his shoulder. "And taking their sweet time."

The woman who'd been speaking with Hunter climbed the ridge toward them. As she got closer, Ella recognized Lisa Flint from the police's media relations team. Lisa reached them and identified herself before giving a brief update, confirming this was the body of a woman in her twenties. Cause of death was suspicious and being treated as a homicide. She had no other details at this time, but there would be an early-morning update.

Ella checked her watch. Derick was speaking urgently on his cell. The story had missed the eleven o'clock televised live news, so online had a chance to break the story if she hurried. She called Canard back and dictated what she had before forwarding a couple of photos and video taken with her phone. The photos and video images were eerie, darkness surrounding the lighted staging area where the body lay covered, men and women in white suits and caps going about their business, looking like space aliens. Yellow police tape encircled the area.

"Photos work. I'll get this story on the website, and social media will pump it out. We haven't had a scoop in a while." He sounded pleased. "Good work, however you did it."

"Just the right place at the right time." She was reluctant to take credit.

"Sure you don't want your old job back?"

"I'm sure. Freelancing works for now."

"Check your Twitter in ten."

Ella tucked the phone inside her bag and stepped back into the shadows on the way to her car. It was past midnight, and all the wine she'd drunk along with the rich meal had made her sleepy. She'd spaced the glasses of wine and had been fine to drive but would be happy to get home and crawl into bed. Perhaps she'd manage a good night's sleep. She was eager to find out. She passed the CBC film crew as they made their way through the gate onto the bike path. The other news outlets wouldn't be far behind. *I win*, she thought.

Odds were that the dead woman was Meilin

Hanon, but Ella wasn't ready to say that publicly. The police would need to notify her family before media broadcasted her name, so even CBC had to respect the protocols. They'd all learn the name tomorrow at the press briefing, and her scoop would be short-lived. Still, she enjoyed the thrill of seeing her byline plastered across social media when she sat in her car ten minutes later, flipping through sites.

———

"Do you recognize her?" Quade asked Hunter. They stood on the fringes of the search site while the photographer took pictures of the body.

"No, but it's not Meilin Hanon — obviously."

"Yeah, this girl's Caucasian." She looked up toward the ridge. "Media is multiplying like birds in that Hitchcock film. Was that Ella Tate I saw earlier?"

"It was."

"Lucky break for her getting here so fast."

"She's dogged." He didn't flinch from Quade's stare. He'd recognized Derick Zukowski from the CBC and knew someone had notified him off the record too, easing his guilt. Leaks abounded on the force.

Quade turned as Auger sidled up next to her. He was dressed in cotton chinos, a black t-shirt, and sandals. Sweat dampened his hairline. "I was playing squash at a friend's condo building when I got word. Any idea who's under the sheet?"

Quade shook her head. "I'm glad you made it. There's no ID, and we don't recognize her."

"Then I'll have a look."

Liam waited a few steps back while Auger and Quade asked the coroner, Brigette Green, to lift the sheet. Auger crouched down and studied the woman's face. He looked up at Quade and said something that Liam was too far away to hear. Auger stood and the three of them conferred for a moment before Quade and Auger ambled over to him.

"It's Meilin Hanon's roommate, Joanne Freemont," Auger said. "She's the one who took Meilin to the party from which she was never seen again. Joanne quit school and went into hiding after a barrage of hatred on social media. We tried to track her down after the initial interview, but she kept avoiding our attempts to meet up. Looks like somebody got to her first."

Liam knew Ella had interviewed Joanne earlier in the week, but he stayed silent. He didn't want his working relationship with Ella to become common knowledge. He'd track her down in the morning to go over her conversation with Joanne and try to convince her to report what she knew to Auger.

"Do we know who and where her next of kin are?" Quade asked.

"Her parents live in Cornwall. I'll get Boots and Jingles to drive down to notify them." Auger took his cell phone out of his back pocket.

"Good. Let me know when that's done so we can

hold a media briefing in the morning. Tell Boots not to reveal her method of death."

"Do we even know?"

"Brigette says she was strangled, and likely within the past twenty-four hours. Whoever dumped her body was extremely unlucky the homeless man's dog found her so soon."

"Or extremely sloppy." Liam nodded at the two of them before he left to find his car. This wasn't his case, but Ella's involvement meant he needed to stay on top of developments. For now, he was simply relieved that it wasn't Charlie McGowan's tiny body lying under the sheet. One silver lining in a night filled with sadness.

———

DAVID WAS late for dinner again, and Ginger wanted to yell at him but didn't dare with her parents in the house. They'd eaten the broccoli, rice, and shrimp her mom had prepared four hours earlier, and David's meal was keeping warm in the oven, likely dried out and inedible. Her anger had grown with every passing minute until she could barely stop herself from boiling over.

"Where have you been?" she hissed when she waylaid him on his way to the kitchen. Her voice was louder than she'd intended, and he took a step back.

His shoulders dropped. "Driving the streets, looking for Charlie. I can't sit at home and do nothing. I've been all over the neighbourhood, searching every side street. I even walked different sections of the Ottawa River, hoping to find him and praying I didn't." His eyes filled with tears, and he rubbed his forehead as if massaging away a headache. "I just don't know what else to do."

Guilt replaced her rage. What was wrong with her, always thinking the worst? Her voice softened, an attempt to smooth over her unfair attack. "I just missed you here, that's all, and you didn't answer my texts. It's almost eleven o'clock, and I was getting worried about you. I'm sorry you were out there searching alone. This is the worst time for me to be so pregnant, or I'd be out there too. Dad's crotchety about you being gone so much, and he's driving me and Mom crazy. If you could patch things up with him, we'll all rest easier."

"How much longer are they staying?" They were standing closer now, whispering into each other's ear.

"I've told them to go back to Halifax, but they don't want to leave until there's word about Charlie."

"All the more reason for me to be out there looking." He gave a wry grin before pulling her into an embrace. He spoke into her hair. "I'm sorry, babe, but it's better I'm not here all day with your dad. We're not good for each other or anybody else."

His familiar sandalwood scent lingered on his skin, and she pressed her face into his neck. "I'm guessing you didn't find anything?"

"No, but I've talked to lots of people, and they've all promised to keep an eye out." He rubbed a hand slowly up and down her back. "I should have checked my phone more often. Time got away from me. How are you holding up?"

"I'm becoming resigned. The victims' support person phoned but didn't come today. It seems like they've given up on the ransom call."

"Nobody's given up. We'll never stop looking." He pulled back and put an arm around her waist. His voice strengthened. "We're going to find him. We'll bring Charlie home." They walked into the kitchen together. Madeleine was pulling David's supper out of the oven, and Richard sat reading the paper at the table, keeping his eyes focused on the page.

"Your meal has dried out. Would you like me to heat up something from the freezer?" Madeleine asked.

"No, this will be fine. I'm not all that hungry anyway. I grabbed a burger at a drive-through at some point in the evening so I could keep searching for Charlie. I covered a lot of ground today and hope some of the people I spoke with will eventually see something and get back to me."

Richard raised his head, and he and Madeleine exchanged glances. He cleared his throat. "I'm sorry for being so bad-tempered. Madeleine has reminded me that I can be overbearing when I'm stressed, and this hasn't been easy for anybody."

"No need to apologize." David sat down at the table and thanked Madeleine as she set the plate of wizened food in front of him. "I'm glad you're both here to look after Ginger while I'm out pounding the streets."

"I'm pleased you feel that way." Richard folded the paper and stood. "Mad and I are going for a walk to wear ourselves out before bed. That way, we might stand a chance of sleeping through the night. I guess none of us has been getting much shuteye."

"Don't worry about the dishes," Madeleine added. "I'll clean up when we get back, or they can wait until morning." She followed Richard's rigid back into the hallway, and they made a noisy exit, slamming the door behind them.

Ginger sat and watched David eat with her chin resting on her hand. His movements were jerky, fatigue making him seem wilted and sad. She noticed the dark circles under his eyes and his dishevelled hair, so uncharacteristic for a man always in control. He caught her staring and reached over to grasp her free hand. He held on while he ate, and she felt the familiar stirring of desire that came less often now that she was pregnant. He was windswept, his skin golden from the hours in the sun looking for Charlie. He took one last forkful and pushed the plate away. "That really was godawful." He grinned. "What say we follow up with some dessert upstairs to make up for this terrible meal?"

"We could do that." She wanted nothing more than to lie with him and feel something other than grief and fear. He needed the closeness too, she realized. They were both struggling and trying to handle their pain the best they could. All the while she'd thought the worst of him, he'd been trying to bring their son home. She'd been wrong to blame him for being so closed off and retreating into his work. She squeezed his hand and leaned in to kiss his mouth. "Let's go to bed while we have the house to ourselves. Maybe we can wear each other out enough to sleep through the night too."

CHAPTER 23

The media briefing started at 11:00 a.m. in the station's main conference room. Quade was spokesperson, with Liam and Auger on hand for questions. Liam scanned the groups of reporters but didn't see Ella as Quade took the mic. It wasn't until Quade named the victim, Joanne Freemont, that he spotted Ella leaning against a pillar at the back of the room. He hadn't given her the victim's name ahead of time, not wanting to cross more lines. She looked ill at ease in jeans and a windbreaker, the humidity having lifted overnight and the heat wave blowing out of the Ottawa Valley. A cold rain had started before sunrise, and he'd woken to the boom of thunder directly overhead. The sudden shift from stifling heat to rain and below normal temperatures was a shock to the system. Sadly, this cool relief was only expected to last a day.

Sherry Carpenter entered the hall and made her way to Ella. They appeared to be a tag team for *The*

Capital. Rumour had it that Ella was mentoring Sherry and responsible for her getting the crime beat. They made an unlikely pair, Ella resembling a Charles Dickens waif and Sherry made up like she was straight off the cover of *Vogue*. Liam forced himself to tune in to Quade's voice, luckily in time to answer a question from a CTV reporter about the stalled Charlie McGowan case. The briefing wrapped up a few minutes later. Quade drew him aside on their way out.

"What do you think Joanne Freemont's murder has to do with Meilin Hanon's disappearance?" she asked.

"If I had to guess, Joanne knew something. She was killed to keep from talking."

"When will people learn it's safer for them to come forward than keep secrets? Blackmailers and abusers only have power over someone if they don't talk."

"Whatever Joanne knew likely put her in a bad light too." Liam had wondered earlier if there was more to Joanne going into hiding than simply online harassment. It looked like his misgivings had merit.

"Well, she *was* working as an escort and took Meilin to that party. Sketchy at best. It's too bad Auger didn't manage to speak with her in any depth."

"Ella Tate met with Joanne last week."

Quade stared at him. She didn't ask how he knew, but he could see the wheels turning. "Can you follow up? No need to bring Auger into the loop at this point."

"I could do that. Ella usually tapes her interviews."

"Well do your sweet-talking best to get your hands on the tape. We need any lead we can get."

"I'll see what I can do."

He looked for Ella in the last of the stragglers, but she'd already left the building. He sent a text asking to meet up. She responded a few seconds later. *Daisy's?*

On my way. He tucked the phone into his pocket and detoured to retrieve his jacket in the office before going to the parking garage for his car, unexpectedly pleased to be seeing Ella again. She was nowhere near his type, if he had a type, so there was no point trying to think any more deeply about why this woman with the mesmerizing green eyes intrigued him more than any of the others he'd dated lately. Why he automatically looked for her in every crowd of reporters and was disappointed when she wasn't among them, well, this was a puzzle best kept for another day.

————

ELLA LOOKED through the grimy plate glass window and spotted Hunter waiting for her in their usual booth. His text to meet up had surprised her until she remembered that she'd told him about her interview with Joanne Freemont. He hadn't been that interested in the details because Meilin's disappearance wasn't his case, but now that Joanne had been murdered, the interview took on new importance.

She entered the diner and slid across from him

into the booth. Daisy hustled over with a pot of coffee. "There you two are," she said, filling their mugs. "What can I getcha, darlings?"

"Grilled cheese for me," Ella said.

"Club and fries." Hunter waited for Daisy to move out of earshot. "The name of the victim came as a shock, I imagine."

"Completely. Joanne was nervous and fearful when we met. She said people at the party were 'connected,' whatever that means. She appeared to be in hiding primarily because of the death threats and vitriol on social media." She pictured Joanne on the couch in her apartment. She'd been so vibrant and lovely, neither of them knowing she only had a few more days to live. Her loss hurt, and Ella blinked back the image, trying to refocus. "I thought the body on the Parkway was Charlie at first. Meilin was my second guess. It never crossed my mind that Joanne Freemont was under that sheet." She fiddled with the handle of her coffee mug. "You want my interview tape."

"I'd appreciate listening to it."

"Normally I wouldn't share my material, but since she's dead, I think you should hear the tape in its entirety. I'll send the unedited file to your Dropbox."

"Thanks. I'll owe you one."

"Let's call us even."

The sandwiches arrived, and Hunter scraped some fries onto her plate with his fork. "I can never eat them all." He lifted his eyes and smiled for a split-second before picking up a sandwich quarter and digging in.

She stared at him. They'd become collaborators, and she knew nothing about him. She picked up a fry. Ate half her sandwich. Swallowed. "So what's your story?"

"Pardon?"

"We're working together, and you've shared zip about yourself while you know everything about me. Where did you grow up? Do you have any family here?"

He took a moment before speaking, seeming to drag the information out of himself. "My sister and I emigrated from Belfast when I was fourteen and she was fifteen." He paused. "Hannah has two boys."

"And your parents?"

"They died in a car crash in Belfast a month before we came to Canada. Hannah and I were sent here to live with an aunt. Everyone felt we'd have a better chance of recovering and starting afresh."

"How sad that must have been."

"We managed to make it through. It was a long time ago."

She could picture him as a boy, grieving and lost in a new country. He'd had to grow up fast. "Is your sister still in Ottawa?"

"She is. Her husband died a few years ago. Cancer. We live quite close to each other. She looks after my cat when I've been working a homicide."

"That's so tragic. She's still very young."

"A widow at thirty." He smiled and shrugged. "Sorry not to have a happier story to tell."

Ella let his words sink in, at a loss how to respond. Hunter ignored her stare and picked up the last sandwich wedge. He bit into it without looking at her.

"I don't see you with a cat."

He raised his eyes to meet hers. "A stray that I adopted one cold winter night. I appear to have a way with wild creatures."

She broke eye contact first as Daisy approached swinging the coffee pot gently back and forth in front of her. "Another round, ladies and gents?"

Hunter shook his head. "I've got to get back to work. Stay and have another cup if you like, Ella. Lunch is on me since I called the meeting."

"No thanks, Daisy. I have to get moving too." Ella ate one last cold fry and reached for her rain jacket on the seat next to her. Hunter was at the cash, and she studied him for a moment before sliding out of the booth. She could picture him with a Rottweiler before a cat, but it just went to show. Surface judgments never told the whole story. She'd pegged him one way and now had to reevaluate. He was like a picture she'd grown accustomed to going out of focus. Disconcerting, but in a nice way.

CHAPTER 24

Sara read about the murdered woman on the Internet. Pictures of Joanne Freemont were trending on Twitter with Ella Tate's article the top story. Sara studied Joanne's picture from all angles. She'd seen the dead girl before. Was she a DQ customer? Sara tried to picture her in the store, paying for ice cream at the counter. The image didn't hold.

"Put your phone away and eat your dinner." Her mom waited until Sara shoved her cell next to the ketchup bottle and picked up her fork.

"Is Uncle Ivan coming over tonight?"

"No, he's busy."

Roddy clumped into the kitchen and dropped heavily into his chair. "Fish sticks again?"

"Well, thank you for joining us, your royal highness. Yes, fish sticks again. If you don't like my cooking, then you're more than welcome to take control of the menu."

"No, that's okay." He slouched over his plate and began eating without looking at her.

Sara felt the familiar tightening in her chest when she was with the two of them. She wasn't sure how they'd gotten to this dysfunctional place, but she hated the nasty way they talked to each other. She wished they were a different family yet had no idea how to get from here to there. "Are you going out tonight, Mom?" she asked to break the silence.

"Not tonight. I plan to watch television and put my feet up. What are you two doing this evening?"

Roddy shrugged. "Video games," he mumbled between forkfuls.

Trying to remember where I saw the dead girl, Sara thought but said instead, "I'm staying in too. Maybe we can watch a show together."

Her mother picked up her empty plate and stood. "We could if you're spending a night at home for once. Sometimes I feel like I'm living all alone in this house."

Roddy grunted. "You're not alone with Uncle Ivan here day and night. He moving in or what?"

"No, he's not moving in, smarty pants. Why would you even ask that?"

"He's always hanging around like a bad case of herpes." Roddy looked over at Sara. "Dad texted again. He wants you to call him."

Their mom slammed her plate into the dishwasher. With her back to them, she said, "Ask your father when he's going to pay for the bloody air conditioning like he promised. We shouldn't have to suffer through these heat waves while he and his bimbo are living in cool comfort."

"I'll ask." *No empathy for the missing Charlie.* Claudette's anger had grown so entrenched that she couldn't see beyond it. Sara's phone dinged. She opened the message from her DQ supervisor. She sighed. "I've been called into work. The regular just phoned in sick. Sorry, Mom. We'll have to watch a show together another night."

"Fine." Her mom wiped furiously at the counter with a damp sponge but seemed to gather herself as she worked. She stopped and turned. "Maybe bring home some sundaes when your shift ends. If the rain stops, we can sit outside and eat them before bed. It's already six degrees warmer than this morning. Tomorrow's going to be a sauna once again."

"Strawberry?"

"Yes, and I'll have a medium. Take the cooler."

It was hard to believe they'd been close once, back when her dad was still in the picture and her mom hadn't been drinking. In those good old days, Roddy wasn't hiding out in his room all the time, and she didn't feel like such a loser. Still, her heart lightened at the thought of the sundaes and spending some time together without Uncle Ivan hanging around. She'd make a large hot fudge with whipped cream for Roddy and lure him away from his computer. Maybe she'd even get the two of them to talk to one another like they used to before Ginger and the divorce.

———

"OH MY GOD, DAD!" Ginger stared at her laptop in disbelief. She clamped a hand over her mouth. "The ransom note."

Richard leapt up from his chair and joined her on the couch. "Let me see." He pulled the screen toward him and read silently. "They give details about Charlie."

"Few people know the name of his special teddy or his favourite song. This has to be real. He must be alive, or how would they have gotten this information?" She allowed herself a flicker of hope while knowing that nothing was for certain.

"It's a good sign all right." Richard thought for a moment. "They want $15,000 in Bitcoin sent to the address in the link and will let Charlie go at the Bayshore mall. I'd have thought they'd ask for more, but maybe all the media attention softened them."

"We need to tell the police."

"The message says not to involve the cops or we'll never see Charlie again."

"I didn't read that far." She took the screen back. Her initial elation disappeared as she read. "What if this is a scam? How can we be sure they'll give him back?"

"Hush. We can handle it. I've easily got that much in my savings account." He laid a hand on her forearm. "Involving the police will only cock things up. Let me make the arrangements."

"But we have to tell David. He should—"

"Nonsense. The less people involved, the better our odds for success. Trust me. I've dealt with so many problems running a company that I'm best placed to handle this. I'll make sure they let Charlie go before they see one cent of the money."

"Dad, if anything happens to Charlie, I don't know if I can bear it."

"All the more reason to let me bring him home."

She swallowed all the arguments as to why this wasn't a good idea, because it might be their only chance, and she was so exhausted. Wrung out like an old dish rag. Her father had the money, and she and David would have difficulty raising this much quickly, even if he'd put up the reward being publicized in the media. They'd need to cash in some bonds or GICs, which would require a bit of time. It was easier to let her father take over as he had when she was a child. Easier to go along and hope. Yet common sense and caution made her reluctant.

"We're taking a big chance not involving the police. I think we need to tell Detective Hunter at the very least."

"We'd be taking a big chance involving them. Trust me on this, Ginger. The cops always bungle things up. They have their own agenda. This truly is our best shot."

The baby inside her kicked, and she rubbed a hand across her belly. The doctor had told her to avoid stress. The idea was almost laughable. She made her decision. "All right, Dad. If you're willing to risk losing the money, this could be our best opportunity."

"That's my girl. Now hand me your machine, and

I'll pretend to be you and will send a message to the creep. With any luck, I'll have Charlie home by this time tomorrow."

The thought of holding her little boy again made her want to weep in gratitude. She nodded as she passed him her laptop, not trusting herself to keep from crying. He liked to take charge as he had throughout her life, and for once, she was thankful to let him.

CHAPTER 25

Cher pumped through the floorboards, belting out a song about turning back time and making somebody cry — Tony's way of telling Ella he wasn't in a good place. She lifted her fingers from the computer keys and sighed. She hadn't seen him since the dinner party. She was a terrible friend, too self-absorbed for her own good.

It was half past midnight, and he knew full well she was awake; otherwise, his music was meant to get her up. She took one last glance at the piece she'd been writing and pushed away from the desk. If she didn't go see him now, she'd never be able to sleep.

She pounded on his door with the side of her fist until he turned down the music. "Are you trying to wake the dead?" she asked when he opened the door, holding Luvy. She followed him down the hallway into his living room and sprawled across his velvet couch. Her eyes focused on a nearly empty bottle of red wine and the full glass he held as he dropped onto the other end of the sofa with Luvy in his lap. "I'm surprised Finn hasn't been up to chew you out."

"Adele and Lena are visiting her parents in Belleville. Finn likes my music when he's home. I believe he's still out."

"Lucky him. Did you work today?"

"Of course."

"That was a lovely dinner you served us, Tony. I'm sorry Hunter and I had to leave so quickly without a proper goodbye." She was easing into possibilities, trying to get him to say what was bothering him without having to ask.

"The evening ended abruptly, but at least everyone made it through dessert. You and Hunter left together. I'd say the evening was a win." Tony rested his head against the back of the couch and closed his eyes. His voice was small and sad. "I believed I was your partner, and you've shut me out of the investigation."

"Is that what this is about? You think I've forgotten we're working cases together?"

He turned his head sideways and looked at her. "Well, have you?"

"Noooo. I need you to locate someone, as it turns out. I was going to talk to you about it tomorrow first thing."

He straightened. "I've taken the week off to figure out some stuff, so I can get started right away. Who am I tracking down?

His eagerness helped ease her lie and made a lump rise in her throat. He'd been struggling with

Sander gone for good, and she hadn't been around much. He deserved better from her.

"Her name's Yina Zhao, and she's friends with Meilin Hanon. They're both Chinese exchange students. Yina arranged my meeting last week with Joanne Freemont."

"The woman whose body was found on the Parkway."

"Yup, and Yina seemed as scared as Joanne. I'm worried for her safety."

"How did you find Yina before?"

"I hung around Carleton University until she showed up for a lecture. She's taking summer courses. She moved off campus after Meilin went missing and rarely attends class in person, so it took a while. She gave me a phone number, but I have no idea if it still works. I'll send you a photo I took of her and the number."

"What should I do when I find her?"

"Keep her in your sights and call me. We can talk to her together."

"You got it. What will you be doing?"

She'd planned to track down Yina herself, so now her day was wide open. "I'll be following another lead and working on a podcast. I intend to put one together on Joanne's death and Meilin's disappearance. The mystery in progress. I don't want the public to stop watching for her. It also wouldn't hurt if some of those social media trolls felt some guilt for hounding Joanne so mercilessly."

"Good luck with that." He set his glass on the

coffee table and stood to walk her to the door. "No more wine or Cher for this boyo tonight," he said with a grin. "I'll need my wits about me tomorrow." He followed her to the front hallway. She turned to face him.

"Thanks for helping me out, my friend. I'm lucky you were free tomorrow."

"Don't you know it, girl."

He shut the door behind her, and she stopped for a moment to smile before climbing the steps to her apartment and a first attempt at sleep.

———

THREE MESSAGES from Sara's dad to start the day: a sunny, warm morning with not a cloud in sight, yesterday's rainstorm over and forgotten. Sara tossed the phone onto the passenger seat and started the car. He was on his way here if the last message, sent ten minutes ago, was correct. She had no desire to see him and turned left at the stop sign instead of right so their paths wouldn't cross. Should she find a place to park and watch for him out of sight? She could follow his car and see where he went next after not finding her at home. The idea was tempting, but if he caught her, he'd be angry and she'd have no explanation.

She pulled a U-turn and swooped over to the curb behind another car parked one street over. Leaving the engine running, she stepped out and walked back to the stop sign. She looked up the road toward her house, keeping out of sight behind a maple. It was less than five minutes before her dad's car cruised to a stop across the street from the house. She could see him craning his head to look inside the living room window. He'd notice her car gone, and she bet her bottom dollar that he wouldn't get out of his Beamer to face her mother. Sure enough, he kept driving, and she was back in her car before he reached the stop sign and turned right. Now was the time to decide whether to carry on with her day or follow him. *What the hell?* she thought, pushing aside the idea of him spotting her. *I've got nothing else to do anyway.*

He drove fast, but she was able to stay a distance behind without losing him. It didn't take long for her to realize that he was going to his office, and she dropped even farther back, eventually pulling over and stopping. *Now what?* She had six hours until her DQ shift started at three o'clock. Going home held no appeal. The Queensway west ramp was a short drive away. She could zip across the city and spend some time at the beach, keep an eye on her dad's house, and follow Ginger if she went out. It was something to fill in the time.

She hated people knowing that she had no friends and nothing going on in her life. The idea of someone finding out and feeling sorry for her was worse than being alone. She'd had a friend once, Katie Stevens. They'd played together in the schoolyard and gotten together on the weekends. All that ended in grade seven when Katie got pulled into the group of girls who used to ignore the two of them. She was always busy or with her new friends, and Sara found herself on the outside with no opening to join. Instead, she'd hung around with a couple of girls at lunch, but they never met after school. They didn't have anything in common and didn't even like each other all that much. The only bond was their geekiness.

Loch Isle was quiet. No police cars or reporters in front of her dad's house. She doubled back and parked on the other side of the dead end. She got out and walked through the woods to the beach, crossing to her usual spot in the shadows at the edge of the tree line, angled so that she could see the peak of her dad's house above the pines and balsam. This was a scrubby bit of beach, never cleared, almost as if Mother Nature kept it wild for her alone. Two towering cottonwood trees provided additional protection from people seeing her, halfway between the water and the steps to her dad's back gate. Sometimes she walked the length of the shoreline before returning to peek inside his yard through an opening in the fence. Today she stayed where she was and stretched out on the sand, using her tote bag as a headrest after she took out her journal and a pen.

She added her dad's visit to her house into the log, followed by his drive to work. Then she flipped back and reread the entries from the past month. She recalled his meeting with the two men in the restaurant and shivered at the memory of the man watching her pass by the window. It was then that she remembered the video. She hadn't watched it yet. She took out her phone and replayed the clip, which had captured the two men greeting her dad clear as a bell.

Neither was familiar, and she wondered why he was meeting them. Work? Not likely at that time of night.

She blinked and replayed the video again. The man staring at her … she *had* seen him before. She'd followed her dad to a hotel some months back but hadn't waited around for him to emerge. This same man — the one staring her down in the restaurant — had gotten out of a car in front of that hotel her dad had entered that night as she idled at the light. He'd glanced her way, and she'd liked his eyes then, dark and intense, and the toned shape of him under a cream-coloured suit jacket. She hadn't associated him with her dad at the time, but now… She made a note in her book and tucked it safely back inside her bag. This could mean something, and she planned to find out what. *P.I. Sara McGowan on the case.*

An hour later, after a brief doze, she got up and shook the sand from her shorts. She was hungry, and there was a Tim Hortons not far away where she could get a sandwich. She reached her car and paused with fingers on the door handle as she looked back at her dad's house. The front door had opened, and Madeleine and grumpy Richard were on the top step, talking to somebody inside. Sara bent and scooted closer, staying behind the protection of the shrubs. A moment later, Ginger emerged through the front door and followed her parents into the driveway. Richard kept looking at his cell and waving his free hand at Ginger. He handed his phone to Madeleine when they reached Ginger's car, and they got in, leaving Ginger standing alone at the edge of the driveway.

Richard backed the car onto the street and rolled down his window to yell at Ginger before driving away.

"We'll be home as soon as we have him safe and sound."

Sara wasn't sure she'd heard correctly. Had they located Charlie? Where were the police, if so? She looked at Ginger's face as she turned away from the road. She'd been crying and seemed worried, but there was hope in her expression too. Sara didn't think she was imagining it. She watched Ginger lumber up the driveway, climb the steps, and disappear inside the house.

Something was going on. Sara was too late to chase after Ginger's car, being on the wrong side of the dead-end barrier, so she'd have to make do with paying her stepmother a visit now that she was alone. She wouldn't rest easy until she knew what was going on, even if none of it concerned her directly. Charlie was her half-brother, though, and everyone she knew had been acting strangely since he disappeared. She had to make certain her suspicions had no basis in reality. She needed to cut off the doubt growing inside her about her family's involvement because maybe they weren't the most wonderful of people, but they were all she had.

———

GINGER OPENED the door with trepidation. Relief flooded through her at the sight of Sara standing on the stoop, looking awkward as always in a too-big t-shirt and baggy navy shorts, her shoulders hunched in as if waiting for another blow to her back. Her hair was mousy brown and split at the ends, and her eyes bulged out just enough to give her an ogling gaze that disconcerted on first encounters. It had taken her a while to warm to the girl. She always seemed to be silently watching and assessing, but Ginger eventually put this down to her large, pale blue eyes. "She's got fish eyes," David once said. "Gets them from her mother." But Sara had treated Charlie kindly, even when she didn't know Ginger was close by and listening. That counted for a lot in Ginger's book.

"Sara, your dad isn't at home right now. He's gone to work."

"That's okay. I came to see you — to find out if you need my help for a few hours before I have to go to the DQ at three." Sara's eyes skimmed over Ginger's big belly before settling on something in the hallway behind her right shoulder.

Ginger forced herself not to turn around to see what she was staring at. She was about to say no, but Sara seemed so gawky and ill at ease in her own body. David said it was hell for the kids living with their mother. She opened the door wider. "Come in and keep me company. There's nobody else here."

"Well, for a little while."

They entered the kitchen, and Sara made tea while Ginger set out a plate of cookies, homemade by Madeleine before she and Richard left for Bayshore. Richard had confided in Madeleine about the ransom request on Ginger's insistence. She wanted her mom to agree with paying, if only for a third point of view, not to mention it was their nest egg being depleted. Her mom hadn't hesitated to risk the money.

"Where're your parents?" Sara asked before biting into a ginger cookie.

"Gone to the mall. They had an … errand." If they came home with Charlie, she'd tell Sara about the ransom. She'd already decided to inform the police either way. Even now, she didn't feel comfortable with her dad's decision to go this alone. If someone was scamming them, they deserved to be caught, and for that to happen, the police had to be involved. If this person really did have Charlie and returned him, the police would demand to know why.

"My dad's been trying to reach me. Do you know what he wants?"

Ginger forced herself to concentrate. "No, he didn't tell me anything. Maybe he's going to ask you to join him in his search for Charlie. He's been driving the streets, looking for any sign of him. He missed supper last night." The look of incredulity on Sara's face before she dropped her eyes to stare at the table startled Ginger. What was going on in this girl's head? Did she know something about David? Ginger shelved the idea as soon as it crossed her mind. Sara wasn't around enough to know anything.

"I could fix us some lunch," Sara said after eating three cookies. "I make great grilled cheese sandwiches if you're hungry."

"I'm not really, but why don't you make one for yourself?"

"No, that's okay. I had a big breakfast." She reached for the last cookie. "Have you heard anything about Charlie?"

"No."

"That really sucks."

The indigestion that had started when Ginger woke up was swirling around in her stomach, making her nauseous. A cramp hit her in the midsection. She grabbed her belly and gasped.

"Are you okay?" Sara set down the cookie and jumped to her feet, genuine concern on her face.

Ginger gasped and the cramp passed, but something felt strange. She looked at the liquid running down her legs and pooling on the floor. "Oh no. My water broke." She moaned. "It's too early." She staggered up from the chair and grabbed on to the counter to keep herself upright. "Fuck, this hurts."

"I'm calling 911." Sara had her phone out, and Ginger heard her repeating their address through a fog of pain. The cramp eased and she straightened up. Beads of sweat covered her forehead. "Calling 911 seems premature, Sara. Can you drive me … ugh." She doubled over again.

"The dispatcher said five minutes, tops. Can I get you anything? Your purse or a suitcase. Do you have stuff packed for the hospital?"

Ginger shook her head as she came up for air. "I have another month. I shouldn't be in labour."

"I guess the baby has other ideas. I see your purse on the hall table."

"Call David and tell him to meet me at the Queensway Carleton Hospital. Oh my God, another one." She gritted her teeth and counted to ten. This baby was in a hurry to get out. The contraction passed and she lifted her head. Sara had her cell phone resting on her ear but wasn't speaking.

"It goes to his voicemail." Sara left a message and was watching her with a concerned expression. Ginger tried to smile and speak normally, relieved to hear a vehicle pull into the driveway a few minutes later. Sara raced across the kitchen and down the hallway to let in the paramedics. One was leaning on the bell and knocking with the side of his fist at the same time.

Ginger had made it to the hallway and watched the two paramedics enter. She assured them that she could walk to the ambulance. "Stay and tell my parents where I've gone," she said to Sara over her shoulder. "Tell them … to … call me with their news."

She groaned and stumbled as another contraction struck. The paramedics kept her upright, all the while moving her toward the door. The pain eased, and she shuffled between them, down the steps, and across the lawn to the waiting ambulance.

"Wait, wait!" Sara leapt down the front steps and ran across the space to pass them Ginger's purse. She touched Ginger's hand and leaned in before they eased her on to a stretcher in the back of the ambulance. This time, Sara's eyes found and held hers without her usual evasiveness. Her voice was soft but strong enough for Ginger to latch on to even as another contraction rolled through her belly.

"Don't worry, Ginger. I'll make sure you're the first to know if Charlie comes home. I won't let anything else happen to him if they've let him go."

CHAPTER 26

Auger caught up with Liam on his way to get coffee at the Happy Goat a few blocks north of the Elgin police station. It was late in the day, and Liam needed some caffeine to make it through the next hour.

"You appear to be going my way," Auger said and fell into step.

"Any new leads on the Joanne Freemont murder?" Liam glanced sideways at him as they waited at a red light.

"Autopsy says she was strangled somewhere else and dropped on the Parkway. My working theory is that one of her clients got carried away, panicked, and tried to distance himself."

"What about Joanne being Meilin Hanon's room-mate? How do you figure that connection fits in?"

"Might be a red herring. What kind of murder mystery would it be without at least one?" Auger grinned. "Don't worry, we're studying all angles, including her ties to the missing roommate." The light changed, and they started across the street. "Rumour has it Greta might not be returning anytime soon."

"I hadn't heard that." Liam waited for Auger to work his way around to the reason he'd followed him onto Elgin.

"You been partnered long with Julie Quade?"

And there it was. "A couple of years."

"She makes an okay placeholder, but I can't see her being staff sergeant permanently. Job will be up for grabs if Greta decides to transfer." Auger was looking at him now. "You got any designs on applying?"

"Nope, and Quade is more than a placeholder. She's a seasoned detective and has all the skills to run Homicide. She passed the sergeant course in the fall."

"Good to know she's got one fan." Auger pulled his phone out of his pocket. "Sorry, I have to take this." He dropped back, and Liam carried on alone into the coffee shop, unsettled by the encounter, knowing Auger was going to stir up shit right where Greta left off.

His own phone rang as he stepped outside the Goat with coffees for the team. He set the tray on the sidewalk and answered. Rosie Thorburn's voice was louder than normal when she told him that Ginger McGowan was in the hospital and asking to see him. "She's in labour and says that she has something to tell you. I think it's important."

"On my way," he said before clicking off.

———

LIAM MET Richard and Madeleine as he stepped off the elevator on the maternity ward floor. They looked upset, Madeleine's eyes rimmed red and Richard's jaw set.

A sinking feeling filled him. "How's Ginger?" He didn't want to think that she'd had more heartache, knowing the baby hadn't been due for a few weeks at least.

"She's fine. A baby girl. Six pounds, two ounces." Madeleine smiled, but the attempt was shaky, and Richard took her by the arm.

"We're on our way for coffee. Can we get you one, Detective?" His voice was friendlier than usual.

Odd, Liam thought. *He's almost sheepish.* "Thanks, but I've had my coffee fill for the day. See you in a few minutes."

Ginger was propped up on pillows, holding her newborn, when Liam poked his head into the room. The taut muscles in her face relaxed into a smile as she motioned for him to enter. "Thanks for coming, Detective Hunter."

"Your parents tell me you've had a healthy baby girl. Congratulations." He looked down at the swaddled pink blanket and could see a tuft of reddish hair sticking out the top but not much else. "Is David here?"

"He's on his way. He's going to be gutted to have missed the birth, but she arrived like a high-speed train."

"That's a shame for David, but I'm happy everything went well." He paused. "So why did you ask to see me, Ginger?"

"My parents tried to do the right thing. Dad thought he could handle the ransom himself and bring Charlie home." Her eyes were pleading for him to understand. "The message came yesterday through my email. They wanted fifteen thousand in Bitcoin and said they'd let Charlie go in Bayshore mall. The message warned us not to involve the police."

"You were conflicted about what to do."

She nodded. "Dad and Mom went to the mall this morning, and they thought they saw Charlie, so Dad transferred the money to the email."

"But it wasn't Charlie."

"No, the blond little boy was not Charlie. He was there with his mom, and she was alarmed when they descended on her but said she understood after they explained. If I'd been there, I would have known it wasn't my son, but they hadn't seen Charlie in months. They wanted it to be him so badly."

Liam could see in her eyes that she knew there'd be fallout. "We likely won't be able to retrieve the Bitcoin. This was someone taking advantage of your situation."

"Yeah, I figured. My parents were prepared to lose the money, even though their intent was to get Charlie back. The sender's email address doesn't work anymore. Dad sent a nasty message a few minutes ago, and it bounced back. I wanted you to know."

"If this happens again —"

"You don't have to tell us. You'll be the first one I call."

"Did David know about the ransom note?"

"No. In fact, I haven't told him yet and am not looking forward to sharing this bit of news. He and Dad already don't see eye-to-eye on much."

"I'll need to have one of your devices so we can try to trace the sender." There was no point in getting angry. He sympathized with their ill-advised attempt to pay the ransom. Ultimately, they had paid the price for ignoring the police warnings. The good news was that Richard seemed less involved in the kidnapping than he had before paying out the money. The fact that he'd been in Ottawa when Charlie went missing and never admitted to it had been a niggling loose end.

She reached into the bedside drawer and handed her phone to him as David flew into the room. He stopped, panting at the foot of the bed to look at her and the baby, his hand over his heart. "My God. A girl?"

"A girl."

Liam saw the joy on both their faces and quietly took his leave after telling them both he'd be in touch. They needed this time to celebrate and regroup after a week from hell. He walked toward the elevator but didn't meet Richard or Madeleine on the way. They could be hiding in the cafeteria until he left, not wanting to face him after falling victim to the scammer. He'd search them out anyway and get their statements before letting Quade and the team know about the ransom scam, not that any of this would help locate Charlie.

CHAPTER 27

Ella spotted Sara working alone behind the counter. She swirled scoops of ice cream from the machine into two plastic bowls and added toppings. It looked like the elderly couple waiting by the cash was getting butterscotch and pineapple sundaes with sprinkles and whipped cream. Ella's mouth watered at the sight of the two of them walking outside and licking their spoons a few minutes later.

The evening was warmer than the day, an unusual weather pattern settling into the region as the sun set. Not as humid as it had been before the twenty-four-hour cold spell, but sultry nonetheless. The DQ had a line-up extending into the parking lot, so she remained in her car and waited. Closing time was in half an hour, and the line would thin eventually. She'd put the car windows down, and a light breeze wafted warm, fresh air across the front seat. People chatted and laughed as they sauntered past, a typical relaxed summer evening. Sara waved goodbye to the last customers at three minutes to eleven, and Ella hopped out of the car and got to the front door as Sara lifted a hand to turn the lock. She hesitated but reached down and pushed the door open to let Ella inside.

"Am I too late for a hot fudge sundae?"

"I'll make you one."

They walked to the counter, and Sara slipped behind. She got busy and added extra toppings while Ella watched her work. She wasn't sure why she'd come to see Sara tonight. A hunch, maybe. That and a genuine sympathy for the girl. Sara was a loner duck, much like Ella, although her own solitariness was a choice. She could see "bullied" written all over Sara, from her inverted shoulders to her inability to hold eye contact.

"You've outdone yourself," she said, accepting the sundae and taking a bite. "Plans after you lock up?"

"Home. Been a long day. I was with Ginger when she went into labour."

"I heard. Great news."

"A baby doesn't replace Charlie, but yeah, a reason to celebrate." She smiled, and Ella realized how seldom she'd seen the girl happy.

"You have a little half-sister."

"I know, right?"

"Are you heading home now?"

"Yeah. Mom's asked that I bring her an ice cream cake. Maybe it helps with her hot flashes." This time Sara's face lit up in a cheeky grin, and Ella chuckled. "I like your haircut." Sara's gaze focused on the top of Ella's head. She looked lower into Ella's eyes and then past her. "Did you want to ask me anything? Is that why you're here?"

"Did you know about the ransom message to Ginger? And thanks," Ella added, tucking a strand of hair behind her ear.

"Not exactly, but I figured she got one. I stopped by as her parents were driving off, I guessed to bring Charlie home from somewhere. I thought they were being taken for suckers. Was I right?"

"Unfortunately, yes."

Sara bent to pick up the spray bottle and rag from under the counter. "I need to do some cleaning before I leave. If you're ready to go, I can let you out."

A not-so-subtle dismissal. Ella turned at the door to face her. "Say, my next-door neighbour is the hairdresser who fixed up my hair mess. Would you like me to make you an appointment? Not that your hair is a mess." Ella mentally kicked herself. Talk about putting her foot in it.

"I can't … I'm saving for school."

"You know, I wanted to find a way to thank you for talking to me, so this would be my treat. Can I set something up? We live just over the bridge in the Glebe on Percy."

"I don't think so." Sara moved around her and unlocked the door. "I usually cut my own hair."

"I know all about that. Tony gave me my first haircut in years except for the ones I give myself. You and I aren't that different."

"Yeah. Yeah, we are."

"Sara, if you ever need help with anything — at school or home — I'm a good listener and sometimes a creative problem-solver."

"You're a reporter. I know better than to deviate from my prepared media lines."

Ella was beginning to like the kid's dry sense of humour. "I wouldn't be listening to you as a reporter."

Sara hesitated. "Well, maybe there is something you can help me with. I took a video of my dad meeting some guys in a restaurant on Elgin, and I can't place them."

"Do these men worry you?"

Sara shrugged. "I'll send the video to you, and you can tell me if I should be worried or not. I know I've seen one of them somewhere before but can't remember where. He's the one staring into the camera."

"I'll wait to receive the file and will give it a look. I've met a lot of people over the years working for the paper."

"That's what I thought. Thanks."

After leaving the shop, Ella sat in her car, eating ice cream and watching Sara clean up through the plate glass window. *You know something*, she thought. *I don't have any idea how or what, but you've got me mighty curious.* She scraped the last bit of chocolate off the cup with her spoon and into her mouth before starting the car. As she took one final look inside, Sara set a cake on the counter and disappeared from her sightline. Ella took a moment to relive their conversations. Sara was smarter than she let on. Introverted. A watcher.

They really did have a lot in common. "I'm going to find out what you know," Ella promised out loud as Sara crossed in front of the window. "And maybe, just maybe, help you out at the same time."

———

SARA WAITED for Ella to drive away before she locked up the shop and slipped out the back entrance. She walked through the darkness to her car in the farthest corner of the parking lot and carefully set the ice cream cake into the cooler on the front passenger seat before rounding the car to climb in. A breeze had kicked up, but it was still humid, and the heat was a shock after working in the air conditioning all evening. The house was going to be a sweatbox again tonight. Her mom would be in a foul mood without a doubt. Hopefully the cake would help.

She drove to the parking lot exit and was looking both ways before pulling onto Bank Street when she saw him — the scary man from the video. A car passing by lit up his face for a moment in the driver's seat of a car parked directly across the street from the DQ's front entrance. The man had his head turned sideways, looking in the direction of the DQ's main door. Her hands froze on the steering wheel. This couldn't be another coincidence. She forced the panic down. She normally would have turned left and passed by him, but she stepped on the gas and merged onto Bank going in the other direction.

Once she'd crossed the bridge, she pulled into the

parking lot at Billings Bridge shopping mall. She circled the parked cars, all the while checking her side mirrors to see if she was being followed. This might not have been the best plan, since it was late evening and the parked cars were few and spaced out. She turned off her lights and drove along the outside row until she found a spot between two cars. She backed in and scrunched down in the seat, keeping watch in both directions.

She had to find out who this man was and why he was watching her. Doing nothing was not an option. She fumbled through her bag with a shaky hand. It took a moment to grasp her phone. She searched through the photo gallery until she located the video she'd promised Ella that she'd forward after her shift. Her finger on *Send*, she paused for a moment. Could she trust Ella? She was a reporter out for a story, not a friend. Yet if not Ella, who? Not her mom, definitely not. Her dad or Uncle Ivan? Not in this lifetime. Roddy wasn't even a consideration. That left … nobody. She hit *Send* and set the phone down next to her, almost immediately regretting having done it.

A car's headlights were going up and down the nearly empty rows as if searching for someone, and Sara sank even lower in her seat. She waited until the car turned down a row heading in the opposite direction and pulled out of her spot, leaving the lights off and driving along the last line of vehicles toward the exit. She was certain it was the same car that had been parked across from the DQ. The driver turned right and started back toward her, but two rows over.

She stepped on the gas and narrowly avoided hitting a shopping cart before making it to the end of her row. She sped toward Bank Street and didn't turn on her headlights until she merged into traffic going south, away from the downtown.

Should she go home, or could he possibly know where she lived? He certainly knew where she worked. *Think, Sara, think,* she ordered herself. *He knows your dad and must have figured out who you are.* The video showed his expression as he watched her, and she hadn't imagined his anger when he saw her lower her phone. On the replay, he started to get up from his seat, as if he was going to chase after her. That had to be why he was following her. Somehow, he'd realized who she was. Maybe her dad had told him that he had a teenage daughter by his first marriage and shown him a photo. She had no doubt they were in cahoots about some business deal, otherwise why the late-night rendezvous? Whatever they were up to had *illegal smell* all over it, especially if this thug — because that's what he looked like — was upset about being filmed with the other two. The feeling of panic made her want to throw up. She couldn't go home and risk this man doing something to her mom or Roddy.

Her mind scrambled through the most horrible scenarios. Her mother had told her often enough: people, specifically men, were capable of committing unspeakable atrocities against girls. A young woman's body had been found on the Parkway yesterday, the roommate of the university student who'd gone missing in November. The uneasy feeling returned from last year when she'd first learned the university student had disappeared walking home from a party in a downtown hotel. She'd watched her dad and the man now following her enter that same hotel separately on the night in question, but linking the girl's disappearance to her dad had been unfathomable. He was a lot of things, but he wasn't a killer. She knew that in her bones. What she hadn't known was that her dad and this man knew each other. The realization that he was the same man she'd seen entering that hotel in November and again with her dad in the restaurant this week had her mind spinning in horror.

She double-checked that nobody was following her by driving down a random side street and parking in front of a house. When nobody turned onto the road behind her, she picked up her phone and texted her mother, telling her that she'd be spending the night at a girlfriend's and not to worry. *Sorry about the ice cream cake.* Then she texted her DQ manager and booked off the rest of the week, saying she was sick with the flu. Half an hour later, when she was certain she'd lost the man with the creepy eyes, she backtracked, wove down side streets to Bronson Avenue, and took the on ramp to the westbound Queensway.

CHAPTER 28

"Someone's here to see you. A reporter." Rosie Thorburn stopped in front of Liam's desk, where he was typing a report. "Want me to get rid of her?"

Liam stilled his hands and raised his head. "Name?"

"Emma or Leah or something. I didn't catch her last name."

Or her first, obviously. "I'll deal with her."

"As you wish."

He watched Thorburn amble over to Auger's desk. He hadn't figured her out yet. She was efficient, but where did her loyalties lie? Greta and Auger had brought her into the unit, which was reason enough to be careful around her. He grabbed his jacket from the back of the chair and got to his feet.

Ella was standing by the main doors in the lobby, bouncing from foot to foot, when he exited the elevator. She was wearing large, round sunglasses and a scarf that covered her hair and hid her identity for all intents and purposes. She motioned for him to join her outside.

"Heating up again out here," he said as they began walking north on Elgin. It used to be that the hottest time of day was noon, but now the heat peaked late afternoon, when it peaked at all. It was going on four and stinking hot once again. He regretted putting on his jacket. They cut across the road at the lights and started down a side street. Ella ripped off the scarf and mopped her face with it. She appeared on edge, energy radiating off her like a sweaty perfume. She stopped under the shade of an elm tree and turned to face him.

"I think there's more to Charlie McGowan's disappearance than we first thought."

"What do you mean?"

"Sara … David's daughter sent me a short video she shot the other night. I believe she was following her father without his knowledge. He met a couple of men in a restaurant on Elgin, and Sara filmed the encounter as she walked past. She told me that she'd seen one of the men before but couldn't remember where. She seemed worried, even if she downplayed the incident, and asked me to try to identify the two men with her dad. I got the video around eleven thirty last night."

She pressed *Play* and passed Liam her phone, waiting for him to finish watching. She studied his face as he handed the phone back to her. "The man on the left is Wes Gilbert. He's the owner of the escort service where Joanne Freemont was employed. I have no idea who the other guy is. Do you?"

It was as if a shot of liquid adrenaline had been pumped through Liam's veins, the same feeling he got every time a big piece of a murder puzzle slotted into place. The connection among these three men could be the key to breaking open both cases. He could see that Ella realized the importance of the video as clearly as he did. "I'll try to find out. If the third man has a record, we'll be able to match him. Forward the tape to me, if you don't mind sharing."

"Good, I will. I've been following Gilbert, hoping he'd lead me to Meilin, if she's still alive. What the hell could he be doing having a meal with David McGowan?"

"A very good question. I'll have to turn this over to the lead investigator on the Hanon case. Are you okay with that?"

Ella took a second to think through what he was asking. She nodded. "As long as you don't say where you got it or that Sara filmed her father. I don't want him to find out."

"Agreed."

She grabbed his arm and gave it a shake. "Shit, Hunter. If my gut isn't lying, this video could break things wide open."

He had an unsettling premonition. "You need to let us handle it. We have no idea what these men are involved in or what they're capable of doing. Promise me you'll stop digging until we know who the third man is."

"Awww, Hunter. You're worried about widdle me. Isn't that sweet." Her slow smile beamed amusement for a moment before her face turned serious. "I work the crime beat for three reasons, Detective. One, I'm not foolish. Two, I don't scare easily. And three, I never make promises I have no intention of keeping, so I'm not going to tell you that I'll stop digging."

"Then be sure to keep me in the loop. We can help each other here." He paused. "I'm going to check in with Sara and warn her to stop following her dad. Luckily, she has no idea what she's stumbled upon."

Ella nodded. "I'll send a text telling her not to worry any longer and to delete the video from her phone."

———

LIAM WAITED HALF an hour before sending the video to Auger. He hoped Rosie wouldn't make the connection between the timing of Ella's visit and the appearance of the video but knew he couldn't hold off sharing this evidence with the team. He cc'd Quade and suggested David McGowan's meeting with Wes Gilbert at the restaurant could be a link between the two disappearances that they hadn't so far considered.

Quade strode out of her office ten minutes after

he sent the video and called him and Auger's team into the meeting room. "Hunter, I know you're reluctant to reveal who filmed this video, but are you certain it's legit?"

"It's legit."

"We're going through files trying to identify the third man." Auger nodded at Liam. "Thanks for bringing this to my attention."

"It potentially impacts both our cases."

"You have to interview David McGowan again and find out why he's having a meal with Joanne's — I want to say pimp — but boss will have to do." Quade looked from Auger to Liam. "Since it crosses cases, I suggest you're both in on the questioning."

"Let's wait until we find out who the third man is. We should be able to identify him today." Auger looked across the table at Liam. "Might give us a better idea of what's going on before you stumble around in the thick of it."

"Did you have any sense that McGowan was into something nasty?" Boots asked.

"No, but we've been probing. Any word on his financial audit, Rosie?"

Her face reddened. "The report came while you were downstairs, and I never had a chance to share it. His company's in good shape and his personal finances are decent, dare I say healthy. I printed the figures for you and have the sheets on my desk. I didn't see any unusual activity that would strike a warning bell."

"So much for kidnapping his own kid for money." Jingles sounded disappointed and gave a wry smile.

"He had no need to kidnap Charlie, since he wasn't in debt." Rosie spoke to him as if she were explaining a simple concept to a child. "It would make no sense."

Jingles regarded her from under lowered brow but didn't comment further. Boots and Liam exchanged glances before looking away.

She's humourless, Liam thought. He'd have a word with her later about forwarding documents to him as soon as they arrived. It would give him a chance to see how she handled criticism. He suspected she was the type to run to HR at any perceived slight. He hoped he was misjudging her.

There was a tap on the door, and all faces turned as the desk sergeant poked his head into the room. "Sorry to interrupt you folks, but there's a woman in the lobby saying her teenage daughter's gone missing. I thought you'd want to get on it right away given the other stolen persons cases."

"Shit," Quade said. "Just what we need." She pointed at Liam. "Come with me, and we'll get the details. Everyone, make whatever arrangements you need with your significant others in preparation for another late night at work. I'll sign off on the overtime later."

Liam glanced back as he followed her out the door. Auger was openly staring daggers at him and Quade. Auger was the more logical choice to carry out this interview, given his work on the Hanon case, but Quade didn't appear to care. Liam hoped she wasn't making a mistake sidelining Auger. He reminded Liam of a cobra, coiled and watching from its hiding place, making plans to strike when the time was right.

CHAPTER 29

"It's Claudette McGowan, David's ex-wife," Liam said to Quade when he spotted her sitting in the waiting area. His heart lurched. Sara McGowan had to be the missing teenage girl.

Claudette stood at their approach. Black mascara had caked in watery rivulets on her cheeks. She was wearing a bright pink tank top and wrinkled orange shorts that might have fit her once. She looked as if she'd bolted down here without a thought to her appearance.

"Sara sent me a text last night that she was staying at a friend's. See?" She held out her phone screen for them to read the message. "I was suspicious because she doesn't name the friend, and she's never stayed away from home overnight except at her father's. Roddy, my son, was as surprised as I was. Then I find out she cancelled her shifts at the DQ for the week, saying she had the flu, which is an out and out lie. Plus, she'd promised to bring an ice cream cake home. It's not like her to forget something like that."

"Did you phone your ex-husband to make sure she's not there?" Quade asked.

"Of course. They haven't seen her since the other day. Somebody's got her."

"Now, we don't know that for certain." Quade's voice was firm, reassuring. "However, you were right to be concerned with all that's gone on, and we're going to be proactive. Detective Hunter will arrange for another officer to take down your details somewhere more private, and we'll notify our officers to be on the lookout for your daughter."

"We can start interviewing her friends and contacts right away," Liam added. "I agree with Acting Staff Sergeant Quade. This is not the time to panic. Sara could be with a friend."

Claudette swiped at a tear. Her expression hardened. "All well and good, but why isn't she answering her phone? I called and texted, and she hasn't responded even once."

Liam held her gaze, but a ripple of dread gripped him. It was more and more urgent that they figure out what was going on with David McGowan and why his family was being targeted. Now a second one of his children was missing. What were the odds of their disappearances being unrelated?

"Man, this is a mess," Quade said when they had a moment alone. She'd moved Claudette into a meeting room where Thorburn was taking her statement. "Any idea what's going on?"

"Sara taped the video of her dad meeting Wes Gilbert and the other man." He had no choice but to tell Quade with this new development. "She appears to have followed her dad that night for some reason. She also asked my source to find out the name of the man we're trying to identify from the footage. My contact says the fact Sara reached out means she had to have been really worried. Likely scared."

"So David McGowan is involved somehow again. Can you go inform him that Claudette officially reported their daughter missing and get his reaction? We'll keep Claudette busy a bit longer to give you time to drive to Rocky Point. I imagine she'll be beating down his door after she leaves here."

"On my way. Should I mention the video or hold that back? I can keep Sara's name out of it."

Quade shook her head. "Auger strongly suggested that we keep that nugget up our sleeves until he identifies the third man, so I'll bow to his instincts for now. You said that David didn't know about the scammer ransom request for Charlie?"

"That's what Ginger believed."

Quade gave him a sideways smile. "Find out if your video source knows anything more."

"As soon as I leave the McGowans."

"Good. Phone me when you've got something to report, and if you can't locate Sara, I'll get another AMBER Alert started. Let's hope nobody else goes missing in the meantime."

———

IT WAS good to be home, with her mom taking care of the baby while she snuggled in her own bed. Maybe it was the hormones, but Ginger wasn't as anxious as she had been before giving birth. She missed Charlie like crazy, and the worry remained constant, but holding baby Krista had miraculously stilled the worst of the raging panic.

She rose from a long afternoon nap and took a quick shower before going downstairs. David was lying on the couch with Krista sleeping on his chest. He gave her a lazy smile and held out a hand. She crossed the room and clasped her fingers around his, sinking to her knees on the carpet and touching the soft down on the baby's head with her free hand. "She's so perfect."

"*And* a good sleeper." He left unsaid that Charlie hadn't been, and she felt a pang of guilt at this small betrayal. He squeezed her hand as if reading her mind. "We'll get him back. Stay strong, my love."

Madeleine entered the room with three cups of tea on a tray. "I heard you in the shower." She handed around the mugs and sat in a chair facing them. Ginger got up from the floor and wedged in at the end of the couch next to David's feet.

"Where's Dad?" Ginger asked before taking a sip of tea.

"He went for a drive earlier and said he was meeting up with a business friend for dinner. He might have to return to Halifax tomorrow, but I'll stay on another week if that's okay with you both."

"Of course. I'm so pleased to have your help."

Ginger thought the tension in the house would lessen with her dad gone. David rubbed his foot along her thigh. The baby stirred, but before she could work up a full-throttle wail, David handed her to Ginger for a feeding. Krista was falling back to sleep, her head resting against Ginger's chest, when the doorbell rang.

"I'll get that." David was on his feet. Madeleine had returned to the kitchen to finish making supper.

Please be good news, Ginger silently prayed. *Please tell me you've found Charlie and are bringing him home.* She listened to the murmur of voices in the hallway, and a few seconds later David returned with Detective Hunter. She couldn't get a read on their expressions but thought David's face seemed pale. She straightened her shirt and shifted into a more comfortable position. "What's happened?"

"Sara's really missing. I can't believe it." David ran a hand through his hair. "I thought Claudette was blowing smoke when she called earlier looking for her." He turned toward Liam and rolled his eyes. "She's been something of a drama queen over the past few years."

"Can you think of anyone Sara might be with?" Liam asked.

"Not really. We rarely see her, and when she's visiting, Sara doesn't talk about her friends or what she does when she's at her mother's. Did you check her DQ job? She has afternoon shifts."

"She called in sick for the rest of the week."

David exploded. "Now why in God's name would

she do that?" He took a deep breath and added more calmly, "She's always been so reliable."

Ginger let out a cry, pulling herself to the edge of the couch cushion. "That's two of your children gone, David. Could the same person have taken them both? Is somebody threatening you?"

"Of course nobody's threatening me. That's crazy talk. I can't even believe you'd think that, let alone say it."

"It's too early to determine if Sara is missing or with a friend." Liam pulled his stare away from David's face to look at Ginger. "She might have decided to spend some time alone. The police are watching for her car and have her picture. We'll get a warrant to track her phone if nobody hears from her soon. She likely hasn't gone far."

"Jesus. Can anything else terrible happen to this family?" David dropped into the nearest chair and leaned forward, his hands covering his face.

Liam watched David dispassionately, trying to assess the sincerity of his reactions. He waited for David to look up. "Ginger wasn't wrong to ask. Do you know of anybody who has it in for you, whether for business or personal reasons?"

"No. My business is doing well and the clients are happy. Ginger and I lead a simple life, although she's right in saying that I put in too many long hours at work." He stared at her. "That's going to change, Gin. If nothing else, this past week has shown me what's important, and it's not being in the office."

"I hope you mean that."

"I do. Life is too precarious." He thought for a moment. "Have you talked to Roddy? He and Sara have always been close."

"I received a text from an officer who just spoke with your son, but Roddy hasn't shared anything concerning her whereabouts. The officer reported that he appears as confused as everyone else."

"Then I don't know what to tell you. The last time I spoke with Sara was a few days ago. She was worried about Charlie but okay otherwise."

Liam wanted to bring up the video and was of two minds about waiting to identify the third man. "Ginger, do you have anything to add?"

She bit her bottom lip and glanced at David before speaking. "No. Sara is a shy girl who shares little with us about her life. She's ... awkward around people." David's jaw tightened, but he didn't comment.

Liam felt for Sara and the picture that was forming of her life. He was no psychologist but thought she'd been caught between two warring parents and had withdrawn into herself. Neither parent appeared to have put Sara and Roddy ahead of their dislike for each other. "Can you both check your phone messages to see if she's contacted you in the last twenty-four hours?"

Ginger reached for her cell on the coffee table and scrolled through the screen. "She hasn't contacted me. David?"

He was already skimming through his messages. "Nothing for a few days."

"How about her room? Has she left anything personal, like a laptop or notebooks?"

Ginger shook her head. "She takes everything with her when she returns to her mom's. My parents are staying in the bedroom she usually occupies on her visits."

"Two of my kids…" David's voice trailed off.

Liam could hear genuine anguish but was also aware that David hadn't offered any information to help find either of his children. Would the man put self-preservation above his family? "If she contacts you, call me," he said. "Anytime, day or night. In the meantime, we'll be searching for her car and speaking to all those in her circle."

"Find my kids, Detective." David's voice cracked, and he sucked in air. "Please bring them home to us so we can end this nightmare and get our lives back."

"We'll do all we can." Liam wanted to believe that the fear David showed was for his kids and not himself, but until more evidence came to light, the verdict was still out.

CHAPTER 30

Ella hit *Publish* and uploaded her latest podcast before leaning back in the chair, hands clasped behind her head. "Outdone yourself again, Tate," she said, pleased with the work on this one. A rap on her apartment door startled her, and she jumped up, punching the air with her fists as she danced across the floor and pulled it open.

"Got some news for you, girl."

Tony and Luvy slipped past her while she stood with her hand on the doorknob. She trailed after them down the short hallway. Tony handed her a glass of red wine before plopping onto the couch with a second glass, and Ella dropped into her desk chair. She saluted him with her drink.

"So what's the news?"

"That student you had me find. Name of Yina Zhao. Well, that girl is on her way to China. She left at four on a flight to Toronto in time to make the international connection this evening."

"How could you possibly know that?"

"Because I drove her to the airport myself and waved her off from the Departures lounge."

"You were supposed to call me when you tracked her down."

"And I would have, except she was hell bent on catching that plane. Some guy in a car was waiting outside the front of her apartment, so we snuck out the back. Luckily, I'd parked a block over, and we scooted down the alley and loaded up her suitcases in my trunk without detection. Deliciously covert."

"Did you see him, this guy in the car?"

"I saw a fellow in a car a couple of doors down across the street and didn't think anything of it, but Yina was inside her apartment freaking out. Said he'd been there almost an hour and she was sure he was waiting for her to come outside."

"Are you saying the man in the car could have been waiting there for somebody else?"

"I suppose, but Yina was awfully jumpy. She refused to let me go knock on the guy's window. I had to play along with her wishes or she would have told me to leave."

"So, she's cut her summer semester short and fled to her homeland?"

"In a nutshell. We had a brief chat that I managed to record for your podcast. She said to use whatever you want after seven tonight when her flight to Beijing takes off. She won't be returning to Ottawa anytime soon." He pulled out his phone and set it on the couch next to him. "Listen."

Yina: *Joanne was scared because of something that happened at the party where she took Meilin. She wouldn't tell me what exactly, except to say that it was bad. Real bad. She said that she wished with all her heart they'd never gone."*

Tony stopped the recording. "Joanne was Meilin's roommate, right? The dead girl they found on the Parkway?"

"Yes." Ella motioned for him to hit *Play*, impatient with him for dragging this out. "What else did Yina say?"

He smiled at her and clicked his phone.

Yina: *Joanne said that Mr. Gilbert told her to get the hell out of there and she'd be okay. She didn't think even he believed what he was saying. Guess she was proved right. Regardless, I don't know what happened. Joanne never told me because she said the less I knew the better. She confessed to me that they'd all lied about that night, and she was having second thoughts. Looks like nobody believed she kept her mouth shut, because someone's keeping track of me. That's why I'm going back to China and never plan to return.* (Background noise and Tony asking a question.) *Sure, I don't care. Your reporter friend can use this tape, but only after I'm out of here.* (More background noise and the recording ended.)

Ella had been leaning forward, elbows on her knees, straining to listen. She straightened. "How did you track her down?"

"I have a contact in the university admissions office. She gave me Yina's address after I explained the situation."

"You continue to amaze."

"People will do pretty much anything for a cut-and-colour."

"You bribed her with a free hairdo. Really?"

"I'm booked up with a long waitlist. She gets to leap over the queue, so yeah, she coughed up the info."

They both jumped as a pounding on the door travelled upward from downstairs. "Expecting someone?" Tony asked.

"Nope."

"Stay here, Ella. I'll go see who it is and get rid of them."

"I won't argue."

She listened to the front door open and the murmur of voices. A minute later, Tony bounded up the stairs with Liam Hunter in tow. "See what the cat dragged in."

Hunter levelled his gaze at Tony. "You're making me think I look as bad as I feel."

He stood in the doorway while Tony returned to his seat on the couch, drawing a sleeping Luvy into his lap. Tony ran his hand in smooth strokes across Luvy's back. "Those are mighty dark bags under your Irish eyes, Detective."

"It's been a long week." Liam stepped into the room, positioning himself in Ella's direct line of sight. She noticed his five o'clock shadow and tired black eyes — he looked exhausted. She almost felt bad for him. "Not good news, I'm afraid. Sara McGowan's mother has reported her missing, and you're one of the last people to hear from her with that video. Has she contacted you since?"

A chill washed over Ella. "What do you mean she's missing?"

"She called in sick to work and texted her mom that she was sleeping overnight at a girlfriend's. Her mom and Roddy say she doesn't have any close girl-friends, and she never stays away overnight except at her dad's."

Her life's far worse than I imagined. Ella wasn't much of a hugger, but she'd have given Sara a big one if she could. "No, she hasn't been in touch since sending the video. I hope she hasn't become a victim of whatever is going on."

"That's my wish too."

They stared at one another. Ella could see genuine distress in his eyes and liked him for it. She began to feel uncomfortable with the length of their eye lock and was relieved when Tony broke the impasse. "Tell us what we can do to find her."

Liam shifted his stare over to Tony. "I was hoping Sara had made contact, and maybe she will yet. I'll need to know right away if she does. Detective Auger has yet to identify the third man in Sara's video, but I'm ready to start grilling the other two, David McGowan and Wes Gilbert."

"Two of David's kids are missing," Ella said. "Hard to believe this is a coincidence." She thought for a moment. "Sara was following her father the night she filmed him meeting these two guys in the restaurant. She appears to have few if any friends and disinterested parents. Do you think she followed her dad on other occasions?"

"If that's the case, who knows what she saw ... or filmed?" Tony's voice rose with the possibilities. "That girl could be in real trouble."

Hunter ran a hand across the stubble on his chin. "Let's hope you're wrong. I'm going back to the station to get things moving. I'll let you know what happens, but please call me day or night if you hear from Sara. I won't be sleeping much until she and Charlie turn up safe."

Ella had a feeling she'd be seeing a few sunrises herself. She saluted him before he turned to leave.

Tony slapped his forehead as they heard the front door slam shut. "I forgot to tell him about Yina Zhao flying home to China."

Ella shrugged. "The cops can figure it out for themselves. Besides, it's not Hunter's case."

"Well, that's a relief. No point sharing information if we don't have to."

"I hear the sarcasm, Tony, but remember, I'm with the press, and we like to break stories, not coordinate them with the police. We're an arm's-length entity."

"Hmmm. That rule seems as flexible as a Russian gymnast when it comes to you and the good detective."

"Never hurts to cultivate someone on the inside."

"Well, your someone looks like he's driving on a two-way street while your sign is pointing stubbornly in one direction, and it's not at him."

"Don't kid yourself. Detective Hunter is only sharing what he needs to impart in order for me to play along and feed him information."

Tony started to respond but seemed to think better of it. He studied her for a moment before standing with Luvy in his arms. "We'll be off then, but on standby. You can call out my name if you need help with any clandestine pursuits. Because you know wherever I am, why, I'll come a-running."

She gave him a look. "Isn't that pretty much a song lyric?"

"Song lyrics are the staff of life, and don't you forget it, girl. Because if it ain't worth singing about, it's just a big ol' sack full of nothing."

"A bit of a leap, but okay." She was still shaking her head when she turned back to her computer screen to begin another search.

CHAPTER 31

Tuesday afternoon. Charlie McGowan missing eight full days with no real leads to his whereabouts. Liam had been through these lulls in investigations on other cases. The frustration never got easier, but he knew now was the time to strengthen resolve and retrace every step for something missed. It could be as simple as looking at the facts and evidence with fresh eyes. He opened the file and began reading.

Auger stopped by Liam's desk a half hour later, looking like a cat who'd lapped up a bowl of cream. "Snap," he said, clicking his fingers and waving his hand back and forth in front of his face. "I figured out the mystery man on the video."

"Oh yeah? Do tell." Liam set down the paper he was reading and bent forward. He found Auger's use of the singular pronoun telling. This was a man who'd take the credit for his team's work without a qualm.

"He's none other than Denis Razzuto, member of

the Montreal mob dynasty, living a quiet, criminal life in Trois-Rivières."

"Begging the question, what was he doing in town with Gilbert and McGowan?"

"Obviously not happy to be captured on camera with them since he saw Sara McGowan filming with her phone." Auger paused. "Patrol found her car abandoned in the Rideau Centre parking garage an hour ago."

Liam's stomach dropped. He felt nothing but pain for Sara, who'd naively stumbled into a dangerous criminal world without any defenses. "No sign of her, I'm guessing?

"Nada."

"Evidence of a struggle?"

"Nope. We've got someone checking the parking garage video, so we should know more at some point if they were within range. Unfortunately, the camera at the entrance had been buggered with, so our chances aren't great."

"What next?"

"Quade's called us into her office for a planning session. You're invited, if you missed her email."

"Has anyone informed Claudette McGowan that her daughter's car was located?"

"Not yet. Why, you want the honours?"

"I don't mind telling her."

"Well, let's see what Quade wants to do. She's the one handing out the favours."

His grimace was half-smirk. Liam didn't react, even though Auger waited a few beats before continuing toward Quade's office. Thorburn approached Liam's desk as he was locking up files and preparing to follow Auger.

Her eyes tracked Auger's retreating back while she spoke. "Sara McGowan's car was towed, and Forensics is going through it. I should have a report by tomorrow, which I'll get right to you."

"Perfect, thanks, Rosie."

She picked up a pencil from his desk. Set it down. "Auger wants — that is, he — oh, never mind. I'll figure it out."

"Something I can help you with?"

She pushed a strand of hair behind her ear that had escaped from the tight bun at the nape of her neck. "I don't think so." She started walking toward her desk but stopped and turned to look back at him. "I'll see you tomorrow, unless you need me to stay late?"

He shook his head. "Thanks for offering, but have a good evening, Rosie. I'll catch you up on any developments in the morning."

"Yeah, I can use the night off. A few drinks in front of the television is about all I want to do right now."

"Sounds like a good plan." It'd be nice to do the same, but he doubted that would be in his cards for a while.

Liam entered Quade's office. She waited for him to settle in the chair next to Auger. Her gaze held his. "This is a troubling turn of events. We now have three missing individuals, two of them children, and one dead university student. The common link appears to be David McGowan, hard as this is to fathom."

"Either someone is sending him a message by taking his kids, or he's part of it," Auger interrupted. "I'm leaning toward the latter."

Quade glanced at him and back at Liam. "What do you think?"

"I have trouble believing McGowan kidnapped his own kids. He's likely involved in something that's got somebody worried. Stealing Charlie and now Sara could be a message. I'm not sure yet what's going on and believe it's time to shake him down."

Quade bit her bottom lip while thinking over their comments. It didn't take long for her to reach a decision. "Hunter, bring in McGowan and see what you can get out of him. Auger, you can tackle Gilbert. Maybe, he knows more about Meilin Hanon's disappearance than he revealed at the time. Joanne Freemont's murder should also be top of mind in your questioning. If you can link Razzuto to any of this, we can haul him to the station later. Call in whoever you need to assist, and tell them not to worry about overtime. I'll sign off afterwards."

"What, and spit in the eye of the bureaucracy?" Auger voiced mock dismay. "Surely, you tempt the fates."

"I'm willing to risk it." Her mouth rose in a half-smile. "You'll find that I'm not the pushover some people think I am, Auger. The fates should be more worried about me coming after them."

———

LIAM PHONED David and gave him the option of coming to the station of his own accord for a chat or getting a police escort. Liam didn't need to fabricate a reason. David's two missing kids was more than enough. David agreed to be there within the half hour. Liam used the time to walk up Elgin to buy a coffee at the Happy Goat. Twenty minutes of fresh air and a jolt of caffeine would help get him through the interview.

The sun was still warm and humidity high as he strode toward the coffee shop, but he enjoyed the brief reprieve from the office. He bought a large house brew and a chocolate chip cookie, taking his time on the walk back, stopping to check his phone under the shade of the same elm tree where he'd spoken with Ella. Hannah was home from Toronto and on her way over to feed his cat. He sent a quick thank-you and promised to check in when he could. All too soon, he reached the station and took one last deep breath before entering. He checked his watch when he reached his desk. Nearly seven o'clock. He'd been working twelve straight hours and had missed supper. It was time to stop focusing on himself, though, and turn his mind to David McGowan and figure out the best way to get him to share what he'd been holding back.

The call came from downstairs, and he watched as an officer escorted David into a small meeting room on the second floor. Liam waited a few minutes before joining him. David sat relaxed in the chair, arms folded across his chest. He appeared calm, but his eyes were wary as he silently watched Liam take the seat kitty corner to him. A camera in the ceiling and a microphone on the desk would record the encounter.

"Thanks for coming in to clear up a few questions. You aren't currently considered a suspect, but we will be recording this conversation." Liam opened up the folder he'd brought with him.

"I *guess* I'm not a suspect. How inane would that be? I'll do whatever it takes to bring my kids home. Sara … I can't believe anyone would hurt her. She's as harmless as — I don't know — a mouse."

Liam kept his face impassive, but inside he grimaced. "When's the last time you saw your daughter?"

"A couple of days ago, before the baby came. She slept over and helped Ginger. I invited her to stay as long as she wanted, but she had a DQ shift and left late morning. She was there when Ginger went into labour but I didn't see her."

"Did she seem worried or upset about anything?"

"No. Sara doesn't appear to have strong feelings about anything, really. She keeps her thoughts to herself unless I manage to pry something out of her. Even then, it's not a lot."

"Is somebody blackmailing you, Mr. McGowan?"

David's eyes narrowed. "What the hell are you asking me? Am I the kind of person who looks like he's involved in something criminal, Detective? I'm a family man, business owner, and philanthropist. I resent your question. Of course nobody's black-mailing me."

"It's a strange coincidence that two of your children are missing, wouldn't you agree?"

"Strange would *not* be my choice of adjective. Evil, despicable, horrific. Try picking one of those."

"Would it come as a surprise to learn that Sara followed you one evening and filmed you through a restaurant window on Elgin Street? You were joining two other men at a table next to the window."

David stared at Liam, struggling to control whatever emotions were at war inside of him. "She did *what?*" he asked through gritted teeth.

Liam pulled out his phone and set it on the table with the screen facing David. He pressed *Play*, and the video brightened the screen. David watched and visibly recoiled at the part where Razzuto stared at Sara through the window. "Could one of these men have harmed Sara?" Liam asked.

David groaned and ran a hand through his hair. "How did you get this tape?"

"Sara sent it before she disappeared. She was trying to find out who the man is that you see staring at her toward the end. We think he scared her. What connection do you have with Denis Razzuto and Wes Gilbert?"

"What in the hell was she thinking?" David shook his head and inhaled deeply before continuing. "We had a meeting to discuss hiring my firm for their financial investments. I'd never met either of them before this encounter that my daughter allegedly filmed — because I only have your word for it that she did. Mr. Gilbert suggested meeting at a restaurant where we could relax over a drink."

"Did they hire your firm?"

"Not as of yet, and we don't have a second meeting scheduled. I'm reluctant to take on Mr. Razzuto, if truth be told. He's not from the most upstanding of families. The jury's out on Gilbert."

"You didn't know that about Razzuto before you met?"

"No. This was to be a preliminary chat requested that morning by Mr. Gilbert. With everything that was going on with Charlie, I didn't have time to carry out any research. I agreed to meet only to keep from going crazy with worry. Work has always been my salvation, but I'm finding even that's not helping the longer my boy is missing." His eyes widened. "Could this Razzuto have gone after Sara?"

"You tell me."

"Our meeting was a nonstarter from my perspective. He'd have no cause to track down my daughter."

"This is all very puzzling," Liam said. "Can you think of any reason that one of these two men would harm Sara ... or Charlie, for that matter?"

David slowly shook his head, keeping his gaze fixed on Liam's face. "Believe me, Detective, I have nothing to hide. This was a one-time business meeting that went no deeper than drinks and superficial chitchat. Neither of these men has any reason to take my kids. I'd tell you if the facts were otherwise." His stare was unwavering, not even a blink to break contact.

"Have you any idea who could have taken Charlie or Sara?"

"None whatsoever. I'm as in the dark as you are. All I know is that this has been my worst nightmare, and I'll do anything to get them home."

———

AFTER A FEW MORE QUESTIONS THAT led nowhere, Liam let David leave the station before walking down the corridor and joining Quade on the other side of the two-way mirror, looking into a second interview room. They stood shoulder to shoulder, watching Gilbert where he sat facing Auger.

"McGowan appears adamant he's not the reason his kids are missing," Liam said.

"Auger and I saw most of your exchange." Quade turned her head to look at him. "Good work. You got him on tape denying he knew Gilbert and Razzuto beyond that one introductory meeting."

"If he was lying, he's practiced at it."

"Yes, I found myself buying what he was selling until I remembered, oh yeah. Doubt everybody who meets for drinks with a known pimp and a member of the Razzuto crime family."

They stopped talking and listened to Auger questioning Gilbert, who again denied knowing anything about Meilin's disappearance after the party. As Liam had expected, the interview elicited nothing new about Joanne's death or the disappearances of Sara and Charlie. Auger was still probing forty minutes later, but by the look on his face, even he appeared to realize that continuing was useless. Gilbert was sticking to his story without any attempt to elaborate.

"Well, fancy that. The exact same version as his dinner companion about their meeting in the restaurant." Quade butted Liam's arm with her shoulder. "We're done here. Time for you to head home for some shuteye."

"And you."

"I've got bit of upward briefing to do, but I won't be far behind."

Liam took a deep breath. "I keep thinking time's running out for those kids. We're spinning our wheels and no closer to figuring out what's going on than when we found out Charlie was missing. This is as maddening a case as I've ever been involved in, and that's saying something." He couldn't remember feeling as hopeless at this point in an investigation. They had no leads and nothing on the horizon. A headache had started in his temples as he was interviewing David, and a lightheadedness now made him nauseous.

Quade rested a hand on his forearm and squeezed. "To quote somebody smarter than me, it's always darkest before the dawn. Keep the faith, my friend. Those kids have to be somewhere, and we won't stop looking until we find them."

He considered her words. "You're right. It's not time to throw in the towel yet, to quote another smart person. But it is time to get some supper, followed by uninterrupted sleep. I'll see you in the morning."

"Bright eyed and bushy-tailed, I hope. Give these cases a rest for the evening, Hunter. Let the night crew shoulder the weight for a few hours."

CHAPTER 32

Liam stopped in at Hannah's townhouse on his way home. He hadn't seen the boys in a few weeks and needed a shot of normalcy. Six-year-old Jack and eight-year-old Hugh greeted him at the door and flung themselves into his arms. Spitting images of their late dad but with Hannah's dark hair and rosy cheeks.

"You've been doing some growing since I saw you last," he said, tousling their hair in turn before letting them go.

"You're here in time to read us a bedtime story!" Jack hopped from one foot to the other.

Hannah appeared in the hallway, wiping her hands on a dishtowel. "Upstairs, boys, and into your pajamas. Two stories tonight if you're quick." They scrambled to beat each other to the stairwell and giggled their way to the second floor. Hannah reached Liam as he straightened from pulling off his shoes and gave him a hug. "I can read to them if you're too tired."

"No, I'd like to snuggle in with the boys for a few minutes. Just make sure I don't fall asleep."

He read for half an hour before tucking them in and turning off the lamp. They shared a room, and he could hear their chatter as he trod down the stairs. Hannah was sitting at the kitchen table with a pot of tea and two mugs. She poured him one as he sat down. A thick roast beef sandwich and salad were on the placemat in front of his chair. "You're losing weight," she said. "How many hours today?"

"Fifteen. Thanks for this."

"I'll be glad when your life settles down again. Jack and Hugh keep asking when we're going to have a meal together."

"I wish I knew." He ate and sipped tea and his headache began to lift. "We have another girl missing. The half-sister to the little boy who disappeared nine days ago."

"How old?"

"Seventeen. Her car was found in a parking garage, but nobody's heard from her since yesterday."

"Does the body discovered on the Parkway have anything to do with these disappearances?"

"The dead girl was the roommate of the Asian student who went missing last year. We're not sure if all these cases are linked or not, although we've uncovered a tenuous connection."

"What a tragedy for everyone involved."

She was looking at him with a mixture of compassion, worry, and exasperation. He smiled. "You don't need to fret. I'm staying objective."

"You never manage to, though, do you? These poor victims and their loved ones eat away at you, but you always brush off the toll it takes, as if you're Superman or something. I hate what this job takes out of you, Liam, time and time again."

"What I go through is nothing compared to what the victims endure." He finished his sandwich and tea and stood. "Time to get home to the cat and my bed. Thanks again for all you do for me."

She looked up at him. "When are you going to give that cat a name?"

"How about I leave that task to Jack and Hugh? Tell them to draw a picture with whatever name they choose so I can post it on my fridge."

"They'll like that, but be prepared. You might not like the result."

"I'm curious to see what they come up with."

She walked him to the front door, and he pulled her into a long hug. "I'll spend more time with you and the boys soon, Hannah. This can't go on forever."

"Do what you need to do, my stoic, soft-hearted brother, but remember to pace yourself. That's all I ask."

"I'll see what I can do."

"And come by for Sunday dinner this week. Put us in your daytimer, and don't let anything else cancel out your family. You need a life beyond murder and crime-solving."

THE CAT WAS NOWHERE in sight as he stepped through the front door. He took off his boots and headed down the hallway and into the kitchen. The cat bowls were filled with food and water, and Hannah's efforts at cleaning were evident everywhere. He opened the fridge and saw she'd left him a plate of lasagna under foil, a new loaf of bread, and a tray of brownies. He wasn't the only one who needed to get a life. The time she spent looking after him was time she could be using to form other relationships, to develop a social life that might include a new partner. He wanted that for her. She deserved to be happy again.

He was still too wired to sleep, even though exhaustion filled every square inch of his body. He poured a shot of brandy from a bottle he kept above the stove and stretched out on the couch, pulling an afghan over himself that Hannah had made him last Christmas. He tugged the phone out of his pocket and checked messages, the blue screen the only light in the room.

There was nothing worth answering, and his finger hovered over the last email from Ella Tate. He could update her about tonight's interviews but should do so in person, not in a text or email. No paper trail. He had to remember only to share with her what she needed to know to keep her digging. They were a team with boundaries. He set his phone within reach on the coffee table and took a long draught of brandy before setting the glass next to his phone at the same time as the cat jumped onto his chest, purring like a lawn mower. He rubbed her back, and she tucked her head under his chin.

Three hours later, Liam woke from a dead sleep, and the cat was nowhere to be seen. He dragged himself upstairs in the dark to bed, threw off his clothes, and climbed under the duvet. He was asleep again before his head hit the pillow.

CHAPTER 33

At 2:00 a.m. Ella looked up from the computer screen and rubbed her eyes. She'd managed two hours of sleep on the couch after supper but had woken at midnight with her mind revving. "Where are you, Sara?" she'd asked aloud into the empty living room. To quell her anxiety, she'd spent the past two hours searching online for information about the girl. She wanted to learn as much as she could about Sara's social media and Google presence.

She clicked on Sara's Facebook page, but she'd made it private since they last spoke. *Smart cookie,* Ella thought. She sent a friend request, knowing it was a long shot, because according to Hunter there'd been no activity on Sara's phone since she went missing. Sara also had a Twitter account that she posted to infrequently. Only thirty-nine followers, although she followed four hundred and fifty-five. Ella clicked on every connection, every interaction, trying to find out more about Sara and the people in her life. She found Instagram and TikTok accounts that Sara rarely posted on.

Ella got up, stretched, and began pacing in the cramped space. She stopped as a thought struck her. Perhaps, the key to Sara lay in what wasn't on public display, the things she wasn't showing about herself. In their brief encounters, Ella had found Sara to be intelligent, the expression in her eyes reinforcing the impression that she grasped ideas quickly and found amusement in situations, even if she didn't react. She hid herself while watching the world from the side-lines. She was like a silent voyeur, easy to overlook or underestimate, as her father had.

Sara's behaviour was understandable. A broken home with parents at war with each other, nobody paying attention, a homely appearance by today's beauty standards. The lack of friends and limited interests only reinforced the idea of her low self-esteem. She'd taken a summer job at the DQ. It meant working alone with brief interactions with customers. No chance of forming relationships or being open to ridicule. Ella had no doubt that Sara had been bullied and ostracized by the girls at school. You only had to study the inward slope of her shoulders and her reluctance to make eye contact to know.

Ella resumed pacing. Roddy was the only one of David's children, with the exception of the new baby, who wasn't missing. Was this important? Was Roddy safe? She'd have to speak with Hunter first thing tomorrow and raise her concern. He was likely a step ahead of her, but sometimes details got overlooked. For now, she'd climb into bed and close her eyes and try to sleep. Fatigue had worked its way through her system, making her sluggish. She'd need all her wits about her to chase down the story and maybe help solve Joanne's murder and find the missing children.

———

THE PHONE STARTLED her into consciousness at 8:00 a.m. She fumbled to pick it up and hit *Receive* before leaning against the headboard. "Yeah?"

"I hope I didn't wake you."

"No, I was up," she lied.

"I want a more in-depth article on the latest missing kid. Sara McGowan. Carpenter's working the Parkway murder, so that leaves you." Canard didn't pause long enough for her to answer. "I'd like a story to post by lunchtime. Include some quotes from her family and friends."

"I'll get something to you."

"Good."

The dial tone hummed in her ear, and she tossed the phone onto the bedside table. The water pipes were quiet. Either she was up in time to beat Tony to the shower, or he'd already taken his while she was asleep. The former would mean hot water and the latter a chilly wake-up. She crossed the hall to the bathroom and turned on the taps. It seemed this was her lucky day because she luxuriated in a steamy scrub for an entire ten minutes.

She was happy now that she'd spent so much time researching Sara the night before. It was early in the day to waylay her family for interviews, so she made a cup of instant coffee and began typing the bare bones of a story, combining what she'd learned from Hunter with facts she'd gleaned about Sara from the Internet, including her school and other tidbits of information. The pickings were slim, but she elaborated, working to make Sara into a well-rounded and sympathetic victim.

At nine o'clock, she phoned Claudette McGowan and set up an interview for 10:00 a.m. She was cutting it tight for timing but would finish her story in the car on her laptop afterward. Claudette had only agreed to meet her because Ella convinced her that an article might help bring Sara home. She'd asked that Roddy be around too if possible, and Claudette said in all likelihood he would be because she wasn't letting him out of her sight.

Baby Lena's howls travelled up from the main floor as Ella got ready to leave. She clattered down the stairs twenty minutes later with Lena's wails still pulsing through the wall between the hallway and Adele and Finn's apartment. Ella stopped outside their door and debated whether or not to check in. She could spare a few minutes, and Adele could probably use a word of encouragement. She knocked and waited for Adele to pull the door open. After fifteen seconds, she knocked louder and leaned an ear against the wood to listen. She couldn't hear Adele moving around and decided she must have her hands too full with Lena to answer.

She left the house and got into her car parked in the driveway. The heat wave had broken again for a few hours at least, and the air felt cool in comparison to what they'd been living through most of the last two weeks. The skies were clear, and the sun would heat up the city by lunchtime. With the humidity gone, this was going to be one of Ottawa's perfect midsummer days.

She stopped at the first intersection and peered down Third Avenue, straining to see past the first block. She could have sworn she spotted Adele sauntering toward her, carrying a shopping bag. Surely, she was mistaken. The driver behind her tapped his horn, and she waved a hand over her head as an apology before easing forward.

Disturbed at the idea that Adele had left Lena alone in the apartment, she nearly turned back, but time was getting tight for her appointment with Claudette. She'd need to be very certain of what she saw before confronting Adele because to wrongly accuse her of leaving Lena alone would be the final nail in the coffin that constituted their friendship.

Just one more damn thing to worry about in a week already chock full of problems, she thought as she turned right onto Glebe Avenue.

———

CLAUDETTE LED her into a cluttered living room and invited her to sit in the recliner while she settled on the couch in front of a large picture window. Both pieces of furniture were angled to watch a flat-screen television balanced on a stand. No offer of tea or coffee was forthcoming.

"I know you must be frantic about Sara, and my article will help to get people looking for her." Ella tried to get comfortable in the lumpy chair.

"That's the only reason you're in my house. What do you want to know?"

Ella took out her phone and indicated to Claudette that she'd be taping their conversation. "It will help to ensure I get the details right."

"Fine."

"When did you discover Sara missing?" She needed a quote from Claudette to demonstrate how worried she was for her daughter's safety.

"Sara texted late Sunday night after she locked up at work that she was staying at a friend's overnight. Then I find out she cancelled her shifts for the entire week at the DQ. I knew right off something was wrong. When she didn't come home Monday morning, I called everyone I could think of before I went to the police."

"That must have been a terrible feeling, not knowing where she was." Ella paused to give Claudette some room to answer. Had she triggered Sara's disappearance when she'd visited her at the DQ? This seemed unlikely. Sara hadn't been upset when they'd spoken. Was somebody waiting to waylay her when she left after her shift? This seemed the more likely scenario, and Ella cursed herself for not sticking around to make sure Sara got home safely.

Claudette's voice dropped. "It was one of the worst moments of my life." Her face crumpled for a moment before she regained her composure.

Ella could see that Sara was loved by this woman, and the overwhelming sadness she'd felt for the girl lifted slightly. "What would you like people to know about your daughter?"

"Sara's a good person, would never hurt a fly. She's smart and kind and doesn't complain."

"Does she know what she wants to do after high school?"

Claudette gave a hoarse laugh. "Funnily enough, she talked about joining the police. She likes all those true crime shows on TV and she reads a lot of crime fiction, especially the hard-boiled books. Mickey Spillane, Raymond Chandler — those kinds of stories. Oh yes, and she's a great chess player. She plays online and enters competitions. She's rated twenty-sixth in the country for her age group."

Footsteps clomped down the stairs, and a moment later, Roddy appeared in the doorway. "I thought I heard voices," he said, the light in his eyes fading when he saw Ella. He scowled at her, but not before she saw disappointment cross his features. Ella realized that he'd thought she was Sara.

"I'm sorry about your sister and half-brother." She waited for him to make eye contact. He was a dishevelled teenager, hair uncombed and angry red acne on his cheeks and forehead. His sweatpants and a stained Foo Fighters t-shirt had seen better days.

"Yeah, thanks."

"Tell Ms. Tate about your last conversation with your sister," Claudette said, pointing to the empty spot on the couch next to her. He ignored her and remained standing.

"It was Saturday at supper, I guess. She got called into work and I never really saw her after that."

"Did Sara ever sleep over at a friend's or have any close girlfriends?"

Roddy's eyes darted from his mom to her. "Last week, she came into my room and told me to let Mom know she'd gone to a movie with a friend, if she asked. Mom and Uncle Ivan were drinking in the kitchen."

Claudette looked straight ahead but didn't say anything.

"Did you believe her, Roddy?" Ella asked.

"No. She didn't have any friends except me."

"Where do you think she went?"

Roddy shrugged. "She liked to drive around. She spent a lot of time in her car. I thought she'd come back when Uncle Ivan left."

"Her father bought the car for her last summer," Claudette said in a flat monotone. "He helps with gas, insurance, and maintenance. He got the alimony cut to nothing and child support halved a year ago, so this was an uncharacteristic show of generosity."

"He told me I'd get a car too when I got my licence." Roddy's face lit up.

"And like I said, don't count your chickens. He's been known to change his mind." Claudette looked at Ella. "Sara isn't overly fond of her uncle being here as much as he is. He's taken a few weeks off from his roofing job because the heat makes him ill. He's needed my support this past while."

"Are you working, Claudette?"

"I'm on stress leave." She barked another hoarse laugh. "You could say I need Ivan's support as much as he needs mine. I'm hoping to go back to my government job in September. I'm a computer programmer at Canada Revenue Agency."

"Do you enjoy it?"

"It pays the rent."

"Just not the air conditioning." Roddy pushed himself away from the door jamb where he'd been leaning.

"I told you, Roddy. I don't have that kind of money lying around for something we'd only use occasionally."

"And I told you that the summers are getting hotter. Climate change."

"Don't be smart with me, young man." Claudette glared at him, and he walked out of their sightline into the kitchen. "Being a single parent isn't all it's cracked up to be," she said to Ella.

"David—"

"Has very little to do with his oldest son." She lowered her voice. "I've given up asking him to be more involved. I've been self-absorbed lately, but I love my kids." She looked at Ella's phone. "I think that's enough for your article. Please don't put in that last part about David."

"I won't." Ella shut off the recorder and handed Claudette her business card. "My focus will be on Sara and getting people to look for her. Do you have a recent photo or two that I can include? I'll need them right away. The article's due at noon."

"I'll send some to you as soon as you leave. Check your phone." At the door, Claudette said, "Sara's a private person. She'd hate this attention, you know."

Ella smiled and tried to impart some of the compassion she felt for this family. "You can count on me to look after Sara in my article. I won't let her … or you, down."

CHAPTER 34

Ella had parked on a side street in the shade of an oak with the windows down while she finished typing the article. She sent it to Canard with seconds to spare. His feedback arrived a few minutes later. He said it was a good piece and would be posted within the half hour on *The Capital's* site. It would also make the hard copy edition the following morning if nothing changed in the meantime. She lowered her phone satisfied and thought about lunch. She hadn't eaten breakfast, and her stomach was rumbling.

She turned toward the downtown and drove until she reached Bank Street. The DQ parking lot was nearly empty, and she slid easily into a vacant spot near the back in the shade. The sun was beating down, and the air had warmed considerably since she'd set out in the morning. The afternoon would be another sweatbox. Through the large plate glass window, she could see a man and a teenage girl moving back and forth behind the counter and hoped he was the owner. She entered and placed an order before getting the man's attention. His name was Barry, and he was indeed the owner. He left the girl in charge to join Ella at the table where she'd taken her burger and fries.

"Thanks for talking with me about Sara," Ella said. She clicked *Record* on her phone and laid it on the table between them. "I always tape my conversations to get the facts correct."

"That's all right then. Yeah, I was surprised when Sara emailed in sick for the entire week. She's been my most reliable employee the last two summers. She takes the shifts nobody else wants." Barry was middle-aged, with a receding hairline and expanding belly that pressed against the buttons of his dress shirt. He had a kind face, and Ella warmed to him. Another person in Sara's world who cared about her.

"Did she seem worried about anything? Mention anyone bothering her?"

"God no. I would have taken action if that was the case. I've been clear to all my staff that I won't put up with any harassment from the public. They only have to call me if I'm not on site, or 911 if it's a problem they can't deal with. Sara never came to me with any issues."

"Did Sara ever talk about her life when she wasn't here?"

"I know she lived with her mother and brother and didn't spend much time at her father's. She said her parents weren't on good terms, and her dad was more interested in his new family than his old one. She didn't seem all that broken up about it, though."

"How so?"

"Let me try to remember what she said. It was a few weeks ago. Oh, yeah. 'My dad has a problem with the truth. My mom doesn't realize it yet, but divorce is the best thing that could have happened to her.' I'd say Sara was mature beyond her years."

"Do you know if she had any close friends?"

Barry was quiet for a moment. A greenish vein throbbed in his temple. "I wouldn't know about friends, but three girls from her class came in one day and ordered burgers and ice cream. Sara seemed flustered — well, flustered for Sara. She was a bit clumsy and dropped one of the sundaes and had to start over. They acted snotty toward her, bossing her around. No please or thank you. They spent their time giggling and staring at her from that table over there while they ate. I wanted to tell them to leave but knew Sara wouldn't have appreciated the gesture. Kicking them out would have embarrassed her and made going into school tougher for her than it already was."

"That's typical bullying behaviour. What was her mindset overall?"

"I could get her laughing with corny jokes, so she wasn't depressed." Barry smiled at the memory, but his expression sobered quickly. "She seemed resigned, if that's the right word. Never asked for anything, and like I said, took the lousiest shifts. I encouraged her to speak up for herself, but she always told me she was fine. If something bad's happened to her, I don't know if I'll ever get over it. She doesn't deserve this."

Ella was not certain that laughing at corny jokes meant Sara wasn't depressed, but she kept the thought to herself. She said, "Don't give up hope. I haven't."

"And I pray you're right." He pushed himself up from the table. "Well, if that's all, I'll let you finish your meal in peace. Thanks for dropping in."

"Thanks for the chat."

Her phone rang as she was walking to her car. She stopped and leaned on the trunk as she answered. "Hey Sherry, what's up?"

"I'd like to talk about your meeting with Joanne Freemont, if you have a few minutes."

"I was on my way home. We could meet there."

"Can you confirm the address? Been a while."

"Sure. Two-twenty Percy. I'll be there in ten minutes."

"Perfect. I won't be long behind you."

Ella rounded the car and hopped into the front seat. She glanced at the two large black garbage bins and the line of bushes bordered by a tall fence that circled the back of the lot. A few straggly cedars provided shade. The decomposing stink of rotting food emanating from the bins was strong, the week's heat helping to accelerate the gag factor. She kept the windows up until she reached Bank Street but rolled them down to let in fresh air once she turned toward home.

SHERRY'D BROUGHT a chilled bottle of white wine, and Ella poured them each a glass before joining her on the couch.

"Cheers to us," Sherry said, clinking glasses. She looked around the small, under-furnished living room. "Ever think about getting more chairs … or a carpet? Maybe a couch with springs intact?"

"I don't like to get attached to stuff.

"I would never have guessed. That cop who died left you some money. Might not hurt to spruce up your digs a bit."

"Thanks for the advice, Dear Abby, but I like my digs just the way they are." Ella didn't make an effort to hide her annoyance. "So, what do you want to know about Joanne Freemont?"

Sherry smiled, as if she'd expected Ella's reaction. She took a gulp of wine. "I've made little headway into Joanne's murder. Do you have notes on your meeting with her?"

"You listened to my podcast?"

"I did."

"Well, those are my notes."

"Surely you kept something back?"

"Not really. The unedited tape is with the police, but there's nothing else of interest. She said she went into hiding because of the vitriol on social media. According to her, Meilin had a great time at the party and left before she did."

"Was she lying, do you think?"

"Possibly. Probably, if what Yina Zhao revealed to Tony is accurate. Yina is another Chinese exchange student and Meilin's friend. She said Joanne told her that everybody was lying about that night. We'll never know now unless someone else at the party comes forward."

"What do you believe happened to Meilin?"

"I think someone at the party's involved. My mind leaps to human trafficking, but I have no proof of anything, only this sick, queasy feeling whenever I think of Wes Gilbert."

"He was brought in for questioning, yesterday along with David McGowan."

Ella's head swivelled to look at her. "First I heard of it. Did the police uncover anything?"

"Not as far as I know. The two of them were released an hour or so after they arrived at the station."

She'd have to check with Hunter and find out if either man had revealed new information. Sherry reached for the wine bottle on the floor and topped up their glasses. "Do you think David was screwing Joanne?" she asked as she set the bottle down. "Might explain why he was in tight with Gilbert."

"He appears to be happily married to Ginger." Ella pondered the idea a moment longer. "But he screwed around on his first wife with Ginger, so…"

Sherry nodded. "A cheating rat doesn't change its stripes."

"A mixed metaphor if I've ever heard one, yet

somehow accurate. Wes Gilbert would know, but I doubt he's talking. However, I like a challenge."

"He's a slimy guy, so be careful. If you need backup, I'm available."

"Good to know." Now two people wanted to be her backup, three if you counted Tony. She'd have preferred none but couldn't deny one of them might come in useful at some point.

Sherry drained her glass and made a show of pushing herself off the couch. "Well, I'll say one thing, Ella: your furniture matches your wardrobe. Both are functional but terribly lacking in style and anything approaching beauty," She held up a hand before Ella could answer. "But if you're happy as you are, who am I to judge? There's some who would say — although I'm not one of them for damn sure — that creature comforts are highly overrated."

"I've got all I need, and it's more than a lot of people in this world have."

"God invented caviar, spas, and pedis for a reason, my friend. Too bad he forgot to give you the gene that appreciates them."

CHAPTER 35

David flipped the burgers on the barbecue and Ginger sat in the lawn chair, rocking the baby in her arms while she tried to figure out how to broach the subject of his interview at the police station. He'd been closed off since he got home the evening before. "I don't want to relive it yet," he'd said when she met him at the door. "They were fishing to pin something on me, but Lord knows what exactly."

"They can't seriously believe you had anything to do with Charlie's and Sara's disappearances. You'd never do anything to harm your own children. My God, you're as frantic as I am."

"Of course I wouldn't hurt my kids. I'd lay down my life for both of them in a heartbeat. Whatever the cops were digging for wasn't obvious, something to do with my business. We can talk about it later, if you don't mind. I need time to recover from this afternoon."

She'd slept on her questions overnight and tried bringing up the subject again two hours earlier. "I can't discuss it yet," he'd said. "Maybe after a stiff drink."

Since then, he'd had three stiff drinks before lighting the barbecue. She'd wondered if he was safe to breathe anywhere near an open flame but decided to keep a watchful eye instead of stepping in. He was in a mood she'd rarely, if ever, seen — morose and angry at the same time.

"Richard got away okay?" he asked with his back to her.

"Dad caught a taxi and made his flight in time. He texted when he arrived in Halifax."

David half-turned, holding the flipper in his hand. "And your mother? When is *she* leaving?"

"Five more days, I expect. Mom's no trouble."

David's silence was answer enough. He scooped the burgers off the grill onto a plate. "Time to eat."

"I'll put the baby in her crib for a nap and will be right down."

She took a moment to watch Krista after laying her on the mattress. Her round blue eyes slowly closed, and her rosebud mouth made sucking noises as she drifted off to sleep. "You are so gorgeous," Ginger whispered, settling a light blanket over her legs. "I wish you could see your big brother." She steeled herself to go downstairs. It was draining to keep the conversation going between David and her mother, upsetting whenever he was drinking. Thank goodness her dad was gone and she didn't have to mediate those two as well.

"There you are. Sit. Sit." Her mom jumped up from the table when Ginger entered the kitchen and fussed about preparing her plate.

"You don't have to wait on me," Ginger protested, even as she slid into the seat across from David. "I'm not an invalid."

"Enjoy my pampering for a few more days." Her mom placed the meal in front of Ginger before settling back into her own chair at the head of the table. "So, David, have there been any developments?" She picked up her fork and looked at him. Her mouth was set in a grim line, as if channelling her husband.

David raised his head to stare at Madeleine as he put a forkful of potato salad into his mouth. His expression was combative, and Ginger inwardly cringed. There was no telling what he'd say when alcohol lowered his filter. "You're asking about my trip to the police station. It seems two men I met for a business meeting about looking after their financial portfolios are linked to illegal activities. The police found out about our interaction." He held up a hand. "And before you ask, I'd already decided they weren't my kind of client and turned down my company's financial services."

Ginger leaned forward, both elbows resting on the table. "Could one of them have stolen Charlie?"

"Not likely, babe. We parted on friendly terms

with no promise to do business. I wish there was better news."

"And Sara." She couldn't go on and took a drink of water to compose herself. She set down the glass. "This is the tenth day since Charlie went missing." Odd how quickly hope could turn to despair. She'd been thinking a lot lately about the universe and fate. She'd been instrumental in David leaving his wife and first family, and she thought perhaps Charlie's loss was cosmic payback for her self-centredness. She'd slept with David while overlooking the fact that he was cheating on his wife. He'd been so grateful to her for saving him from his miserable marriage — how many times had he told her that — but she hadn't given a thought to his wife or his other two children. What better way to teach her a lesson than to steal her child?

David was watching her with a quizzical expression. "Are you all right?" he asked, lowering his voice. "Are *we* all right?"

"Of course." She reached across the table and squeezed his hand. "The police are doing all they can to find Charlie and Sara, and we have to roll with the process. If this means answering questions about our associations and relationships, then so be it. Maybe the answers lie somewhere we never considered."

"Or a stranger's behind this," David said. "They haven't excluded that possibility."

"No, they haven't." She let go of his hand and picked up her burger. She wasn't hungry but knew she had to keep up her strength. Her mother had sat silently throughout the exchange. Ginger glanced over at her. She'd been frowning at David but smiled when she noticed Ginger's eyes on her. She picked up her fork and lowered her head rather than comment.

They concentrated on eating without mentioning the police again. David was the first to get up from the table. "I have some work emails to answer, but I shouldn't be long." He kissed Ginger's cheek, and she listened to him walk down the hall and enter his office.

"He's trying," she said to her mother. "He's even delegated a chunk of his work to free up some time."

"Your father and I wonder if you and Krista would like to come to Halifax for a while to take a break from all the stress."

"How would being in another city change anything? Anyway, I need to be here when Charlie comes home."

"You could catch a flight back to Ottawa within a few hours. I hate to think of you alone in this house without any support."

"I'm fine, Mother. David gives me all the support I need."

"If you say so." Her mom stood and started gathering the plates but paused before walking over to the counter. "Our offer is open-ended, Ginger. You can change your mind at any time, and we'll have your old room ready. We'd love to have you. And that's the last I'll say on the matter."

CHAPTER 36

Streaks of orange and pink blushed the morning sky as Sara trudged up Third Avenue to Percy Street. She'd stayed concealed by the bushes behind the DQ until an hour ago, when she finally judged it safe to leave her hiding place. She was tired of being on the run and was starting to believe she might have overreacted to the man in the car. In fact, she'd been about to come out from the bushes and go through the back exit into the DQ to talk to Barry when that reporter had shown up yesterday afternoon. Sara had decided to wait until she left and stayed hidden behind the garbage bins. Overhearing Ella give somebody her address had seemed too good to pass up — a sign. Afterward, when she went for a walk by the river to stay hidden and kill time, Sara recalled Ella telling her she lived across the bridge in the Glebe 'hood, a half hour walk at most. Ella had invited her to get a haircut from her downstairs neighbour, so it wasn't like she was precious about her privacy.

Sara had spent the last three days staying out of sight. Her phone had died soon after she sent the video, and she was foolishly without the charger, so she couldn't even check the news. She passed the nights inside the DQ after Mandy locked up following her shift. Luckily, Sara had the key and knew the code for the security system that bypassed the monitoring service. Even more fortunate for her, Barry hadn't fixed the broken security camera on the front door. The DQ was easy enough to get into, but she didn't want to spend any more sleeps on the floor in the storeroom. Last night was the worst. She'd only managed a few hours, listening to all the noises and jerking awake with her heart pounding in panic three or four times. Outdoors felt safer somehow, and this morning she'd slipped out of the DQ through the back door well before first light and waited for morning to arrive in the safety of the bushes.

In the middle of the night, staying hidden had seemed crazy. Beyond crazy. Then she thought about the man following her — and the fear. She'd remembered more about that evening in November when he'd entered the same hotel as her dad. He'd shaken hands with the third man in the restaurant video, and they'd walked into the hotel together. The online news had reported that the Chinese girl's roommate had brought her to a party in that hotel on the same night. The roommate who was putting herself through school as an escort. The two men from the restaurant and her dad must have been at the same party and had to know what happened to the missing Chinese student. Her dad … she wasn't sure and didn't want to believe him capable of anything so evil. And yet — why else was this guy following her?

She reached the corner and turned south, looking at house numbers as she walked. Ella's house was third in from Third Avenue. *A bit of synchronicity there*, she thought. The house was three storeys, red brick with a peaked gable roof. The second floor had a screened-in balcony. The front yard was small, with a few bushes and a tree that was as tall as the top floor. She kept going past the house to the end of the street, checking behind her at regular intervals.

She began to relax and started back toward Ella's place, not sure if she lived in the entire house or if there were apartments. The front door opened as she reached the intersection at Fourth Avenue. A tall, slender man in a Hawaiian shirt, white denim shorts, and sandals stepped outside carrying a little wiener dog. The man wore dark sunglasses, even though the sun was barely up, and his bright orange hair was wet and combed back from his forehead. If this was Ella's boyfriend, he dressed the exact opposite of her. Sara watched as he set the dog on the sidewalk and they meandered down the street, the dog sniffing and peeing on whatever bush the leash would let it reach.

She'd asked for a dog after her dad moved out. Her mom had said definitely not. She wasn't having a dirty animal messing up the house. "And I'm for sure not replacing the dirty dog that left with a new one."

Sara had been checking the Humane Society website every morning to see the available dogs looking for homes but stopped after that. She'd have to wait until she moved out and got her own place.

It was time to make a decision. She'd be stupid to think that she could keep on hiding, especially since she hadn't been threatened or harmed. Who would even believe that a man had followed her from the DQ into the parking lot at Billings Bridge and driven up and down the rows looking for her? Even she was having trouble accepting it actually happened as time passed and the terror faded.

The guy with the dog was walking toward her and was almost at the corner. She picked up her pace and cut him off before he started up the sidewalk. He stopped, and she thought he was movie star good-looking when he smiled. The dog jumped up on her legs, and she bent to pet its head. "Luvy likes you. Are you looking for somebody?" he asked. His gaze was curious but friendly.

"I'm here to see Ella Tate. Does she live in this house?"

His eyes focused on her face and widened. "Sara? Sara McGowan? Oh my God, child, we've been so worried about you." He grabbed her around the shoulders and clasped her to him in a hug. The dog barked and jumped on the back of her legs. He let her go and stepped away. "Where have you been, girl? The media has been running your photo and the cops are searching for you."

"I was — I wanted to — it's just—"

He patted her cheek. "Don't tell me now. Let's get you inside and cleaned up. Are you hungry? Ella will be over-the-moon happy to know you're safe, but she's still in bed, so come to my place and I'll get her up in a bit. She's not been sleeping well, and this is the only time she gets in a few straight hours. We can call your mom. I hear she's worried sick."

His words tumbled over each other, and she took a moment to absorb everything he was saying. "I don't want to call anybody until I talk to Ella." She was on the verge of tears. The fear and lack of sleep had caught up to her. "Please, she was … helping me with something, and I need to speak with her before anybody finds out where I am." *Otherwise, what was the point of the last three days?*

He shrugged. "What could another half hour hurt?" He scooped up the dog and led her into the house. They skirted around a baby carriage and climbed to the second floor. His apartment was sunny and smelled of cinnamon and brown sugar. "You're a lucky girl. I just finished baking carrot muffins and cinnamon swirls. Would you like to clean up before you eat or after?" His eyes were kind, and she started to relax.

"After."

She looked around on her way to the kitchen. The living room was filled with bright, modern furniture and art. There was a large dining room table where the man told her to sit.

"My name's Tony, by the way," he said as he set a mug in front of her. "Coffee?"

"I'd love a cup of coffee. Thank you."

"Can I scramble up some eggs?"

She nodded, and he went back into the kitchen. It wasn't long before she was digging into a plate of eggs and bacon and fresh baking. Tony sat watching her eat while drinking a cup of coffee. He typed on his phone and told her he'd asked Ella to come down as soon as she got up. "Feeling any better?" he asked.

"A bit. Do you mind if I clean up now?"

"I'll get you a towel and washcloth. You can take a shower and wash your hair." He turned in the doorway. "I could give your hair a trim while we wait for Ella. I'm a hairdresser."

"That's okay."

"Nonsense. I'd love to. It'll make you feel better, and it'll make me happy."

The bathroom was all slate and stone with a gigantic showerhead and jets that came at her from every angle. She thought about Tony as she washed her hair. He was probably an outsider, like her. She'd bet he'd been bullied growing up. Kids were cruel if you were different.

He had her sit in a chair and tied a tea towel around her neck after she got dressed. He talked the entire time he combed and clipped. She didn't need to say a word. Finally, he mussed up her hair with one hand as he spritzed. He styled with a brush while he used a blow dryer. "You look fabulous," he said after he shut it off. "One would hardly know you've been on the lam for three days." She took the hand mirror from him and moved her head from side to side.

"I've never had a haircut like this."

"You can come back anytime. I like to keep my friends coiffed."

She froze at the sound of a door opening.

"In here, Ella!" Tony called, whipping the tea towel off from around her neck and shaking the hair onto the floor. "Time to get things moving," he whispered to Sara.

Ella stopped in the doorway as she took in the scene. A look of pure delight crossed Ella's face as she caught sight of her. "You're here! I can't believe it." One moment Ella was standing in the doorway and the next she'd crossed the floor and grabbed Sara into her arms. "Oh, thank God." Ella pulled back, the joy gone from her face, replaced with a curious frown. "So where have you been? Why didn't you let anybody know where you were?"

"That man in the video I sent to you. Do you know who he is?"

Ella studied her. "His name is Denis Razzuto. Does that mean anything to you?"

Sara shook her head.

"He lives in Trois-Rivières, Quebec, and he's part of a mob family that controls much of the Eastern Townships. Now, tell me why finding out his name is so important."

"He's been following me."

Ella's gaze sharpened. She looked at Tony. "Did anybody see her come inside?"

"I wasn't paying attention."

"Nobody followed me. I made triple sure." Sara

tried to keep the wobble out of her voice. "That night when you came to talk to me, he was waiting outside the DQ, so I went south on Bank instead of driving past him. He must have seen me, because he was behind me going over the bridge. I went to the Billings Bridge mall and parked in the lot. He was going up and down the rows looking for me, but I snuck out with my lights off. My phone died soon after I sent that video to you, and I didn't have a charger."

"You left your car in the Rideau Centre's underground parking." Ella seemed to be confirming rather than asking.

"I thought it would be safe there. It seemed better to be on foot so I could hide places."

"The police have it. It's safe." Ella looked at the floor and back at Sara. "Tony gave you a haircut. Looks great."

"Thanks. He let me take a shower, too, and fed me breakfast."

Ella smiled at Tony before she pulled a chair out from the dining room table and told Sara to sit. She took the seat facing her. "Why do you believe Razzuto was following you?"

"Because I filmed him, and he knew." She chewed on her bottom lip. "I'd seen him before."

"Where?"

"He was in front of the Blue Sapphire Hotel. I ... followed my dad there. That other man in my video was there too. They met up outside and went in together."

"The other man is Wes Gilbert. He's a businessman and runs an escort agency. Do you know what day you saw them at the hotel?"

"Yes. It was the same day that Chinese student went missing in November. I didn't wait for them to come outside, but when I asked Ginger later, she told me that Dad was out late that night. She said he was wining and dining some clients." Sara had decided while on the run that she'd tell the truth if it helped to bring Charlie home. "My dad is a compulsive liar, but I can't believe he'd hurt anybody. He'd never do anything to Charlie or let someone else hurt him either. He must have gotten drawn in with these people without knowing what he was getting into." She met Ella's stare without backing down. She knew it looked bad for her dad, but she wasn't going to throw him to the wolves.

"I know that wasn't easy to share."

"All I want is for Charlie and that missing student to come home." She wrapped her arms around herself. "I'd also like that man to stop following me. I was scared to go home in case he hurt my mom or my brother."

"We're going to make certain that he stops bothering you." Ella typed on her phone. She looked up. "Detective Hunter is on his way. Should we contact your mom to let her know you're safe? She's been worried out of her mind."

"She has?" Sara had convinced herself that she'd bought some time cancelling her shifts and telling her mom that she was at a girlfriend's, that nobody would be all that concerned anyhow. "I'll try her now if I can borrow your phone, Tony."

"I think that's a good idea."

"The world is unfolding as it should," Tony said after Sara went into the living room to make the call. "I'll just put on a fresh pot of coffee, shall I? It looks like we've got company coming."

"I could sure use another cup. I'm still trying to absorb that she's safe. Thank goodness she didn't decide to stay hidden any longer."

"The girl's a bit sheepish about her decision to go incognito, from what I can tell. She's far from stupid, so she must have been terrified to behave as she did."

"And that worries me. Let's hope Hunter figures out why she was being followed — and how to keep her and the rest of her family safe."

CHAPTER 37

Liam spent an hour speaking with Sara McGowan and then drove her home, where her mother and Roddy greeted them in the driveway. He left the family with their arms around each other's waists, walking back toward the house and made it to the office in time to debrief Quade before joining Auger downstairs. They stood shoulder to shoulder, watching Denis Razzuto and his lawyer through the two-way mirror. "Our mafia guy's looking a tad on edge," Auger said. "How much longer do you want to leave him stewing?"

"Let's give him ten more minutes." Liam needed the time to swallow the disgust he felt for this man before questioning him. He'd have to keep professionally distant, even if what he wanted to do was drag him outside and pummel him black and blue until he spoke the truth.

"You believe everything David McGowan's daughter said?"

Liam glanced at Auger. "Why, you don't?"

"She spent three days hiding out because she imagined this man was following her. Sounds kind of, I don't know," Auger made a spinning motion with his index finger near his temple, "whoo whoo. From what's been said about her, she could be vying for some of the attention her missing little half-brother's been getting. Wouldn't be the first time an overlooked kid made up stuff to feel self-important."

"Sara's credible. She was honestly terrified and doesn't strike me as somebody who wants the limelight."

"If you say so. I'm just having trouble picturing Razzuto caring about a nothing-looking teenage girl over a harmless video." Auger turned away from him. "I'll meet you in the hall in ten."

Auger grabbed the knob at the same time as Quade was pushing the door open from the other side. He stumbled back a step, and Quade strode past him. "Stay for a minute," she said over her shoulder to Auger on her way to Liam. He watched Auger hesitate before he let the door swing shut and walked toward them.

"David McGowan's in interview room number two. We haven't tracked down Gilbert yet." Quade paused, including them both in her gaze. "How do you want to proceed?"

"I believe if we get David to crack, we could use whatever he tells us to get to Razzuto," Liam said.

"So, let Razzuto and his high-priced lawyer sit for

another hour while you break down David?" Quade grinned. "I like it."

"If that's what it takes to get one of them talking. What do you think, Auger?" Liam didn't honestly care but was being careful not to give Auger a reason to feel excluded.

"McGowan's in this up to his neck. Get him to talk and all will fall into place."

"Good enough." Liam exchanged glances with Quade. She gave him a half-smile.

"Talk to David alone," she said to Liam. "He's used to being interviewed by only you. If we add Auger, he might get defensive. We'll watch from behind the glass."

"I'll try to convince him that telling me what happened that night in the hotel is in his best interest."

"Shouldn't be too tough," Auger said.

Liam left them and entered the interview room. He settled across the table from David McGowan, who had not yet requested a lawyer. He didn't appear unduly concerned about being asked to visit the station again. He set down his coffee cup and looked at Liam. "I can't believe Sara was hiding out all this time, worrying us sick. What was she thinking? Well, she wasn't thinking, obviously. Is that why you asked me here? To pick her up?"

"Not exactly. She's at home with her mother and Roddy." Liam paused for effect. "I want to talk to you about that video I showed you the other day, the one your daughter filmed of you meeting Denis Razzuto and Wes Gilbert in the Elgin Street restaurant. It's obvious Razzuto saw Sara recording on her phone as she walked past." Liam set the phone on the table in front of David and hit *Play* so David could watch the video again. He studied David's expression as Razzuto's eyes tracked Sara walking by the window with her phone held at chest level recording their encounter. You could make out her reflection in the glass on the video.

"Jesus." David rubbed his forehead with his fingertips. "I still can't believe she did that."

The clip ended, and Liam slid the phone back toward himself. "How did Razzuto find out she was your daughter if you only met the one time?"

David's jaw tightened. "No idea."

"It wasn't the first time, though, was it?"

"What do you mean?"

"The two of you attended a party hosted by Wes Gilbert at the Blue Sapphire Hotel on the evening of November 30 of last year. The same party where the now-dead Joanne Freemont and her roommate, the missing Meilin Hanon, were on the guest list." Liam held up a hand. "And before you deny it, know that we have eyewitness evidence."

"Not bloody Sara again." He gave a weak grin.

Liam stayed silent and watched the wheels turning behind David's steely blue eyes. This was a man for whom lying was second nature, if what Sara had said about him was true. He must have been caught out before and would have tried-and-true methods to extricate himself from tricky jams. Liam didn't have to wait long for him to come up with one.

"All right, I was at the hotel, but only to schmooze and pick up new clients. I wasn't friends with Gilbert but had met him the week before at a networking event. He invited me to the party."

"Did you know he ran an escort agency?"

"Of course not. I would never have gone if I had. I met Razzuto for the first time that night at the hotel, but we said about ten words to each other. Gilbert introduced us in passing."

"So the meeting in the restaurant—"

"Entirely set up by Gilbert, who knew I was working to build my business. As I said, it was the reason I went to the party in the first place. Gilbert was attempting to link me up with Razzuto, but I left the restaurant uneasy and found out later about his family connections. I didn't agree to take him on as a client."

"You must have wondered about him after the party."

"Boys will be boys." He flashed another grin. "Yeah, I didn't like what I saw there either. I felt I had to meet him and Gilbert, though, so they wouldn't think I was a threat, you know, to talk about what happened that night at the party. It was my chance to make sure they weren't involved in the Chinese girl's disappearance."

"And were you convinced?"

"It never felt like the right moment to bring it up."

"Where was the networking event when you first met Gilbert?"

"I'd have to check my calendar, but I can't remember if I have the date marked. Britt was always getting on my case for forgetting to tell her about my meetings."

Liam let a few beats pass. "What happened at that party, David?"

David looked down, pursed his lips, and removed all trace of emotion from his face. "Nothing I want to talk about."

"We have Razzuto in the other interview room, waiting for me. He's not a man who'll sacrifice himself for you or anybody else. This is your chance to beat him to the punch by telling me what happened, especially…"

"Especially what?"

"If he's blackmailing you by taking Charlie."

David straightened. "You think he has my boy? No way. If he had, why wouldn't he have already told me to keep me in…" He shook his head, perhaps realizing he was about to implicate himself.

"He was following Sara. He scared her enough that she went into hiding. Why would he do that?"

"It appears my daughter was spending her free time tracking me around the city. God knows why, but I assure you that I intend to find out. Razzuto's a private man. He must have been trying to figure out what she was up to, filming us together."

"Did you tell him you have a teenage daughter?"

David stared at Liam for a moment before replying. "If Razzuto was interested in having me as his financial advisor, he would have researched every corner of my life. Men like him have to know all the skeletons when it comes to people they're dealing with. He'd have loved to find something in my life to give him leverage over me."

"Which brings us back to Charlie."

David flopped back in his chair and rubbed his mouth with the knuckles of one hand while he thought. "You can't tell him any of this came from me."

"I can try to keep your name out of it." *Maybe.*

"If he took Charlie..." David closed his eyes and sighed. "I have no choice, I guess. He gave that Chinese student a drug of some sort in her drink. Seemed to loosen her up, because she was dancing and laughing and having a great time."

"Razzuto slipped a drug into Meilin Hanon's drink the night of the party?"

"Yeah. She was this shy, wallflower kind of girl when she first entered the room with Joanne. Attractive, though, with killer black eyes and a sweet body. You couldn't help but notice her. Razzuto started chatting her up almost immediately. He got her a drink, and she began to relax the emptier her glass got."

"So you don't know for certain that he drugged her?"

"Well, I didn't see him put anything in her drink, but her behaviour spoke for itself. He topped up her wine a few times over the next few hours, and she sure acted like she was on something."

"Where were you when this was going on?"

"Mingling. Drumming up clients. I talked to Joanne Freemont, mainly about financial investments, when our paths crossed. At first she appeared pleased Meilin was having a good time, but she started to get concerned toward the end."

"How many people were at this party?"

"Forty-five, maybe sixty people. Gilbert had rented the penthouse suite, and there was lots of room to circulate."

"You said Joanne was concerned toward the end. What do you mean by that?"

"She asked me if we should intervene. Said Meilin was in over her head. By that time, Razzuto was moving in for the big finale, if you get my drift."

"No, tell me."

"Kissing her and running his hands all over her body. They started slow waltzing, and it looked as if he was holding her up. You gotta picture it, though. The lights were dim, the music was loud, and lots of people were dancing and fooling around. It was kind of chaotic. Joanne said she was going to get Meilin out of there."

"Did Joanne go speak with her?"

"Before she could, all hell broke loose. Meilin started having a bad reaction to the drugs or the alcohol, maybe both. She began convulsing and flopping around, foaming at the mouth. Razzuto let go of her, and she fell onto the floor. Hit her head hard. I heard the crack from where I was standing."

"You saw all this?"

"I was watching the two of them, so yeah, I saw it all happen. Someone turned up the lights, and the music stopped. People were stunned, standing around with their hands over their mouths. At that point, she'd stopped convulsing and had gone completely still. Gilbert yelled at people to clear out, and nobody argued, Joanne included."

"And you?"

"I left too. You have to understand how shocked we all were. Nobody knew what to do, so we followed Gilbert's instructions and went home."

"Was Meilin Hanon dead when you left?"

"I looked back at her before I stepped out of the suite, and she hadn't moved, but I can't one hundred percent confirm that she'd died. You'll have to ask Razzuto and Gilbert what happened to her after that."

"Did nobody try to revive her?"

"Again, I couldn't say. We were hustled out of there."

"You spoke with Razzuto and Gilbert after the party because you met at the restaurant. What did they tell you?"

"Actually, I spoke with Gilbert the next day. I was worried about the girl. It was before she was reported missing. He told me that she rested for a bit, started feeling better, and walked out on her own steam. Like

I said, nobody mentioned her disappearance when we were at the restaurant."

"Yet she never made it back to the dorm."

"Gilbert said something must have happened to her on the way home. He said she had insisted on walking and told him she was fine. I wanted to believe him."

"But you didn't."

"Not after her disappearance was all over the media. However, I had no proof that she'd died at the party or even that she'd been drugged. Razzuto isn't someone you feel comfortable challenging."

"The others at the party—"

David laughed. "Nobody was about to say they'd been there, and if they did, they knew better than to point a finger at Razzuto. Everyone in the room had something to lose. Ginger won't be happy to know I was with these people either, if I'm honest, even if I was working to bring in new clients for the business. I'm fortunate she sees the big picture."

"Are Razzuto and Gilbert blackmailing you to keep quiet, David? Have they threatened to harm Charlie?"

"No. Absolutely not. I'd never let that happen."

"Do you know who killed Joanne Freemont?"

"No, I've told you everything. I'm sorry I didn't speak sooner, but you can understand my reluctance. Can I go home now?"

Liam stood and looked down at him. "I'll be back once I speak with Razzuto. Until then, sit tight. We'll see if he tells the same story."

CHAPTER 38

Liam took a brief break before joining Auger to tackle Razzuto. He checked his phone. Ella had left a text with a request to call her. He stepped into the hall and hit her number on his speed dial.

"Ella. What's up?"

"I'm on my way to David McGowan's office to see if any of the staff have more to say about the company's business associations. I'm hoping they'll feel more comfortable speaking with me second time around."

"Good idea. Fill me in on what you find out. We've got David McGowan and Denis Razzuto here and are trying to find out more about that night at the hotel when Meilin went missing. We should meet up later."

She was silent, and he could hear the faint sound of traffic in the background. She raised her voice, and he pictured her speaking into her hands-free phone.

"Okay, I'll check in and we can arrange to meet when you're available."

He wanted to say more, but she'd logged off and he was listening to dead air. Visiting David's office should be safe enough. There'd be people around. *At least she checked in*, he thought. *One step in the right direction.*

—————

RAZZUTO and his lawyer glared at Liam and Auger when they entered and took their seats. After Auger went through the preliminaries, Razzuto's lawyer voiced a protest about being kept waiting so long.

"So noted," Auger said before pulling out his notepad. He took his time asking the first question while Razzuto and his lawyer stared bullets at him. "Why were you following Sara McGowan in your car after her evening shift at the DQ four nights ago?"

"I wasn't."

"You waited for her outside her workplace, the Dairy Queen on Bank Street, and after her shift ended at eleven o'clock, followed her into Billings Bridge parking lot. You drove up and down the rows of cars searching for her." Auger lifted his eyes to Razzuto and let the silence stretch.

"I might have been downtown, but I wasn't following her."

"We can check your phone and get your exact locations that night."

Razzuto's lawyer whispered in his ear. Razzuto straightened. "I was curious about her and why she was videotaping me with her father at a restaurant on Elgin a few evenings earlier. Let's say I'm sensitive to that kind of thing."

"How did you find out her identity?"

"Her father and I had business dealings. She looked familiar, and I remembered seeing her in a family photo when I researched David. I might add that I always find out as much as I can about a new business associate, so McGowan was no different. I put two and two together when she walked past the window filming us. Thought maybe her father put her up to it, to be honest."

"This wasn't the first time you met David McGowan?"

A flicker of wariness entered Razzuto's eyes. "We'd encountered each other before." He leaned sideways and said something to his lawyer.

"How many times before?"

"Once."

"On November 30th at the Blue Sapphire Hotel at a party hosted by Wes Gilbert." Auger waited for confirmation, and Razzuto nodded.

"Please say that for the tape."

"Yes, we were at the same party November 30th. Wes Gilbert introduced us that evening."

"Did you interact with Meilin Hanon, the Chinese exchange student?"

"The missing girl? Yeah, we danced a bit."

"I understand she became ill."

"Shit, yeah. She had an epileptic fit or something. Began convulsing and fell on the floor. It was frightening. Grotesque."

"Had she taken any drugs?"

"Who knows? Anyhow, Wes cleared out the party, and she recovered enough to walk home. She said she was fine and the fresh air would do her good."

Auger checked his notes and let the pause lengthen. He raised his eyes to stare at Razzuto. "Did you put a drug in her drink without her knowledge?"

Razzuto bared his teeth in what could be taken as a grin. "No."

Auger waited until the silence stretched into the uncomfortable range. "You'll swear to that under oath?"

"Of course."

"Meilin was living on Carleton University campus, which had to be a two-hour walk. It was the end of November and the weather was five degrees and drizzling overnight. She'd fallen and hit her head. Are you adamant that she walked home alone, and nobody offered her a cab or a ride?"

"She was with Wes Gilbert when I left, so…"

"You're saying Gilbert was the one responsible for getting her home."

"I am."

"Did you meet Joanne Freemont?"

"In passing. David McGowan was glued to her side all night."

"Were they—"

"More than acquaintances? John and client? Most likely, from what I saw."

Liam sensed the interview slipping away. It had dissolved into Razzuto's word against David's. They'd each given enough of the truth to absolve themselves while implicating the other. They'd both wedged Wes Gilbert into the middle of whatever had gone on. Liam tapped Auger on the arm. "I'll be outside." He needed to track down Gilbert and hope his version of events shed light on the truth, see which one of them was the most eager to throw the other two under the bus.

He joined Quade in the hallway. "Are you going to keep David McGowan or send him home?" she asked.

"We can't hold either of them. They back up each other's stories to a certain extent, implausible as they are. We need to speak with Gilbert before one of them finds him first."

"Why don't I have another go at McGowan while you track down Gilbert? It'll give you some time and maybe I can rattle David."

"Good plan."

Quade motioned toward the two interview rooms. "It's appearing likely that Meilin died that night and they got rid of her body. Do you believe Razzuto killed Joanne as well to keep her from talking?"

"It fits, but we have no proof of either. We need to find Gilbert and get him to spill his guts."

"What a mess. Charlie's abduction has to fit in somewhere as a warning to David." Quade started walking toward the stairs. "I'm taking a coffee break before I tackle him a second time. Send a text when you've located Gilbert."

"You got it."

CHAPTER 39

The office was quiet as Ella stepped into the reception area. There were no ringing phones or clicking of computer keys. Vanessa wasn't at her desk, and Ella debated whether she should walk down the hallway to the row of offices or stay where she was and see if someone showed up. As she stood considering the options, Vanessa sauntered into view from the direction of the lunchroom, carrying a mug of steaming tea. Her expression warmed when she recognized Ella standing in the middle of the waiting area.

"I didn't expect you back. David's out of the office for the day."

"I'm only here to confirm some new information. Is Olivia Jones-Briggs available for a quick chat?"

"She should be. I'll check." Vanessa settled in at her desk and placed a phone call. Lowering the landline receiver, she pointed down the hallway. "Olivia is free now. Her office is last on the left."

"Thanks." Ella passed a line of partially open or shut doors until she reached Olivia's office. Olivia met and ushered her inside, inviting her to sit in the chair across from her desk. She had one of the larger offices, on the opposite side of the hall from David's corner suite. Ella had peeked in before tapping on the door.

"Thanks for seeing me. It's quiet here today."

Olivia took her seat and smiled. "David's at a meeting off-site, and about half our staff are working from home. The modern workplace in action."

"You've been left to hold down the fort."

"Wouldn't be the first time." She leaned back in the chair. "So how can I help you today?" She was dressed more casually than on their first encounter in a white tank top under a gauzy red blouse. Navy capris completed her outfit. The blonde highlights in her freshly streaked hair shimmered under the fluorescent lighting. Expertly applied makeup accentuated her eyes. Ella thought this was a woman who would fight aging with every tool at her disposal. So far, she appeared to be winning. Olivia held up a hand glittering in delicate gold, diamond, and ruby rings. Silver bracelets slid down her arm. "Before we start, has there been any progress finding Charlie? I hate asking David because it's so hard on him. From what I can see, he's barely keeping himself together."

"No, Charlie's whereabouts remain a mystery. You do know that David is being questioned by the police at the moment?"

"I know. We're pretending he's at an off-site meeting. No need to upset the rest of the staff. Pulling him in to the station seems like salt in an open wound, in my opinion. To have a child missing and then be suspected of harming him — I can't think of anything more obscene or painful."

"It's not a good position to be in, certainly." Ella had decided before sitting down that Olivia was a woman to be dealt with head-on. She ran the office and had seemed no-nonsense on their last encounter. "Britt left on good terms, I understand."

"She did."

"Was there any office gossip about her and David?"

Olivia's steady gaze broke away. She looked down at the red, polished nails on her right hand and sighed. "David and Britt had a flirty kind of relationship when not in meetings. I wouldn't know if they took it further offsite." She looked at Ella again. "How could that be important?"

"It might not be, but his behaviour could be key to figuring out why Charlie was taken."

"*If* he was taken. From what I understand, it's still possible he's in the river."

"The police think it unlikely but not impossible, yes." Time to try a new tack. "Does your company do business with either Denis Razzuto or Wes Gilbert?"

Olivia thought for a moment before shaking her head. "No, David had background done on both and said neither was a good risk." She paused and her brow furrowed. "There is something odd, though."

"What would that be?"

"I shouldn't … I feel bad about saying anything. Oh, just forget it."

"Whatever you tell me is in confidence. Is it something the police could uncover anyway?"

"Probably." She tilted her head from side to side as she weighed options. "Oh, what the hell… We aren't working with Wes Gilbert, but his girlfriend Jocelyn Langdon is a client. David deals with her file exclusively, so I can't tell you much, only that she hired David to manage her money about two years ago."

"So Gilbert's a risk, but his girlfriend isn't? Is that normal business practice?"

"Let's say I was surprised when I found out." Her expression turned worried. "I want you to swear that you didn't hear this from me."

"Rest assured I never reveal my source. Is there any way to have a look at Jocelyn Langdon's file — off the record?"

"The police will need to get a warrant, I'm afraid. Not even I have access."

"Would Vanessa?"

"Good question. She's David's gatekeeper, so maybe." Olivia sat forward and rested her elbows on the desk. "I haven't told him yet, but I've had another job offer that pays more with decent benefits. I'm thinking it's time for me to try something new."

"I can understand wanting a change."

"Still, it feels like I'm leaving David and the company at a vulnerable time. I've got my resignation letter finalized. I only have to hit *Send*." She took a deep breath and let it out slowly. "I've been waffling, but I have to think about my career and future. I've taken a back seat for much too long. It is hard to let go, however."

"Change is always tough, but it's the only way to grow."

"Thank you for being so understanding. We're still women clawing and scratching our way in a man's world. We have to learn to make decisions with our heads and not our hearts."

"It's the only way."

Ella left her and went in search of Vanessa, who'd returned to the lunchroom and was standing with her back resting against the counter, holding a butter knife. There were dark circles under her eyes, and the energy she'd shown at their first meeting was not in evidence. "Are you on your way?" Vanessa asked as a bagel popped out of the toaster behind her.

"Yes, but I wanted to ask you about one of David's clients, Jocelyn Langdon. What can you tell me about her?"

Vanessa looked puzzled for a moment. "Jocelyn Langdon? I've seen the name on David's calendar, but she's never been to the office. He has a few files that I don't work on, and she's one of them."

Interesting. "Do you have access to her file or any of the others?"

"Not as of yet. David said he prefers to look after these clients all on his own and keeps the files in his home office. Of course he works on them with our accountant at some point before year-end. I have enough to do without them, so…" She spun around and opened a container of cream cheese, dipping in the knife. "I'm not complaining."

"Great." Ella turned to leave but stopped. "Are you feeling okay, Vanessa? You seem tired."

"I am a bit. Taking care of the office with David not around is a lot of work." She dropped her voice. "Everyone is so unhappy, and it's hard staying positive, you know? Most of the advisors are working from home so they don't have to be here. Something has to change soon or they'll all be looking for other firms."

Ella nodded but didn't mention Olivia's imminent departure. It wasn't her news to tell, and Vanessa would find out soon enough. "Well, take care. I hope things will get back to normal soon."

"You and me both."

———

ELLA SENT HUNTER a text asking him to call her before she drove home to the Glebe. He still hadn't made contact by the time she pulled into the driveway. The day was hot, but clouds were scudding across the sky, propelled by a westerly wind that promised a cold front and thunderstorm late afternoon. Those without air conditioning, like her, would welcome the relief.

She spotted Adele rounding the corner onto Percy

and walking toward the house. She looked summery cool in a billowy white dress and oversized sunglasses. Lena was nowhere in sight. Adele hadn't spotted her sitting in the car, and Ella took a moment to ponder how best to approach her. She eased out of the front seat before Adele started up the walkway, carrying a tote bag from one of the clothing stores on Bank Street. She jumped when she heard the car door slam and saw Ella walking across the lawn toward her.

"Hi, Adele. It's a great day, isn't it? Where's Lena?"

"Oh, Ella, what a surprise. Lena's good." Adele pasted on a smile that could double for a grimace.

Ella pointed at Adele's bag. "You've been shopping."

"There was a sale, and this dress I'd been eying was forty percent off. Couldn't resist."

Adele led the way up the steps and opened the main door. She half-turned. "Well, see you later." She'd crossed to her apartment by the time Ella entered the foyer and was inside with the door shut seconds later. Ella followed and stood with her fist upraised to knock, wondering if this was the right moment to confront Adele. The idea of Lena being left alone gave her no option. She rapped sharply on the wood and waited.

Adele took her time answering. She opened the door halfway and stood blocking entry. Her voice had an impatient edge. "Did you need something, Ella?"

Ella looked past her down the hallway. Lena's bedroom door was closed. Nobody else appeared to be in the apartment. "Adele, I know you've been going out and leaving Lena alone. I'd be happy to come sit with her when you need to run errands or meet a friend for an hour or two. Anytime I'm around, you can ask me."

Adele stared, her eyes defiant. "You're dying to tell Finn, aren't you? This is what you've been waiting for. A chance to make me look bad."

"No, I'm not planning on telling him. I'm only concerned about Lena and you. I know having a baby changes your life and can be a difficult adjustment. I want to help out."

"I don't need your help or your pity. Find someone else to make your charity case."

"I really mean it about babysitting if you want to go out. I'd love to spend time with Lena."

"And I'd rather you were nowhere near her."

Adele moved back and slammed the door. Ella stood still, shaken by her response. Had she overstepped? Made things worse? She thought about knocking again and apologizing but had no stomach for a second round. She climbed the stairs, running Adele's angry words through her head, not certain she'd handled the outburst correctly. Should she tell Finn about Lena being left alone or stay out of it? Both choices had a downside. Adele appeared to be struggling, but Lena should not be left alone, even for an hour. Ella wasn't a kid person, but even she knew the basics of keeping a baby alive.

Her phone pinged as she was reaching into her pocket for the apartment key. Hunter was parking and would be at the front door in five minutes. Adele and the dilemma would have to wait, and Ella was momentarily thankful for this bit of reprieve. She opened the door and hurried inside to use the washroom before she had to head back downstairs to let him in.

CHAPTER 40

"You've bought a new chair." Liam stood in the doorway to Ella's living room. "Special occasion?"

"The only part I had in its purchase was when Tony talked me into writing the cheque. He picked it out and had it delivered yesterday. I haven't sat in the thing yet, but Tony and Luvy have already claimed the spot."

"You're kidding. I can't believe you wouldn't want to give it a test run. Well, I for one enjoy a new leather smell." He crossed the room and made a show of settling in. "Passes the comfort test. Tony has taste."

"You sound like Tony … talking about Tony." The kettle whistled, and she left to make instant coffees. He listened to her rummaging around in the kitchen while he surveyed her compact apartment. Computer equipment took up all the space on a heavy oak desk positioned next to the open window that was high up on the wall. The second-hand couch where he normally sat was the only other furniture. A faded Bart Simpson poster on the wall in front of the computer passed for artwork. His eyes returned to the window and the urn sitting on the wide ledge. Ella's brother Danny, murdered almost a year ago.

She entered with two coffees and tracked the direction of his gaze but didn't comment as she handed him a mug. Turning the floor fan in his direction, she took her seat at the desk, swivelling the chair around to face him. "Sharing time," she said before taking a sip.

He set his cup on the floor and pulled out a notebook and pen. "By all means, ladies first."

"If you insist." She put her coffee on the desk as she organized her thoughts. "I got some interesting information from Olivia Jones-Briggs, the woman who runs David's office while he's off wining and dining clientele. She's outlasted all the other employees but told me that she's handing in her notice today. Seems she's had enough. She let slip that David McGowan has some clients that he keeps separate from his business, Gilbert's girlfriend being one. He keeps the files at home, and nobody has access."

"The girlfriend's name?"

"Jocelyn Langdon. I researched her on my phone. She's a server at a downtown bar and models lingerie on the side. Twenty-four years old and has a separate address from Gilbert. They might be living together, though."

"It would be hard to believe she makes enough to warrant VIP attention from David McGowan. Gilbert could be laundering money through her. I can't imagine he's declaring all the earnings made through his escort agency."

"I agree. Razzuto has to be in on the action, if he's not funding it. The three of them appear to have a relationship that Razzuto doesn't want filmed. He must be awfully jumpy to have followed Sara around the other night. He might have been trying to scare her, or he could have wanted to find out what she was up to — maybe he thought David recruited her to record them together. In any case, I'm starting to believe there's a lot at stake, whatever they're involved in."

Liam nodded. "Razzuto mentioned that he thought David was setting him up by having his daughter film them. I believe having you talk unofficially to David's employees has paid off. Good work. I'm thinking a warrant to seize his files is in order, but I'll have to drop by his business and get this intel firsthand from Olivia Jones-Briggs."

Ella smiled. "Or I can forward the recordings of my conversations to you now."

He returned her smile. "You're ahead of the game. Send them along, but I'll make the trip after I leave here. It's time I met the staff in person. I've spoken to Olivia and Vanessa Lo on the phone but kept my distance so David didn't get jumpy. You can bet he's nervous now after being grilled at the station today. Once I've visited his office, I'll head back to HQ and get the warrant going. Another long day."

"So, since this is a share session, what have you got for me?"

He swallowed his conscience and told her what he knew. "Razzuto strongly suggested that David and Joanne were more than platonic. He said they spent all evening glued to each other at the hotel party in November. Both David and Razzuto reported that Razzuto was dancing with Meilin Hanon when she had a seizure, fell, and hit her head hard. David suggested Razzuto drugged her and planned to have sex with her later, but Razzuto denied this."

"Of course he did."

"Yeah. David claimed he left when she was lying on the floor unconscious … or dead. Apparently, Gilbert cleared the room after telling everyone the party was over. David said the next day he contacted Gilbert because he was worried about Meilin, and Gilbert told him that she'd regained consciousness after everyone left, felt better, and insisted on walking back to residence alone. Razzuto backed up the key parts of David's version when we interviewed him today at the station."

"I'm not buying it. Are you?"

"Nope, but we need evidence to disprove their two accounts. My best guess is that she died at the party and they disposed of her body. I've spent the last few hours trying to find Wes Gilbert but without success. We need him to turn on Razzuto."

Ella rubbed her forehead. A shadow crossed her face. "I so wanted her to be alive."

"I know. Me too."

They stared at each other, and Liam had the strangest urge to cross the room and give her a hug.

Instead, he took a drink of coffee until the feeling passed. "Any one of them could have killed Joanne Freemont. David would not have wanted his wife to find out if they were indeed having an affair. Gilbert and Razzuto had lots to hide as well."

"Joanne was a convincing liar when I interviewed her here in my apartment, I have to say. She never mentioned David and told me Meilin was alive and happy when she last saw her."

"She must have realized that telling the truth would put her in grave danger. The irony is that by staying silent, she was in even more danger." He drank the last of his coffee before standing and striding the few steps toward the hall. He stopped in the doorway and looked back at her, still sitting at the desk. "I'll check in later. Thanks again. We make a good team."

He left without giving her the opportunity to reply, uncertain why he'd linked the two of them in such a way, already regretting that he had. It was one thing to steer her inquiries now and then — look out for her interests — but linking them together as equals was a slip he had to be careful never to make again.

CHAPTER 41

L iam waited for Vanessa Lo to click through a file on her computer screen. Her forehead furrowed in concentration as she searched for information that wasn't there. After a furious round of typing, her fingers stilled and she looked up at him, puzzled. "Olivia didn't enter her new address into the system. She moved recently, I think she said into a townhouse. I could call David?"

"Worth a try." He'd arrived at the office too late to witness the shouting match between David and Olivia, but Vanessa was still shaken enough to tell him all about their argument, which ended with Olivia packing up her personal possessions and stomping out. David left soon after without telling Vanessa where he was going. She had confirmed the existence of the handful of clients David kept separate in his home files, so speaking with Olivia wasn't as urgent, but he'd still like to have a chat with her.

Vanessa picked up the desk phone and hit a

button, examining the chipped nail polish on one hand while she waited. She lowered the receiver. "He's not picking up. I can send Olivia's new address to you once I get it if you like."

Liam nodded and recited his own phone number, which she wrote on a notepad. He added, "A text is fine. You said she lived in a downtown apartment up until a few weeks ago?"

"Yes. She was in the same building as my friend Britt on Nepean. Olivia was living in this downtown high rise and told Britt about a vacancy. Britt's the reason I heard about this job too. She recommended me when she handed in her notice to David." She frowned as if the referral might not have been a good thing. "I could give her a call. She probably knows where Olivia moved to."

"I need to leave, but why don't you keep trying to locate her address and text it to me once you have it." The hour was getting late, and he still had to return to HQ. Thorburn was working on the warrant to confiscate David's home files and computer, but he'd have to check it over before she filed the paperwork with a justice of the peace. Weariness had threatened to overtake him a couple of times already today, and he'd resorted to drinking three strong cups of coffee to keep going. It wouldn't have taken much for him to have fallen asleep in Ella's new chair and let the world slip away for a few hours.

He took the Queensway and reached the police station as the clock struck five. Quade spotted him walking through the door and waved for him to come into her office. He took a quick detour past Thorburn's desk. She stopped typing.

"I'm almost done the warrant."

"I shouldn't be long. We can go over it after I meet with Quade."

"I'll be here."

Quade had poured them each a dram of whiskey from the bottle she kept on hand. She slid the glass across the desk as he sat down. "Looks like you could use this."

"It has been a long few weeks." He drained the glass in one go and let the warmth spread into his chest. "I hear you didn't keep David long after I left. How about Razzuto?"

"We have nothing to hold either of them … yet, and we've had no luck finding Wes Gilbert. I'd be worried about his safety if he were a nicer person."

"His girlfriend around?"

"Yup, but she's not talking except to say that he'll show up. She appears to be living in his condo. When do you plan to collect David's financial records?"

"Thorburn's got the warrant started, so we'll get it to a justice of the peace shortly."

"Good, let them know this is part of a murder investigation to speed up approval, but wait until morning to execute it. The gatekeepers will not approve the overtime for this one." Quade threw back her drink and set the empty glass next to his on the desk. "Let's talk about your new partner."

He took a second to realize she was referring to Rosie. "No issues."

"Except that you're using her like an admin assistant. She needs to get out of the office, help you with the investigation and interviews."

"I was thinking of her as placeholder until you return."

"I know, but she's not, and I might not be." Quade's expression softened. "Show her the ropes, Hunter. You're the best one to do it."

"Do you trust her?"

"The way she looks at Auger is giving me reason to hope. I'd say he's not her favourite person."

Liam stood. "Then consider Rosie Thorburn my detective in training."

"I knew you'd rise to it."

He left the office and noticed that nearly everyone had gone home. Thorburn was alone in her corner, and he walked over to her desk. She handed him the warrant and watched as he sat in the visitor chair and went through the pages. "Good work," he said finally, looking up at her. "Tomorrow morning I'll take an officer over to David McGowan's to collect this stuff. Would you be able to drop by Sara McGowan's house to see how she's doing and find out if she remembers anything that could help with the case?"

Rosie's eyes brightened. "I'd be happy to."

"Great." He felt a stab of guilt at the pleasure on her face, knowing he'd been thoughtless to assume she was content doing desk work. "We can grab some lunch afterward and catch up, maybe brainstorm next steps."

"I'll leave my lunch hour open. So, if you don't need anything else—"

"Head home, and thanks for staying late to finish this up. Tomorrow should be another long day, but I feel like we're starting to make some headway on the cases. Good work on this warrant, but it's time you got out in the field."

"I'll do whatever is necessary." She beamed at him before ducking her head and turning away to pick up her bag from the floor.

CHAPTER 42

The police dropped Sara's car off mid afternoon about the time she was feeling hemmed in by her mother's hovering and fussing. She told her mom that she was zipping over to see Ginger and left before she could put up an argument. Her dad had sent two text messages to call him, so she drove to his office first hoping he was there, since the other option was his house at the other end of the city, and she didn't really want to visit Ginger and the new baby today. That had been only an excuse to get out of the house.

She parked in the back lot of her dad's office building, relieved to see his car in its reserved spot near the side door. Should she wait for him to come out or go inside and risk annoying him, because really, she had nothing pressing to share? He wanted to talk to her, but did he want to see her? Those were two different things entirely. There was also the matter of the video — which he had to know about — and she could only imagine his displeasure with her for following him around the city. While she sat chewing on a fingernail, deciding what to do, the side door slammed open, and the blonde woman from her dad's office whose name she had forgotten strode outside carrying a cardboard box. She opened the trunk of a black Audi and thrust the box inside before getting into the driver's seat. She sat for a moment with both hands on the steering wheel, head bowed and shoulders shaking.

Sara sat very still, realizing the woman would not want anyone seeing her so unguarded and upset. As Sara watched, the woman turned sideways and appeared to be rummaging in her handbag. A moment later, she dabbed at her eyes with a tissue before putting on sunglasses. Her car engine started and the Audi began backing out of the spot. Sara waited until it pulled out of the lot before turning on her own car and following a distance behind. She hadn't really needed to speak to her dad, and finding out what was up with Olivia — she remembered her name all of a sudden — seemed much more entertaining. She had time to kill, and there was nothing more exciting than tailing a mark and staying out of sight. The surge of adrenaline reminded her of how much she loved the thrill of the chase. P.I. Sara McGowan in training. This was when she felt most alive. The time when she forgot how completely shit-awful her life was.

———

SARA JUST MADE it home in time for dinner, as she'd promised her mom. Uncle Ivan was sitting at the head of the table, beer bottle halfway to his lips, when she entered the kitchen. She dropped onto her seat at the same time as Roddy slumped into the one across from her. He raised his head high enough to glance at their uncle before rolling his eyes at Sara. She pursed her lips tightly to keep from reacting.

"Well, isn't this nice? All of us together," her mom said as she crossed the kitchen and set down a plate of sliced roast chicken and a bowl of potatoes. She'd already put bowls of stuffing, green beans, and dinner rolls in the centre of the table.

"A special meal to celebrate having Sara home safe and sound," she said, sitting at the end of the table directly across from Uncle Ivan. "I thought we could all watch a movie later while we eat pie and ice cream. I got a nice apple one from the grocery store."

"You should go into hiding more often," Roddy said to Sara, picking up the plate of chicken.

"Roddy." Her mother raised her voice and slammed the end of her fork on the table, but Sara grinned.

"It's okay, Mom. I know he's kidding."

"But do you really?" Roddy said before stabbing a potato from the bowl. "A week without no-name spaghetti sauce and fish sticks in exchange for a few days on the run?" He pretended to weigh each option with his hands.

"Yeah, I get it," their mother said. "No need to get rude. Things will be better around here. I phoned work and told them I'll be going back start of next month."

"Are you feeling up to it, Mom?" Sara had seen her mother at her worst and hadn't noticed much improvement since the spring.

"We need the money, even if your brother won a few hundred dollars playing video games." She smiled at his bowed head. "Roddy has donated it to the family finances, and we should have air conditioning installed early next week. I called and set it up this morning."

"Really?" Sara's eyes darted between her mom and Roddy, who had just shovelled a heaping forkful of stuffing into his mouth. He shrugged and swallowed.

"Trophy's coming next month. I beat the nine others who made it into the final."

"There's a future in gaming." Uncle Ivan waved his knife in Roddy's direction. "Always knew you'd go far, son."

"Then you're the only one." Roddy smiled to temper his self-deprecating sarcasm.

"I have to leave as soon as I finish eating." Uncle Ivan looked across the table at their mom. "Things to do."

"When are you getting a job, Uncle Ivan?"

Sara shook her head at her brother. He's asked the question innocently enough, but she knew he was being a dick.

Uncle Ivan's voice remained jovial. "Who says I'm not actively employed?"

"Uh, Revenue Canada. Our grocery bill." Roddy stood and picked up his plate. "Chicken dinners don't come free. I'll finish eating in my room, Mom. I'm working on a computer program and will also skip the movie."

"Roddy—" Their mom began but stopped herself and shook her head at his disappearing back. "At least he sat with us for a few minutes. So Sara, what are your plans for tonight?"

"I'm watching TV with you. We have the second season of *Bridgerton* waiting for us."

"And so we do." Her mom smiled at her before picking up her beer bottle and taking a swig. "More potatoes, Ivan?" She slid the bowl toward him, and the rest of the meal passed in a pleasant silence.

———

SARA TURNED off the television and placed a blanket over her mother, who was snoring softly next to her on the couch. She'd fallen asleep during the extravagant ball scene and hadn't woken again. Sara climbed upstairs and saw the light on in the space under Roddy's door. She knocked, and he called for her to enter. He was typing on his computer but closed the page as she stepped closer. He turned around to face her.

"You had Mom worried," he said. "Was some guy really after you?"

She sat on the edge of his bed. "I thought so at the time. Now, I'm not so sure."

"Where were you the last three nights?"

"I slept at the DQ and kept out of sight during the day. Wasn't that hard. You got any idea if Mom and Uncle Ivan are up to something?"

"Like what?"

Kidnapping Charlie, she thought, but said instead, "They're barely ever here and seem ... evasive."

"I'm hardly here either. Do you suspect me of doing something bad too?"

"No, have you?"

He shook his head, but a bright red spread upward from his neckline. "Unless whacking off is a crime." He laughed.

"God. You can be disgusting." She stood. "See you in the morning then."

He called her name when she reached the door. She stopped with her hand on the knob and half-turned. "What is it, Rod?"

He hesitated before waving her away. His voice barely rose above a mumble. "Nothing. Just nice hair-cut. I'm glad you're home."

"That's not nothing." She smiled and stepped into the hall, pulling the door closed behind her. Sometimes he wasn't the pain he pretended to be, and these were the moments when she loved him the best.

CHAPTER 43

Rosie woke early and slipped out of bed without waking Brad. He'd worked the overnight shift and wouldn't be up before noon, giving her time to meditate, linger over a cup of tea, and get ready for work without interruption. She liked when he was on nights.

She wasn't certain the exact moment when she'd started imagining her life without him, but the idea was coming more frequently, and she wasn't sure what she should do about it. They'd been together since high school, with the exception of a few "breaks" and leaving him would be difficult, but the restlessness she'd been feeling was getting harder to ignore.

This morning she cut her meditation short and showered quickly before settling with tea and toast in front of her laptop. She closed her eyes and said a silent prayer before opening her messages. Only two from Auger's private account. Was he losing interest at last?

She opened the first and enlarged the photo with forced detachment. He was getting creative with the camera, she'd give him that. The angle made his penis look dangerously huge. She saved the picture in the file she'd created and opened his second message. Three words: *You want it.*

"No, no I don't," she said under her breath and closed the laptop. She sipped her tea and thought over options. Reporting him was the bravest course of action, but he'd been far from stupid executing his campaign of sexual intimidation. The phone number he used to send her messages was untraceable. He'd never sent a photo or message that gave away his identity, even though she'd seen his genitals from every conceivable angle. He'd been careful in the office too when others were around. He'd wait until the two of them were alone to sidle up next to her and lay a hand on her shoulder or run his fingers down her arm and whisper something crude into her ear. Her mistake had been letting him get away with touching her the first time.

The tightness in her chest eased as she stood and stretched, thinking about her only out-of-office assignment since she started in Major Crimes. It was a follow-up visit, but it was a start. Perhaps Liam Hunter would take her seriously and give her a chance. He'd be the first since she completed police training and got a job in Auger's unit nearly a year ago. It had been a hard pill to swallow when she found out why Auger had picked her over the other candidates. The man knew a victim when he saw one.

A noise and she spun around. Brad was standing in the doorway in his pajama bottoms, scratching his chest and yawning. "What are you doing up?" she asked.

"Had to pee and was checking to see if you'd left. On your way?"

"Yeah, I'm interviewing someone and was waiting until eight thirty to get on the road. How was your shift?"

"Typical of nights. Three overdoses and a heart attack. We managed to stabilize all four before getting them to emergency."

There was a time they would have crossed the space to hug and kiss before parting for the day. She couldn't pinpoint when their ardour for each other had faded. Even sex had dropped off to once every few weeks. Maybe her restlessness was tied to his waning interest.

He grinned. "Well, have a good one, supper will be ready when you get home."

"Oh that's right. You're on days off." She blew a kiss before he turned to leave, already preparing for the drive ahead, plotting her route to the east end. Like everything else in her life, she'd compartmentalize their relationship until she couldn't ignore the problems any longer. Even then, it would take a miracle to make her push back or make a change.

————

ELLA WALKED QUIETLY DOWN the stairs and stood on the bottom step, listening for sounds of a baby crying. She startled when the apartment door opened, but it was too late to scoot across the foyer to exit by the front door. Finn smiled when he saw her, and she relaxed. *Not Adele.*

"Off to work?" he asked.

"I am. I'm surprised you aren't at the gym."

"I've hired someone to help out a couple of mornings a week. Adele and I had a talk, and she wanted to start her yoga classes again. I'm going to pick up some coffees and bagels and will be right back so she can head out."

"That's great." Relief flooded through her. She wouldn't have to say anything to him about Adele leaving Lena alone.

He took a step into the hall. "Say, have they found that little boy yet? I haven't read much in the news about him lately. It's been what, two weeks?"

"About that. No sign of him yet."

"How devastating for his parents. It would kill me to lose Lena, and I don't say that lightly."

"It's been hard on his parents. His mom is really struggling." She pulled out her car keys. "I have to get going. Do you want a lift to Bank Street?"

"No, I'm looking forward to the walk. Catch you later?"

"Later."

She thought about Finn as she started the car and drove toward the east end. She wanted him to be happy but couldn't shake her unease over Adele's behaviour. It was one thing for Adele to dislike her for no reason — that she could deal with — but quite another for her to leave the baby unattended. Perhaps she'd confessed her morning outings to Finn, and he'd realized she was struggling. It would be good to think so. She wanted so badly to believe that Adele's yoga classes were all she needed to become a good mother. It was only fair to be patient and give her time to adjust, much as Ella's gut told her to confide in Finn. Adele was a teacher and worked with kids, but being responsible for your own child, twenty-four-seven, had to take a mental shift. Ella remembered Finn telling her before Lena was born that Adele worried about being a crappy mother and didn't think she could do it. They'd both believed she'd feel better about everything once she held her baby. Maybe it wasn't that simple.

She took the Queensway and traffic was moving well. She began to relax and enjoy the drive. Twenty minutes later, she turned onto Sara's street. A green car she didn't recognize was in the driveway, so she parked across from the house and strolled up the sidewalk, all the while surveying the yard and windows for anything out of the ordinary. She rang the doorbell and heard footsteps before the door jerked open.

"They're in the living room." Roddy was wearing headphones, and his voice was louder than normal as he spoke over whatever music was blasting into his ears.

Ella saluted and trailed after him down the hallway. He kept going into the kitchen, and she paused in the entrance to the living room. Sara saw her first and motioned her to enter. She sat facing a young woman Ella couldn't place although she looked vaguely familiar. She was attractive — early thirties, auburn hair tied back, wide hazel eyes — and wore a conservative navy pantsuit, the jacket buttoned at the waist over a white shirt. The room was hot, and beads of sweat glistened on her forehead. She looked uncomfortable, sitting forward on the edge of the couch.

"Sorry to intrude, but Roddy said to come in."

"Are you here to see Sara?" The woman fiddled with the page of a notebook in her lap, her gaze meeting Ella's.

"I'm Ella Tate, Sara's friend and a contract reporter. Sara came to my apartment yesterday for help. And you would be…?"

The woman's eyes registered recognition when she heard Ella's name. "Oh, right, sorry. I'm Rosie Thorburn, working with Detective Liam Hunter in Homicide. That is, I'm his partner, well, sort of partner until they assign someone else. I'm checking to see if Sara remembered anything more about the man following her. Detective Hunter sent me to have another chat."

"Does this mean Julie Quade has the staff sergeant job?"

"For now."

"You can sit, Ella," Sara said, pointing to the empty chair next to her. "You know everything that's going on anyway."

"If it's okay?" Ella looked at Thorburn.

"Sure, why not? I was asking Sara if she remembered anything more about the man," Thorburn checked her notepad, "about Razzuto and the times she saw him."

Sara worked her bottom lip but didn't speak. Ella and Thorburn exchanged glances. Ella pulled her chair closer to Sara and hunched over, elbows on her knees. "Why were you following your dad those nights he met Razzuto in the hotel and the restaurant, Sara? Was it something you did regularly? Because it would be an odd coincidence if the only times you followed him were the ones when he met Razzuto."

Sara flushed and grimaced. "It isn't as creepy as it sounds, but yeah, I was following him and Ginger. I'm not sure why except that it felt like a game, you know, keeping out of sight like a P.I. or something." She chewed on a fingernail. "I didn't have much else to do."

Ella thought how best to phrase her next question. Sara might retreat if she felt her father was in jeopardy. Thorburn sat quietly, letting Ella control the conversation. "Do you remember if your dad met with anyone else whom you believed suspicious or … unusual?"

"Is he in trouble?"

"No, but maybe he met someone who had a motive to take Charlie. That's the only reason we care about the people he dealt with. Anything you remember could help."

Thorburn opened her mouth to say something but

stopped when Ella held up a hand. Ella shot her an apologetic glance, and Thorburn shrugged. They waited to let Sara think through whatever it was she was reluctant to tell them.

Sara looked at the floor and sighed. "My dad bores easily when it comes to family life. If Ginger thought she was saving him from a loveless marriage and ungrateful teenagers, she was duped. Dad only left Mom for her because she was pregnant, probably why he hasn't moved on yet since Ginger got knocked up again." Sara raised her eyes to Ella's. "I followed Dad several times to an apartment last fall where he was sleeping with his new secretary."

"Britt Flambert?"

"Yeah. She's young, pretty and adoring." Sara shook her head. "Mom is Dad's equal intellectually, but she's lost the other three qualities he admires. He forgets that she took a government job to keep them afloat while he went to university. The deal was for her to get a degree after he started working, but I came along and she shelved all her dreams of becoming an engineer. She's younger than Dad and was pretty in those days. I have photos…" Sara sighed and shifted positions. Ella waited a moment.

"Did you actually see your dad with Britt?"

"No, but I know she lives in the apartment building he liked to visit on Nepean. He stopped going there, though, when Ginger got pregnant again. Britt also left his company suddenly, so it adds up. If not her, then who else?"

"Do you think he wanted to make a go of his marriage to Ginger?" Thorburn asked.

Sara smiled. "That would have been a nice fantasy, but no. He started seeing someone else a month after he broke it off with Britt."

"Who?" Ella suspected and Sara confirmed her guess.

"That university student who died this week, Joanne Freemont. He didn't seem to care if anybody saw them together either. I watched them meet up in the ByWard Market and other places downtown. If I didn't know him better, I'd say my dad had real feelings for her. If Ginger had found out what my dad was up to — well, maybe she wouldn't be surprised because he's cheating on her like he cheated on our family. I wonder if Ginger knew in her gut he was being unfaithful and chose to ignore all the signs, or maybe she hoped he'd get over the latest fling. But what I do know is that nobody reacts well to being discarded. She signed a prenup and probably regrets that now, even though she'll get half the house. She'll have to fight for everything else. Just ask my mom. My bulldog of a step-grandpa is another loose cannon who never liked my dad." Sara's gaze focused in on Ella, and she visibly flinched, clamping her mouth shut as if she hadn't realized she was speaking her thoughts aloud. She slumped back in the chair.

Thorburn's eyes widened as they met Ella's. She seemed to be having a hard time believing either what Sara was telling them or the fact she had stated her father's business so dispassionately. Ella wasn't surprised, though. Sara was a smart girl who'd learned to cope with an egocentric, philandering father and a bitter, self-destructive mother. Ella identified with Sara on more levels than she was comfortable admitting.

"I'm sorry, Sara," Ella said. "None of this can be easy for you."

"My dad's not a killer." Sara sounded exhausted, but her voice gained in strength as she straightened and looked Ella in the eye. "He's a lot of things, but I know in my heart he could never kill anybody. Whoever took Charlie to get to him knew what they were doing. Dad isn't the greatest father by a long shot, but he loves us in his own limited way. Stealing Charlie was the best way to hurt him, if that's what somebody set out to do."

CHAPTER 44

Liam waited impatiently in the coolness of the office air conditioning for the justice of the peace to sign off on the warrant. He'd lined up a forensics technician and a uniformed officer to go with him for the search. Detective Pope in the Fraud Division was on standby. Liam glanced at the clock. Nearly 10:00 a.m., and the morning was slipping away. He was about to go buy a coffee when his cell rang.

"Show time," he said, lowering his phone as Quade stopped in front of his desk.

She pumped her fist in the air and said, "Justice Peterson comes through again. This is going to make your David McGowan an awfully nervous man."

"Only if he has something to hide. Any word on Wes Gilbert?"

"Surveillance reported in twenty minutes ago. No sign of him, but his girlfriend hasn't left his condo yet today."

"Is that unusual?"

Quade nodded. "She normally goes to the gym for 10:00 a.m. and meets a friend afterward for coffee. This is the first morning she's missed since we started watching the place. I'll keep you in the loop if anything changes."

"I'll keep you informed as well. Thorburn's gone to visit Sara and will try to get more information out of her. I'm convinced she knows more about her father's business than she's revealed."

"Can you blame her? He might be a weasel, but he's still her dad."

"Let's hope he hasn't had a hand in his son's disappearance." The idea of his possible involvement saddened Liam.

Quade rubbed her forehead. "Now that would be an egregious, heinous, despicable bit of nastiness if he has. I pray to the god of common decency that he's not involved."

"We need to be prepared for anything."

"Unfortunately, yes. Well, round up your team and good luck. It feels like we're closing in on the reason Charlie was taken, and maybe this will lead us to him."

"*If* he was taken. We haven't ruled out the river." He'd learned the hard way not to draw conclusions without evidence, although he didn't blame her for wanting a good outcome. Hope was all they had to go on until they uncovered the truth, good or bad.

———

GINGER HELD the baby in her arms as she stood in front of the window and scanned the street. David was in his downstairs office, and her mother had taken her car to the grocery store. She'd been reluctant to admit to them both that she'd all but given up on seeing Charlie again. The spark of hope she'd been keeping alive had died, replaced by a paralyzing sense of dread. She found herself waiting and watching for the hammer to drop, afraid to let Krista out of her sight.

She and David had found each other in the predawn darkness after she'd fed the baby and returned to bed. It was too early yet in her healing after the birth to make love, but they'd gotten creative and he'd held her afterward with her head on his chest, staring into the darkness while she listened to the strong beat of his heart. A wave of sadness rushed through her with searing force, and she'd focused on the light shining through a crack in the curtains while fighting back tears. *It's Charlie,* she thought. *He's not coming back to me.*

She'd slept fitfully after that and awoken sweaty and exhausted. David was already up. She found him in the rocking chair in Krista's room, holding her against his shoulder and rubbing her back. She stood in the doorway watching him in this unguarded moment. He was humming a lullaby and kissed the top of the baby's head before he spotted her. She stepped closer.

"I was trying to keep her occupied so you could

sleep in." He smiled up at her as he passed Krista into her arms. "I'll go put on the coffee while you feed her."

"Deal."

Breakfast had been subdued. Her mom didn't join them, saying that she was getting dressed and then making a run to the grocery store to stock up on some items so Ginger would be set for a while. David scrolled through his phone while wolfing down eggs and toast before excusing himself and disappearing into his office down the hall from the kitchen. After he'd gone, Ginger moved her nearly full plate aside and tried to solve a crossword puzzle on her laptop, eventually giving up, unable to concentrate on the clues. Krista's cries as she was cleaning up the dishes proved to be the distraction she needed.

She climbed the stairs and changed the baby's diaper and then sat in the rocking chair to feed her. Once Krista stopped suckling on her breast and her eyes closed, Ginger stood and moved in front of the bedroom window, patting Krista's back in slow, soothing circles. She was about to turn away to put Krista into her crib when two cars pulled into their driveway and parked one behind the other. A horrible premonition filled her when she recognized Detective Hunter getting out of the first car. Would so many police come to tell them Charlie had been found alive?

She called to David before laying Krista on the mattress and was still yelling his name as she hurried downstairs to the front door to let the police inside. Detective Hunter stood on a step above the other two officers. He gave her a quick smile that disappeared as he held up a piece of paper. "We have a warrant to take David's work files and computers. Is he home?"

She stared. "What are you talking about?"

"I have a warrant to take your husband's work files."

"I don't understand." Her mind scrambled. "Has this got something to do with Charlie? Is this why he was taken?"

"We can't draw any conclusions until we have a look at David's clients and accounts." He seemed to relent as he studied her. "Finding a motive to help locate Charlie is always top of mind."

"Shouldn't you be at his office then?" She was honestly confused. David worked from home, but everything business-related was kept in the east end. She let out a groan as she looked past Detective Hunter and the men gathered behind him. Her car had appeared on the road at the bottom of the driveway, and her mother was straining to see the house as she backed up to park on the shoulder. Ginger opened the door wider and stepped aside. "Come in, then, and get what you need. David's working in his office off the kitchen." *Let them do what they have to and get out.*

"We shouldn't be too long," Detective Hunter assured her on his way past. "I'm sorry."

David met them in the hallway, and Ginger went outside to help her mother with the groceries. She needed a few minutes to pull herself together. The police wouldn't have shown up with a warrant unless they had proof of something. Was David involved in a shady business deal that got their son kidnapped? She tried not to let her mind go there.

"What's happening now?" Her mother handed her a bag from the trunk and reached in for two more.

"The police are here for David's business records. I have no idea why."

"Has this got something to do with Charlie?"

"How could it?" The anger in her voice was for David, but it was enough to make her mother go quiet as they walked up the driveway and climbed the front steps. They took the bags to the kitchen, and her mother put the cold items into the fridge while Ginger unpacked the canned goods. She could hear the rise and fall of David's and Detective Hunter's voices in his office, but she couldn't make out what they were saying.

"I'll be in my room," her mother said. "Call me if you need anything. I can watch Krista if you have to go out."

"Thanks, Mom."

Her mother stopped and turned before leaving the kitchen. "I'm booking my flight for tomorrow. Your dad called and could use my company. Seems he's struggling with the stove and the dishwasher." She smiled. "He's a dinosaur, but he tries."

Ginger felt a sinking in her chest. "That's fine

then, Mom. I'll drive you to the airport, and thanks again for all you've done."

"I just wish we'd be here when Charlie comes home." She hesitated. "Your room is always available if you need to get away for a bit."

"I know."

After the sound of her mom's footsteps disappeared up the stairs, Ginger followed her and checked on Krista, still sleeping in her crib. She lingered for a moment, watching her beautiful child who slept so innocently without a worry in the world, before returning downstairs to wait on the couch in the living room. Detective Hunter and another officer climbed the stairs with David, and she heard them go down the hall to the den where he worked when he wasn't in his downstairs office. Another officer carted David's computer from the back of the house through the front door. He returned again to take out a box of files. It didn't take long for the two working upstairs to descend with David's laptop and more files. David trailed after them and joined her in the living room. His face was mottled red with anger.

"I have no idea why this is happening. They appear to be under the delusional belief that my business has been operating illegally."

"Well, that's simply crazy. I can't believe they're doing this when Charlie is missing. Why can't they put their energies into finding him?" She was close to tears again. "Why can't they leave us alone?"

"I'll go downtown with them and try to sort this out. Will you be okay?"

"Mom is here, so yes. Call me as soon as you know anything."

"I will." He pulled her up from the couch and hugged her hard. "Try not to worry. I'll be home as soon as I can. This is nothing but a big misunderstanding."

CHAPTER 45

"Well, I was *not* expecting a log of her father's after hours' activities," Thorburn said, flipping through the notebook that Sara had thrust into her hands as they were leaving her house. "Do you think he had any idea she was following him?"

"I'd say no. Unfortunately, he doesn't even seem to see her when she's standing right in front of him." Ella didn't know which emotion was winning out, the sadness or the anger.

"She's documented the night he went to the hotel when Meilin went missing and the night David met Razzuto and Gilbert at the restaurant on Elgin." Thorburn looked up. "Is this weird that she followed him around and kept notes or what?"

Ella considered the question seriously. "A psychologist would have a good answer for why Sara behaved as she did. I'm only making an uneducated guess, but to me, this speaks to a lonely girl who can't let go of her father, even though he has no time for her. Can I have a look?"

"Sure." Thorburn passed over the notebook. They were standing behind her car with their backs to Sara's house. Ella turned pages, skimming the dates, times, and locations written in Sara's neat script. She stopped and flipped back a few pages. "Her dad made regular visits in the evenings to the apartment building on Nepean where Britt Flambert was living, or that's what Sara noted in the margin. He appears to have stopped late autumn last year. I wonder what that could mean?"

"He might have found out Ginger was pregnant? Maybe Britt was putting pressure on him to leave his wife, and he broke it off?"

"You could be right." Ella continued reading, turning pages and absorbing dates and locations. "He stopped his night-time outings for a few weeks but started going to the ByWard Market a couple of times a week at the beginning of November. Sara noticed him with a younger woman she describes as having long reddish-brown hair, tall and slender…" She scanned the next pages. "But she doesn't record them being together after the party at the hotel in November. The woman fits Joanne Freemont's description."

"He might still have been seeing Joanne, but she was in hiding, if I read the police reports correctly. That party spooked them."

Ella nodded. "He'd have been extra careful, and Sara obviously wasn't chasing around after him all the time." She came to the last entry made the day before. "Sara followed Olivia Jones-Briggs yesterday to a house outside the city."

"Let me see." Thorburn took the book from her. "Hunter sent an email this morning asking me to track down Olivia after I finished speaking with Sara. He went to the office to talk to her yesterday, but she'd quit and Vanessa — David's new admin assistant — didn't have her address. Olivia moved recently and hadn't given it to anyone. Hunter's tied up with the warrant."

"Warrant?"

Thorburn flushed. "I shouldn't say until I get clearance."

"That's okay. You probably shouldn't."

Thorburn typed on her phone with speedy thumbs. "Just sending Hunter a text to let him know I've got a lead on Olivia."

"You think she's living at the address Sara followed her to?"

"She might have been visiting someone." Thorburn brought a map up on her screen. "Geez, Sara tracked Olivia halfway to Cornwall. Hunter's busy, so he won't be happy driving forty minutes out of the city for no reason. I guess I'll make the trip and check it out."

Ella glanced at the map. "Yeah, it is a ways out. Well, I'm attempting to track down Wes Gilbert, so I'll be off."

"It was nice to meet you, Ella."

"And you, Rosie. I'm guessing our paths will cross again soon."

———

THE MORNING HAD SLIPPED into mid afternoon before Liam made it back to the office. He met Boots and Jingles chatting by the printer.

"What's the news?" Boots asked. "Arrest anybody?"

"David McGowan will be spending the night in lockup. Forensics uncovered fraudulent activity in his business dealings. Money laundering, for starters. He has a couple of clients he was keeping separate from his company, including Wes Gilbert's girlfriend."

"Any evidence linking McGowan to his boy's disappearance?"

"No, although his clients appear to have reasons to use Charlie as leverage against him." Liam looked over at Auger, who was talking on the phone. "Has Rosie put in an appearance?"

"Not yet. We thought she might be with you," Jingles said. "Quade's in a budget meeting and told us not to expect her back until late afternoon."

"I'll bet she's loving that." Liam continued over to his desk, puzzled by Thorburn's absence. He checked his phone, but her last text had been sent around 10:00 a.m., telling him she had a lead on Olivia and would check it out before returning to the station. He sent a return text asking where she was and read his email while he waited for her reply. Auger called his name and motioned him over. Auger lowered his cell phone as Liam reached his desk.

"So Gilbert's girlfriend left his condo twenty minutes ago and caught a cab. Surveillance is following and say she's on the Airport Parkway."

"Getting out of Dodge. You picking her up?"

"The warrant is being signed as we speak. Thanks for keeping me in the loop on the money laundering scheme, by the way. Looks like Jocelyn Langdon will soon be regretting letting her sugar daddy use her to wash his and Razzuto's money. We're holding off cuffing her until we see if Gilbert is meeting her at the airport. The Quebec Sûreté is organizing to pick up Razzuto at his home in Trois-Rivières. The hope is that McGowan, Gilbert, or both will cut a deal and pin Joanne Freemont's murder and possibly Charlie's abduction on Razzuto. Gilbert could back up McGowan's story about Razzuto drugging Meilin, and we'll nail him for that one too. We've got all three on financial fraud at the very least."

"The bargaining chip."

"Exactly." Auger grinned.

"And what if Razzuto isn't responsible for Joanne's and Meilin's deaths or Charlie's abduction?"

"Then I'll convince either Gilbert or McGowan to talk in order to save their own neck. That's how these people operate."

Liam wished he shared Auger's optimism. He wanted to find Charlie safe and sound, but the possibility had faded to remote. "Have you heard from Thorburn today?"

Auger shook his head, his expression souring. "Quade made her your partner, remember? No reason for her to contact me."

"Except our cases are connected, and you've been working together up until a couple of days ago."

"She's never shown any initiative before, so not sure what she'd have to contribute to my case. I'm beginning to believe I made a mistake recommending her to Greta, let alone hiring her in my unit last year, so thanks for taking her off my hands. Perhaps you can get more work out of her than I did. The promise Thorburn first showed hasn't panned out."

Liam let his comments pass, although the fact that Auger disparaged his employee so openly was disturbing. He checked the time as he walked back to his desk. Ten after four. He clicked open the message app on his phone, but Rosie hadn't opened or answered his text. He sat and punched in Claudette McGowan's home number. Roddy picked up on the third ring.

"Hey, Roddy, I'm looking for Officer Rosie Thorburn. She was by your house to see Sara this morning. Did she say where she was heading afterwards?"

"Nope, but she was outside talking to that reporter last time I looked out the window."

"Ella Tate?"

"I guess, if she's that spiky-haired blonde with the smoking green eyes."

"Is Sara home?"

"DQ shift. Mom's driving her in. Scared about her opening or closing up alone."

"Okay, thanks."

Liam put the phone into his pocket and stood. He called across to Auger. "I'll be out for a bit, but you can reach me on my cell."

"I take two creams and a sugar," Auger said, "if by out you mean the Happy Goat."

"Not where I'm heading, but good to know."

Liam left the office and took the stairs to the main floor on his way to the parking garage. It appeared Ella was the last one to speak with Rosie. It would take ten minutes for him to arrive at her apartment. He wouldn't rest easy until he knew where his new partner had gone after leaving Sara McGowan and why she hadn't returned to headquarters.

CHAPTER 46

The kettle whistled, and Noreen poured boiling water into the teapot and plunked a tea cozy over top. Olivia entered the kitchen a moment later, her normally perfect hair damp with sweat.

"That about does it," Olivia said, looking around the kitchen, knowing she'd soon be gone. She'd planned to stay another week at least but was learning to improvise when necessary.

"Her car?"

"In the back shed, ready to dispose of tonight. The licence plates are nicely muddied. Did you arrange to stay over at your friend's?"

"Yes. I told her that I'll drop by after supper and will spend the night. You have the other car lined up?"

"It's waiting for me in the rental lot under the name Gail White. I'll drop my Audi off at a parking lot in town and pick up the rental nearby before crossing the border. Piece of cake, really."

"You are one organized woman."

"Apparently the reason David kept me around."

"Tea?"

"I'd love a cup."

They took their seats at the table, facing each other. "This is a lot of change happening to you very quickly," Noreen said, picking up her mug. "How are you feeling … really?"

"It's time I took control of my life. I'm positive and hopeful, all things considered." Olivia gave a sideways grin. "That morning when Charlie wandered outside the gate and I took him changed everything. By taking advantage of the opportunity, it made me feel as if I hadn't given up all my power."

"Speaking of him, he's sleeping a long time today." Noreen's voice wasn't judgmental, but Olivia knew her well enough to recognize the subtle edge of disapproval

"It's only until we make it across the border. I won't need to drug him again after tomorrow."

"And David—"

"Is out of my system for good." Olivia didn't know how to explain the lightness she felt, the certainty that she could start over.'

"This last one, the policewoman, I've got a bad feeling. Her colleagues will come looking for her."

"And they won't find her. Chances are she didn't tell anybody where she was going, and even if she did, we'll stick to our story."

"I still don't understand how she tracked you here."

"It *is* a mystery. She was stupid to come on her own, but this must mean nobody suspects me of having David's kid."

Noreen nodded. "I'd have to agree. She didn't appear suspicious at all until she saw the toys lying on the living room floor. I should never have bought him that damn teddy bear."

"And we dealt with her, so stop beating yourself up. The only way anyone would think I had a motive would be if David talked about us, and he's not about to do that, is he?"

"He's proven that, certainly. It was quite ingenious to direct the police to his home office."

"Only a matter of time before Denis Razzuto and Wes Gilbert figure out their investments are gone, and David's life will be over anyway. I've syphoned off enough for us to live on for a very long time."

This time, Noreen shook her head. "The arrogance of the man. Thinking he could toss you away after all your years of devotion and not consider you'd ever retaliate."

"He believes I'm still loyal, although he's become more tentative around me. If he ever suspected I took Charlie, he dismissed the idea because I've given him no reason. He hasn't even an inkling of my rage." She lifted up the teacup with a shaking hand.

"Well, he's a fool." Noreen straightened. "I hear tires on the gravel. Are we secure?"

"We are. I did a sweep and all his toys are in the basement with Charlie."

They sat staring at each other when the doorbell chimed, followed by a fist pounding on the front door. "Stay calm," Olivia cautioned as she got to her feet. "We can do this."

She opened the door and pasted a puzzled look on her face. "Can I help you?"

"I hope so. I'm Detective Liam Hunter, and this is Acting Staff Sergeant Julie Quade. We're looking for my partner Rosie Thorburn. The last we heard she was coming to speak with you, Olivia. It would have been mid- to late-morning."

"Oh yes, you and I have spoken on the phone, Detective." Olivia gave him a quick smile before feigning concern. "She was here, but that was hours ago. She told us that she was making certain I was staying at this address and you'd be in touch soon for a chat. I've been living with my friend while my new townhouse is being renovated." She spoke over her shoulder. "Noreen, did that police officer who stopped by earlier say where she was going?"

Noreen got up from her chair and stood in the doorway to the kitchen. "Not that I recall. She did ask if there was a restaurant nearby, since it was past lunchtime, and she'd skipped breakfast. I told her if she drove about twenty more minutes, she'd have lots to choose from in Cornwall."

"By any chance did you see which direction she headed when she left?"

The detective was the dark, brooding type Olivia

liked. A bit young for her but easy on the eyes. "I didn't notice, did you?" She half-turned toward Noreen.

"No, sorry."

The female detective spoke for the first time. "I wonder if I could trouble you for the use of your washroom?"

"Oh, of course." Olivia stepped back and pointed to the second floor. "There's only the one at the head of the stairs."

"I won't be a minute."

Olivia knew full well that the bathroom visit was a pretense to check the bedrooms, but she wasn't worried. The staff sergeant would find nothing of interest up there. Sure enough, she could hear stealthy footsteps moving down the hall overhead, even as Detective Hunter asked Noreen questions about living in the country. She pretended to be listening to Noreen's answers. A few minutes later, they all looked up as the other detective descended the stairs.

"Would you like to stay for a cup of tea before you head back to Ottawa?" Noreen asked. "It won't take but a minute to boil the kettle."

"No, but thank you. We need to be on our way." Detective Hunter waited for his staff sergeant to reach him. "If Officer Thorburn gets back in touch, please tell her to check in at headquarters."

"Of course. I'll let her know that you're worried about her."

After the two detectives had walked down the path to their car, Olivia shut the door and leaned against it.

"Change of plans," she said to Noreen. "You'll be coming with me to Connecticut. We can't chance them returning with a warrant."

Noreen looked at a spot on the floor, and her shoulders heaved in a sigh. Her face was resigned when she looked up at Olivia. "I'll let my friend know I won't be staying overnight, and I'll go pack a few things."

"Pack everything of importance, because there's a good chance you'll never be coming back."

Olivia felt a momentary pang for her old life and for the love she'd nurtured for the past six years. The same love David had feigned but hadn't felt for her. She'd fallen into the "other woman" cliché but hadn't allowed herself to become a victim too. *Fool me once…* Whoever said revenge was hollow hadn't gone about it properly, because she felt wonderful. Ready to take on the world with her new child and a friend, albeit a reluctant one, along for the ride.

———

"ANYTHING AMISS UPSTAIRS?" Liam asked as they reached the car.

"Not a thing." Quade checked her phone as she walked. "Goddamn it. I have to get back to the station. Another fire to put out."

They pulled open the car doors at the same time. Liam checked the back seat. "Now where has Ella gone?"

He scanned the property and spotted her sauntering toward them, keeping close to the lot line of trees and bushes. He'd almost forgotten how she never followed directions when she was chasing a story. He started the engine and waited for her to slip into the back seat. "I thought you were staying out of sight in the car," he said, turning to stare at her.

"And I thought I'd check out the yard. The property goes a long way back, and there's a big shed that looks like a small barn or garage at the end of a nearly grown over track. I couldn't see through the windows, and the door was padlocked."

"Did you hear anything coming from inside."

"No, but…"

Quade held up a hand to stop her. "Auger just messaged me. He received a text from Rosie Thorburn. She went for lunch in Cornwall and was taking the rest of the day off, since it's getting late. Says she lost track of time."

"So we've made a wasted trip." Liam let irritation override his relief. Thorburn had agreed to lunch with him after her visit to speak with Sara. He'd been preoccupied with everything going on but would have made time once she returned to the office. Was she so flighty that she forgot, or had she decided to blow him off? Neither was a good option.

"I'll have a chat with her tomorrow," Quade said. "She's got to understand the need to let us know her whereabouts at all times when she's out in the field."

Ella stayed silent in the back seat. She was staring out the side window when Liam looked at her in the rear-view mirror. He wondered what she was thinking but let it pass as he backed out of the driveway and turned toward home, not sorry the trip had ended the way it had. Thorburn was new to field work and needed guidance, but this could be easily dealt with … hopefully. He'd have supper with Hannah and the boys and come back to the office with his patience restored in the morning. He'd speak with Rosie then and mentor her as Quade had asked. Everybody deserved a chance to screw up. God knows he'd needed some second chances himself and could draw from that well of experience.

CHAPTER 47

Ella stood for a moment in the late afternoon heat and watched Hunter and Quade drive to the stop sign at the corner of Percy and Fifth and turn right. The air above the pavement radiated upward in wavy lines, baked by the relentless sun. Even she was beginning to feel drained by the hottest summer in history, the humidity making being outdoors for any length of time close to unbearable.

She ambled up the sidewalk and climbed the steps to the apartment door, using her key to enter. She'd spied Finn's truck parked around the corner as they drove past on Percy and stopped to listen in the hallway outside his door, wondering if he'd given Adele the entire day off from minding Lena. Perhaps, Adele would find her equilibrium with more support from him. Ella had no doubt that Finn would step up once he realized Adele needed his help. He was a caring man, loyal to his family and friends.

The hall was cooler than outdoors, but not by

much, and Ella didn't look forward to climbing upstairs to her small, stifling apartment in the eaves. Her footsteps were heavy on the creaky steps, and Tony thrust his apartment door open wide when she reached the second-floor landing. "Time for an *aperitif, ma cherie, avant le souper?*"

"*Mais oui.* Thanks, *mon ami.*" She entered his hallway and bent to rub Luvy behind the ears before following him into the living room. Frank Sinatra crooned from the sound system speakers hidden somewhere out of sight. Relaxed music must mean a relaxed Tony. She took a seat on the emerald-green couch and watched him add gin to a shaker.

"Gimlets tonight," he said, plopping ice into the shaker with silver tongs. "A drink first invented to prevent the scurvy. You and the delicious detective out on a case?"

"Not exactly." She kicked off her shoes and tucked her feet up under her on the couch. "His new partner named Rosie Thorburn was checking out a residence halfway to Cornwall, and nobody heard from her all afternoon. We set out to find her whereabouts. I had an idea of the location because she'd shown me … oh, never mind. The details aren't important, but they took me along as the guide."

Tony added fresh lime juice and syrup and began shaking their drinks while he stared at her. "And…?"

"Rosie sent a text to another detective at the station that she'd gone into Cornwall for lunch and was taking the afternoon off." The unease she'd felt walking around the property returned. The garage or shed or whatever it was at the back of the rutted track had felt off. The windows were blackened out, and she'd gotten a strange shiver up her spine when she tried to look inside.

"So what's eating at you?" He strained the drinks into two martini glasses, added a wheel of lime to each, and crossed the floor to hand her a glass. "Cheers." He took a sip. "Oooh, now *that's* a gimlet worth its vitamin C." He set the drink on the coffee table. "Are you sensing something awry?"

She tasted the drink. "No, it's lovely. Thanks for this."

"Not the drink, girl. The missing officer. Is your intuition not convinced she's okay?"

Ella stilled. She couldn't deny the heaviness in her stomach. She tried to put her unease into words. "It just seemed too convenient that Thorburn sent a text immediately after Hunter and Quade were at the door asking about her. There was also a big, locked shed at the back of the property that gave me the creeps."

"Naturally, you were scouting around the acreage while they had the homeowner's attention."

"Would you have expected anything less?"

"Your reckless consistency is a comfort, Tate." He left her for a moment and returned with a plate of shrimp and cocktail sauce and a bowl of cashews. "Drink up, and we'll make a drive back to this worrisome homestead. I always like a jaunt out to the country on a hot summer evening. We can take my car. The air is set to the perfect temperature."

"You don't need to—"

"But I do. What kind of an assistant would I be if I didn't support your hunches?"

She nodded and realized how tense she'd been on the drive back to Ottawa. The worrisome feeling would keep her from sleeping tonight — she knew this in her bones — so there was no choice, really. She threw back the drink and stood. "We can bring the snacks to eat on the way."

"And I'll toss in a plate of cheese and crackers to keep us topped up."

———

LONG RIDGES of shadow stretched across the road when Ella pointed out the driveway to the house where Olivia was staying. "Hunter said she's there with a friend named Noreen who's renting. That's likely Olivia's Audi halfway up the drive. Noreen's car is in front of it, nearer to the house."

Tony slowed but kept going. "I want to scope out the area and find a place to tuck my car out of sight."

Ella craned her neck to look at the other side of the road. "It's fenced off farmland by the look of it. Cows would be my guess."

Tony drove to the next driveway three minutes down the road before turning around. "Why in the name of Walmart would someone live out here in the middle of nowhere? I couldn't imagine being this far from a Big Mac."

"I couldn't imagine you eating a Big Mac."

"*Touché.* Ahh, here we are." He eased off the highway and backed onto a dirt track, positioning the car so it was half in some bushes before he turned off the engine. "If the farmer is checking the fields, and Lord only knows why at this hour, he can get past us easily. The house you pointed out is only a few hundred metres on the other side of the highway."

Ella opened the passenger door wide enough to slip out. She reached for her bag on the floor.

"Where are you going?" Tony asked.

"To check out that shed. I brought a flashlight and a lock pick."

"Of course you did. Well, wait for me."

The driveway to Olivia's house was visible and would take less than a minute to reach. "What's that noise?" Tony checked over his shoulder as they walked. Darkness was settling around them, and a carpet of stars glowed in the inky sky. A truck zipped past, heading toward Ottawa.

"I believe that would be the chirp of the cicada, which you might recall we also have in the city."

"They sound a lot louder out here. They're probably gathering like the birds in that Hitchcock movie, getting ready to peck out our eyes."

"You can always wait in the car."

They heard an engine start up in the driveway at the same time and had only a couple of seconds to react before headlights caught them. Ella grabbed on to Tony's arm and drew him over the edge of the shoulder onto the grassy incline. They flattened into the dirt and tucked their heads. Ella chanced a look toward the road. The headlights of two cars blinded her as the first car turned onto the highway in the direction of Cornwall. The second vehicle followed closely behind.

"Quick, we have to follow them." She waited until both cars had driven a short distance up the road before scrambling onto the shoulder, ignoring the gravel digging into her hands. She pushed herself upright and started running with Tony a step behind.

"What about the shed?" Tony called.

She kept her eye on the retreating taillights. "It'll still be there if this is a wild goose chase. Hurry so we don't lose track of them. We have to find out where they're headed."

CHAPTER 48

"Another piece of cherry pie, Liam?" Hannah brandished the knife in his direction.

He patted his stomach and groaned. "I can't eat another thing." He stood and began gathering up plates and cutlery to take to the dishwasher. "This has been great, sis, but next time, I'm going to treat you and the boys to supper out. Name your restaurant."

Hugh jumped up from his seat. "Napolis pizza! Napolis pizza!"

Jack joined him in a run around the table, and Hannah watched in amusement. "Decision made," she said. "Don't you have something to tell your Uncle Liam, boys?"

Jack stopped and stared at Hugh. "Oh yeah." They both raced for the door, pushing and shoving. Liam listened to them rustling around in the next room. A minute later, they were back. Hugh held a piece of paper that he dropped into Liam's hands.

"We named your cat," Jack said as he hopped from one foot to the other.

Liam turned the page over. He recognized a disproportionately large interpretation of his pet drawn in black and brown crayon. He kept his expression serious as he studied it. "Gorgeous work, lads."

"Hugh drew her. He said my picture was stupid." Jack leaned on Liam's arm, his breath warm on Liam's cheek. "But I wrote the letters." He traced one with his finger.

"Mom made me let Jack name her because I tore up his picture." Hugh frowned. "She said it couldn't be Snot Nose or Farty, so he had to pick something else. Can you read her name, Uncle Liam?"

"Sure I can, but how do you pronounce it, Jack?" Liam bluffed, not certain he wanted to know. The squiggles could have spelled anything.

"I told you he wouldn't be able to read it." Hugh scowled at his brother.

"Lucky." Jack ignored his older brother and wrapped an arm around Liam's neck. "Her name's Lucky 'cause she found you, and you love each other."

"Lucky," Liam repeated, relieved and touched by Jack thinking the cat and he were meant for each other. He hugged Jack around his waist and looked across at Hugh. "She has indeed found her home. Good choice, my boyos."

"We thought of it together," Jack said generously.

Liam's phone buzzed, and he excused himself from the table. "What's up, Boots?" he asked into the receiver as he walked toward the living room.

"Thorburn's boyfriend called. She hasn't made it home. He's worried."

Liam ran a hand through his hair. "Give me his number, and I'll phone him. She hasn't by any chance contacted Auger again?"

"I'll try him while you try the boyfriend. Name's Brad Gregoire."

Brad picked up on the first ring. "This isn't like her. She always answers her cell when she sees my name on call display."

"She texted a colleague that she was having lunch in Cornwall and taking the afternoon off. Does she have a friend she might be visiting?" Liam strived to keep his voice reassuring, not certain he succeeded.

"I've tried everyone I could think of, and nobody's seen her."

"What kind of car does she drive, and do you know the plate number?"

"Sure. A green Honda Accord. BTLJ 241."

"I'll get officers keeping an eye out for it. Sit tight and I'll check around with the others on the team."

"Rosie would have texted me if she planned the day away. Something's wrong."

"I know it's hard not to think the worst, but we've a long way to go before that. I'll be in touch when I know something. Call me at this number if she shows up or you hear from her."

Boots phoned back a few seconds later. "Auger says nothing since that one text. What do you think is going on?"

"I'm not sure. Put out a bulletin to city and

provincial patrol to keep an eye out for a green Honda Accord. Licence plate BTLJ 241. Call me if anyone sees the car."

"Will do. Anything else?"

"I don't know Rosie well enough to have any idea about her habits. Her boyfriend says he's tried calling all her friends. We'll have to sit tight for the time being. If she's still missing in a few hours, I'll go talk to him."

Hannah had cleared the kitchen table, and Hugh was shuffling a deck of cards when Liam returned. He'd promised to play War and Go Fish after dessert and couldn't back out, especially since he had no clue how to help track down Rosie. He took his seat and ruffled Jack's hair while Hugh dealt.

"Everything okay?" Hannah asked, picking up her hand. "You look worried."

"An open book, am I?" He grinned at her and worked to concentrate on his cards. "My new partner's boyfriend hasn't heard from her, and she's not answering her phone. Even if she took the afternoon off, you'd expect her to touch base with him." Speaking the words aloud gave them weight. He knew something had to be wrong. "I'll have to take off after a few rounds," he said over Jack's head. He couldn't simply sit still without trying to help find her. She was his partner, even if a placeholder, and he felt a responsibility. "I'll need to leave story time in your hands for tonight."

Hannah let out an exaggerated sigh. "Text if you need me to feed the cat or water your plants."

"Lucky should be fine for a few hours, but thanks." Liam high-fived Jack and Hugh. "The cat's going to love her new name."

————

TONY HUNG BACK, sometimes losing sight of the second car's taillights when they rounded a corner, but only for a moment or two before spotting them again. A series of four vehicles going in the opposite direction whizzed past on the two-lane road, but traffic remained light for the most part. Houses were set back, few and far between, separated by farmland and woods. The road lay shadowed in pockets of pitch darkness. "They're heading toward Cornwall," Tony said. "Maybe going out for a late supper." He glanced sideways at her.

Ella sat hunched over, watching through the front windshield. "Why not take one car?"

Tony hesitated. "I suppose it's odd, but there could be a number of plausible explanations."

"They're up to something. I can feel it in my bones. Don't lose them."

"I'm like a leech on their backside."

They rounded another corner and reached a long, straight stretch of highway. Her warning now seemed prophetic. The two sets of taillights were nowhere to be seen. "Where'd they go?" Tony asked.

Ella scanned the length of highway and both sides of the road but didn't see them. "Slow down, Tony. They must have pulled off somewhere." She continued searching, her head swivelling from one side of the road to the other. She leaned into the windshield and gave a yelp, pointing past Tony to their left. "They're heading down that dirt road into the woods. I see a set of taillights."

"What should I do?" Tony had slowed to a crawl. Luckily, no vehicles were coming up behind them. "If I follow, they'll see us for sure."

"Stay on this side and pull over ... there's some-body's driveway up ahead. Back into it and turn off the lights." She checked the time on the car dash-board and pulled out her phone, opening the maps app. "This road isn't on the map. It's got to be a farmer's track that doesn't connect to another road. They'll have to come back this way."

"That's a bit of a gamble. Maybe the map's just not detailed enough."

"Let's give them ten minutes. The road might lead to someone's house if they've gone for dinner. We can drive up to see and then double back and look in that shed on their property if they're staying for a visit."

"*And* the night does not get any less creepy."

Tony rolled down the windows before turning off the engine. The air was filled with the sound of cicadas, humming like a Hendrix guitar solo, long and sizzling in the end-of-day heat, even if the air felt slightly cooler in the country. A light breeze had kicked up to make the wait comfortable, if not pleas-ant. "Have another shrimp," he said, passing her the plate.

Ella popped one into her mouth and watched across the road as she chewed. She raised a hand. "I hear a car."

Tony squinted. "I don't—" He slumped and flattened against the seat as a car's headlights swept into view from the direction of the road where they'd seen the two cars disappear. "That's the Audi," he said as it turned onto the highway and zipped past them. "I counted two women in the front seat."

They looked at each other. "So where's the other car?" Ella asked.

"They've ditched it and are continuing on to Cornwall together. Should we follow them or go in search?"

Ella debated chasing after them, but the clenching in her stomach was getting worse. She chewed on a fingernail. "Let's gamble and drive up the dirt road. I want to see where they left the other car." She checked the dashboard. "They drove twelve minutes since leaving the highway, so taking into account the time required to drive back to the highway, we should find the car about six minutes in, unless they only drove a short way and got out to talk or something."

Tony started the engine. "We should find the car within six minutes max along the road. That narrows it down. Good forward thinking, girl."

The road was unpaved but pothole-free. Tony drove slowly while he and Ella peered into the bushes and trees on either side. No sign of a car on the first pass. At the five-minute mark, the road ended at an overgrown driveway that led to a house with the roof caved in, a black, hulking mass set in a clearing now thick with tall grass and bushes. Tony parked and they circled the building on foot, their eyes adjusting to the gloom and moonlight. They met in front of his car. "It can't be safe to go inside. We should just leave." He took a last glance toward the house and shuddered as he reached for the car door handle.

"I'm going to have a quick look." Ella opened the passenger door and bent to reach inside, grabbing the flashlight out of her bag on the floor.

He groaned, but she heard him following behind as she scrambled up the incline to concrete steps leading to the main entrance. The front door opened with a bit of elbow grease, and she swung the flashlight beam around the hallway. Dirty didn't begin to describe the listing walls and grimy floor. Scurrying noises and the stench of decay made her gag. She focused the beam along the torn-up floorboards. No footprints or signs of recent activity in the dust. She swung the light to the stairwell, noticing the filthy, torn carpet on the steps and the broken banister. She turned to look at Tony. "There's no possible way they got a car in here. It doesn't look like anyone's been inside for a long time."

"Oh my gawd. What is that smell?" He held his nose and backed away. "We cannot get out of this house of horrors fast enough."

"Maybe we can catch up to Olivia on the highway, although I remain curious about where they ditched the other car."

"And I remain uneasy about this entire enterprise."

Tony drove a little faster on the return trip, but the narrowness of the road and the darkness kept him at a low speed. Ella continued to scan the bushes, finding it difficult to make out more than shapes in the darkness. A minute in, she caught the grey glint of metal in the headlights as they swept around a bend. "Tony, stop! There's something in that copse of trees."

"I don't see anything." He hit the brakes and waited in the car while Ella leapt out with the flashlight. She found the car nestled into the bushes between two pine trees, nose first with barely enough room to walk around it. This car, which on closer inspection was a Honda, didn't appear to be the one that had been parked in Noreen's driveway in front of the Audi, although it looked somewhat familiar. Ella checked the interior with the flashlight as Tony thudded up behind her.

"Anything?" he asked.

"No." She hesitated. "The doors are locked. Why would they park the car here unless they meant to hide it? We need to look in the trunk, much as I'd rather not."

"Wait here." Tony raced back to the car and returned with a wire coat hanger. "I have a friend who's always locking the keys in his car. Shine the flashlight on the window."

He had the lock lifted within seconds and swung the door open as wide as possible through the long grass. He bent and lifted the lever to open the trunk.

Ella waited for him to join her at the back of the car. They exchanged looks before she yanked it open.

"Oh my God. Is she dead?" Tony whispered.

Ella took a split second to recognize the police officer she'd been speaking with that morning at Sara's house, part of her face visible above the duct tape covering her mouth. The tape didn't cover her nose, so there was a chance. Ella felt her neck, relieved to find it warm to her touch. "It's Rosie Thorburn, the missing cop. This is her car. I think she's still breathing. Help me get her out."

"Stand back. I've got her." Tony scooped his arms under Rosie and lifted her against his chest. He carried her to his car while Ella rushed ahead and opened the back door. She scrambled in and reached for Rosie as Tony lowered her. Rosie's hands were tied behind her back with a rag, and Tony struggled with the knot while Ella steadied her body sideways. He held up the rag after removing it from her wrists. Ella cradled Rosie's head and took a deep breath before ripping off the duct tape in one quick motion. Rosie moaned, but her eyes stayed closed. "The nearest hospital's in Cornwall." Ella met Tony's eyes, and he nodded. "Hand me my water bottle before you start driving. I'll moisten her mouth and try to cool her down."

"You got it. Don't worry, I'll get us there lickety-split."

"And I'll call Hunter to stop Olivia and her friend before they cross the border, because that's the only reason I can think of for why they're making the run to Cornwall." Ella looked down at Rosie's fluttering eyelids and wondered why Olivia and her friend had shut her in the trunk and left her to die, as she surely would have in tomorrow's heat. What had Rosie walked in on, dangerous enough that they couldn't allow her to live?

CHAPTER 49

Olivia finished securing the car seat and plunked the sleeping Charlie, now named Gabriel, into place. She buckled him in and slammed the door. Noreen shut the trunk and they both got into the front seat of the rented car, Olivia at the wheel.

"Shame you have to give up your Audi." Noreen reached for the seatbelt. She stole a glance at the kid before facing front.

"It's just a car … and stop fussing." She adjusted the mirror to check on Gabriel, his head lolling against the cushioned back. She had to remember to think of him now as Gabriel, not Charlie. "He's fine. I lowered the dose, and he'll be awake by the time we reach Burlington."

"I'm not worried about him."

"Good, because we can't start doubting each other."

"I wouldn't." Noreen's bottom lip trembled, and

Olivia felt the familiar irritation at her weakness. Noreen's constant need for affirmation was getting tiresome. Olivia wondered how long she'd have to put up with her in the new town. She'd meant to leave her happily behind and start a new life without any reminders.

Noreen wouldn't meet her eyes. "I've decided to go to my friend's, and she'll drive me home in the morning. I won't be going with you to the States." She said the last sentence with an unusual hint of defiance.

"Are you sure?" The words came out almost like a threat. Olivia wasn't sold on this change in plans, reluctant to let Noreen out of her sight.

"Think about it, Olivia. I'll be a yoke around your neck in the long run. You'll be less easy to track down without me along. Besides, it will look like we're both on the run, while if I stay in the house, I can get them off your trail. Karen's waiting for me with a bottle of wine, and we're ordering pizza." She gave Olivia a long, searching stare. "You're better on your own with the kid. I'd be a constant reminder of all you're working to forget."

Odd for Noreen to be so perceptive. Olivia thought she'd heard a quiver in Noreen's voice that she'd tried hard to cover up with a light-hearted tone. She knew then that Noreen was right. Their partnership, or friendship, such as it was, had worn out its welcome. She liked the idea of travelling light. "As you wish," she said as if Noreen had the final say. "What's your friend's address?"

The tension in Noreen's shoulders relaxed as she gave directions, and twenty minutes later they pulled up in front of a townhouse. The delay irked Olivia, but getting rid of Noreen was worth forty minutes of pain now that she'd decided to dump her. Olivia's phone pinged as she stopped next to the curb.

"That guy I sold my Audi to texted that he picked it up, so that's one worry gone. He's driving it into the chop shop as we speak."

"Your phone?"

"About to go in the garbage. I was waiting for this final call."

"It's all under control then." Noreen hesitated with her palm on the door handle. "We're even now, Olivia. All square in the debt department. I'll never be able to thank you enough for getting me out of my abusive marriage, but I think helping you with this — project — means we never have to look over our shoulders. We'll be old friends who lost touch from here on in."

Olivia nodded. "Take care of yourself, Noreen. Make sure the next guy you get involved with doesn't need disposing of like Phil. He did prove a challenge." She was reminding Noreen that she was equally culpable in all they'd done. If one went down, they both would.

"And enjoy the rest of your life with your new son. David owes you at least this after jerking you around for so many years. I still can't believe he made you have an abortion and promised to leave Ginger so you could start a proper family."

A rush of anger made Olivia clench the steering wheel until her hands hurt. She forced her voice to stay even. "Let's say her second pregnancy opened my eyes, and his infatuation with that university-aged hooker … well, she was the last straw. Maybe one day he'll put it all together, but by then I'll be long gone and he'll have the rest of his life to rue his sins. He'll be charged for Joanne's death once their ill-fated relationship comes to light, and I, for one, will celebrate that day." She still flinched when she remembered David saying he'd found the one. The one! A slut of a university girl who'd grow older just as she and Ginger had. She'd done the girl a favour ending her life while she was still young and desirable. Before David tossed her aside for an even younger model.

"I can join you once you're settled, if you send word." Noreen didn't put much enthusiasm into the offer.

Olivia drew herself back and focused on Noreen's face. "This is goodbye, I'm afraid. I won't be contacting you again."

Noreen tried to hide her reaction by turning away, but not before Olivia saw the relief in her eyes. Noreen's voice sounded even lighter. "Then you take care, Olivia. I don't regret all we've done, but I'm not sorry to put it behind me."

She got out of the car and hurried up the driveway while Olivia watched. Had she made a mistake letting her leave so easily? She'd wondered a few times about Noreen's displeasure at having Gabriel in the house, and her nervousness over his abduction. Her lack of backbone had always been a worry. She honestly was one wimp of a woman. Well, too late now, and soon it wouldn't matter.

Olivia looked behind her at the still-sleeping Gabriel before putting the car in gear. The border should be quiet this time of night, and she'd find a fast-food drive-through on the other side. Not much longer before she was done with this old existence and on to an exciting future with her new son. Hurting David and Ginger was lessening in importance as she envisioned her life with Gabriel. He was worth everything she'd sacrificed, the baby she'd aborted. The revenge had been sweet, but raising him would make her time on this earth mean something, help her to start over without David, the man she'd wanted to spend her old age with before he'd shown his true colours. She angrily blinked back the tears that gathered in her eyes as she drove down the road toward her new life.

CHAPTER 50

The American border guard looked at Olivia's photo and back at her face from his seat inside the booth. She smiled through the car's open side window, but he didn't react. He leaned forward and peered into the back seat and flipped to Gabriel's passport. "Sleepy guy," he said, handing back both documents. "Where you two headed?"

"Visiting family in Florida."

"How long you planning to stay?"

"A week. My mother's celebrating a big birthday."

He clicked on his computer. "Drive and park in the spot directly in front of the building over there. You've been randomly selected for an inspection."

"I hope this won't take long."

He didn't answer, and she drove in the direction he'd pointed and pulled into the parking space. "We'll be on our way soon, Gabriel," she said, turning to look at him. He stirred and one arm waved in the air for a moment and then dropped onto his tummy. She waited half an hour before a different border guard exited the building and strolled in her direction. He reached her as she stepped out of the car.

"Is there a problem, sir?" she asked. "You've kept me here a long time."

"We had a shift change. Open the trunk, madam," he said without cracking a smile.

He hadn't offered an apology, but he hadn't shut her down either. She walked with him around the car and used the key. He opened her two suitcases and riffled through them while she stood a few steps behind. Leaving the trunk open, he moved to the driver's door and got inside, feeling under the seat and opening the glove compartment. "Do you own a car, ma'am?" he asked.

"I do, but it's not in the best shape, so I paid for a rental. This ride is more comfortable for a long drive."

He finished inspecting the front seat and lifted his head a few times to stare through the window of the building. She began to get a bad feeling. Finally, he heaved himself up and out of the car. "I need you to come inside and sign a document. Will your son be okay for a minute?"

"He'll be fine. Could I use the washroom first? Would you keep one eye on him?"

He focused on Gabriel and nodded. "My boy's about this age." The first crack in his official reserve. She wondered if she'd misread the situation, but her gut told her she hadn't. He'd been stalling for time and only ended his search when someone had signalled to him from the other side of the plate glass.

Inside the small washroom, she looked for an escape route. The windows were block glass and too high up, even if she could squeeze through. She suspected the customs officer was waiting outside the door for her to exit, so no chance to duck out a back way. They'd catch her before she'd taken ten steps. She stood in front of the mirror, fixed her hair, put on fresh lipstick, and squared her shoulders. She'd blustered her way through difficult situations before. The U.S. officials had nothing on her and no reason to single her out. Getting past this nosy customs officer shouldn't be an impossible task.

He met her outside the washroom door as expected, leaving no opportunity for her to slip past him into her car. She stood a better chance of escape behind the wheel, but was it time to make a run for it or stay and act innocent? She had no choice for now. Her gaze shifted past him and froze. Standing near the counter were the reporter Ella Tate, holding Gabriel in her arms, and the Irish cop who'd identified himself as Hunter. He'd come to the house searching for the missing policewoman. Was it only that afternoon? All eyes turned to stare at her while a hot flush rose up from her chest like a fever. The detective stepped forward and blocked her path while the customs officer stood close behind to stop her from turning tail and running.

"I've come to escort you and Charlie back to Ottawa." The hard black flint of Hunter's eyes said as much as the flatness in his voice. "Your friend Noreen Smithers is already on her way to the station. She wisely thought better of what you've both done and turned herself in. She said this was her first opportunity to break free from you."

Charlie picked that moment to waken and shriek, his face contorted in rage. "Mama. Want Mama." He twisted in Ella's arms, and she rubbed a hand up and down his back, uttering comforting noises. Over his head, she stared at Olivia with a look of disgust oddly mixed with pity.

Olivia stood taller and glared them all down. "Noreen is a snivelling liar. I've done nothing wrong. David's the one you ought to be arresting, and I won't say another word until I speak to my lawyer." She should have heeded her inner voice when she saw the fear in Noreen's eyes. It was a warning sign that Noreen didn't trust her to stay away. Had Noreen only been stringing her along, scared of being a loose end? Had she told them about the cop they'd left in the trunk of her car? She never should have let the cunt go. "Noreen's the one who needs to be in handcuffs. She's the one who forced me to help her."

"We'll get to the truth, don't you worry," Hunter said as he pulled a set of handcuffs out of his jacket. "But rest assured, we will need to hear how Charlie McGowan came to be in your car as you attempted to use fake passports to cross the border. You'll be driving with me. Ella, her friend Tony, and Charlie will follow us in your rental to the police station in Ottawa. We've got another long night ahead of us."

CHAPTER 51

Ginger accepted Liam's offer of a ride home from the Ottawa Children's Hospital after Charlie had been examined and discharged. He was groggy from the sleep medication Olivia had been feeding him, but the doctor had assured Ginger that there'd be no lasting effects. Already, Charlie was snuggling into her neck with his arms wrapped tightly around her as they exited the hospital by a side entrance to avoid the media. The sky had lightened since she arrived in a police car in the dead of night, and Liam could see that weariness was beginning to overtake her elation.

"I'm sorry you've had to go through this." He could imagine the torment she'd experienced over the past few weeks. His comment could have referred to any one of a number of tragedies: her missing son, David's screwing around, her failed marriage. He'd shielded her as much as possible from David's deceit, but her questions had demanded answers that he couldn't avoid.

She tried a smile. "My boy's home and my baby girl is healthy. I can deal with the rest." She paused. "What will happen to him?"

"David?"

"He's lied about so much. It appears obvious that his deception caused Olivia to behave as she did."

"David didn't know she'd abducted Charlie, but there's evidence he was involved in some illegal business dealings. We're holding him overnight at the very least. Again, I'm sorry."

"I'm still in shock. When I worked for him, there was no hint of this. His work ethic and dedication to clients were reasons I was attracted to him." She rubbed a hand up and down Charlie's back as they walked. She stopped and faced him at the entrance to the parking lot. "Could you do me a favour?"

"If I can."

"Tell David not to come home. I don't want to see him … not yet. I need some time."

"I can pass along your message."

"Tell him that he owes me this, at least."

He nodded and watched her kiss the top of Charlie's head. It felt wrong to leave her in the dark any longer. "Olivia took Charlie on a whim. She'd come over that morning to tell you about their affair, and he was standing outside the open gate."

"She told you this?"

"Her friend Noreen Smithers has been talking. She claims Olivia showed up on her doorstep with

Charlie, completely frantic about what she'd done. She initially planned to only keep Charlie a day or two to make David squirm."

"Something must have happened to make Olivia change her mind." Ginger's eyes pinned him. "I need to know, and David won't tell me the truth. Please."

He rubbed a hand slowly across his forehead. "This isn't easy to take."

"But I need to know."

His gaze searched her face, and her eyes didn't waver. He took a deep breath. There never would be a good time to add to her pain. "According to Noreen, David told Olivia that he planned to leave you, that he was in love with Joanne Freemont. He didn't appear to realize how this news would devastate Olivia with whom he'd had a relationship for six years."

"No, he's never been one to worry about fallout." She closed her eyes and swayed. Liam grabbed on to her arm to steady her. "I shouldn't have told you."

"You had to tell me." Her eyes widened. "Joanne. The university girl found dead on the Parkway. Did David…?"

He jumped in before she could finish the thought. "I don't believe he had anything to do with her death. Noreen claims Olivia was responsible."

Ginger's expression was a combination of relief and revulsion. David was a liar and a cheat, but not a killer or kidnapper. "Thank you," she said. "I appreciate that you told me the truth, however devastating."

"It's the least you deserve after all this."

He was pleased to see Ginger's mother waiting for them on the front steps when he pulled into her driveway. Ginger would have support to get through these next few days. Despite the early hour, cameras and reporters had returned across the street, and he attempted to shield her and Charlie from view as he hustled them into the house.

Ginger handed Charlie over to her mother before she turned to look at him. "This isn't over yet, is it?" Anguish lined her face in the harsh overhead lighting.

"I won't tell you that it will be easy, but time will help. The media will go on to another story, and your life will return to normal."

"Your dad, sister, and I want you to come with us to Halifax, at least for a while. You can take the time you need to sort out what you want to do." Her mom rested her head against Charlie's cheek as she spoke. "Oh, my dear boy."

Ginger turned to him. "Can we leave Ottawa if I give you my parents' contact information?"

"I'm not in charge of the investigation, but I can ask on your behalf. I'm certain that something can be worked out."

"I'll still have to face David at some point, but I'll be happy to leave that for the distant future. For now, all I want to do is hug my children and count my blessings in peace."

Her mother added in an unusual show of defiance, "And all I want is for David to leave my daughter and grandchildren the hell alone."

———

LIAM DROVE to Britannia Beach and parked in the empty lot. It was 5:00 a.m. He got out of the car and walked across the sand and down to the water's edge. The previous day's heat had dissipated, and a light breeze off the bay cooled him. The sun, barely over the horizon, was partially hidden by clouds that were scudding in and foretelling a storm that might or might not blow over.

He didn't know if he'd be able to sleep. The knowledge of what could have happened to his partner if Ella and Tony hadn't been so dogged unsettled him. He'd unwittingly sent Rosie on a trail that could have ended in her death, and guilt rested heavily. Charlie was home and safe and this lifted one burden, but even there he hadn't been the one to figure out the truth. He had not protested when Quade assigned Auger to handle the interviews with Olivia and Noreen, because he was drained and shaken by the near escapes.

His cell rang as he turned to walk back to his car. He glanced at call display before accepting. "You still at the station?" he asked, stopping to turn and look out over the water.

"On my way home. Hang on." He could hear the rustle of Quade's clothing and a bang. "Sorry about that. My hands-free got jolted. Charlie and his mom doing okay?"

"They are. Ginger wants to take the kids to

Halifax to stay with her parents, so she'll likely be checking in later today."

"I don't see a problem. Rosie is doing better. Her boyfriend and parents are at the hospital. I spoke with her briefly, and she's asking to return to work tomorrow. I told her to take the week at least. She's going to have to see the police psych to get some counselling." There was a break in conversation punctuated by swearing at her end. "Someone cut me off. Can you imagine at this time of the morning? Anyhow, I hope you aren't upset by Auger taking over the questioning. Noreen Smithers has verbal diarrhoea, so it's really a matter of recording what she's telling us. She said Olivia poisoned Bud Smithers, her abusive husband some fifteen years ago, as if doing her a favour. His murder kept the two of them in a troubled alliance because Noreen couldn't prove she wasn't in on his death. On her part, Olivia keeps saying David and Noreen are responsible for everything and then shuts up. The fraud squad has taken over David's case, with Razzuto and Gilbert also in their sights. Did I mention the team picked Gilbert up at the airport on his way to the Bahamas? No sun in his future for a while. He and Razzuto are being held for Meilin Hanon's death and cover-up. The charges on that one should be interesting. Likely manslaughter for Razzuto, but still to be determined. Gilbert wants to cut a deal to confirm what we pretty much figured out in exchange for a lighter sentence. He's been watching too much American television."

More static and cursing before Quade resumed

talking. "Where was I? Yeah, Noreen says Olivia found out where Joanne was staying by listening in on a call between her and David. Olivia lured Joanne to a Parkway parking lot, pretending to be a go-between for David. Noreen knew the details we were holding back, so there's that to confirm her story. She said that Olivia threatened her if she didn't go along. Hunter, are you still there?"

"I am."

She seemed to focus on his silence for the first time. "You kept all the lines open … with Ella Tate, the families. You can take credit for Charlie being found in time."

"I missed something. Olivia and Britt lived in the same apartment building. We assumed David had the affair with Britt because she's younger and easier to seduce. It feels—"

"We all missed that and more. People hold secrets and lie about the truth. Our job is to keep digging until the answers are found. You never stopped digging. Don't regret what you couldn't possibly have known. Get over yourself, Hunter."

"Is that an order?" He smiled.

"It is. Go home and get some sleep. I don't want to see you before ten tomorrow. That's an order too."

"On my way, and Quade?"

"Yeah?"

"Thanks."

"It's me who should be thanking you." She clicked off before he had a chance to contradict her.

He flipped through his messages when he reached

the parking lot, his heart quickening as he opened one from Hannah. She didn't usually contact him while he was working unless it was an emergency. He relaxed and smiled as he read. She'd been asked out on a date — dinner with a coworker — and wondered if Liam would have Friday free to watch the boys? He sent a thumbs-up emoji and a heart. At last she was taking a step forward. She called as he put the key into the ignition.

"What are you doing up, Hannah?" he asked, hesitating.

"I couldn't sleep and realized you're still up too. The case?"

"Charlie McGowan is home safe and sound, and we've made an arrest. My missing partner has also been found and is going to be okay."

"Oh, thank God. Three miracles in one day."

"I'm guessing you accepting a date is the first."

Her infectious laughter had him joining in. "Now all we need is for you to go on a date too for a miracle quad."

He thought about Ella Tate and his inexplicable attraction. At the very least, they could both do with a decent meal. "I'll sleep on it," he said. "Tell the boys I'll be making my special mac and cheese with hot dogs on your date night."

"Grand. They're going to split with delight." Her laughter again. "I'll put some black stuff in the fridge for you. See you Friday around six."

"A couple of Guinness are all the payment I need. See you Friday."

CHAPTER 52

Ella opened her door at eight thirty the next morning to find Tony holding a tray with apple and cinnamon muffins and two cups of coffee. Luvy scooted through her legs and disappeared around the corner. "You're up early," she said as Tony slid past.

"Thought we should recap last night's festivities. Any word on that cop, Rosie Thorburn?" he called over his shoulder.

"The news reports say she's awake and going home today."

"Wonderful."

She followed him and plopped down on her desk chair, Luvy lying at her feet. Tony had set a plate with two muffins and a cup of coffee in front of her computer before settling himself on the new chair.

"Cutting hair today?" she asked before biting into a muffin warm from the oven.

"First client's at 10:00 a.m. Are you still on the

adrenaline high from last evening? I could barely sleep a wink."

"I didn't sleep much either, but it was because I was working on an article for *The Capital*. I hit *Send* a few minutes before you tapped on my door." She picked up the coffee cup, grateful for the jolt of caffeine. "I'm going over to check on Sara after we finish up. I'm hoping she'll agree to be interviewed for my podcast."

"Angle?"

"Abduction and return of her half-brother Charlie. The effect it had on everyone involved. Also, I want her to speak about her own three-day disappearance. I think people are still confused by what occurred."

"Now that's a podcast I'll definitely tune in for. I heard from one of my cop friends who was here for dinner the other night. Seems the hunky officer Stefan was quite smitten by you."

"Really? I can't imagine why."

"He's going to be calling to take you out, so I'm here to encourage you to accept. You're not getting any younger, girl."

"Thanks for stating the obvious." She rolled her eyes and shrugged. "Maybe I'll give him a try. It's probably time I got back into the social swing."

Tony clutched at his shirt. "Be still my heart. Just when I believe I have you figured out — *snaaap* — you throw a curveball. You never cease to amaze."

"My goal in life is to confound you."

"Then I will encourage Stefan to give you a call."

They finished their coffee, and Tony returned to his apartment to get ready for work. Ella had a shower and checked the weather. The heat wave had entered its final week. Thunderstorms were expected to rumble in by the weekend. She put on one of the summer dresses that Tony had picked out for her and slipped on leather sandals. Walking downstairs a half hour later, she paused on the bottom step, staring at Finn and Adele's apartment. Should she check in or let things be? The door opened while she stood waffling, and Finn stepped out holding baby Lena. His face was unshaven, and his eyes were tired.

"Everything okay?" she asked, concerned, taking a step toward them.

"Adele's gone."

"Gone shopping?"

"Gone finding herself. I have no idea where."

"Oh, no." She'd been wrong to think Adele was getting better. "What are you going to do, Finn?"

"Look for a nanny. Wait for her to come home. Not sure what else I can do."

"Did she tell you she was leaving, or did you find out afterward?"

"She left a note. I knew she was having a hard time, but this ... she said she wasn't fit to be Lena's mother. She never threatened to harm herself, so I don't fear that way. I just don't know what to do."

"Oh, Finn." She leaned forward and put an arm around his neck, pressing her cheek against his. "If there's anything I can do. I have to go out for a bit, but I can watch Lena after lunch."

"Would you mind? I need to get to the gym for one o'clock if possible."

"Of course. I'll be sure to be back in time."

"I've called her friends and parents and hope she's in touch soon. The ball's in her court, as they say. I have to pray this time away will make her miss us, and she'll find her way back home. Even if she wants me out of her life, Lena needs her."

———

SARA'S EYES snapped open to sunlight pouring through her bedroom window. She tried to pinpoint what felt wrong before remembering that the air conditioning had been installed the day before. She wasn't hot, and the sheets were cool instead of damp with sweat. She relaxed and took a moment to replay Ginger's phone call to her from the night before. Charlie was safely home, and a woman from her dad's work was in custody for his kidnapping, the woman she'd followed to that house off the highway. No word about or from her father, which she found strange, but Ginger had avoided bringing him up except to say that he was as shocked as she was to find out who'd taken Charlie. Ginger had invited her over today to see him before they left for Halifax late afternoon. Sara guessed her father wouldn't be going with them. She couldn't imagine him spending any more time than he had to with Richard and Madeleine.

She'd tried texting and phoning her dad after Ginger's call, but he hadn't responded. She sat up and reached for her cell. Still nothing from him. She clicked on *The Capital* news app and scrolled through the stories, stopping at one written by Ella Tate. Her eyes widened, and she reread the part about her dad. He was being questioned about fraudulent dealings with the owner of an escort service and a Quebec mobster named Denis Razzuto. A picture of the three of them together was inserted into the story halfway down. Razzuto was also implicated in the death of the Chinese foreign student in November. Wes Gilbert had confirmed that she was deceased. Sara looked up. The two men she'd filmed in the restaurant. The man who'd chased her that night into the Billings Bridge parking lot. Did this mean she could stop worrying about him coming after her? No wonder Ginger had avoided speaking about her dad. Sara had no doubt though that he'd squirm out of whatever trouble he was in. He'd always landed on his feet before. He had no conscience about lying and always found a way to extricate himself.

Roddy was in his room when she passed by his door. She stopped and knocked, entering before he answered and flopping onto his bed. He shut down his computer screen and swivelled his chair to face her. "So what's up?"

"You heard Charlie's home?"

"Yeah. Good news."

"I'm going over to see him. You wanna come too?"

He glanced back at his computer. "I got stuff to do. Next time maybe."

His face had reddened, making her curious. "Dad's in shit. His business is being investigated."

Roddy nodded. "I read all about it. He'll get off, though. He always has answers for everything."

She wasn't surprised Roddy viewed their dad's problems the same way she did. They had firsthand knowledge of how he operated. "Has Mom gone out?"

"Yeah. She's using some of my winnings to buy work clothes. I think she's happy about going back. Uncle Ivan got a job in Kingston and leaves on the weekend. No more drunken pity parties in the back-yard." He grinned.

"I haven't seen your trophy yet."

"There's been a delay. Something about customs and paying duties. I'm not paying, so not sure if I'll ever see it." His fingers tapped on the desk like they did when he was nervous … or lying.

The redness in his neck had definitely darkened.

Sara thought over the timeline of his sudden good fortune, and an ugly thought took hold. She stared at him until his eyes met hers. "You were the one who got that ransom out of Richard. Ginger told me that he paid the money from their savings."

"No." His denial was feeble, spoken without conviction. Her stab in the dark took on substance. Roddy had the computer skills to pull it off and certainly reason to take advantage of their father.

"What you did was wrong, Roddy. You could have gotten into a shitload of trouble."

He held up a hand to stop her. "But I didn't. All I

wanted was Mom to get some of what Dad owed her. Are you going to tell?"

"Mom doesn't know?"

He shook his head. "She honestly believes I won the money."

Sara considered what to do. Roddy had done wrong, but he'd used the money to help their mom. "What else have you spent it on?"

"Nothing. It's stashed where nobody can trace it to me."

She debated what to do and finally lit on an idea. She made her voice stern. "I think if you donate the rest to a woman's shelter, we can forget it ever happened, but you have to promise me you won't do anything like this again."

"I don't know about that."

"You can't turn out like Dad."

"When you put it that way…" He gave a smile that made him look all of ten years old. "He's the last person I ever want to be like."

"Then donate the money so I don't have to tell Mom."

Sara didn't smile until she left his bedroom and was halfway down the stairs. Her brother had put one over on that prick Richard and restored a fraction of the imbalance between their families. Maybe Roddy's bit of revenge was like a ladder tossed into the dark hole they'd sunk into since their dad left. After all, Charlie was home, and the air conditioning was installed. Nobody had been harmed either way.

She opened the front door, and the heat struck her

full force. She was singing by the time she reached her car and climbed inside. She'd stop at Tim Hortons on her way to see Charlie and Ginger, who had to know where her dad was holed up. She had time to track him down before her shift began at the DQ. She'd have to remember to ask the cop for her notebook back or buy a new one. She began humming and reached over to turn on the radio.

Sara McGowan, P.I. in training, is back in the game.

ACKNOWLEDGMENTS

My husband Ted always said that the true test of coaching a team was how many players came back the following season. Well, if this is the yardstick, I'm delighted to say that all my beta readers returned, plus two. Thank you to my trusty critique team — Mary Jane Maffini, Susan Rothery, Derek Nighbor, Carol Gage, Darlene Cole, Alex Brett and Lisa Weagle. Your enthusiasm and the time you took to go through an early version of the manuscript have been instrumental to the final book. It really does take a village.

Thank you also goes to Allister Thompson, editor extraordinaire, and creative cover designer Laura Boyle. I've also been so pleased to meet and work with the talented Heather Williams, who narrated both books in this series. Heather also lives in Ottawa where she hosts an evening radio show and works as a voice actress on various projects. I'm so thankful we found each other!

So one evening while sitting around with my curling team after a game, I mentioned that I was setting part of this book in the Rocky Point neighbourhood. To my surprise, one of my teammates said that he lived on Loche Isle Road, the very street I'd randomly chosen for the McGowan family home. Dave and Ann Anderson generously provided lunch overlooking the Ottawa River in their back yard one hot summer day before taking Ted and me on a tour of the street and waterfront. Thank you to both for all the insights into the neighbourhood and a lovely afternoon. I used my imagination to create the McGowan house, but quite a bit of the local geography is faithfully told.

I've also been blessed with a neighbour who works at the Ottawa Police Services, who never fails to stop on his way past our house with his dog to answer my police procedural questions. He also took the time to read an early version of *When Last Seen*, helping to ensure that I get things right - a huge thank you, my friend, for all this invaluable support. Any factual errors are mine alone.

Of course, my gratitude extends to each of you, my readers, without whom I'd still be tucking manuscripts into my desk to collect dust. Your words of encouragement, kind emails and reviews, not to mention purchases, keep me motivated to continue writing and publishing. A special thank you to Jim Napier, Joey Taylor, Vicki Delany, Dawn Rayner, and Lita Boudreau. Also, my sincere gratitude to my family, near and far.

Finally, thanks to my daughters, Lisa and Julia Weagle, and my husband, Ted — your love and support are reason enough.

ABOUT THE AUTHOR

Brenda Chapman is a crime writer who has published over twenty books, including the lauded Stonechild and Rouleau series, the Anna Sweet mysteries for adult literacy, and the Jennifer Bannon mysteries for middle grade readers. Brenda's work has been short-listed for several awards, including four Crime Writers of Canada Awards of Excellence. A former teacher and senior communications advisor in the federal government, she makes her home in Ottawa.

Manufactured by Amazon.ca
Bolton, ON